"To say nothing, especially when speaking, is half the art of diplomacy." — Will Durant

ZVR DIPLOMACY

"All diplomacy is a continuation of war
by other means."
— Zhou Enlai

ZVR
DIPLOMACY

Illustrated by Michael Dubisch

Edited by Jeff Conner

"The principle of give and take is the principle
of diplomacy—give one and take ten."
— Mark Twain

"Diplomacy is the velvet glove that cloaks the fist of power." — Robin Hobb

ZVR ALT-LIT

EDITOR/DESIGNER: JEFF CONNER

ASSOCIATE EDITOR/TZVR: CHRIS RYALL

ASSOCIATE DESIGNER: ROBBIE ROBBINS

ZOMBIES VS. ROBOTS

CREATED BY ASHLEY WOOD & CHRIS RYALL

IDW founded by Ted Adams, Alex Garner, Kris Oprisko, and Robbie Robbins

ISBN: 978-1-61377-646-9   16 15 14 13   1 2 3 4

Become our fan on Facebook **facebook.com/idwpublishing**
Follow us on Twitter **@idwpublishing**
Check us out on YouTube **youtube.com/idwpublishing**

www.IDWPUBLISHING.com

Ted Adams, CEO & Publisher • Greg Goldstein, President & COO • Robbie Robbins, EVP/Sr. Graphic Artist
Chris Ryall, Chief Creative Officer/Editor-in-Chief • Matthew Ruzicka, CPA, Chief Financial Officer • Alan Payne, VP of Sales
Dirk Wood, VP of Marketing • Lorelei Bunjes, VP of Digital Services

СОДЕРЖАНИЕ

Introduction

Jeff Conner

THE WORLD OF *Zombies vs. Robots* is vast and varied, dangerous
and disgusting, brutal and bloody. Most of its stories are set in
the United States; a logical situation since the pernicious Z-virus
was first introduced by American scientists. Also stamped *Hecho
en USA* are the hastily banged-together warbots; wise-cracking
walking tanks tasked with containing the gnawing zombie hordes.
Thus, the domestic bias of our ZVR stories is quite understand-
able.

Unlike our brain-addicted zombies however, IDW's plucky ZVR
scribes originate from all parts of the English-speaking world, and
beyond—namely Canada, Australia, the UK and Russia (with an
ex-pat or two now based Stateside). Through happy circumstance,
of the thirty-plus stories brewed up in IDW's Lab of Loathsome Literature, four are set in the United Kingdom, and four in Russia.
How can one resist the urge to match up these tales of rot, rust and
resistance into an international ZVR Fight Club? A battle of the
bands sort of deal, with you the reader being the ultimate winner.
(Clearly, this editor succumbed to this temptation of terror and ad-
venture on beleaguered foreign shores!)

"Diplomacy" is the way that governments negotiate with each other; even when at war (which is what usually happens when diplomacy fails). Will Rogers, the great American philosopher and humorist, "joked" that without diplomats surely wars would end much sooner. (He also described diplomacy as saying "Nice doggie" while looking for a rock.)

"Diplomacy" can also refer to how people (rather than *peoples*) negotiate interpersonal relationships. In this sense *everyone* is a diplomat, some more skilled than others. The endless ebb and flow of personal diplomacy, that symphony of strategy and emotions, generates most of our drama, both commercial and personal.

But what does *diplomacy* mean in the ZVR context? Clearly the robots and zombies are not negotiating much of anything. The zombies want human brains and nothing else, so their interest in their robot foes is basically zero. You simply can't reach an understanding with unthinking brain-eaters found in ZVR, while the chatty warbots solely exist only to slaughter said zombies (and you best try to keep out of the crossfire). In other words, it takes two to negotiate—and by definition these two parties have a failure to communicate; it's more likely that they can't even conceive of it.

Aside from the geopolitical undertones (and we'll get to them in a moment), what this collection most concerns itself with is how the beleaguered humans in ZVR world negotiate with *each other* (or *oneself*, in some cases) when confronting dead folks walking. Can human relationships (as we normally understand them) prevail in the face of such horrific onslaughts? Well, that all depends, as the definition of "human" can be awfully elastic during such times.

Now, one would think that if science can eradicate small pox and polio, even commute the death sentence of AIDS, then the Z-virus could also be dealt with in some fashion. And yes, some of our protagonists are trying to do just that (there's no shortage of test subjects). Obviously mere science cannot cure the zombie plague; a military element must be involved as well. Test tubes and flame-throwers, working together like labor and management.

So it's not the terms of peace that inform *ZVR Diplomacy*, but the terms of survival. People can be pretty tough when the zombies are at the door, but societies and civilizations crumble regularly, often from self-inflicted wounds. What will happen once all the brains are eaten, Mr. Zombie? Will you develop a taste for large animals? Or will our warbot would-be saviors ultimately prevail before their power cells run dry? Is it only after human extinction that the Z-virus will finally burn itself out, its zombie hosts permanently bereft of brains, whithering away to dust and allowing our ravaged planet to return to its pre-human Eden state?

As noted, this book's menu of Russian and British responses to the zombie pestilence (and its subsequent warbotic rejoinder) was not consciously planned. All the better I say, as unintended inspiration is usually the most pure. And these stories are pure inspiration of the finest order.

This collection's presentation of such rarified purity features: Steve Lockley's tale of farmers and soldiers making a last stand against waves of shamblers (Steve is from the UK); Rio Youers' adroit depiction of British patriotism in the face of the undead invasion (born in England, Rio lives in Canada); Robert Hood's chiller about a man's soul trapped in a warbot (Robert hails from Australia); Gary McMahon's evocative look of how a priests efforts to cope with the zombie plague contrasts sharply with his government's (Gary is from the UK); Ekaterina Sedia's meditation on honor and love in the face of horror (born in Moscow, the story's setting, Ekaterina now calls New Jersey home); Simon Clark's giddy revelation about a warrior nun's ultimate sacrifice (Simon is a UK resident); Dale Bailey's pulpy Chernobyl meltdown (Dale lives in North Carolina); and Simon Kurt Unsworth's revealing take on British pride colliding with American imperialism (Simon lives in the UK). And it's all held together by the giddy art of versatile master artist, Mike Dubisch (who lives in Arizona).

Saying and doing nasty things in a nice way is one description of diplomacy, *ZVR Diplomacy* achieves that and more.

ZVR DIPLOMACY

A Zombies vs Robots Collection

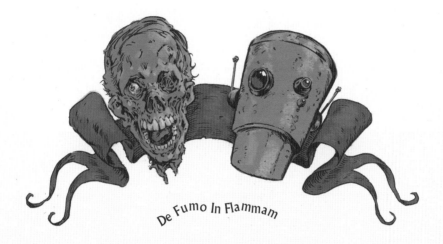

De Fumo In Flammam

Edited by Jeff Conner

Illustrated by Mike Dubisch

IDW PUBLISHING
San Diego, CA
2013

THE LAST DEFENSE OF MOSCOW

Steve Lockley

A FIGURE STUMBLED through the trees and a shot fired out. The bullet had caught him in the shoulder but he stayed on his feet, stumbling through the snow. Another shot and another, until the figure fell to the ground and did not move again. There was a cheer from the ranks; row upon row of conscript and professional soldier alike. And then there was nothing but silence as they waited in case the body started to move again.

"Gromyko!" The young man heard his name being called out and he saw a uniformed officer calling for him. He hoisted his scythe so it was above the heads of the men he had to pass to get to the end of the line and made his way slowly towards the soldier.

"Sir," Gromyko said when he reached the man.

"They tell me that you grew up near here," the man said. This was General Levitch, the man given command of the battle that was about to take place. They all knew that there would soon be a mass of the zombies stumbling from the woods now that the first one was dead. It was only a matter of time

"Yes sir," he confirmed. He had grown up on a farm that skirted the forest, and now he worked it with his father, scraping out a

1

living but little more than that. He had thought many times of leaving, of going to Moscow to find a new trade, but he knew that he could not abandon his father.

"The enemy will soon be upon us Gromyko and I have a job for you."

Gromyko waited, not knowing if he needed to acknowledge the statement or ask what was needed of him. He didn't want to be here, none of them did, but every man woman and child in the area who could walk had been brought here. The fit stood in the front ranks while the old, the young and the weak were back behind the lines, safe from the conflict but unlikely to offer food for the zombies should they reach their homes. A stray creature would find no one on the farms and in the cottages to feast on today.

"Go with Captain Varos. He will tell you what is required. It is your job to ensure that he completes his mission. Do you understand?"

He didn't, but he acknowledged the order. Nothing made sense any more, least of all him being given something to do other than stand in a line with the men he had known all his life, knowing they might not all be alive at the end of that day. In fact there was every chance that none of them would survive if the threat that was about to emerge from the forest proved to be as unstoppable as many suspected. The zombies had swept through the continent like a plague, their ranks growing with every town and city they passed through and now a horde of the fiends was about to threaten the very heart of Mother Russia and they had to be stopped. The Russian winter had stopped Napoleon and Hitler, but would it be sufficient to stop the ragged corpses that could not feel the cold from reaching Moscow?

Gromyko led the way up the hill away from the massed ranks that stood ready to stop the zombies in their tracks, following Varos' instructions to take him as close to the edge of the woods as they could while taking the high ground. If Varos had walked alone he would almost certainly have fallen foul of one of the ditches that were now covered in snow, each step a potential broken ankle. But even in the snow Gromyko knew where they ran and where the run-offs gouged scars in the ground beneath the blanket of white.

Glancing back down the hill the scale of the assembled troops was even more impressive than down there on the ground. At the front were the farmhands and factory workers called upon to swell the ranks, behind them the uniformed solders with rifles at the ready. Though it was only from this standpoint that Gromyko could see the truth of the situation. The soldiers could not shoot at the zombies, even if such a tactic was likely to prove fruitful, while the peasants with scythes and pitchforks stood in front of them. They were not there to kill zombies but to deter deserters. On long winter nights by oil lamp, Gromyko had read about the tactic being used in ancient times; the Romans had placed forces gathered from defeated tribes into the front ranks of their army to draw the fire of the enemy. Cannon fodder before cannons had been invented.

To one side, away from the immediate danger were huddled the old and the infirm, the women and children and behind them the great hulking machines that their defense may ultimately rely on; the robots. The great brass and steel machines, which wheezed and squealed with each motion, were impervious to the attacks of the zombies and unstoppable. They had not been called upon for years but now they had been called back into action, prepared to see action at last. At the moment their engines were silent, their hydraulics relaxed and they stood like puppets whose strings have been momentarily relaxed.

Varos urged him on, drawing Gromyko from his thoughts and he pushed on, the soft snow making the going more uncertain. On the crest of the hill stood the farmhouse he had lived in all of his life, the house empty now and the animals left unattended in one of the barns. His father had wanted to leave the doors open in case they should not return to feed them. He could not dare to imagine them starving to death or the pigs turning on themselves when the food ran out. Gromyko convinced him to keep them safe, for without the animals there would be no future for them; nothing to fight for, nothing to protect.

As they skirted what they knew would soon be the battlefield the tree line grew closer. The creatures were supposed to move in a fairly straight path. They would continue in the valley towards the lines of defenses, the rows of sharpened metal farm implements ready to be used against the zombies.

"How did the gunshot manage to stop it?" Gromyko asked, pointing at the fallen body just beyond the edge of the tree line. "And how come there's only one of them? Where are the rest?"

"They will be here soon enough," the young officer said.

"But a single shot?" he could not believe how easy it had been stopped.

"He was not a zombie; not one of them."

"Not one of them?"

"If he had been one of them the gun shot would not have stopped him. It was Dimitri. He was sent into the forest to see how far away they were."

"And someone shot him?" Gromyko could not believe what he was hearing. They had killed one of their own and no one seemed to care, but was it by mistake or just in case?

Varos said nothing, just lowered his head and followed carefully in Gromyko's footsteps. "We have to position ourselves at either end of the trench." He pointed to the dark scar that ran for almost a quarter of a mile; a ditch that had been dug with the sweat of soldiers and peasants alike and filled with brushwood and valuable straw that had been soaked in petrol. "When the zombies come out of the woods we set fire to it. Not before."

"And then?"

"And then we run. If we can rejoin the ranks then so be it, but the General has made it clear that ensuring that the fire burns is more important than our safe return."

"That's very nice of him."

"He is confidant that his plan will destroy enough of the creatures that we will not be needed in the ranks. If they get through then the poor sods standing at the front will be caught between the devil and the deep blue sea. They will have to kill or be killed. If they are bitten the soldiers behind them will be only too quick to make sure that they don't get the chance to infect anyone else." He drew a finger across his throat and that was all Gromyko needed.

THE FIRST OF the zombies stumbled from the trees and despite being hit by rifle fire it did little more than lose its footing for moment and slow its momentum before moving again. This was the real thing; it was going to take a lot more than that to stop it. Gromyko was already in position at the far end of the trench and on Varos' signal set fire to the oil-soaked brushwood barrier that sat in the trench. He could not believe that the zombies had so little residual intelligence that they would walk straight into it, but that was not his concern. He had a job to do and no matter how he looked at it he could be one of the lucky ones who would have the chance to walk away.

A great gout of flame rose up, sucking the oxygen from the air, singeing Gromyko's hair and scorching his face, but he managed to hold on to the piece of wood he had used to ignite the barricade. He grabbed a handful of snow and used it to cool his skin before following the line of brushwood, touching the flame to it at intervals to ensure that the whole length was quickly ablaze. Snow and ice fizzed as it melted and evaporated in an instant in the heat that burst out, turning the ground where Gromyko was standing to slush beneath is feet when previously it had been hard as iron. Once he passed the halfway point he had reached the stretch that Varos had set fire to and they both threw their wooden torches into the inferno before running back the way they had come.

Even as they watched, back on the bank and pausing to catch their breaths, what must have started as a trickle of ones and twos of the zombies coming from the woodland had become a torrent, a great surge of stumbling corpses, a tide that had nothing to direct it and it moved inexorably towards the fire.

"Perhaps it will work," said Gromyko.

"Perhaps. It may thin out the numbers but I do not think it will be sufficient on its own."

The first of the zombies reached the burning barricade but did not even break its stride as it stumbled in the fire, its ragged clothes bursting into flame and its flesh burning as it fell onto the bonfire. It was followed by another and another, each one pushed by the mass of bodies behind. There was a great cheer from the ranks as the defense seemed to be doing its job and from their standpoint at least, it must have looked as if they would not be called into battle today. Gromyko could see that their celebrations would be short lived. The flames destroyed some of the bodies that stumbled into them but the mass of bodies that was still pouring from the trees would eventually break through the defense. The flames though, would mask the size of the horde from those who waited, until it was too late.

"We have to warn them."

"Warn them about what? The fire is doing its job for the moment at least. Any that manage to break through will be ablaze and easily dispatched once the robots are sent into the fray."

Gromyko wished he shared the other man's confidence. All he knew was that many of his friends would believe they were safe now and that the enemy would soon be defeated. The walking corpses continued relentlessly moving onwards, their bodies adding to the pyre as the brushwood began to sink into the trench sending sparks flying into the sky. Rotting flesh burned and filled the air with a stench more acrid than that of the burning oil, human fat rendered turning rags and bones into walking human candles, oblivious to what was happening to their bodies, until muscle and sinew burnt to nothing and they collapsed to the ground unable to move but still dangerous.

The weight of bodies, still thrashing in the flames, pressed heavily on the quickly charring barrier until the fire seemed to consist only of fallen corpses. Still they poured from the forest, a never ending tide until at last the weight of bodies began to dampen down the fire and clambering over the smoldering corpses the zombies emerged from the smoke. First in ones and twos but then a torrent of them stumbled through until it was as if the barrier no longer existed. Even Varos was surprised by the effect that the sheer weight of numbers had. Gromyko wanted to point out that he was right to have doubted the defenses now that the fate of Moscow could lie in the hands of peasants and farm boys.

AT FIRST THERE was the sound of fear and panic as the hope that they would not be needed to fight was dashed. There was still some distance between them and the hoarde but that was closing slowly. Another trap had been laid; a second trench covered in brushwood that the zombies would fall into but it was unlikely to account for the zombies in great number. It would soon fill with bodies to make a human bridge for those that came behind. Nothing could stop them unless the living's greatest weapon could deal with them and with the sound of escaping steam and the groan of metal on metal the engines of the great machines were fired into life. Pneumatics powered the joints of articulated limbs and the robots rose from resting positions, ready for action. Gromyko had never seen one of them before today other than in the museum. It was hard to think that something built so long ago could be relied upon to provide the defense that was needed; a weapon that could fight the zombies without risking human life.

The earth shook as the first of the machines took a tentative step and began to walk. Another cheer came from farmers and soldiers alike. Many wondered why they had been held to the sides of the ranks like cavalry on the wings of set piece battles, but that was the very reason they were there. With the enemy's potency relying completely on close-quarter battles it would be foolish to ignore the tactics that had been employed in ancient times when Roman armies had conquered entire nations even though they had inferior numbers. This was where you placed your faster, mobile units that could make lightning strikes and break the lines of the enemy forces

"Now we will see the strength of Mother Russia. We know that the foolish westerners have fallen to the hordes in places but it will not happen here. We will be victorious and when this is all over we will be the most powerful nation in the world. Let the zombies lay waste to the Americans with their inadequate machinery," said Varos.

Gromyko was sick and tired of hearing this rhetoric. What was wrong with the way of life in the west? This was a new world; a new age and the whole world had a common enemy. It made sense that everyone should be fighting together, not looking for ways to come out ahead at the end of the conflict. If an end ever came.

By the time the first of the zombies stumbled from the second trap the robots were in position, their great iron feet stamping on the walking corpses, arms sweeping through them two and three at a time slicing through corpses and breaking bodies as if they were playthings. More cheers, more shouts of joy from the ranks. Could the robots really deal with all of them though, or would they be overwhelmed by numbers? Gromyko glanced back towards the forest, hoping against hope that the last of the zombies had emerged and that the true size of the enemy could be at last assessed. Although the flow had slowed significantly there was no sign that it was about to come to an end. The flames of the first trench had almost lost their potency but still served to slow some of them down. It was essential that the robots complete their work quickly and efficiently if this battle was to be won. The farmers and soldiers were ready to play their part, but in truth they only wanted to be involved when the battle was already won.

"We should get back," said Varos.

"I thought you said that we didn't need to?"

"Our act of bravery and heroism," he mocked, "has excused us from the need to fight but that does not mean that I do not want to be part of the victory. I don't want to receive my medal for this if I spent most of the time standing ankle deep in snow and watching the fun without even being able to take part if I was needed."

"What about me?"

"That's up to you, but if you have friends and family down there you might want to join them."

What started as a brisk walk turned into something resembling a run as the incline of the bank made them move faster and faster despite uncertain footing. They were barely able to stop themselves when the first crash came, followed by a universal intake of breath. One of the robots had fallen and in moments the zombies were scrambling over it as if it was just one more obstacle to pass. Then another crashed to the ground and the snow fell from the branches of trees near where Gromyko stood and in a heartbeat later the bot exploded, sending shards of metal and body parts into the air and showering down into the snow.

"You still think that these things can be beaten?" Gromyko yelled but his companion was lost for words. He was rooted to the spot, barely able to believe what he was seeing, as if his whole world was falling apart in front of his eyes.

"We have to do something," he said at last.

"Do something? What on earth do you think we can do? Do you think that we can defeat these things with scythes and swords?"

"Maybe…maybe the rest of the robots will be enough. Maybe there are more on their way."

"If there are more coming, why aren't they here already?"

Another robot hissed and ground to a halt frozen in a moment of time while everything else moved around it then in slow motion it started to topple over.

"You know what it is, don't you?" said Gromyko.

No reply. The man's brain was not working on all cylinders, just like the robots. They weren't just being overwhelmed by the number of bodies, though there was little doubt that was the cause of their collapsing; they were failing and Gromyko knew why. These machines had never been built to deal with terrain and conditions like this. There may have been those who dreamed of using them against decadent westerners, of building a great army that would crush any enemy underfoot, but they had forgotten their original purpose. These robots had been built to quell uprisings from within the Soviet Union, from the rebels in satellite states who wanted independence and as a defense from the greater land threat which would come from China. They were built for operating in a warmer climate than this. Gromyko knew about machinery, he had kept tractors running through the depths of winter but knew to his cost how sometimes the diesel grew waxy and the engines would no longer operate. He suspected that in their arrogance, the politicians and military leaders had not consulted with the mechanics and engineers to ensure that the robots were fit for the purpose and had merely serviced them and tested that they functioned before transporting them here. Now they were little more use than statues, the diesel turned waxy in their engines.

"Do you want to do something about this? Do you really want to be a hero?" He asked Varos. "Or was that just bravado? Joining the fray down there will not help; we will be just two more poor idiots who won't stand a chance."

"I'm not running away." There was genuine fear in his eyes but it was tempered by a strong sense of loyalty, of the need to obey orders, to be a good soldier.

"We are just going to fetch something that might just change the tide, or at least buy a little more time for someone to do something about this. But we will need help."

THE GENERAL WAS barking orders to a small group of officers braced to attention, his uniform stretched tight and a ceremonial sword at his side. Gromyko had seen soldiers like this before. There were the ones who would carry out orders without a moment's thought, without questioning anything they were asked to do. Varos was not quite one of them but it was clear that he wished that he was. He was a career soldier and this unswerving loyalty was what it would take to rise up the ranks.

"Varos. It appears that your good works were not sufficient to deal with the enemy."

It sounded to Gromyko as if the General was blaming them for the trap not having done everything it was intended to do, as if they had failed in their mission, even though they had done exactly what they had been ordered to do.

"Gromyko has a plan sir."

"You are not here to have plans Gromyko, you are here to fight.

You are here to defend Moscow. You are here to save Mother Russia from the fiends that are knocking on her door. It is not your place to make plans."

The General turned his back on them and watched as the soldiers headed towards the gathered women and children, the old and the infirm who had been held back. They were brought to him, herded like sheep until they were close enough for him to address them.

"Comrades," he said. "You are to serve your country well today. This is your chance for glory and the time to mark your place in history."

They looked confused. They thought they had been brought there for safe keeping but now it seemed as if they were going to be called into action after all. They were frightened and huddled together for mutual protection.

"What is he going to do with them?" Gromyko asked. They could not be asked to fight; they would be no more effective than a single stalk of grass in the wind. Even together they would not stand a chance.

"He's going to sacrifice them," Varos said.

"What?" Gromyko could not believe what he was hearing. Did the General think it was possible to appease the zombies in some way? Did he think that they would go away and leave them alone if some kind of offering was made?"

"He wants to slow down the zombies but a little extra time, maybe even make them easier to kill while they are feeding."

"That's madness. These are people, not sheep or cattle to be done with as he pleases. Besides, doesn't he risk their ranks being swelled by these people?" He waved a hand in their general direction, then saw that his father was standing at the front holding onto a woman who looked as if she as barely able to stand.

"That's why he wants to use the weak. If they do become like the zombies they will be easier to kill than if they were resurrected fighting men."

"We've got to stop him."

"He's right," a voice said behind Gromyko. He had no idea that anyone had been listening to them but he was glad to see a familiar face when he turned around. Sergei Andropov was a well-known face in the area, a great burly man who had once killed a bear with his bare hands when it had threatened his children. Gromyko had been afraid of him when he was younger; the great scar on his face a constant reminder of the fight that could so easily have killed him, but as he grew older he had learned that the gentle giant of a man had never hit another in anger.

"Will you speak to him?" Andropov said.

"Me?" said Varos, looking up at the big man.

"Who else?"

"He won't listen to me."

"Perhaps not," Gromyko said. "But there are enough soldiers who might. Let me take my father and we will fetch something that might help. Will you come with us?" He asked Andropov, but the big man shook his head.

"I will stay and fight for as long as I am able. If your father has something that he thinks can help then that is good enough for me. He is a very clever man."

Gromyko had never heard his father called clever before. He was good with his hands and could tell by smelling the air when the best day to sow and the best to harvest had arrived, but never clever. He could keep a machine working long after it should have outlived its usefulness and even though he did not claim to be a mechanic, other farmers would often ask him to look at tractors that were not running properly, threshing machines that jammed too often. And in his barn was his great machine that he had built out of fear of this very moment, but his offers to bring it had been brushed aside just when it looked like it might be needed.

Gromyko pulled his father from the crowd though he was reluctant to release the woman he supported. Someone else took his place and led the woman away. No one stopped them as Gromyko and his father walked away, calling another man to follow them, it was as if there was some kind of stand off as the General and a few of the soldiers barked orders but no one moved, not even the rank and file soldiers who had been waiting for their instructions. These men might be prepared to kill their enemy; to lay down their lives to stop the zombies that were stumbling towards them, but they would not turn on their own people. They were here to save Mother Russia and without its people a country was nothing. If its people were killing each other then that made it less than nothing. First one then another, and another moved to stand in front of the unarmed elderly and infirm. Then they were joined by more, standing defiantly between the General and the people he thought were disposable. The General continued to shout orders, his face growing red with anger and frustration but even his closest officers refused to fire upon their own men and they lowered their weapons.

"We have to build barricades to hold them at bay until more help arrives."

"There is no more help coming," said the General. "Don't you see? The people in power do not care if we live or die. All they want to do is buy time to give themselves the chance to flee Moscow and if possible, allow as many others who wish to, to make their escape, but that is not their main concern. We will stop these things here and we will do it now."

"But not your way!" said Andropov. "We will fight until our last breath but we will not sacrifice our wives and children to do it. That would make us no better than them. No, it would make us worse. They kill, not because they choose to do it, but because something is making them."

The General shouted and screamed but no one was taking orders from him any longer. His gun had been taken from him but then he drew his sword, brandished the ceremonial weapon in the air without threatening anyone in particular. Few were taking any notice when he screamed the cry to attack and ran towards the zombie horde, oblivious to whether anyone was following or not.

Gromyko trudged through the snow as fast as his father could run, making sure that the other old man was not left behind. Gromyko had called the man Uncle Ivan for as long as he could remember even though they were not related. He had seen the old men working on the machines in the barn together and there was no doubt that Ivan knew as much about what they were capable of as anyone else did. They could hear the increasing sounds of battle behind them as the barn at last came into view.

It took both Gromyko and his father to open the barn doors, pushing aside the newly accumulated snow as they did so. Uncle Ivan rested for a moment, lighting a cigarette as if that would aid his breathlessness, bringing on a bout of coughing.

"Will he be alright?" Gromyko asked.

"Ivan? Of course, he'll be fine."

"We should leave him here. Let him rest."

"No I need him to help me operate this thing."

"You've got me."

"But you don't know how to work it."

"I can learn. It can't take long."

"Too long. Every moment we waste is another of our friends we risk losing."

"Then Uncle Ivan can ride with me and show me how everything works while you drive. We can let him off before we get there. No time lost."

"Will you please stop talking about me as if I was almost dead?" Ivan said, the cigarette stuck to his bottom lip, one eye barely open as smoke drifted into it. "I was driving these things before you were born."

Gromyko glanced at the combine harvester with the extra attachments that the two men had fitted to it, then back at Uncle Ivan. It was impossible to tell which of them was the oldest. Whichever it was, he suspected that the machine had been looked after better than the old man.

THE ZOMBIES WERE held at bay but it would only be a matter of time before they surged over the final barricade that the farmers had built to defend themselves and their families while they reached over with scythes and spades swinging and hacking, severing heads and limbs from bodies. As a man tired another stepped forward to take his place. The army tried to fend off those zombies drifting to the sides but some of them fell prey to the creatures. It would not be long before they were back on their feet again having changed sides like some undead defectors turning on their masters.

There was no sign of the General. Within moments of charging into the horde with his sword swinging and hacking heads from shoulders he had fallen, engulfed by the overwhelming number of bodies. He had made little difference to the fight against the fiends, cutting down no more than a few of them before he succumbed himself, lost to the fight.

The combine harvester rocked and rolled through the snow, snagging the barbed wire fence, pulling posts from the ground as if they were no more than matchsticks. Gromyko sat perched on the back of the machine, listening carefully as Uncle Ivan tried to make himself heard above the growl of the engine. The old man demonstrated how each of the controls worked and what each mechanism was capable of doing. Even though none of the knobs and levers had any identification it was not difficult to understand what their purpose was.

Ivan clutched at his chest as the machine lurched forward, cresting the hill and starting its descent. Gromyko grabbed hold of him to make sure that he did not fall from the machine and into the equipment that was intended to save them.

"You have to stop!" he yelled to his father, but there was no sign that he had any intention of even slowing.

"I told him to ignore you," Uncle Ivan said, clenching his teeth and clutching a hand to his chest to fight back the obvious pain. "We don't have the time to stop even for a moment."

"You're in no fit state to do anything."

"If you abandon me here I will not stand a chance either. Sooner or later those things will get me, and as long as I'm with you then at least there's the chance that I will be able to take some of them with me."

It was hard for Gromyko to argue with that, but he still didn't like the idea of Uncle Ivan putting himself in greater danger than he needed to. He could go back to the farmhouse and lock himself away. Even if the zombies won this battle he suspected that they would just push on towards Moscow without looking for victims who were not standing in their way. He would be safe, but there was no way that he was going to let Gromyko send him from the field of battle. Uncle Ivan was a proud man who would not want to hide away from the danger.

The combine harvester lurched on, cresting the last brow of the hill before starting down again, building speed as it hurtled on towards the horde of zombies. Gromyko's father wrestled with the steering wheel, trying to keep the great machine under control as gravity pulled and the wheels struggled to keep their grip in the snow and ice.

There was a shudder as they reached the bottom of the hill and the great cutting cylinder was almost buried in the ground and prevented them moving any further, but with a creak and a groan it was raised until it did little more than scrape through the top layer of snow. After a moment of struggling to regain momentum it began to build up speed, slewing erratically from side to side as one wheel then another found better grip in the ground.

Gromyko was unaware that they had reached the first of the zombies until the machine hit it. He tried to look past his father's shoulder while still holding onto Uncle Ivan and almost lost his footing on the icy metal strip he was standing on. If he had fallen he would have slipped beneath one of the great wheels at the back of the vehicle while the great blades at the front of the machine turned and chewed into one of the fiends that had fallen into the rotor. The vehicle slowed but continued to push forward as it ploughed into the edge of the mass of bodies, which seemed oblivious to the threat that the combine harvester posed to them.

The arrival of the machine had a galvanizing effect on the men and women who had been holding the barricade, desperately trying to resist the unstoppable mass of flesh and bone that was moving with no sign of being stopped. They were being beaten; every ounce of strength had already been given, but now they found something more. The old men and the women stepped forward, giving those who had been fighting longest, those whose faces were splattered with gore a moment of respite.

Uncle Ivan pulled one of the levers and a blade extended from either side of the machine, slicing into bodies as they moved forward, cutting at neck height and severing heads from ragged bodies, thinning out the numbers and giving the defenders time to dispose of some of the others. The rotor shuddered as too many bodies were caught in the blades, threatening to bring the whole machine to a halt for a moment. The motor groaned and strained against the resistance until the cutting edge eventually sliced through the obstruction. The moment was enough to allow the zombies to advance and reach the side of the machine. Uncle Ivan tried to fend one of them off but he was too weak to do more than offer ineffectual swings with the machete he had kept at his side. Gromyko clambered over him and hacked at the fiend, severing an arm from its shoulder and it fell back to the ground just as they began to move forward again. The tread of the great wheel ground the zombie into the snow and the last sign Gromyko caught of it was its head as it disappeared beneath the tread.

From the crowd emerged the General, his dress uniform torn to shreds, his face and exposed flesh smeared with blood and gore, though which was his and which came from the zombies he had tried to destroy was impossible to tell. The great rent in his neck was the tell-tale sign that it was too late for him. Even if he was not one of them already, he would be very soon. But what Gromyko saw in his eyes was rage, pure red hot rage. His mouth opened as if to speak but nothing intelligible came out of it, only a deep guttural sound that caused blood to bubble from the wound.

The thing that had once been the General grabbed at Uncle Ivan and the old man did not resist, instead he slumped, clutching at his chest, not resisting as he was pulled from his seat.

Gromyko screamed, snatching at the old man's clothes, trying to stop him from falling to the ground. Uncle Ivan let out a feeble scream as the wheel rolled over his leg but it was lost in the sounds of battle. Gromyko released another cry and hacked at the General who was trying to pull himself on board, ignoring the closeness of the wheel. Gromyko slammed the metal blade against the General's arm, severing his hand which still held his sword, but it made little difference; there was no sign of panic, no cry of agony, just a frantic waving of the ruined arm as it tried to gain purchase. Gromyko swung the machete again, this time burying it deep in the zombie's neck; his arm shuddering as it struck bone before the creature fell to the ground and was lost in the mass of body parts that had been chewed up by the rotating blades.

They had bought the soldiers some time, but clearly it was not going to be enough. They had forged a way thorough the mass but the gap was closing behind them like the tide rolling in. The combine harvester had almost reached the far end of the sea of bodies and they had disposed of many of the creatures, but it was not enough; it was never going to be enough. They would have to turn at the far end and make their way through the bodies once more as if they were cutting down wheat at harvest time. Gromyko's father was obviously unaware that Uncle Ivan was no longer on board, Gromyko patted him on the shoulder and took his place where Ivan had been. With too much debris caught in the cylinder, the blades were not moving smoothly. Gromyko's first thought was to get down from the machine as it turned to try to clear some of it before they tried again but there was no time. If they did not complete another run it would be too late, but the decision was taken out of their hands when something in the engine snapped and with a loud bang, black smoke shot through the exhaust. It was over. There was nothing more they could do but hope. Gromyko looked at his father, who had slumped over the steering wheel and he knew that everything was lost. If it was something that could be repaired quickly the old man would already be tugging at the great metal tool box that he kept stowed beneath the seat.

"That's it," the old man said rubbing his hands across his eyes.

"There must still be something we can do. Anything."

"Nothing. It's had it. We could strip down the engine, maybe replace the broken part but not now, not today." He turned and looked at the zombies that were still threatening to overcome the defenders who were still holding their own but only just. They needed as much help as they could get.

"Maybe you could do something about the robots? Maybe there's a way to get them started again."

"Perhaps. But it will be too late."

"We have to try," Gromyko pleaded until he realized that there was a new sound in the air, the sound of engines moving towards them. He looked up to see a row of farm vehicles moving down the hill towards them; tractors and combine harvesters, making their way through the snow and ice and behind them an old bulldozer belching black smoke. The farmers had seen what they had done and had gone to get their own vehicles

Maybe they had done enough after all. Maybe they had bought enough time for the other farmers to come to their rescue.

"We can do it, Dad. *They* can do it." He pointed towards the other farmers who were doing everything they possibly could to save their community, maybe to save Moscow and Mother Russia herself.

The old man clambered to the back of the vehicle and retrieved a metal fuel can from the back. He held it in two hands and the sound of liquid sloshed inside. "Should be enough," he said. "Bring the toolbox."

Together they made their way to the nearest of the fallen robots. Gromyko had no idea what his father had in mind, but he knew that the can would contain the diesel he used in the farm vehicles, maybe a gallon at most. Perhaps it would thin the diesel already in the robots. It was a long shot but it had to be worth trying

The old man ran his hands over the great machine, the saviors of the Russian people that had fallen in battle so easily, defeated by the one thing that had defended them so many times from invaders. He grabbed a rag from the toolbox and used it to grip the fuel cap which he located in the robot's back, then with the aid of a battered funnel added fuel from the container.

"You think it will work?"

"Maybe." He pressed the starter button and the engine tried to turn over but failed. The farmers were grinding the zombies underfoot but there was no guarantee that it would be enough. They needed to get at least one of the robots moving again if they could. He pressed the button again and this time the engine coughed into life. It sputtered and groaned, threatening to die once more but then at last the machine started to budge. Gromyko had no idea how the robots were controlled but they had at least done everything they could. The machine's joints began move, stretching and testing connections until it began to right itself. Unsteady at first, it took a moment for the machine to find its balance but then it was moving, lumbering slowly towards the zombies until it caught up to those creatures that had only just reached the back of the mass, those whose bodies were most decayed and held together by little more than perished tendons. The robot swept them aside, the fragile bodies falling apart as great metal hands swung through them like scythes. The tractors did their best to defend the barricades, thinning the crowd that was forcing its way to the barricades, buying extra time and limiting the number of zombies they were having to deal with at once. Soldiers stood shoulder to shoulder with farmhands, old men with children and together they were holding back the tide.

Gromyko wanted to help and followed the robot's progress. It beat its own path through the zombies, destroying everything in its wake and giving hope. By the time Gromyko reached the mass of ruined bodies there was little more to be done. So many of the dead had been standing beside him when this had all begun, destroyed by the zombies or bitten and changed, then destroyed by the people they had stood beside. He recognized many of them, knew most of them by name. In the mass of corpses he came across the General's sword, half buried in gore. He looked around for the man's body, needing to see it to be sure that he no longer posed a threat, but then he saw movement, a man struggling to free himself from the remains.

"Uncle Ivan!" Gromyko cried as he saw who it was who was trying to free himself. His walk changed to a run, but then Uncle Ivan turned and Gromyko saw that his face was ruined and most of one arm missing. He stopped in his tracks, slipping in the blood-soaked mush that now lay underfoot. The fiend that had once been Uncle Ivan closed the distance, stepping on former friends and foes alike. Gromyko tried to get back to his feet but all he did was slip and slide in the icy mud. He called for help but knew that no one would be able to hear him or come to his assistance, and the great robot was too busy with dealing with the enemy itself. He reached amongst the bodies hoping to find something he could defend himself wtih but his hands failed to close on anything he could use. Just as he thought that death had come to him he caught sight of a metal blade slicing through the air, then severing Uncle Ivan's head from his shoulders. The body stood motionless for a moment before sinking to the ground and falling across Gromyko's legs. He hauled himself free, pushing against the corpse to move as far away from it as he could, but cried out in terror as a hand was offered to help him to his feet. He looked up, surprised that his savior was his own father, who held the General's sword with the dead man's hand still firmly attached. He dropped it to the ground and held his son in an embrace that Gromyko hoped would never end. The last of the zombies were being cleared away by the robot and soon the bodies would be built into a pyre and burned. Lessons had been learned about what the robots were capable of, but also one of their greatest weaknesses.

⚜

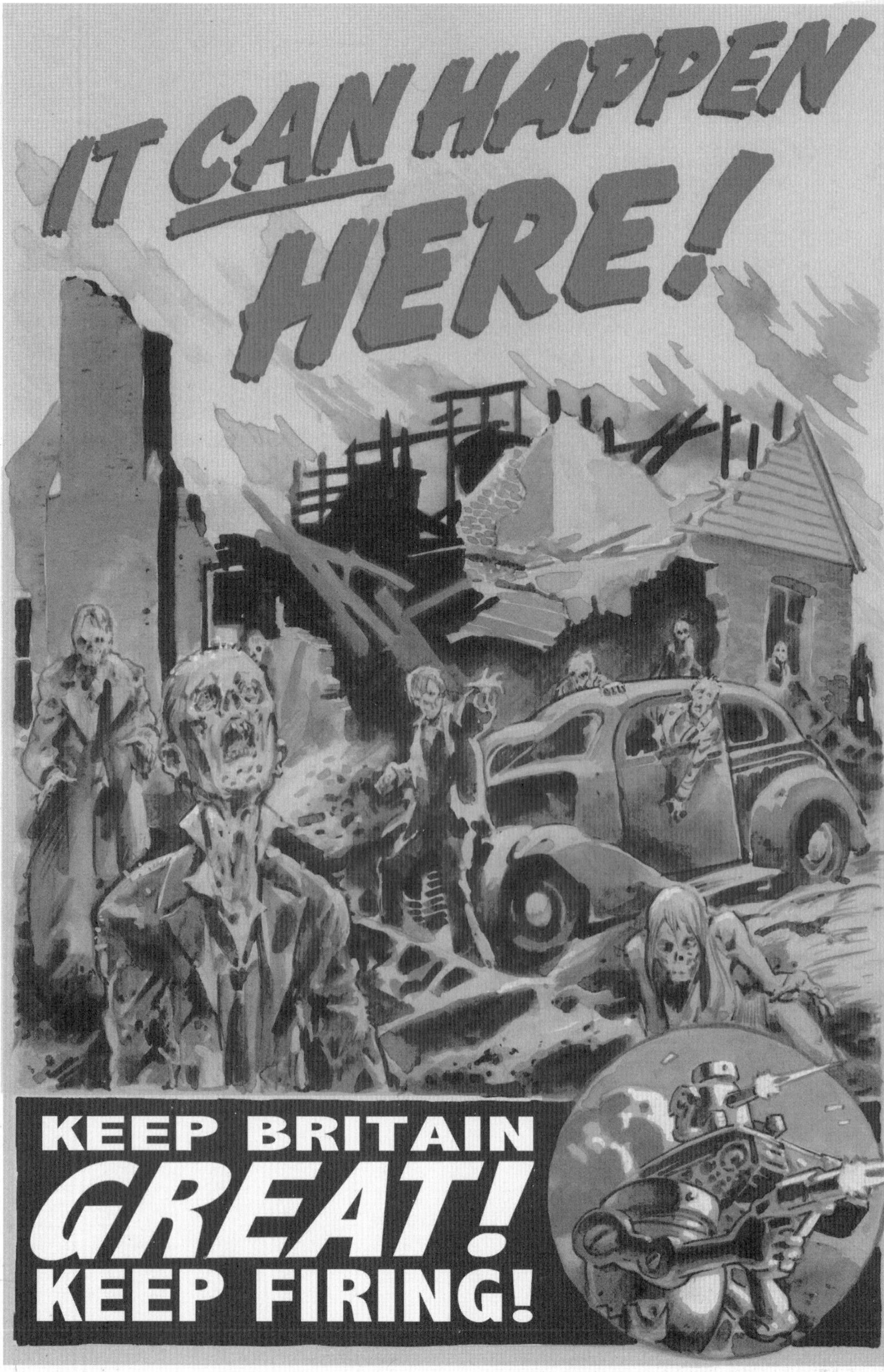
IT CAN HAPPEN HERE!
KEEP BRITAIN
GREAT!
KEEP FIRING!

FOR KING AND COUNTRY

Rio Youers

A ND SO THE missiles flew.
From above, a safe distance—where the solar system bleeds into the rest of space, say—the earth resembled a microbe undergoing some violent chemical reaction. Strips of vapor criss-crossing the atmosphere as doom rained down. Huge welts appearing, boiling fallout. Land mass reshaped and blackened. Islands wiped out by toxic mega-tsunamis. Entire continents ruptured, obscured by clouds as dark as ash. It was—as Skull Face, the MK 6 warbot that pushed the button, so eloquently put it—a total reboot.

Zombie scum scrubbed from the face of the planet.

Along with everything else.

Almost.

AFTER.
KIRTLAND UNDERGROUND MUNITIONS STORAGE.
NEW MEXICO.
EVERYTHING BLOWN TO rags and dust. A soulless desert stretched beneath nuclear haze, and a sun that glared, cold and useless, like an empty eye socket. Deep in the mountains (but not deep enough),

the fifteen billion-dollar WMD storage facility lay in fifteen billion pieces. Only the durability of Paleozoic rock face kept it from being entirely vaporized, although the fallout from stored nuclear warheads and a shoal of other weaponry caused unthinkable devastation.

Only fair, as this was the place where it all began…where Dr. Phillippe Satterfield and his team developed their Trans-Dimensional Gateway. A portal to new worlds—to discovery.

Or so they had hoped.

New worlds…yes. Discovery…yes. But of a terrifying nature. Their misjudgment was to prove grave indeed. Worldwide destruction. Seven and a half billion dead.

Well, sort of dead.

The Gateway remains. Kinked out of shape, like an old buckle, and as useless as the sun behind that scrim of deathly cloud. Walk through it and you'll go nowhere. But on the other side—the goddam zombie side—the discharge of nuclear energy has created a permanent rift in time and space. A window, if you will, all but invisible…but every now and then some undead thing slips through.

Most of the time that undead thing passes into nothingness: a future unimagined, or a past that doesn't exist. But every now and then the seam aligns with a place of light and life, and the zombie virus fights to take hold. Sometimes it is extinguished within a matter of moments. Other times—in worlds parallel to ours, for instance—it finds a way to survive.

And so it was for one monstrosity—lost in the brain, its stomach like a scooped-out oyster, teeth still gnashing—that shuffled unwittingly toward the seam, trying to pull from its shoulders a dusty, dented warbot (one of Dr. Herbert Throckmorton's resilient contraptions) with orders only to destroy. Into the rift they tumbled…

POOT—

…and found themselves in the city of Warsaw, Poland. And from there, like a raging army, the invasion spread.

* * *

IN A WORLD MUCH LIKE OUR OWN…
BUCKINGHAM PALACE, RESIDENCE OF KING GEORGE VI.
LONDON, ENGLAND.
WITH ITS TRACKS squeaking and oil smell puffing from its lower
ventriculated exhaust, the king's servicebot careened through
splendid hallways of arched ceilings and marble floors, each
adorned with the riches that only sovereignty can provide. Its engine sputtered and a single warning light flashed on its dull casing.

"IMPERATIVE: Must reach >*ztssk*< his majesty's private apartments. One hundred and twelve feet until >*pzzt*< destination."

It rumbled and backfired, occasionally getting its wires crossed
and trundling in the wrong direction.

"U-turn when safe. One hundred and >*spoink*< eighteen feet
until destination. DANGER: Grand Staircase ahead."

This servicebot—affectionately named Harold by the king and
his people—had seen better days. A Centum Series 6, once a glimmering model, the pride of the king's robots: a cuboid-form stain-
less steel body with hydraulic arms and continuous tracks, standing
less than three feet tall, powered by a two-fifty horsepower engine
and stamped with the Royal Coat of Arms. No weaponry. Not even
a .22. Its singular function was to serve, and that's what it did. It
used to do it so well, too, without sputtering and spoinking, but
with the war raging the king had been forced to commit his engineers to battle, and Harold suffered—degenerated into near disre-
pair—as a consequence.

"For king and >*preep*<…warningsystemoperatingat…twelve feet
until…> *fzzk*<…country."

It clattered through the great hallways, occasionally slowing as it
juggled multiple processes, sometimes running into walls or adorn-
ments as its navigation system faltered. A larger bot would have
caused significant damage, but Harold left behind only a few scrapes
and dents, doing most of the damage to itself. Just as well the hallways were all but empty. There was a time when they bristled with
bots and humans: secretaries and doctors, technicians and guardbots, maids, cooks, engineers, and various other servicebots. Those

days were history. The king had kept the minimum number on hand and committed the rest to the war effort. Man, woman, and bot. It was a time of great need, of valor and fortitude, when the people of Great Britain had to stand together and fight. "We are a proud nation," the king declared in his address. "Made great by the courage and tenacity of its citizens. In this, our darkest hour, we must prove these qualities, commit as one to the cause, and show the invading undead that our glorious land will not be taken without a fight."

Thus…empty hallways.

"Seventy-six >*teenk*< until destination."

If only the rest of Europe had shown this level of resilience, the zombie invasion would almost certainly have been quelled before it took hold. But weak and ill-advised resistance had allowed it to spread, and quickly. More like a wave than an invasion, growing larger, gathering momentum, as it swept across Europe.

Now it was almost impossible to stop.

It began in Poland. A single undead organism that shambled through the streets of Warsaw and leeched on a number of healthy individuals before being captured for testing. At this point the entire country should have been quarantined, with military blockades placed along its borders. This didn't happen, of course. Poland was crippled within a matter of days, and from there the invasion snowballed across the rest of Europe. Germany fell. Then Scandinavia and Belgium. Scenes of disorder and mass hysteria: terrified citizens fleeing their homes; looting and rioting; tanks rolling through once peaceful streets; armies and militant factions driven back by waves of the undead.

Guns blazing…ineffectual.

People…eating people.

Chaos.

The greatest virologists in the world worked (and ultimately failed) to understand the infection, to find a cure, while scientists and engineers developed task-specific automatons to A) counterbalance the depleting population and B) join the fight. These bots were modified versions of the contraption found clinging to the zombie in Warsaw—so determined a piece of machinery that it was deemed the perfect ally. Mass production was prioritized, and in a short space of time warbots, guardbots, and tankbots were rolling from weapons facilities across Europe. Why further the loss of human life (and the spread of infection) when a robot could be sent to do the grunt work?

Docbots and servicebots followed. Scibots and sniperbots, too. Each with elementary programming, one of two prime directives: destroy or serve. They joined the campaign in a clanking wave of bolts, cogs, and springs. But the zombies kept coming, tripling— quadrupling—in number in the blink of an eye. Armies fought alongside the bots, trusting the machines by their sides as much as the machines in their hands. Men of all ages were enlisted, handed rifles, sent to the frontlines. Yet the zombie wave pressed onward. An unstoppable sea of the dead.

"With our neighbors in dire need," Great Britain's prime minister said during an emergency wireless broadcast. "We extend a hand of friendship and solidarity, and commit ours—the bravest soldiers, and the finest robots—to the battle in Europe. And though the way will be dark, and the fight long, we shall not rest until the undead threat has been eliminated. People of Great Britain, as of this moment…we are at war."

The War Cabinet felt confident assigning much of its hardware to the European mainland, believing the English Channel would prevent the infection from spreading into Great Britain. The objective, in any case, was to eliminate every last zombie before the Channel theory could be tested. Unfortunately, stopping the zombies proved more problematic than anyone could have guessed.

There were just so *many* of them. Not enough good men to stop them all. Not enough bots and bullets. And while the Channel slowed the spread of the infection, it couldn't halt it for good. The zombies entered the water, were swept out by the current, dragged down, pushed along like so much kelp, and washed up (sometimes in pulsing, twitching pieces) at various points along the English coastline. The first victim was a ten-year-old boy who'd been fossil-hunting on a beach in Dorset. He'd uncovered from a slew of shells and pebbles what he thought to be a rock from the Jurassic era, but which turned out to be a disembodied head. The boy screamed and dropped the grotesque object, but not before it could spin in his hands and bite off the tip of his index finger. He dashed home, bleeding, weeping, *changing*…tore out his sister's throat and opened his mother's skull like a clam.

And from there…

"EMERGENCY: System critical. Shutdown >*bzzk*< imminent. Must reach his majesty's >*pleenk*<…twenty-one feet until destination."

Production of bots and military hardware increased, with women of all ages running the factories 24/7 while the men (and some of them were really only boys) went out to fight. London was barricaded, its perimeter patrolled by the most advanced guardbots. Sentries and watchtowers were posted every three hundred meters, with checkpoints at all routes in and out of the city. There was a secondary barricade around Buckingham Palace. Within, it was secured by a formidable military presence whose one directive was to protect the king.

And although Southern England slowly succumbed to the zombie invasion, it was believed the Capital would not—*could* not—be breached. The king would live, by Jove! He would not become a brain-dead, shambling corpse.

Never!

For as long as there was a king…there was a Great Britain.

Harold jounced and sputtered onward, its tracks leaving oily marks on the marble floor. It coughed a filthy clod of smoke from its frontal vents and its warning light fizzed unsurely.

"Ten feet until destination."

Two guardbots outside the king's private apartments. Human form, cast iron casing, eight feet tall with PX-90 25mm chain guns for arms. They aimed their cannons at Harold and spoke in unison:

"STATE PURPOSE."

"To see the king," Harold replied, drawing to a rattling halt.

"IDENTIFICATION."

"It's me…>*spoink*<."

"IDENTIFICATION INVALID."

The chain guns hummed as their motors cranked to life.

"Wait!" The servicebot's warning light flashed faster. It raised hydraulic arms and scanned the two towering guardbots. "It's Harold. The >*pzzzt*< servicebot…"

"INDENTIFICATION INVALID."

The humming got louder. The cannons' bores trembled.

"Centum Series 6, model number November-Kilo-Charlie-six-eight-eight-niner-Tango-Romeo."

A puff of foul-smelling smoke leaked from its exhaust.

">*Ploop*<."

The chain guns cooled as the guardbots lowered their arms.

"INDENTIFICATION VALID. ACCESS GRANTED."

The doors to the king's private apartments swung open. Harold tracked slowly forward, trembling.

"GOD SAVE THE KING."

"God >*fzzk*< the king," Harold agreed meekly.

His majesty sat alone at the dining table. He spent most of his time alone, having sent the queen and the two young princesses to Balmoral when the zombies first lurched onto British soil. He stood as Harold entered the room and stepped quickly toward the sputtering servicebot.

"What is it, Harold?"

"News, sir," the bot replied. "Rather >*breep*< frightful, I'm afraid."

"Yes?"

"It's the >*ztssk*<…>*frrrt*<…"

"Oh, spit it out, you useless box of bolts."

">*Cloink*<."

The king delivered a sharp, open-handed blow to Harold's casing. Its emergency light winked out and it teetered on its tracks, then fell with a sound like a toolbox falling off a workbench. Another greasy cloud of smoke ballooned from its vents.

"Thank you, sir."

"The news, Harold!" the king demanded.

"Yes, sir…it's…it's the zombies, sir."

"What about them?" the king asked.

Harold's hydraulic arm whined as it pushed itself back onto its tracks. Its emergency light began flashing again, reflected in the king's eyes like rage.

"They're >*fzzzt*< the barricade, sir," it said. "They're coming for you."

AUDIO/VIDEO TRANSCRIPT.
NEWSREAL 122: "PROTECTING THE HOMEFRONT."
MUSICAL INTRO PLAYS to the NewsReal title sequence. Both fade to a low camera shot of British troops and bots marching through the streets of a small coastal village. We see patriotic townspeople waving their Union Jacks and cheering. Cut to close-up of a young soldier, who is distinctly seen smiling and tipping a cheeky wink.

VOICEOVER: *NEWSBOT-15:* "That's the stuff! The British show their pluck as they march to war against advancing zombie hordes. Here, soldiers and robots from the 6th Infantry Division assure the good people of Abbotsbury that the country is in safe hands. That's it, ladies! Wave your flags with pride. Let your men and robots know that you're behind them!"

Sweeping shot of idyllic farmlands, cows in meadows, and gamboling lambs. A young farm girl scattering chicken feed. Cut to shot of a bleak mass of zombies cresting a hill. Hundreds of them. The camera zooms in on their dead, vacant faces, their slack mouths filled with uneven teeth.

VOICEOVER: *NEWSBOT-15:* "Here come the rotters! Waves of the undead descend on a farm in Devon, stinking of decay and dressed in the rags they died in."

We see clusters of zombies shuffling among the farmyard animals. The cows moo and dart in all directions. Chickens scatter, spraying feathers, and the sheep run scared. But the zombies pay them no attention. They are intent on only one thing.

VOICEOVER: NEWSBOT-15: "No roast beef or mutton chops on the menu for these ugly blighters ..."

Another sweeping shot of the fields surrounding the farmhouse, and now they are crawling with zombies. Ten times more than before. It's like watching a fire spread.

VOICEOVER: NEWSBOT-15: "... The only thing they have an appetite for is brains. *HUMAN* brains."

We see the young farm girl drop her bucket of feed and bolt pell-mell for the safety of her cellar. She pulls the doors closed behind her just as the first wave reaches the farmhouse. Random shots of zombies thumping on doors and boarded-over windows.

VOICEOVER: NEWSBOT-15: "Strength in numbers as the undead surge forward, painting Britain's once-green landscape deathly black. Let's hope this young lady has sturdy bolts on her cellar doors, or she'll be joining the ranks of the undead before she can whistle, 'Rule, Britannia!' "

Cut to footage of bots rolling off production lines, lights flickering as they are booted-up for the first time. Engineers consult blueprints and make notes. Warbots, guns fully loaded, take their first well-oiled steps. Cut to grainy shot of robots of unknown directive. They are not warbots or guardbots, but something...different. There must be at least twenty of them, but it's difficult to tell because the screen is mostly blanked out by a banner that reads: TOP SECRET.

VOICEOVER: NEWSBOT-15: "Britain's hopes lie firmly in the character of its people, and the production of bots at facilities across the country. Technology is constantly being upgraded. New bots are faster, stronger, and deadlier than ever before."

An angry-looking technician steps toward the camera, waving his arms to indicate that filming is prohibited.

VOICEOVER: NEWSBOT-15: "Bravo, chaps! Jolly good job! And look, here come the bots now, fighting alongside our boys."

Cut to the sweeping green countryside again. Soldiers charge and fire their Lee-Enfields, with mighty tankbots rolling beside them, booming on their tracks as they unload countless shells. Cut to flash-images of zombies being taken out by chain-gun-wielding warbots—limbs and heads removed in a rain of bullets. A cluster of the undead falling beneath the tracks of a rumbling tankbot. Close-up of a zombie taking a bullet right between the eyes, the back of its diseased head opening like a ripe cantaloupe. Random shots of war and destruction. Endless guns blazing. Robots in ruins, circuits exposed. Smoke and body parts everywhere.

VOICEOVER: NEWSBOT-15: "Battles rage across Southern England as the relentless undead meet the equally relentless might of his majesty's forces. Here we see tankbots from the 28th Division holding off a zombie attack on the outskirts of Southampton. That's it, boys, drive those shambling blighters back to the grave!"

Cue the music as we cut to footage of RAF Spitfires taking off. Squadrons tattoo the sky like migrating birds. We hear the drone of four Merlin XX engines as a Lancaster bomber roars into the frame, propellers blurring, robots in the gunner seats. Cut to street level, where hopeful Brits look to the skies, shielding their eyes from the sun. A grimy-faced boy in short trousers and a flat cap grins and waves a huge Union Jack.

VOICEOVER: NEWSBOT-15: "And what's this? Here come the flyboys to lend a hand. Tally-ho, chaps!"

* * *

Engines screaming, machine guns rattling as the Spitfires swoop low and strafe a shuffling throng of zombies. They come apart like wet paper, chunks of moldering flesh spraying in all directions. Cut to shot of the Lancaster dropping its payload of incendiaries and a 4,000 lb Blockbuster.

VOICEOVER: NEWSBOT-15: "Bombs away!"

Overhead shot of bombs falling, rosettes of fire blooming on the ground below. Cut to images of destruction: streets and fields pocked with craters; rolling clouds of smoke; ruined buildings and burned-out, overturned vehicles; a few stray zombies staggering through the ashes. Cut to a troop of warbots clunking through the smoldering rubble, picking off the undead with their spinning chain guns.

VOICEOVER: NEWSBOT-15: "These British-made warbots certainly know how to rub salt in the wound. I say, old boy, that's jolly good shooting!"

Cue victorious music as we see the RAF squadrons banking right and returning home. Cut to footage of proud British troops marching ever on, tankbots cutting wide tracks across the countryside. Dissolve to image of a Union Jack, rippling lightly, filling the screen.

VOICEOVER: NEWSBOT-15: "The battle may be won, but the war is far from over. With the tenacious undead multiplying by the hour, the road to victory will be long indeed. But rest assured his majesty's forces are armed and ready. Great British men. Great British robots."

Dissolve again, this time to footage of the royal family waving from the balcony at Buckingham Palace.

VOICEOVER: NEWSBOT-15: "God bless this great nation, and God save the king."

* * *

Music and picture fades.

Transcript ends.

LETTERS TO GLADYS.
FROM PTE. WILLIAM POLLEN, 43rd INFANTRY DIVISION.
THE PALACE BARRICADE.
MY DEAREST GLADYS…

How I adore these silences. As I put pen to paper, the sky darkens in shades of purple and the first stars glitter in the east. It reminds me of moments spent with you, walking hand in hand to the sound of evening birdsong, or sitting on Carnation Hill and watching the Steel Rocket huff and puff its way toward Winchester. Such wonderful memories. Alas, in the midst of this terrible war, they seem a lifetime ago. I pray nightly, to God, and to anyone else who will listen, for an end to this darkness…so that I might return to you, my darling, and listen to birdsong again.

Not that I have much faith in God. It appears He has turned His back on us. Now my trust is in my king, my generals, and in the men and robots beside me. With you so far away, they are all I have.

It's a decent group, on the whole, led by Colonel Walters, who expects nothing short of 110% at all times, even when we're sleeping. There's Simpkins from Liverpool, too young to even grow a moustache. Some of the chaps call him "girly-boy," but he takes it in good spirits, as well he ought. Corporal Perkins is quite the character, of whom I have become rather fond. He does a frightfully good zombie impersonation that (although it makes us laugh fit to burst) will probably get him shot one of these days. Then there are the brothers, Roper 1 and Roper 2, from Beaconsfield. They both bleed green, always dismantling and cleaning their rifles, and their boots are so polished you could use them for shaving mirrors. They have each told me that they would rather be on the other side of the barricade, fighting alongside the grunts and robots on the frontline. I, on the other hand, hope to never have to fire my weapon, though we have heard reports of zombies just south of the Thames, so it may only be a matter of time before I am thrust into the fray.

Yes, a decent crew, it has to be said. So you might find it a dash peculiar, then, to learn that I have developed quite the friendship with a robot. That's right, my darling, a robot! A MK 7 guardbot, to be precise. They are, ordinarily, antisocial contraptions, but Arthur is…well, different. His directives are to guard (obviously), and to shoot the zombie rotters on sight. But Arthur may have a few crossed wires. He sings, for one thing (Perkins says he is like a Wurlitzer with a machine gun). "Land of Hope and Glory" is a particular favorite, and his rendition of "We'll Meet Again" would send shivers up your spine. It makes for pleasant accompaniment during those long hours of guard duty, standing at the edge of the barricade and staring at endless empty streets.

"I do enjoy your voice, old boy," I said to him earlier today. We were guarding the northern rim of the barricade, where Green Park meets Piccadilly. Extremely peaceful, now that the city has been evacuated. "As long as you know when to pipe down and fire your weapon."

(The MK 7, in case you don't know, my cherub, is armed with a rear-mounted Vickers .303 machine gun. A genuine feat of engineering!)

Arthur replied by breaking into a haunting verse of "I'll Be Seeing You." His lights flashed happily, as if to assure me that I have nothing to worry about. I could hear his motors whirring as he scanned Piccadilly for unusual movement.

I dare say you find it strange that I refer to a robot—a sexless assemblage of wires and bolts, no less—with masculine pronouns. Indeed, it goes against all logic. I know Arthur doesn't have feelings or emotions. I know he's not human…but I just can't bring myself to think of him as an "it."

He finished singing and all was silent again. A ghost town around us.

"Have you ever fired your gun?" I asked him.

"A total of fifteen thousand, three hundred and twelve rounds fired during phase seven and eight 'Recognition and Targeting' test-ing. Accuracy at 99.7%. Robo-Trac Advanced Defense Manufac-turing, Wetherby, West Yorkshire, England."

"Spiffy," I said to him.

"How about you, old chap?" he asked. "Ever fired your gun?"

"In training," I replied. "A long time ago."

"Accuracy?"

"Well, I…hit a few targets."

"And would you be able to hit those targets now?" he pressed. His lights flickered in a way that made me think, if he had eyes, he'd be narrowing them. "In the heat of battle, with the undead shuffling toward you—and some of them might look like people you know, one of your squad mates, even—would your hands be steady enough to get off a shot…right between the eyes?"

I looked away from him, my mouth opening and closing use-lessly.

"Don't worry, Billy," Arthur said, and his motors whirred smoothly as he went back to scanning the deserted street. "I've got your back."

You see what I mean, darling, when I say that Arthur is different?

I can hear him now, running through his systems check prior to shutting down for the night. And I suppose I should shut down, too. We're up at 0500 hrs—me, Arthur, and the Ropers—to patrol the south barricade, which could get interesting if the rumors we have heard are true. I imagine the Ropers can barely sleep with excitement.

So yes, to my bunk…soon. For now I shall look at the darkening sky, one of the few things that hasn't changed in the least. It's as beautiful now as when we counted stars together, and allows me to believe that everything can go back to the way it used to be.

I need to believe that.

Be safe, my darling.

All my love…Billy.

MY DEAREST GLADYS…

Saw my first zombie today. A most disconcerting sign. This

means that they have breached the Capital Barricade and are heading our way. Of course, it may have been a lone zombie, which is extremely rare, and unlikely, given their tendency to clump. Intelligence suggests that where there is one, there are bound to be more.

It happened toward the end of our watch. We were on Victoria Street, looking from our post atop the barricade toward Westminster Cathedral. It had been a long, uneventful morning (the Ropers were most disappointed) when all of a sudden the little red light on the side of Arthur's casing started to flash.

"WARNING: undead life form crossing Ambrosden Avenue. Three hundred and five feet southeast by east. One hundred and twenty-five-point-eight degrees."

The Ropers immediately sighted down their rifles, but I took a step back, sweat breaking on my forehead.

"Are you quite sure, old bean?" I asked.

"Affirmative."

"I can see it," Roper 1 declared. "Ahh, the blasted thing just stepped behind a tree. Can't get off a clean shot."

"Me, either," Roper 2 said.

"And you're sure it's a zombie?" I said. "It's not just Perkins, is it, on the wrong side of the barricade?"

"Why don't you go out there and find out?" Roper 1 suggested.

I stammered, wiped my brow, and fetched the field glasses from the equipment box. I trained them in the direction of Ambrosden Avenue, saw something shuffling just behind the tree, and watched it lurch into view. Arthur was right: an undead life form—a zombie, by Jove, with its gray face hanging and pale eyes that seemed to stare both nowhere and everywhere. It wore a button-down shirt and one shoe. Nothing else. I could see open sores on its legs, as dark as old meat.

It shuffled toward us.

"By God," I said. "It must have breached the—"

Roper 1 fired his Lee-Enfield. I felt the sturdy kick of the rifle next to me—felt its power—and watched the bullet strike the zombie plum in the middle of the chest. It was driven back into the road with such force that it left its shoe in the middle of the pavement.

"Got the rotter!" Roper 1 said proudly.

"Good shot, old boy," Roper 2 commended.

But the zombie got back to its feet and continued to lurch toward us.

"WARNING," Arthur said. "Undead life form. Still crossing Ambrosden Avenue. Two hundred and seventy-three feet southeast by east. One hundred and twenty-eight-point-two degrees."

"Quite the resilient chap," Roper 1 said.

"You have to aim for the head," Roper 2 said. "Here, I'll show you."

He took aim and fired. Again, I saw the bullet hit, this time to the left of the chest, striking the zombie's shoulder and taking its arm clean off.

"A little low, old boy," Roper 1 said.

"It's these bloody sights," Roper 2 moaned.

The zombie shuffled on, undeterred by the loss of a limb.

Roper 1 fired again and missed completely.

"Perhaps we should radio for a sniperbot," I suggested.

"Perhaps you should take a shot yourself," Roper 1 snapped. "Instead of hiding behind those—"

A terrific rattling sound took us all by surprise. It was Arthur, doing what he was programmed to do and firing his .303. The zombie must have shuffled within range and the bot was giving it what for! I lowered the field glasses and covered my ears. Ropers 1 and 2 squeezed off a few more pointless shots, then stepped back and waited for the dust to settle.

Arthur's red warning light stopped flashing, and a little green light on the opposite side flicked on. "Undead life form eliminated."

I raised the field glasses again and looked toward Ambrosden Avenue, expecting to see the zombie lying motionless in the street. But it wasn't there. I scrolled the field glasses left and right, fine-tuning the focus wheel, and it was only upon closer inspection that I was able to see chunks of flesh and bone splattered from the piazza in front of the cathedral to halfway across Ambrosden Avenue. Arthur had, quite literally, ripped the old blighter to pieces!

I lowered the field glasses and gulped, feeling somewhat foolish for having, only yesterday, questioned the bot's readiness to pull the trigger. (Particularly given my own reluctance.)

Roper 2 snatched the field glasses from me, then he and Roper 1 took turns to evaluate Arthur's prowess with the .303. "Bravo, old chap!" they said, and such-like, slapping his casing as one might slap a fellow on the back.

Roper 1 suggested that the sound of gunfire might draw more of the undead toward us, so we decided to wait a moment to ensure the coast was clear. We all four scanned the streets fastidiously, but there was no further movement. I breathed a sigh of relief. The thought of zombies having broken through the Capital Barricade was quite chilling; they would then be only one step from Buckingham Palace...from us.

There was nothing, though. Not a pigeon taking wing from a rooftop. Not a mouse, nor even a breath of wind. The empty streets looked like heaven to me.

"Just a one-off," Roper 2 said. "A rogue."

"Let's hope so," I said.

We radioed the incident, then moved on to our next post. Nothing to report. Empty, blissful streets. We returned to camp at 1500 hrs, and to nigh-on a hero's welcome. News of our zombie sighting (and subsequent annihilation) had spread like the infection itself. Arthur received many more thonks on the casing, and I a few slaps on the back. Ropers 1 and 2 exaggerated the accuracy of their marksmanship, and I didn't contradict them. Indeed, I'm guilty of my own embellishment, although I commit only the truth to this letter.

I can hear them now. The Ropers continue to regale while Arthur sings: "There'll Always Be An England." I hope he's right, but I have my doubts.

He's dropped a few of the words, which is unlike him. He claims he's picking up interference from another bot. A crossed line, or something. "There'll always be an England," he sings. "Where there's a country >*spoink*< ..." It still sounds beautiful, though. I close my eyes, Gladys, and imagine dancing with you.

I look at the sky, but there are no stars tonight.
Maybe tomorrow …
Be safe, my darling.
All my love…Billy.

MY DEAREST GLADYS…

It has happened. The unthinkable! God truly has turned His back on us—scooped us into His palm and thrown us to hell in the bargain.

The zombies are through the Capital Barricade. Not just one hapless old rogue, either, but an army of the undead. A thousand strong, and coming this way.

This will be the briefest of letters, my cherub. I scribble it now (apologies for the dreadful cursive) while the chaps and bots prepare for battle. I probably won't get the chance to finish. And if this really is the end, you may not receive it, anyway. One of many unopened, unread letters. Glimpses of love and hope. Relics for a future generation…if there is one.

No reason not to write it, though. It keeps me sane when everything else is falling apart.

They didn't just break through the barricade. They overwhelmed it. At Bromley, Croydon, and Hounslow. Vast numbers that the patrols just couldn't keep back. They sent in the tankbots, of course, and we saw the RAF fly over, but to no avail. Colonel Walters said it was like trying to stop a swarm of bees with a flyswatter. What's more, the moment zombies bite or scratch a healthy person, they add one more to their number. It's like that saying: pluck one gray hair and two will grow in its place. My darling, I fear I will have many gray hairs before this ordeal is over.

Are we without hope? I wish I knew what was going on out there. How many towns and cities have succumbed? Are we—within the barricade—the last ones fighting? Are the scientists in Europe any closer to finding a cure … a vaccine? There are so many questions, so many doubts, and it seems the only answers are in bullets and bombs.

One thing is clear: we, and the Palace Barricade (which seems so small and fragile now), represent the last line of defense before the king. As I write this, troops and bots move to points along the Thames' north bank. The hope is that the river slows the zombies' northward progress, and that they can be easily picked off trying to cross. Possible, I suppose, but I'm not altogether optimistic. I remember how quickly the infection crossed the English Channel—a much broader body of water, as you know. There have also been numerous zombie sightings to the east and west, so they can—and will, I'm sure—come at us from all directions.

It all looks rather bleak.

There! Perkins has just ordered me to put down my "blasted pen" and prepare to move out. We're headed south, of course, to man the barricade at Grosvenor Gardens.

There are many miles between us, my darling, and I feel each one of them, like a pain in my heart. But at this moment I am thankful for the distance. I want you as far from this hell as possible.

I hope to write again. I love you...Billy.

THE KING'S PRIVATE APARTMENTS.
BUCKINGHAM PALACE.

HE SAT ALONE, smoking a cigarette and occasionally looking out the window at the chaos surrounding his palace. Fat clouds of smoke rolled in the distance. He could see burning trees. Hear gunfire and explosions. Robots were scattered in pieces across The Memorial Gardens. Even the mighty tankbots—overwhelmed and unplugged. They stood on their tracks, unmoving, like fallen dinosaurs. One day, in many thousands of years, they would be unearthed and pieced together. Studied and exhibited in museums.

"It's over," the king said. He blew a string of smoke into the air and stubbed out his cigarette. Another quick glance out the window. He saw soldiers shooting soldiers—presumably those who had been infected, and possibly, amid the confusion, those who hadn't. Guardbots at the palace gates sprayed bullets at the advancing undead. A tankbot fired its gun at the Victoria Memorial, where a pack of zombies chomped brainlessly on the statues. A direct hit, and they were blown to wet chunks. The memorial cracked into so many small pieces and crumbled out of existence, as if it were a thing of no merit: a sandcastle washed away by the tide.

"All over," the king said again.

Most disconcerting, though, was his view of The Mall—the half-mile stretch of road leading from the palace to Admiralty Arch. It was packed with zombies, bunched in a thick line, stumbling and lurching in his direction. Easy enough to strafe, or even fire a doodlebot (a flying robot armed with a 1500 lb Amatol warhead) at. Get rid of a few thousand of the buggers at one fell swoop. But to what end? They were coming through St. James and Green Park, too. Along Constitution Hill and through the palace gardens. He was surrounded, and they just kept coming…and coming …

He needed something bigger.

It was time.

The king had on his desk a device, a button of sorts, that when he pushed it summoned the servicebot, Harold. He pushed it now and waited. Lit another cigarette and watched the war rage outside his window. No sign of the bot, so he pushed the button again, waited, finished his cigarette…then grabbed the device and hurled it across the room. It struck the wall hard enough to leave a mark, and fell to the floor in two pieces.

"Blasted bot!" The king marched to the door, threw it open, and demanded that one of the attending guardbots summon Harold immediately.

"Harold, sir?"

"Yes…Harold. The servicebot."

"Do you mean the Centum Series six, sir? Model number November-Kilo-Charlie-six-eight-eight-niner-Tango-Romeo… sir?"

"I don't know his bloody number," the king stormed. "Just summon him, damn you!"

"I'm afraid we can't do that, sir," one of the guardbots replied, and the other added, "We're not programmed for that, sir."

"Not programmed?" the king said. "What kind of robots are you?"

"Guardbots, sir," they replied in unison. "Mark twelve. Humanoid form. Assembled at Pulse Automation—"

At that moment Harold tracked into the hallway, puffing and smoking. It stuttered toward the king, lights blinking.

"You have kept me waiting, Harold," The king said. He stepped back and folded his arms.

The servicebot wheezed and leaked oil. "Dreadfully sorry, sir. Still having a few >*pzzk*< problems."

"Quite," the king said, frowning. "I don't suppose it matters. We're all doomed, in any case."

"Sir?"

"Enter, Harold."

Harold nudged into the room and followed the king, who strolled to his chair by way of the window. Outside, the last human soldiers made a stand, while zombies and robots went at each other with singular, relentless intent.

"Barely a working brain out there," the king said.

"A working >*ploomp*<, sir?"

"Never mind, Harold." Another cigarette, lit with trembling hands. His docbot had suggested that cigarettes were bad for his health. A preposterous notion. And even if they were, it made no difference now. The king inhaled deeply, cracked a bitter smile, and dropped wearily into his seat.

"Something I can do for you, sir?"

"Indeed, Harold," the king nodded. "A matter of great importance. In fact, the one that will end this war."

"I'm here to >*zoink*<...GETDOWNBILLY...>*fzzk*<..."

"Harold?"

"Sorry >*fuut*<...touch of interference, sir. It's all rather >*brrip*< ..."

"Who on earth is Billy?"

"No idea, sir," Harold said. Its red lights flashed. "Bit of a crossed line, is all. Nothing to >*spoink*<."

"Another reason to act quickly," the king said. "We're running short of time, Harold. I dare say the zombies will be knocking down my door within the hour, and those guardbots have only a limited supply of ammunition."

"Yes, sir," Harold agreed. Its motor whirred as it slumped on its tracks. "I do wish you'd gone to Balmoral with Queen >*zzzth*< and the princesses."

"A king does not run from the fight, Harold."

"With respect, sir, no king has had to face a zombie apocalypse."

"But I am not the first monarch to face adversity," the king said firmly. "Though I may well be the last."

"The last?" Harold's system light flickered hesitantly. "What do you mean, sir?"

"I mean that it's over, Harold. All hope is lost."

"Not quite, sir. The men are still >*prrnk*<, and there are reinforcements coming in from the north."

"It's over, Harold," the king said, and sighed. "This is not up for debate."

"No, sir. Of course not, sir."

"But I, the king of England, am going to end this war. Not some shuffling zombie scum from the lowlands." The king's hands twisted into hard little fists. "Do you understand, Harold?"

"Of course >*pzzk*<...*ofhopeandglorymotherof*...>*teenk*<."

"I say, are you singing, Harold?"

"Not intentionally, sir. Touch of the old interference, I'm afraid."

The king's brow knitted in another firm frown. He then jolted in his chair as an explosion rocked outside, so close that the window rattled in its frame.

"Time is against us," he said. "Harold, you have access to communications, am I right?"

"Yes, sir."

"Jolly good. Then I want you to deploy the atombots, on my authority."

"The atombots?"

"Yes, Harold." The king shooed the servicebot toward the door. "Do it now, and do it quickly, otherwise these zombies will be having my brains for supper."

Harold inched backward. "But >*fzzk*< ...*godwhomadethee-mightymake*...sir, >*brrrp*< I really don't—"

"The decision has been made, Harold."

Harold buzzed and stuttered. "Yes, sir, but the atombot will decimate the capital."

"Indeed it will," the king said, and his thin lips turned up in a chilling smile. "The zombies, too. Which is why I have ordered you to deploy *all* the atombots, to points right across the British Isles. Every last zombie shall be eliminated. Whatever the cost."

"Yes, sir, but the cost >*cloomp*< ...*pickingsomethingupbilly*... will be the destruction of everything...and >*preep*< everybody."

"The queen and my daughters are safe, Harold, if that's your concern."

"Actually, I—"

"You're still here, Harold?"

"Yes, sir. Sorry, sir." The servicebot reversed its tracks and whirred toward the door, but didn't get far before turning back to the king. One light flickered hopefully.

"The prime minister—"

"Is *DEAD*, Harold. Or *UN*dead. It amounts to the same thing." The king's face bloomed bright pink and another explosion lit the sky outside. "The chubby bugger has smoked his last cigar."

"The deputy prime minister...?"

"*DEAD!* A zombie. So is the Lord President of the Council. The chancellor, too. They're probably all shuffling along Downing Street as we speak."

"Yes, quite," Harold said. Its dented casing trembled. "Dashed bad luck, what?"

"Indeed," the king boomed. He took a stride toward Harold, who tracked toward the door, all parts rattling.

"What are you programmed to do, Harold?"

"To serve you, sir."

"Anything else?"

"No, sir. Only to >*skrrz*< you, sir."

"Then do it," the king said.

"At once, sir."

Harold beeped and bumped toward the door, its tracks leaving grubby lines on the plush carpet. At the threshold it stopped and looked back at its master, who stood framed by the window. A consuming silhouette.

"God save the king," Harold uttered.

Another explosion outside, and for a second it looked like the sky was bleeding—a sick red light that shone on the king and turned his eyes to fire.

"It's too late for that," he said.

LETTERS TO GLADYS.
FROM PTE. WILLIAM POLLEN, 43rd INFANTRY DIVISION.
THE PALACE BARRICADE.
MY DEAREST GLADYS...

We are truly in the thick of it now. If ever I thought that I was somehow cheating the war, enclosed by not one barricade but two, I can think that no longer. Indeed, I recall the Ropers' urgency to join the frontline and get their hands dirty (or bloody, I suppose). Well...wish granted, only it was the other way around; the frontline came to them.

The River Thames couldn't stop the zombies, just like the English Channel couldn't. The undead splashed into the water, and without air in their lungs sank to the river bed, which made picking them off impossible. There they slogged, relentlessly, across to the north bank, where they emerged en masse and attacked the soldiers posted there. Scenes of horror and confusion. Three of the four Horsemen of the Apocalypse at full gallop. Many of our boys were dropped by friendly fire. Others succumbed to the undead, either torn limb from limb or becoming zombies themselves. This, of course, happened the length of the Thames. The zombies also swarmed the bridges and came through the Underground. They came from the east and west, too. There simply were not enough bullets to stop them all.

I write this letter in the ten minutes Colonel Walters has given us to regroup and recoup. Arthur stands over me, his .303 trained on Constitution Hill.

I'm so glad I have him.

It must be a blessing, at times, to have no emotion.

He shot Simpkins—our "girly-boy" from Liverpool—with no qualm whatsoever. A single cartridge fired right through the middle of his forehead.

Simpkins had been scratched, you see, as we retreated from a band of the undead on Wilfred Street. One of the blighters came out of nowhere—crashed through the window of what had once been a charming little pub. It grabbed Simpkins and raked its diseased fingernails across the back of his hand. Roper 1 came to the rescue, but all too late. He shot the zombie and Simpkins broke free. Roper 2 lobbed a grenade into the advancing pack, which gave us enough time get away. We then reloaded and assessed the damage.

The scratch on Simpkins's hand was only small (I've received worse paper cuts), but the skin had been broken and was already beginning to darken.

"I'm fine, chaps," he said worriedly, covering the wound with his other hand. He managed a trembling smile, which made him appear even younger. "It's just a—"

A single shot, fired at point blank range. The back of Simpkins's head opened and I saw the cartridge carry out most of his brains. He dropped to the ground like a rag.

The little light on Arthur's casing flashed green. "Undead life form eliminated."

Wilfred Street is only a short distance from Buckingham Palace. The length of three football pitches, I'd say…which means that, yes, the zombies have broken through the Palace Barricade. They are among us! In small enough numbers to deal with at the moment, but we are receiving reports of many parts of London being overrun, and those zombies are heading this way.

I don't have long, my buttercup, and there is no escape.

Distant explosions. The roar of Spitfires overhead. The sound of men screaming. Lights glow within the palace, and I wonder what the king is doing while his country collapses around him—while people die and robots shut down. I'm sure he's in an underground bunker, surrounded by riches, with food and drink enough to last a thousand years. Still, I have sworn loyalty, will defend him to my last breath. And though I have not yet fired my gun, I will if I need to.

Arthur has just broken into a verse of "Jerusalem." His .303 smokes and shudders as he fires it, flames bursting from the muzzle. I look up and see the undead—so many of them—shuffling along Constitution Hill.

"*And was Jerusalem builded here, among those dark Satanic mills …*"

To war, my darling.

Goodbye.

MY DEAREST GLADYS…

Not quite "goodbye" as yet. There is no reprieve from this hell, but I have found a moment to write to you—this, which will surely be my final letter—while Arthur cools his circuits and rearms, and we await the optimum moment to make our move.

Our objective has changed. And if you should receive this letter—even if it takes ten or fifteen years—then you'll know that we were successful.

Actually, it's not just our objective…*everything* has changed.

I write this from the cover of lime trees in the palace gardens. Zombies shuffle past us, less than thirty feet away, putrid, dragging their feet. Hard to imagine that they were men and women once upon a time, with jobs and houses and children. Now they are little more than shells, drawn toward the lights in the palace because they have no light of their own.

The palace…which we swore to defend, and which we now—much like the undead—are trying to infiltrate.

Allow me to explain …

Remember when I told you that Arthur was different? Well, merely calling him "different" is doing him a disservice. Of all the robots I have encountered, from unrefined workbots to the most advanced scibots, Arthur is by far the most exceptional (and not just because of his singing). I have no idea who programmed him, but there is little doubt they gave him something extra.

I have lost count of how many times he has saved my life in the last hour alone.

The zombies came from all directions. Constitution Hill. The Mall. Green Park. It soon became apparent that we stood no chance. Reinforcements were called, and although we were assured that parabots from the north would be dropping in, we knew they would not reach us in time—that they could do little to stem the zombie tide, in any case. There followed panic, disorder, and much death. Tankbots rolled and fired recklessly. Howitzers boomed, making the very air shiver. I watched a Lancaster thunder over and drop a slew of bombs on Green Park. An effective method of eliminating zombies in huge numbers, only our men and bots were there, too. Intentional fratricide—the cost of war, I suppose, but still harrowing to witness with one's own eyes.

I stood beside Arthur in the middle of the Memorial Gardens and watched the undead lurch toward us.

"Grab a box of .303s, Billy," Arthur said, pointing at a crate of ammunition that had been airdropped in. "And stay >teenk< to me."

The .303 fires at approximately five hundred rounds per minute, and I think Arthur made every one of those rounds count. He blazed, turning on his hydraulic legs and cutting the undead to pieces. I watched zombie hands and arms fly, zombie chests explode, and cabbaged brains spatter the air, thick as London fog. We kept moving, scoping everything around us. I coughed through the fire and smoke, weeping sooty tears, but Arthur kept shooting, his lights flicking between green and red so fast I was sure he'd blow a fuse. I could smell the heat of his gun—could almost taste it at the back of my throat.

"*RELOAD!*"

I grabbed a half-full box of ammo from a fallen warbot and rammed it into Arthur's casing.

More of the undead surged forward. I watched Colonel Walters shoot three of them, then the force from a nearby grenade knocked him off his feet and within seconds he was mobbed. The zombies tore him to shreds. The last thing I saw, before Arthur whirled and fired into the pack, was a naked female zombie licking pieces of brain from her fingers.

No chance of Colonel Walters coming back to eat his former unit.

Perkins, however …

He shuffled from the smoke and ruin, eyes rolled back and jaw slack. I raised my Lee-Enfield, framed his vacant head in the sights, and curled my finger around the trigger.

But couldn't shoot.

"Perkins?"

How could I be sure that he really was a zombie, and not just doing his eerie impersonation? I mean, he'd be jolly foolish to do it at such a time, wouldn't he? But could I risk pulling the trigger—killing a man—without being 100% sure?

"Perkins…this isn't the time for games, old boy."

"*AGGGLE FLAGGLE KLABBLE!*"

"Perkins!" My finger trembled.

He shambled toward me, boots scuffing along the torn ground. The front of his jacket was covered in blood and I could see a gory flap of skin hanging from his throat, rippling lightly, like a little red flag.

My arms trembled. He wavered in the sights.

"*SNARGLL!*"

"GET DOWN, BILLY!"

I dropped to my knees at Arthur's command, clutching my rifle to my chest as the bot unloaded. I felt the power of his machine gun less than four feet above my head. It was like falling through a storm cloud. Spent shells rained down around me, sizzling hot, their tips glowing.

"Undead life form eliminated."

Rather; I looked up and saw one of Perkins's puttees, like a dead snake, lying in a puddle of claret. It was all that was left of him.

"Get behind me, Billy," Arthur said.

He didn't have to tell me twice. I scrambled on hands and knees around the bot and threw my back against his rear casing. I could feel the heat of his engine—everything cranked to full power—even through my woolen jacket and bergen.

Something buzzed and clicked inside him. It reminded me of a record rising into position in of one of those…well, one of those newfangled Wurlitzer jukeboxes.

He started to sing, "Land of Hope and Glory."

His gun rattled like wild applause.

If I didn't know any better, I'd swear the old boy was having a blast!

The zombies approached from every which way and Arthur cut them down. He wheeled in outrageous circles, and I kept my back locked to his. Sometimes the blighters would get so close I could smell their ghastly breath, see the color of their teeth and the blood-shot in their eyes. I was sure they'd reach out and drag me away, but Arthur would always rattle around in the nick of time and drive them back in an explosion of .303.

"*Land of Hope and Glory, Mother of the* >spoink< *…*"

Through the ruin I saw our boys give it all they had, with stiff upper lips and guns blazing. Young men with pounding hearts, torn apart like they were never there to begin with. Robots that had been glimmering models only weeks before, opened up like tin cans or blown to scrap metal by errant grenades.

"*Wider still and wider,* >fzzk< *thy bounds be set…*"

The Union Jack outside the palace flying high, but obscured by clouds of smoke. Tankbots trundling across the battlefield, turrets reeling, guns like thunder. Warbots crippled by hordes of the un-dead, fighting with their last sparks of mechanical energy.

"*God, who made thee mighty, make thee mightier yet…*"

I saw the Roper brothers firing into a swaying crowd of zombies, as thick as rows of maize. Both of them screaming—fear or eupho-ria, it was hard to tell. They frantically pulled their triggers until their ammunition was spent, then threw down their rifles, pulled daggers from their belts, and ran swinging—suicidal—into the

throng. There was a brief furor that reminded me of boiling water,
I watched Roper 2's severed head pop into the air like a champagne
cork, then the crowd swayed onward, still hungry…always hungry.

"*The blood a hero* >pleenk< *hath spent, still nerves a hero son.*"

Arthur sang proudly and blew away the undead and we inched
toward the palace gardens. A breach in the fence allowed us to
enter, and therein we found a moment's respite.

All I could smell was death and smoke. I was trembling—still
am, my darling, hence the shaky handwriting—and sick with fear.

Arthur stopped singing. The muzzle of his .303 glowed like the
tip of a cigarette.

"I'm picking something up, Billy," he said. All his lights flashed
red.

"What do you mean, old boy?"

"A crossed line," he replied. "I appear to be transferring data with
a bot in the palace. And what I'm receiving is not good news, I'm
afraid."

I gestured at the hell all around us. "How can it get any worse?"
I asked.

"Atombots," he said.

"Atombots?" I said with a frown. "What on earth are they?"

"A top secret project, dear chap, and for good reason. Whereas I
am armed with a Vickers .303, the atombot is armed with sixty-
four kilograms of uranium-235, with an explosive yield the equivalent of seventy-five million sticks of dynamite. One atombot alone
will destroy most of the capital. The king has ordered his bot to deploy twenty of them."

"By Jove!" I exclaimed. "And they're all to be deployed here?"

"Negative," Arthur said. "At strategic points across the country.
Britain will effectively be wiped off the face of the map."

"Good grief!"

"Like I said, old boy…not good news."

It was difficult, amid the frenzy of battle, to absorb the impact of
what Arthur was telling me. And then I thought of you, my darling,
with your family in Hornsea—your parents, who smell of old things

and are insufferably sweet, and little Peter, with his bright ginger hair and wonky eye. I thought of all the goodness in your soul, and the way you would hold my hand when we strolled through the meadows in brighter days. I recalled the touch of your lips and the sunshine in your hair, and knew with everything in my heart that I couldn't let those atombots fly. Whatever the cost, I had to stop them.

"Arthur," I said. "What can we do?"

His motors whirred. Ribbons of smoke still drifted from his muzzle. "We have to >*bzzzk*< into the palace," he said. "We have to stop that bot. Or the king. Or both."

Gunfire and explosions. The roar of death. I looked up and saw blood on the Union Jack.

"Let's do it, old bean," I said.

And so here we are, my darling, waiting to make our move, to save this country I love so dearly—to save you, and everybody else.

Arthur's circuits have cooled and he is rearmed. He is humming a tune, so quietly I can barely hear: "We'll Meet Again."

An optimistic soul, on top of everything else.

Be safe, my darling.

All my love…Billy.

THE STATE ROOMS.
BUCKINGHAM PALACE.
"DIRECTIVE: DEPLOY ATOMBOTS. One hundred and thirteen feet until >*kzzx*< destination."

These opulent rooms, dripping with riches, in the most beloved, famous house in the land…all about to be blown to rubble. Perhaps, from the ashes, a new palace would rise, but Harold's processors were unable to calculate the when. One thing was certain, though… it would rise in a very different Britain. One scarred and broken and not so Great.

"One hundred and four feet until destination."

The servicebot wheezed and rattled along, dripping oil, blowing smoke. Through the White Drawing Room and into the Music

Room, where the grand piano trembled musically every time an explosion shook the world outside. Harold's auditory receptors also registered gunfire and screaming, the groans of the undead as they hammered on the palace's windows and doors. They would be in soon, and these grand rooms would be empty no longer.

"System critical >*gzzk*< ...thiswaybilly... >*frrrp*< ..."

Perhaps, Harold computed, the king had not lost his marbles. Perhaps he really was doing the best thing for this great nation. After all, a scorched and empty land that could, one day, be built on again was surely preferable to an island besieged by the walking dead.

Wasn't it?

The sound of windows breaking. More gunfire, this from the direction of the Grand Staircase. All too close.

"Sixty feet until >*grrrk*<."

Harold stuttered, stopped, belched. A tiny mushroom cloud puffed from its exhaust and a short circuit threw its tracks into reverse.

"Sixty-three feet until...sixty-five...sixty-eight..."

It hit the piano and careened, bumped into a wall, wobbled on its tracks, then corrected its line and started heading in the right direction again. Its bolts rattled and sparks leapt from gaps in its casing.

"Fifty-two...forty-nine..."

Slowly...getting...closer.

THE AMBASSADOR'S COURT.
BUCKINGHAM PALACE.

THE GUARDBOTS ASSIGNED to the Ambassador's Entrance were strewn in pieces across the court, which made entering the palace easy. Or *easier*, at least. They still had to work through a maze of the undead. Arthur's .303 didn't stop firing until its ammo stores were empty, then Billy helped it reload and it went to work again. Round after round punched the air, and Billy wondered if he would hear the sound of that gun forever—if, even if they managed to stop the atombots, it would chase him into his dreams.

Arthur blew the zombies out of their raggedy clothes and stepped over the pieces (some of them still twitching) into the palace proper. Billy followed, occasionally looking down the sights of his Lee-Enfield but never firing—never *having* to; Arthur was that quick. More zombies crowded the Grand Staircase, blocking the route to the State Apartments. Arthur (programmed with a little something extra, no doubt about it) ripped into a verse of "Boogie Woogie Bugle Boy" and gunned them all down.

They climbed the sweeping staircase, picking their way through the debris of rotten body parts. At the top Arthur paused, lights blinking.

"What are you doing?" Billy asked.

"There are nearly eight hundred rooms in Buckingham Palace," Arthur said. "We don't have the time, or the ammunition, to search them all. So I'm tracking the servicebot's electrical signal and using its data to get a lock on location."

"There's a good chap," Billy said.

Arthur whirred and clicked. Billy waited, clutching his rifle, occasionally flicking the barrel at any deviant body part that shuffled toward him. Finally Arthur stopped whirring, sang two lines of "Just a Gigolo," and clomped toward the Blue Drawing Room.

"We're close," the robot said. "This way, Billy."

THE BALCONY.
BUCKINGHAM PALACE.

THE KING LOOKED from his ruined country to a sky stained with fire and smoke. Any moment now he would hear the drone of the atombots, and it would all be over. No more zombies. No more war.

No more anything, he thought, but so be it. A desperate disease requires a dangerous remedy, as a wise man once said. It was up to up him—the king, loved by the people—to be brave, step forward, and sound the death knell. He would carve his place in history, like every great king and queen before him. It was his destiny.

But first…one final cigarette.

"Indeed," the king said. He lit one and inhaled deeply. Smoke poured into his lungs while zombies poured into his house. Neither would get the chance to kill him. He gave a royal wave, as he had so many times before from this balcony, to jubilant, cheering crowds.

They weren't so jubilant now.

The king looked at the sky.

"Oh, do come on," he said.

Below him, zombies lurched across the forecourt. He watched a warbot fire its guns until it was dragged to the ground by undying arms. A tankbot crashed into the palace gates, fired blindly, and blew itself onto one side. A single soldier—surely the last man standing—coaxed the zombies close, then pulled the pin on a grenade and dropped it at his feet.

Brave, the king thought, finishing his cigarette and flicking the butt over the balcony. *I'm going to do something similar. Only bigger. Much.*

But where were the atombots?

No sight of them. No sound.

"That blasted robot!" The king said. It had obviously malfunctioned, gone the wrong way, maybe fallen down the Grand Staircase. Either that or it had leaked too much oil and shut down.

"When you want a job doing…" The king gritted his teeth and stepped inside. He walked across the Balcony Room to where his guardbots waited for him in the Principal Corridor.

They stood to attention. Every light bright and chain guns fully armed.

The king didn't even look at them.

"Come with me," he said.

THE BLUE DRAWING ROOM.
BUCKINGHAM PALCE.

A TEMPORARY COMMUNICATION center had been set up against the east wall. Banks of computers, radios and recording devices, teleprinters and Telex machines. It was here—and it seemed so long ago now—that Harold first learned that the undead had breached the barricade.

The servicebot jerked weakly toward the wall of machinery, bleeding oil, almost lost in a cloud of smoke. It managed to jack into the access point, link with the mainframe, and upload the king's security codes.

A light on one of the computers flashed and an automated voice crackled through a radio speaker: "WELCOME, YOUR MAJESTY. AWAITING DIRECTIVE."

Harold sparked and shuddered. "Operation >*spoink*<," it said.

"DIRECTIVE INVALID. AWAITING DIRECTIVE."

"Apologies, old boy…Operation >*kzztk*<."

"DIRECTIVE INVALID. AWAITING DIRECTIVE."

Harold didn't notice the soldier and MK 7 guardbot storm into the room by way of the Picture Gallery, and took no notice when the soldier shouted, "*STAND DOWN, SERVICEBOT!*"

Harold wasn't programmed to obey soldiers.

It rattled and spoinked, and with a final surge of power delivered the king's order.

"Operation…Leonid."

"DIRECTIVE VALID," the automated voice said. "OPERATION LEONID UNDERWAY. GOD SAVE THE KING."

"God save the king," Harold agreed, and then all its lights went out.

ARTHUR'S OCULAR RECEPTORS detected the servicebot it had been communicating with—a dented, clapped-out box of a bot, wired into a flashing grid of communication equipment. Billy shouted at it to stand down, but Arthur knew that it wouldn't…*couldn't*. It was programmed to only obey the king.

This situation, like so many others, required force.

Arthur took aim—a single shot to the bot's motherboard should do it—but before it could pull the trigger …

"…OPERATION LEONID UNDERWAY…"

"Oh dear," Arthur said.

"What is it, old boy?" Billy asked.

Arthur lowered its .303 and watched the servicebot's lights wink out. No sense in shooting it now. The little fellow was offline…permanently.

"We're too late," Arthur said. "The atombots are flying. Approximately three minutes until impact."

Billy took a useless step toward the bank of machinery. "Three minutes," he gasped. "We must be able to do something."

"Well, it's enough time for a song," Arthur said. "Any requests, old boy?"

"Yes, here's a request…" Billy pointed at the computers and Telex machines, their lights flickering happily. "Hack into the system and abort the operation."

"No-can-do," Arthur said. "Hacking isn't part of my programming, dear boy. Now, if I had the king's security codes I'd be able to…" The guardbot trailed off and something ticked deep inside its casing.

"What is it?" Billy asked.

"Codes," Arthur replied. "The king's security codes. The servicebot uploaded them over our crossed line. They should be in my internal storage."

"Can you find them?"

"Already have, old boy," Arthur replied, and clomped toward the communication center. It brushed the servicebot aside, linked itself with the mainframe, and uploaded the data.

"Well, that was easy," Arthur said.

The same automated voice crackled over the speaker: "WELCOME, YOUR MAJESTY. AWAITING DIRECTIVE."

Another voice, behind Arthur and Billy, said, "Not so fast, chaps."

Billy turned around and his first thought was to drop to one knee, only every muscle in his body had locked tight. He couldn't move. He could barely breathe.

The king stood in the doorway linking the Music Room to the Blue Drawing Room. Two MK 12 guardbots towered behind him, their chain guns already spinning.

"Your majesty," Billy croaked.

And then the bullets flew.

* * *

IN THE SPLIT second before the first round struck Arthur's iron casing, it managed to articulate the word, "Abort." In the next two seconds—as it was ripped to shreds in a storm of chain gun fire—it said, "Operation Leonid." And then, as it furiously returned fire and slumped to the ground in a shower of sparks, the automated voice—oh so sweetly—announced: "DIRECTIVE VALID. OPERATION LEONID ABORTED. GOD SAVE THE KING."

And indeed it appeared, through all the gunfire, that God *had* saved the king.

He was the only one standing.

THREE GUARDBOTS SHOT to scrap and a soldier (who didn't even have a stripe on his arm) bleeding all over the floor.

"What a jolly mess," the king said.

"*Arrr...Arrrghh,*" the soldier gurgled, spitting blood and crawling toward his fallen robot friend. He'd been shot in the stomach. In the groin. In the legs. Terribly painful, the king thought.

"*Arrgh...Arthur.*"

The guardbot's ocular receptor dimmed. "We... >*teenk*< ...did it...Billy."

"Not quite," said the king, stepping over his own fallen guardbots. "You forgot about me. I'm more than capable of punching in a few numbers and having those atombots fly. Should have done it myself to begin with."

He strolled across the room (being extra careful not to step in the soldier's blood) to the communication center. Some of the machines had been blown apart by gunfire, but the one he needed—the most important one—was untouched, working perfectly.

"Destiny," the king said, and punched in his security codes. "Now, let's put an end to this."

"WELCOME, YOUR MAJESTY. AWAITING DIRECTIVE."

The king smiled.

"Operation—" he started, but never finished.

* * *

Throughout this entire war, for all the death Billy had witnessed, he had never fired his gun. Not even one bullet.

Until now.

He pushed himself to one knee, teeth gritted and blood bubbling from between his lips. With trembling hands he lifted his Lee-Enfield and socked the butt firmly into his shoulder. He had no second thoughts. No misgivings. His girlfriend's beautiful face flowered in his mind, and he knew without doubt that he was doing the right thing.

He curled his finger around the trigger.

"Now, let's put an end to this," the king said.

Exactly, Billy thought, and blew his majesty's royal brains right out of his royal skull.

For a moment…silence. It was like the war had ended, then Billy heard the thud of an explosion—it sounded like a howitzer striking the palace's west wall—and everything came flooding back. Gunfire and grenades. The zombies groaning and shambling through nearby rooms. Billy dropped his rifle and collapsed, then crawled through the blood to die at Arthur's side.

"Bill… >*fzzzt*< …Billy…"

"Arthur…old chap." Billy placed one hand on the guardbot's ruptured casing. He managed a smile. "You…had my back."

A single light inside Arthur flared brightly, and then started to dim…

And from somewhere inside that smoldering debris came the sound of singing:

"*I Don't Want to Set the World on Fire…*"

Billy closed his eyes and faded with the music.

The communication center—still smoking and splattered with the king's brains—stuttered into life a moment later. The radio crackled and a light on the Telex machine blinked rapidly as it rattled out a brief message:

*** URGENT *** FROM WASHINGTON DC *** THE AMER-
ICANS ARE COMING ***

AUDIO/VIDEO TRANSCRIPT.
NEWSREAL 159: "HOME OF THE BRAVE."
*MUSICAL INTRO PLAYS to the NewsReal title sequence. Both fade to a
shot of US battleships, destroyers, and carriers rolling across the At-
lantic. The camera zooms out and we see that the fleet is huge. It fills
the screen. Too many to count, and all en route to points across the
British Isles.*

VOICEOVER: NEWSBOT-15: "The eagle has landed…the American eagle, that is."

*SHOT OF AMERICAN tankbots rolling through the streets of a northern
mining town, followed by advanced warbots, soldiers and sailors.
Brits crowd the pavements to catch a glimpse of the American heroes.
We see young girls cheering and waving the Stars and Stripes, while
old men in flat caps look on grimly.*

VOICEOVER: NEWSBOT-15: "The might of the US military arrives in Britain, and not a minute too soon. Here are the boys and
bots from the 7th Armored and 5th Marine Divisions. This hand-
some bunch will join British forces in an effort to send the zombie
blighters back to hell."

*CLOSE-UP OF AN American marine, one eyebrow cocked and a garri-
son cap perched on his head. A reporter asks what it's like to be in
Britain. "Well gee, sir," the marine answers with a grin, and his teeth
are perfect. "I guess it's just swell."*

VOICEOVER: NEWSBOT-15: "American enthusiasm on display,
but we'll see how 'swell' he thinks it is when he gets in the thick of
it."

*   *   *

CUT TO SHOT *of the White House, where the Stars and Stripes fly proudly and the North Lawn is blessedly free of death and zombies. Cut to the president sitting in the Oval Office.* "America shall not stand idly by while our friends in Europe suffer," *he states gravely.* "It's time to show these zombies what Uncle Sam can do."

VOICEOVER: NEWSBOT-15: "That's what we want to hear, Mr. President. And from one world leader to another..."

CUT TO THE *country residence of Britain's new prime minister. Several rows of high voltage fencing and huge tangles of barbed wire surround the Tudor mansion. Tankbots and guardbots patrol the barricade, with two sniperbots posted in every watchtower. Cut to footage of the prime minister inspecting his troops, then saluting a US Hellcat that roars overhead. In the next frame we see him bowing to the new queen of England—a fifteen-year-old girl who stands rod-straight and expressionless. She is surrounded by an army of bots that make her look like a doll.*

VOICEOVER: NEWSBOT-15: "Security is paramount as the prime minister meets with Queen Elizabeth II. Many issues are discussed, including America's involvement in the campaign. Before leaving, the prime minister makes certain he lays a wreath at the memorial to our fallen king."

FOOTAGE OF THE *prime minister somberly laying a wreath at the base of a monument that is almost lost in a sea of flowers. He lowers his head in prayer.*

VOICEOVER: NEWSBOT-15: "The king is dead. Long live the queen!"

DISSOLVE TO PHOTOGRAPH *of Queen Elizabeth II, and cue the strident music as we cut to yet more images of war. Man and robot, side by side, firing their weapons as grenades boom and body parts rain from the sky. Strafing from British and American aircraft. Incendiaries falling, blowing gaping holes in the land. Yankee warbots, armed with flamethrowers, blasting through ranks of the undead.*

VOICEOVER: NEWSBOT-15: "I say, old boy, that's one way to do it."

MORE FOOTAGE FROM *the frontlines, with explosions shaking the screen. We see burning buildings, a derailed train crawling with the undead, F6F Hellcats taking off from carriers anchored in the North Sea. Amid the hell and confusion, a single gesture of hope: a brave American soldier flicking a peace sign at the camera.*

VOICEOVER: NEWSBOT-15: "This remains our darkest hour, and many will fall before we see an end to this war. But with hope in our hearts we can—and *will*—prevail."

CUE THE "STAR *Spangled Banner" as we cut to a shot of more Yankee troops rolling through quaint village streets, people cheering and waving from pavements and rooftops.*

VOICEOVER: NEWSBOT-15: "In the meantime, lock up your daughters…"

CUT TO SHOT *of one daring soldier breaking file to kiss a young woman on the cheek. She giggles and blushes as he rejoins the march.*

VOICEOVER: NEWSBOT-15: "…And God Bless America."

Music and picture fades.

Transcript ends.

SOUL KILLER

Robert Hood

Centre for Non-Traditional Technologies Research
Installation 04.1, Bilibinski District, Chukotka, November 1963.

COLD, ALL AROUND him. Andrei Bryukhanov felt it like despair.
A deep cold. Not the raw bite of winter that blanketed the country beyond these walls. Not the natural frigidity of snow and ice.
This was deeper, much more personal than that, compounded of
fear, obsession and inhuman cruelty.

He willed himself to pull against the restraints holding him within
Dr. Vasilisa Leontyev's labyrinthine apparatus. Nothing. He was unable to move. It was as though he'd been frozen into the mechanism.

His tormentor leaned close, dark green eyes staring into his.
High cheekbones. Sensuous lips. Hair tied back, leaving wisps of it
curled onyx and lush against the unblemished skin of her neck. Andrei felt an irresistible urge to release her hair, to run his fingers
through its silky strands and across her shoulder. But he couldn't.
His muscles were frozen.

He dare not anyway. *Dushegubka*, they called her—Soul Killer.
Beauty of a goddess, heart of a devil. Attempts at intimacy by one
of her scientific subjects would not be tolerated.

Besides, he loved his wife Anouska. He could not be unfaithful.

"He is ready, Marovic?"

"Vitals are normal, Comrade Leontyev. The drug worked as predicted." The speaker was Ilya Marovic, Leontyev's direct subordinate. Though he was beyond Andrei's line-of-sight, Andrei could picture the man. Tall, thin and physically taciturn—yet Andrei had seen genuine emotion simmering in his eyes. The windows to Leontyev's soul revealed no such humanity.

"So he's comatose?" queried a softly authoritative voice. It belonged to Yuri Adrianov, an official observer from Moscow. "Unaware?"

"Completely."

"Yet his eyes are open." Andrei had never seen Adrianov; he'd always lurked too far in the background, out of Andrei's line of sight, whenever he visited Andrei in Leontyev's company. But he sounded large and contemptuous.

"He's in a state of profound sensory deprivation, Comrade Adrianov." Leontyev's tone was terse and impatient. "His eyes may be open, but a recent thanatological break-through has helped us to develop electro-chemical techniques for turning consciousness inwards, creating a state of profound ego-death. For the moment the subject exists in a dark, silent place."

"You assume too much," Marovic interjected. "I believe he feels everything, hears everything, sees what is before him—"

"These unsubstantiated beliefs aren't useful, Marovic." Her dark eyes held him in silent warning.

A skeptical grunt was his only response.

"Is he ready?" the Soul Killer's voice added, a few degrees colder.

"He's been trapped within the containment field for weeks. Undissipated psychic energy will have built toward a peak by now." He paused momentarily then continued, "It may or may not be enough."

Leontyev scowled at him. "I need certainty, Marovic. We wouldn't want him to die prematurely, would we?"

"Prematurely?" Marovic took a deep breath as though to prepare himself for the lengthy communication that followed. "Comrade

Leontyev—we have already seen that the intensity of magnetic force needed to stimulate an active psi-response in animal brains disintegrates those brains long before a catalytic level can be reached. Humans are likely to have the same intolerance. Living matter isn't built to take the strain."

"Lectures in procedure aren't required, comrade."

"Is this a serious problem?" interrupted Adrianov.

Leontyev laughed, one humorless *Hah!* "It's irrelevant. Alone, Marovic never achieves significant progress in his work because his sensibilities make him timid. The fact is, Comrade Adrianov, in this experiment we transcend the flesh. Why do we need the living shell when it is incorporeal energy that creates a personality? We are concerned with consciousness, not bodies."

"It would be wrong to let him die," snapped Marovic.

Leontyev's face, almost serene in its hardness, turned back toward Andrei. "*Let* him die? I have no intention of *letting* him die. Nothing can be left to chance."

"I don't see—"

"I will make sure his body dies at *exactly* the right moment to allow us to send his spirit where we need it to go. *He* won't die, but his body must."

Her words increased the chill paralyzing Andrei's muscles. He had known that it would end like this. When he was accused of treason and his wife and child threatened with exile or death, an offer of clemency in return for volunteering to take part in Dushegubka's research seemed a gift from God. Transmigration of consciousness? Such an inspirational concept—how bad could it be? But he had known even then that this gift came from no benevolent deity but from a devil stained by blood and without compassion. God had abandoned him.

"If you keep him alive until the sequencing has begun," The Soul Killer continued, "I will guarantee the timing of his body's death well enough."

"Oh?"

As Leontyev was still facing him, Andrei saw the ruthlessness that formed on her lips. She lifted her hitherto obscured left hand, with its long fingers and black-painted nails. In it, she held a handgun, cold and deadly. She raised it, directing the barrel toward Andrei's chest.

"Bang!" she whispered.

"It may not be instantaneous," Marovic remarked drily.

"The brain will likely go into shock and his consciousness linger. We can relish those few moments of near-death. They add spice."

"Hardly an elegant solution."

The Soul Killer shrugged. "Crude, yes, but effective enough."

Abandoned Kirtland-Chang Research Facility.
New Mexican Territory. The Future.

AN EXPLOSION RUMBLED through the compound's hollow emptiness. Bent over clunky dials and awkward sliders on a computer control bench, Dr. Charlesford Stanton did not glance up as the tremor of the blast bashed at the walls and made the concrete floor on which he stood shudder. Such grumblings were unremarkable within an experimental munitions area.

What Stanton was slightly more aware of, however, was the figure that staggered up to him from behind, though he only flinched in acknowledgement when a trembling hand clamped down on his shoulder.

"Stanton, they've broken through!"

"Careful, for God's sake! Setting these wretched dials accurately is hard enough under the best of circumstances."

"But they're in!"

Stanton glanced back into Karl Donatelli's bloodshot, near-hysterical eyes. "Who's in?"

"The zombies, who do you reckon?"

Stanton straightened, feeling tired muscles stretch and crack. "In where?"

"The compound."

"How?"

"Nakamara's men are undisciplined fools." Donatelli glanced

nervously toward the main door. "Several got bored and ventured outside. Wanted to bag some dead meat as a diversion. Instead the dead meat bagged them. Then their drunken buddies let them back in."

"What's Nakamara doing about it?"

"Not much. Someone tried to stop them with a rocket launcher but their aim wasn't much chop. Nakamara's scattered across the loading dock in a thousand pieces."

"Shit!" Stanton glanced toward the huge bulk of vaguely humanoid metal—scratched, battered and smeared with blood and oil but undeniably imposing—parked in front of the inter-dimensional portal's oval access ring. "We've got to get that contraption into the time stream before the zombies..." He paused, glanced back at Donatelli again. His face was dripping with sweat. "Well, you know. It's our only hope."

"Slim hope, Charlie. We should get the hell out of here."

"And go where?" Stanton began bashing at the control console.

"Anywhere. This place may be fairly isolated, but they've been gathering out there for weeks. With the bay doors blown apart, there'll be hundreds of the bastards pouring in. Maybe thousands. What's the point in staying?"

"If I can align its trajectory accurately, maybe the warbot can stop Fritz Winterbottom back in '08—"

"Before he goes through the portal and brings back the plague, you mean?"

"Why not?"

"They're not programmed to kill humans, not deliberately. It won't work."

Stanton shrugged carelessly. "Maybe. True, I couldn't fiddle with the AI—it was locked down. Would've had to neutralize it completely. But I've fitted the warbot with backup, so to speak. As soon as the bot's AI confirms the presence of Winterbottom, a signal will activate a limited-range thermo-nuclear device—"

"What? You're kidding me."

"Small-scale, Karl—*very* small. It'll be fine."

"It's insane."

"Insane? The whole situation's insane."

"You're screwing with forces you don't understand, man. You could cause a worse disaster."

"How much worse can it get? The explosion will incinerate the bastard, and the zombies will never get a hold on us here. They'll be gone. Poof! We'll be safe."

"You don't know that. The plague was already active in the far future before Winterbottom brought it back. Saying he started it creates a temporal paradox. Chicken and egg, Stanton. It began, somewhere, sometime, whatever else Winterbottom might've done or not done—"

"At least it gives us a chance!" Stanton returned to his calibrations. "You want to run, then run. I'm doing this!"

Donatelli watched Stanton's hands scurrying over the dials like large naked spiders with ADHD. He couldn't see any meaningful pattern in their movement. Was Stanton a hero or just a deluded fool? Both maybe, Donatelli decided. If he wanted to commit suicide, so be it. Personally, Donatelli had seen enough of his friends and colleagues become zombie chow to last him a lifetime, no matter how short that lifetime might prove to be. Death was already scratching and pounding on the lab door.

"I'm taking the Rover."

"Go then!"

"Come with me—"

"Go, damn it!"

What was the point in arguing? Stanton never listened to reason and Donatelli had no desire to sacrifice himself to the man's delusions. He took off toward the service door at the far side of the room, hearing the guttural roar of the dead, bone thudding on steel door, the high-pitched whirr that signaled activation of the interdimensional portal. Fingers on the door handle, Donatelli glanced back—just as the lab's main entrance collapsed. A grotesque mass of torn skin, shredded clothing and grasping fingers crashed through the gap, the breathless snarls of their lust for flesh rising like a tsunami of fury. Lit by sharp light crackling from the portal's ring, the zombies were a vision of Hell.

At the sound of the dead, the warbot's core imperatives overrode Stanton's more recent programming. It turned, gun-arm grinding into place.

"No!" shrieked Stanton. "Into the portal! Now!"

The warbot ignored him. The ammunition cartridges of its in-built machine-gun began to rotate, propelling bullets in a fiery stream across the narrowing space between robot and zombie horde. The corpses tore apart, flesh ripped from bone, splattering walls, floor, lab equipment—but it did not stop the mass of them. More and more of the zombies poured through the gap. They raged across the bloody debris, stumbling over sodden scraps torn from fellow dead while legless torsos dragged onward inexorably, skeletal fingers scrambled for purchase amid the gore and offal, corpse mouths shrieked soundlessly. Not even the warbot's bullets could keep up with the onslaught.

Electrical discharges suddenly shot from the cables connecting control console to portal. Smoke billowed from gaps in its casing. "Stanton! It's overloading!" Donatelli yelled. But Stanton went down under a mass of zombies, arms still flailing at the controls. For a moment his head rose out of the ravenous chaos, mouth open in an almost comical scream. Then the warbot turned toward Stanton and, though intended for the zombies, a stream of bullets ripped the man's head apart. The console burst into flame.

Gut retching, Donatelli slammed down the handle still grasped in his aching fingers. A deep rumble swelled up in the floor beneath his feet. He yanked open the exit door. *Have to get away! Have to run!* But amid the cacophony, he hadn't heard the sounds coming from the corridor beyond. Undead stench struck his nostrils first, followed within seconds by a wall of tearing claws. He staggered back. Fell. Suddenly he was staring point-blank into the dead, opaque eyes of a zombie. Its mouth snapped shut and he felt the side of his face ripped away. Blood and vomit gushed out through the tears.

The last thing he saw through a gap in the wall of dead flesh surrounding him was the warbot overwhelmed by a crowd of angry corpses, forcing it backwards into the portal. As the warbot disappeared through the swirling miasma of the dimensional interface, taking a group of zombies with it, the console erupted into flame and shredded metal. In the seconds before his ribs were crushed in the frenzy and his skull torn open, Donatelli felt the explosion engulf everything, extinguishing the light and plunging his world into darkness.

LIFE HAD ALWAYS had an extra dimension for Andrei Bryukhanov. Even as a child his mind would wander and in its journeying his mind's eye would see things that he should not have been able to see. Places he had never visited were clear in his memory; places far over the sea were as familiar to him as the village square. He could describe to his mother events on a ship at sea or the view from the summit of Mt. Everest. One morning in August 1945, he walked the ashen streets of Hiroshima, Japan, and reported on the apocalyptic desolation he saw there. He could repeat conversations he had overheard from miles away and describe the sensation of tropical heat on his skin even as a bleak winter wind blew snow against the outside walls of their home. Some considered him a saint, others a demon. His "uniqueness" became well known in the town where he grew up and throughout surrounding districts.

Such notoriety was what drew Dushegubka to him. He knew that. When he was denounced as a traitor it should have come as little surprise that she was there to offer him clemency. She had been experimenting on people such as Andrei Bryukhanov for years, seeking ways of fighting from afar the so-called Cold War against the Americans. Andrei was valuable grist for her psychic mill.

Andrei remembered listening to Leontyev as she talked of her latest project—though now, strapped into her spiritual transmigration apparatus, he wasn't sure whether it was in her actual presence or via his long-distance eves-dropping abilities that he'd heard the words.

"To be able to project the will and consciousness of our own agent into the mind of the enemy—and then to control him," she enthused. "With that knowledge, how could we not gain advantage over the capitalist warmongers?"

To prove it undeniably and dramatically, she said, she would put Andrei Bryukhanov into the body of an American agent and make him assassinate the US President, John F. Kennedy. All from a distance, without leaving Bilibinski. Yuri Adrianov would be her witness. He was well respected in the Kremlin.

"There will be no laughing at my ideas then," she said.

Pain flooded through Andrei as the magnetic field around him grew stronger. Leontyev stood dispassionately and watched her victim's body spasm, waiting for sign that his consciousness had loosened its hold over his traumatized flesh. Andrei felt himself slipping away, while around him the energy matrix in which he was encased strained to contain the build-up of psychic power. Screens bombarded him with images of his target vessel—Lee Harvey Oswald, a covert operative of the FBI. Oswald wore an ordinary face, though with asymmetrical eyes and lips that looked as though they were barely holding back the secrets that churned in his head. Oswald had visited the Soviet Union in 1960 as a double agent, itself a blind. Married a Russian woman. Was secretly trained as a shooter, though he didn't know why. He returned to Fort Worth with his "secrets," convinced the KGB considered him a reliable asset. He was currently in Dallas, where he would meet with his FBI superiors, ostensibly collecting intel to bring back to Moscow. He was a nobody, but soon he would be infamous for murdering his President.

Voices whispered in Andrei's ears. *Domovoi*, they said. *Domovoi*. Were they calling him a house spirit? *Domovoi* Bryukhanov, they whispered. The voices described Oswald's movements, giving coordinates, place names—details of a life on the verge of disruption. *Kill the President, Domovoi.* Compelled by the voices, Andrei felt his consciousness wrap around a plethora of facts, embracing them, moving outward from his body to seek their presence in the time-space continuum. He seemed to be hovering then, seeing his own flesh encased in wires, dominated by TV screens and huge magnetic generators—bombarded by their energies. He felt his body dying, becoming a corpse. The beautiful Soul Killer, gun in hand, stood beside him. "Stop this now, Leontyev," said Marovic. "He's clinging to life by a thread." Andrei watched as the woman raised her gun and pulled the trigger to sever that thread. Looked on as the barrel belched fire, wisps of smoke and a metal projectile. As though in slow-motion the bullet spun toward his chest. Cracked his sternum. Exploded through his heart. Spat out a spray of blood and fractured bone.

It should have hurt. There should have been at least a few moments of agony. Andrei, however, felt nothing. He had already left. Pain had become merely darkness.

In the darkness his spirit, ungrounded, scanned the currents of sub-spatial energy, seeking a vessel to occupy.

In the far distance it sensed the presence of Lee Harvey Oswald—a beacon to guide him.

But something stronger and more demanding was coming, riding the currents of both time and space. It drew closer by the moment.

VIOLENT MOLECULAR DISRUPTION accompanied the warbot as it tumbled into a deep temporal vortex. Waves of energy burst over it. The power of the wave-front swept around the metal juggernaut's flailing limbs, burst in through its eyes and scrambled its circuits. In an instant its programming was all but wiped clean. It had become a void. It was swept away, accompanied by flailing dead amidst a cloud of blood and gore.

Drawn by the synchronicity of powerful electro-magnetic pulse and distant energies calling to it over time and space, the warbot drifted in the direction of Chukotka and November 1963. As drifts go, its motion was both rapid and unstoppable. Sixty years before—yet only nano-seconds after falling into the void—it burst through the temporal barrier in a chaotic frenzy that decimated most of the Soviet research lab before the whirlpool of atomic disruption upon which it rode contracted to a glowing temporal anomaly. The carcass of the warbot crashed across benches and destroyed Vasilisa Leontyev's machineries. It came to rest mere inches from Andrei Bryukhanov.

Andrei Bryukhanov was dead—yet he screamed in pain, and because of the vastness of the disruption that wracked his spirit at that moment, failed to notice that the warbot hadn't come alone.

FOR ILYA MAROVIC the arrival of the warbot brought mind-numbing chaos. A sudden violent concussion filled the laboratory with light and a roar like the screams of a thousand tortured men. Marovic was flung back against the control panel of Leontyev's apparatus, tangled in sparking wires torn from the machine by the impact. Fire surrounded him—fire that wasn't flame but instead burned with a chill straight from the blackest depths of time and space. He could hardly make out a thing, as though he had something in his eye, but in that instant he did see the energy surge grab Leontyev, too, tossing her toward the rear wall like so much detritus. A sheet of metal ripped from the top of a bench sliced through fat, bureaucratic Adrianov and the room filled with a swirling red mist. So much blood! More than could have come from even Adrianov's bloated torso. Something huge loomed out of the glare. It seemed to be surrounded by writhing bodies.

Marovic screamed as the energy field engulfing him flared brighter, gouging further and further into his flesh, shattering his bones, entering his nerves and flowing through them into his brain. Ethereal claws tore at his consciousness. Awareness fractured, dimmed, began to flicker toward nothingness.

"Marovic!" roared a voice in his ear and firm hands grabbed him. It was Khrushchev, head of security. Marovic had seen the man enter the lab moments before the experiment began, no doubt intent on evaluating their activities for potential intelligence violations. "Help me!" he groaned.

As Khrushchev dragged him out of the tangle, the energy still flowing through him flared up again, and for a moment Marovic was looking down at his own contorted features—his face ripped along the jawline, a piece of metal tubing glowing with some strange energy embedded in one eye. He tried to scream but he'd been disconnected from his mouth. He could no longer feel his body at all.

Khrushchev stumbled back and Marovic went with him. Left behind on the shattered control panel, his bloody, prostrate body burst into flame.

Then the yellow glare swept away into darkness.

COLD. A METALLIC, unresponsive cold that held him tight and numbed his flesh. Andrei lay in this new cold, alone, unseeing and too insensible to feel confused. After a period of time that might have been a second or a year, he began to hear something. A voice? At first it merely whispered, so low he couldn't make out the words. Yet when he finally made sense of them, the experience was no longer like hearing. It was as though he'd tuned into someone else's memories. They were broken and faded memories.

"Stanton! It's overloading!"

Fire flares. Vast energies course through him. A gun that is his arm roars, spits metal. Dead eyes surround him. Mouths dripping with blood scream their pain and hunger.

Memories of unnatural violence, of dead humanity ravenous for human brains, of civilization in ruins. The emotions accompanying them were flat, neutral—observances rather than responses. Yet Andrei felt a strong need to destroy the hungry dead. There was no passion in the need, merely a sense of necessity.

How can the dead live?

Yet they do. They must be stopped.

He opened his eyes as the whispers diminished into a background murmur of shattered masonry, falling equipment and debris settling into stillness. Beyond an overturned supply cupboard and other jetsam a glow that implied a simmering fire sent shadows flickering over the ceiling, like irritated ghosts. He could sense the radiation from it, not as heat but as sub-space turbulence.

The lab lay in ruins around him. Instinctively Andrei moved his arm. It felt heavy and unwieldy but he was no longer paralyzed or restrained. He turned his head. The grinding sound—metal on broken concrete flooring—puzzled him. But across the rubble he could see a body, torn and broken, like a shattered mannequin. Who was it? He couldn't tell. There was something wrong with his eyes. The world was colorless—sharply focused though strangely distant. He tried to blink, to clear his vision. His eyelids refused to move.

"Stanton! It's overloading!"

Stanton? He'd never heard the name before, yet he knew immediately, intuitively, to whom the name belonged. Stanton was a scientist. A scientist in a world overrun by a terrible plague. He'd been trying to do something with Andrei. Andrei wasn't sure what, but that realization did not surprise him. They all used him. Everyone. Just as his country had used him. Just as the Soul Killer had used him.

He'd almost forgotten about Leontyev. Where was she? She'd been standing over him. She'd—

The gun in her hand spits metal. A tearing pain flares in his chest…

—she'd shot him! Killed him. Confused, he pushed the images aside. Whatever had happened, Andrei knew he had to get away from this *Soul Killer* while he could.

Kill the dead!

In the far corner of the lab, seen through a veil of dust and smoke, a bent human figure stumbled out the door. Andrei watched it for a moment, wondering at the need he felt to annihilate that shambling ruin.

Destroy them all!

He tried to sit up and it was then that he realized that a heavy bench had toppled onto his chest and legs. Strange that he couldn't feel the weight of it. Was that a consequence of the drugs they'd been using to keep him trapped within himself?

Desperately he pushed against the solid, immovable bench, knowing he wouldn't be able to budge it. To his surprise, however, it lifted off him, flew through the dusty air, and crashed hard against the wall opposite. To push it away like that was indicative of great strength, but Andrei had never been physically strong and his recent past had more or less drained him of whatever vitality had survived in his muscles. To do this was—impossible.

When he saw his lower body, revealed by the removal of the bench, the sight came with all the uncanny force of a nightmare.

What had he become?

"Stanton! It's overloading!"

Bulky, metallic armor encased him. He pushed himself up, finding his balance with greater ease than he'd anticipated and staring at the world from a perspective he'd never had before. He was much taller now, and bigger, so much so that his own metal-clad body dominated his peripheral awareness. He lifted his right arm and stared at it. It had been re-constructed into some kind of machine gun.

Kill the dead!

He staggered, his short, lumbering legs sliding automatically into position to re-balance him. He glanced around.

A body, a scorched, still smoldering human body, lay across the transmigration machine's control panel, which had been ripped apart by the explosion. Half the dead man's face was gone and it was badly burnt, but Andrei recognized it as Marovic. That made him sad. He'd rather liked Marovic. Amidst the wreckage, almost at his feet, he noticed another body, this one a slight man covered by a torn and badly scorched hospital gown, here and there bone showing through gaps where flesh had been sheared off by the blast. For a moment Andrei didn't recognize him, but the wound torn into his chest—the bullet hole, the blood and shattered bone—grabbed his attention forcefully and made him study the man's features. Ratty brown hair, hawkish nose, gaunt cheeks, ragged beard, full lips encrusted with dry spittle and vomit.

<I know you,> he said aloud, in a voice that was cold and deep and echoed in the room like the sharp clang of metal-on-metal. <Who are you?>

The body did not answer, but Andrei's memory did. That corpse was his, the dead flesh of Andrei Bryukhanov—heart torn asunder by Vasilisa Leontyev, the Soul Killer. In the same instant, he knew more—

This is no suit I'm wearing, he thought. Not armor. I am the metal casing the way this corpse had once been me. I don't wear the metal, the metal wears me.

He felt the truth of this absurdity with absolute conviction. How it was possible he didn't know, but he knew he had become something other than human—

A robot, an intelligent machine made to hunt and destroy the living dead. Code-named warbot. Warbot Model 3.2. A machine whose nascent AI had been burnt from its wiring, leaving a mere trickle of data to echo memories of its duty into his thoughts.

Andrei had no idea what an AI was, but he knew what it meant. The robot's mind had been ripped away in some cataclysmic disaster, and Andrei's own disembodied spirit had been drawn into the empty circuits. Now the two of them were joined.

Kill the dead!

What he really wanted was to press his palm onto his forehead, to feel the warmth of familiar flesh and find comfort in the soft pressure of his own skin. But the hand that rose toward his head was alien, cold and hard—and he forced it away in horror.

Something moved to his right, a door opening onto this scene of destruction and madness. Through the dispersing smoke, he detected soldiers. Leontyev's guards. They scanned the room purposefully, as though they expected to see something. Was it him they'd expected to see?

The first one to do so started back, crying out a semi-articulate warning. Another shouted a command. They all trained their weapons on Bryukhanov and began shooting, over and over again. Their bullets ricocheted off his body, striking without pain or noticeable effect, at worst denting his exterior. Without thinking, driven by the ghost of the robot's underlying imperatives, he raised his gun-arm and cut them all down. Their bodies thrashed blood into the air and their cries echoed from the walls.

Silence fell. The cold seemed deeper than ever. Once again in control of his "body," Andrei felt the emotional impact of what he'd just done overwhelm him. These men may have worked for Leontyev—and the Soul Killer was cruel and undeserving of pity—but they were not to blame. They simply did their duty as dictated by the Politburo. They had lives, and friends. Loved ones who would mourn for them. Children.

Memory of his own son caused the chaos in Andrei's mind to focus on thoughts of his family: his boy Pavel, his wife Anouska. With thought of them came clarity of purpose. Leontyev was dead. Marovic was dead. The Kremlin's observer was dead. Even Andrei Bryukhanov was dead. None of them could call on him now. They could have no hold over his spirit.

He would go home to where his spirit belonged. He would be *domovoi*—a spirit in his own house. But he would return to his family as a free man. They would welcome him with joy. Melded into the carcass of an alien machine, Andrei Bryukhanov smashed his way out of the compound and set out across the bleak, wintry landscape, seeking to reclaim the life that had been taken from him.

GRIT IN THE air choked Vasilisa Leontyev, rasping in her throat like sandpaper. She coughed, spluttered—and glanced up again to see three or four of the facility's security guards peering at her nervously. None of them was very experienced or overly competent. But they had AK-47s.

"Comrade?"

Lazar Khrushchev, head of the facility's security unit, approached her with a ferocious air. He wasn't related to the First Secretary of the Party, despite whispered rumors to the contrary—rumors that suggested his exile in this less-than-high-profile establishment had been motivated by internal family politics. Leontyev had often wondered if tolerating his frequent impertinence might benefit her in the long run. His face was hard, the muscles of his jaw tensed. His usually immaculate uniform was singed and torn.

"I was in there when it happened," he growled. "Marovic and Adrianov. Both dead. That thing—I've never seen anything like it."

"Whatever it is," she growled, gesturing back toward the bulky armored figure that had appeared out of nowhere amid a raging storm of fire and electricity, "Capture it!"

Khrushchev nodded resignedly, cocked his rifle and gestured for his men to follow. Leontyev watched as they pushed through the door into the main lab, watched as they were cut to pieces by the blazing machine gun on the thing's arm. *No man this*, she thought, seeing it more clearly through a gap in the door and thinning smoke. *A machine*. It had a star painted on its chest—scratched and faded to a monotone gray now. That might have indicated that the machine was of Soviet origin, but there was also English writing on it: "Dead Fucker."

Clearly it was some kind of automated capitalist weapon. But if so, it had lost its sense of purpose. Through the shattered door and the swirling haze, she could see it turn and lumber from the massacre, heading not deeper into the complex but toward the exit. Doubtless she had been the target of its attack, but why had it abandoned its mission now? Did it think she were dead?

Leontyev grabbed the arm of the only soldier to remain with her. "Follow it," she said. "Wherever it goes. But keep your distance. I want to know where it's going and what the hell it's up to."

The soldier disappeared into the smoky shadows. Ahead of him, the machine had smashed its way out of the room.

Alone, Leontyev re-entered the lab to better survey the wreckage, growling curses into the smoky air. Further in, the atmosphere was red, as though drops of blood were suspended in the air. Smoldering fires made the light eerie and the atmosphere foreboding. A radiation leak? She backed out, unwilling to go further. This was disastrous. Her transmigration device had been destroyed, Marovic tangled in it like an electrocuted rat, the experiment terminated. The timing of the machine's attack couldn't have been worse, clearly facilitated by covert intelligence leaked to the enemy by a mole within her own unit. She would have to look into that possibility. Andrei Bryukhanov, the strongest psychic available to her, was dead. Even if his spirit had managed to link with the American double-agent Oswald, the destruction of her equipment had rendered it impossible for her to control him effectively, despite her activation of his brainwashing through the use of a pre-set code word. Was he in America now, more or less a free agent? Years of work, hope of success, credibility—all gone. Could the situation possibly get worse?

She hadn't thought so, but the arrival of the metal assassin heralded a change, one that mutated the world into a place Leontyev didn't recognize at all. She had embraced the possibility of psychic warfare not least for reasons of ambition, but there'd been a scientific quality to the research that mitigated her materialistic skepticism and let her believe in it. This was different.

At first she hadn't realized what she was seeing. The gaunt, shadowy figure that emerged from a pile of rubble didn't look familiar, though that meant little as most of Leontyev's staff were, to her, faceless nobodies. But this soldier wasn't wearing one of the standard uniforms; as far as she could tell his clothes were more like workers' trappings, foreign even for this remote location and perhaps not a uniform at all. What's more, they looked torn and derelict in ways that could not be accounted for by the recent explosion. Most of the bloodstains were blackened and scaly. Where the man's flesh was lacerated, there was no oozing redness, just dark, dried-out meat and the odd festering sore. It made no sense. Then she saw his face, and she knew the truth of it. This man hadn't been injured during the explosion that accompanied the arrival of the death machine; he had arrived at the same time as the robot, already dead but impossibly animated.

That wasn't the worst of it. As she watched, the blood-splattered corpses of some of her guards began to drag themselves up, blank eyes turning toward her. Endowed with an unnatural vestige of life, the dead men swayed for a moment, as though seeking balance, then snarled. As one they turned toward her. Staggered into motion. Hands became claws, gouging at the air. Their jaws opened and closed, shattered teeth grinding as their empty lungs emitted low, breathless moans.

The sight confused her so deeply it wasn't until the first of them had drawn close that she registered the danger to herself. Its presence was unnatural and its intent that of a rabid wolf.

"Stay away from me, soldier!" she ordered in the fiercest and most supercilious tone she could muster. Authority meant nothing to it, of course; she wasn't convinced it could even understand her. She backed away, breathing heavily.

She'd lost her gun during the chaos of the death machine's initial arrival, but a quick glance offered her an alternative. Prying an AK-47 from the fingers of one of her downed guards—the man wasn't yet dead and not yet a monster, and she wondered for how long the last of his warmth would protect him from whatever supernatural plague was resurrecting the dead—Leontyev quickly turned toward the approaching corpse and fired point-blank into its chest. The creature staggered backwards with the force of the impact, but it did not drop. Sporting yet more holes in its body, it regained its balance and came at her again. Luckily the AK-47 was set on full-automatic. She depressed the trigger and held it, letting the assault rifle loose in all its deafening fury. The action threw her off-balance and some rounds went wild. She re-aimed and continued. The corpse's blood flew through the smoky air. Spent bullets sprayed out behind her until the final cartridge was empty; mere seconds had passed, with perhaps 100 rounds fired. It hadn't stopped the dead man, but she'd managed to shatter its hip on one side and the thing could only hobble along on one leg, dragging the other behind it uselessly.

Other dead men were approaching now, maybe twenty of them. Leontyev smashed the heavy butt of the rifle into the closest, dodged its grasping fingers and headed back out the door. More of her security guards had arrived, including Khrushchev.

"You made it out," she observed.

He nodded, looking dazed and disorientated.

"Well, don't just stand there," she snapped, gesturing toward the snarling corpses. "Stop them!"

He was breathing heavily. "Sorry," he managed. "I think I must have been hit by something. I have memory gaps…and there's a voice—"

"Psychoanalysis later, comrade. Those damn things are getting close."

He looked at her, lips not quite forming the sneer that was lurking there, just the near side of insolence. Instead he turned, gesturing for his men to attack.

More useless gunfire. More noise. Leontyev retreated to a safe distance down the corridor and watched the men fend off their dead comrades, the unnatural sight of the ravenous cadavers and their relentless advance undermining whatever combat skill her guards might have been able to muster. The first soldier having his throat ripped out, face torn from his skull by grasping undead fingers, broke whatever resistance remained in them. The men fell back, some turning to run, some firing wildly. Bullets ricocheted off the walls of the corridor. Another soldier was bitten; he cried out and fell, hit by one or two bullets that had been intended for the monster clamped on his arm. Leontyev watched as life left him, and a new life, a pseudo-life, replace it. What an amazing biological weapon this was! *How had the US kept its development secret?* she wondered. Whatever it was, virus or something more arcane, it could decimate civilization across Asia and Europe, destroying the Soviet Union without the need to resort to military action. But wouldn't the capitalist scientists have created some means to protect themselves at the same time as they'd developed the weapon itself? With such protection, their armies could answer the distress call that the UK and its European allies would surely issue, and invade under the pretext of humanitarian compassion. Leontyev determined she could not allow this viral weapon to spread beyond the walls of CNTTR Installation 04.1. She would find some means of re-directing it against them.

"Fall back!" Khrushchev shouted through the din.

Those who heard weren't slow in obeying his order. Leontyev turned to join the retreat but as she did she became aware of someone near her. She reacted in time to avoid the dead hands clawing at her face, dodging clumsily to one side and crashing against a trolley table covered in surgical masks and gowns. Steadying herself on its edge she struck at the corpse's arm. The thing moaned at her, expelling foul odors from its open mouth. Quickly she dodged its hands once again, maneuvering the wheeled trolley between the corpse and herself. She rammed the monster up against the wall.

The corpse wasn't strong. Leontyev found she could keep it pinned there as long as she pushed her full weight against the rim of the trolley. She was just beyond the corpse's reach.

"Don't you touch me, you fucker!" she growled.

That was when she noticed the hole in its chest and, focusing for the first time on its face, recognized who it was—or had been. Andrei Bryukhanov. Dead—and out to kill her.

"Andrei," she whispered, "are you still in there?"

She glanced around. The other corpses seemed to be pre-occupied with chewing on the brains of those of her guards who hadn't been quick enough to escape, or were wandering off down the corridor in the wake of those who had been. She stared back at Andrei's contorting face, trying to see below the surface. The corpse growled half-heartedly and returned her gaze.

There was nothing in those eyes. She was convinced of it. No life. No Andrei. Nothing.

"You need help, Vasilisa?"

Leontyev scowled at Khrushchev's overt familiarity. Only once had they given in to the sexual attraction between them, but since then he had displayed a sense of ownership. It was a lapse of discipline she'd have to correct, and soon. Maintaining pressure on the wriggling corpse, she held out her right hand. "Gun," she snapped.

Khrushchev handed her his weapon—a TT-33 pistol.

"Nothing bigger?" she asked.

He shook his head.

It would have to do. She aimed it at Andrei Bryukhanov's head and pulled the trigger repeatedly, until the magazine was empty. The corpse's skull shattered. Blood, bone and brain splashed over the wall. She stepped back. The corpse continued flailing its arms around, unwilling to give way to stillness.

"Get me an AK," she said.

"Just leave it."

"Now!"

Khrushchev grunted and took a few steps down the corridor. He returned moments later.

"Step back!" he growled.

As Leontyev moved out of the line of fire, he rapid-fired at the corpse until its head disintegrated under the assault. It collapsed to the floor, a mass of twitching blood and bone.

"This isn't going to be easy," he commented. "What now?"

"We get out of here but lock these bastards in the main compound. None can be allowed to escape, Khrushchev. Not one of them."

"Why don't we destroy them now?"

"As you said yourself, it won't be easy. Many of our people have joined their ranks—and besides, there's something else I have to do first. Something of foremost importance."

"Oh? What?"

"Find and neutralize the assassin who brought them here."

BRYUKHANOV HAD NO idea how long he'd been walking. His consciousness drifted as ethereal as the snowflakes that fell through his visual field, caught on currents of wind and melting to nothing before they hit. Being inside the machine had, to an extent, emotionally disconnected him from the world. What was out there couldn't touch him. The beauty of the forests through which he walked, surreptitious shadows that might have been wolves but were smart enough to avoid him, the misty air and occasional smudges of sunlight that should have inspired memories of his wife Anouska and their life together—these meant nothing to him. An almost instinctual drive kept him moving forward, for the moment undercutting the imperatives of the machine he had become. He was going home. That was enough.

For most of the trek—a direct trajectory that took him off-road, across snow-covered fields and through forests—he wasn't aware of meeting anyone, though occasionally memory of firing his weapons brought with it images of shouting, blood and destruction. It wasn't until he reached a village named Ustruya that the familiarity dragged his consciousness into greater clarity. The road through the village was empty, darkness covering houses to either side like low-lying fog. Flickering light and the sound of men talking drifted from behind clouded windows on a building further toward the center of the square. A tavern. Andrei wasn't drawn to its promise of warmth and company; he had other priorities. What were these priorities? They drove him, but he couldn't clarify them. His mind had thinned to a transparent veneer over memories of violence—images of snarling, monstrous faces, blood and torn flesh.

Movement to the right caught his attention. Andrei glanced that way. A man staggered toward him in a barely coordinated manner, voice a broken croak.

Priority override engaged. Zombie target acquired.

The man took an awkward step closer. Despite himself, Andrei raised his arm, allowing his command system to charge the weapon. It activated and the figure's head was torn off in a spray of bone and blood.

The noise of his weapon attracted others. They emerged from nearby houses, crying out, shouting, growling their displeasure. If Andrei had been more in control, more lucid than the moment allowed him to be, he would have understood their fear and what it meant. They halted in their tracks, gasping, drawing away. They were people he knew, ordinary people he'd grown up with. They weren't dangerous. But in the shock of that moment he lost control to the warbot's core programming, damaged and compromised as it was. As it had done with the first villager, it simply reacted without proper analysis of the situation. These weren't the zombies it was meant to destroy—but the warbot was no longer differentiating with any accuracy. Taken out of Andrei's control, the weaponry engaged and the townsfolk died.

He remembered walking on, squashing dead flesh and bone beneath his feet. Then he was elsewhere in the town, standing outside a door not knowing how he'd got there, his sense of time skipping about erratically. This place was familiar and somehow comforting. But what was it that he wanted here? He couldn't remember. Thrusting forward impatiently, he smashed open the door. Inside cringed a woman and a boy. They screamed at him.

<Please,> he said. <Why am I here?>

The woman and the boy kept shouting, pleading, demanding that he leave them alone—threatening, crying hysterically.

<Stop!> he commanded.

His demands had no effect, though it was obvious this pair were terrified, not the threat that the robot's command circuits registered. For a moment Andrei didn't understand such terror. He tried to concentrate on what they were saying and the sliding, squirming sounds they made began to reveal an undercurrent of meaning, to inject emotion back into his consciousness. The woman's eyes, bright with tears, drew him toward her. There was a hidden imperative in them. He felt it drag him back to himself.

<I am Andrei Bryukhanov,> he said in a voice that made the flimsy walls tremble.

"USTRUYA?" LEONTYEV RECOGNIZED the name of the village, but for a moment couldn't place it. Unexpectedly a report had come through from the rookie soldier she'd sent to shadow the robot during the chaos that consumed them in the aftermath of its assault on her lab—Brodsky or some such was his name. She'd neither expected him to obey her so determinedly nor, if he did, to survive the experience. That he had succeeded in his mission was a miracle—or perhaps tribute to the fear her "Soul Killer" persona could evoke in underlings.

But Ustruya? The robot-assassin had headed straight to some pissant shit-hole in the middle of nowhere. Why would it do that? What was in that backwater that could possibly interest it?

"Isn't Ustruya village famous for something?" said Khrushchev. "I've heard the name recently. In regards to one of the dogs in our care perhaps?"

His query jolted something in Leontyev's memory. She suddenly knew what the town was famous for. Her subconscious mind had already gathered the pieces into a nebulous whole, but that seething mass of speculation had been disjointed. This one new piece of information connected the threads and brought it all together. It seemed obvious. Her psychic test-subject, Andrei Bryukhanov, was a native of the provincial village. It was where he'd been born and where he'd made so famous a name for himself that Leontyev's esoteric interests had compelled her to recruit him. Was it mere coincidence that the experiment had been interrupted at the moment Bryukhanov had departed his body and she had killed the empty vessel left bound into her apparatus? Probably, but that being the case, what if the sudden arrival of the mechanical assassin had deflected Bryukhanov from his intended target in distant Texas? What if his consciousness had been drawn instead into the nearest psychic vacuum, perhaps damaged by the transition? Could the robot have acquired Bryukhanov's memories, even his desires?

"This may be a vindication," she said, not really speaking to anyone but herself.

The security officer frowned at her. "Vindication?"

"Of my research. We must hurry to Ustruya. Now."

When Khrushchev insisted on remaining, wanting to finish off the monsters that were still shuffling through the research complex before doing anything else, she reluctantly conceded. The dead killed anyone they saw, their numbers growing moment by moment. The process fascinated Leontyev and she had vowed to herself to investigate it further once they'd secured the robot. She needed to understand how it worked. But for now, it was vital to find the mechanical assassin quickly rather than let it wander. It was too valuable to lose.

"Take Viktor as my second-in-command." Khrushchev gestured toward a young man standing self-consciously to one side.

Leontyev raised one well-groomed eyebrow.

"He's more effective than he looks. You can rely on him."

"If you say so."

"And you should reconsider calling for back-up," Khrushchev

added. "I suspect you'll need more than standard-issue equipment."

"Absolutely not." She scowled at him. "We've had this discussion, Khrushchev. Until we figure out what's going on, I want to keep it quiet." In truth, she could see advantages for herself in studying the robot without the interference of the Kremlin's more favored scientists. If they learnt of this, she'd never get near it again. But would Khrushchev betray her?

"Then I should come with you, Vasilisa," he said.

"Stay and deal with the dead." She relaxed into tentative trust. "Just keep at least a few of them alive for study later. I'll be fine—"

"A dangerous tactic, comrade. Should they break out, the plague will spread quickly."

"It's a high security installation, Khrushchev. Strong enough to keep dead men in, I'd assume. And I have absolute faith in your ability to make sure nothing escapes that shouldn't."

"I'm flattered, but for all we know some of the creatures got out before the lock-down. No one was keeping tabs."

She dismissed his concern with a wave of her hand. "I'll deal with any corpses we stumble across. They seem to be connected to the robot somehow. I suspect if there *are* any out there, we'll find them when we find the death machine."

"I'm not..." A look of distraction swept over his rocky features. "I'm...not convinced that's how it works—"

Suddenly Khrushchev grasped and clutched at his head. "What?" he screamed. "What do you want?" He collapsed to one knee, moaning and muttering inarticulately. Then he gasped, fell and lapsed into unconsciousness. By the time one of his men had found a medic, however, he was awake again. A brief examination revealed nothing.

"Migraine headache," he muttered, breathing in erratic gasps. "Came on suddenly."

"Concussion perhaps," suggested the medic.

"It's likely enough. I was hit on the head earlier." He looked up at Leontyev, his eyes bloodshot and haunted. "I'll be alright," he added. "Go!"

Leontyev left with the majority of the available guard and set out toward Ustruya—a doctor of psychiatry and a dozen scared and psychically battered toy soldiers, with high-powered weapons and too much imagination for their own good, bumping and sliding along the snow-sodden roads in the only truck they'd been able to get access to. A tank would have been useful, but the Kremlin felt no great need to supply Bilibinski Installation 04.1 with heavy artillery. The Politburo displayed limited faith in the importance of her work. The platoon of raw recruits that had formed her staff was only there by virtue of a nuclear reactor being built nearby. Paranoia, not scientific faith, drove those in power.

"What's that ahead?" muttered the driver.

Leontyev squinted through the filth that covered the truck's windscreen. The road was littered with red-tinged snow and what might have been bodies. A burnt-out car smoldered to one side. "Looks like there was trouble."

Even as they came to a stop and she and Siyankovsky, Khrushchev's second-in-command, climbed out of the truck's cabin to take a closer look, Leontyev could see that most of the bodies had been cut to bits by machine-gun fire. The burnt-out, blackened vehicle was riddled with bullet holes.

"What do you think?" said the young soldier.

"I think the death robot's been here," she answered drily.

Movement in the surrounding trees drew their attention, vague forms solidifying out of the misty foliage. Siyankovsky swore. He called for his men and a few of the soldiers in the back of the truck overcame their fear sufficiently to get into a defensive position. The approaching figures revealed themselves as a living man—a farmer, pursued by a group of corpses. "Help me!" the man screamed, running toward them. "Please!" One of the soldiers primed his weapon.

"No!" Leontyev shouted. "Don't shoot!"

The soldier looked at her, eyes almost manic.

"I said no, soldier!" she repeated.

He lowered his gun and the farmer ran past, cringing behind the guards near the side of the truck.

The pursuing corpses drew closer. They were making low growl-ing noises and shambling even more awkwardly than Leontyev had seen in previous specimens. Perhaps it was the cold. One of them was dressed in the tatters of blatantly foreign clothing. Of the other two, one looked like a provincial policeman and the other a peas-ant.

"Kill them!" ordered Siyankovsky.

Kill the dead, Leontyev thought. Not likely.

Her guards began firing at the approaching corpses. Their bullets missed totally as often as not, and the ones that didn't tore holes in the monsters' flesh but failed to stop them. How had they come to be in this spot? Along with the torn-apart scraps of bone and flesh scattered over the road, a group of five or six men must have stum-bled upon the robot, perhaps opening fire on it like good little cit-izens. It appeared to have defended itself accordingly. Yet if the robot caused the dead to become voracious, why were three of its bullet-riddled victims still lying motionless on the road? To one side, she noticed, a dead man was sprawled in the mushy snow and mud. His skull had been torn open and the cavity emptied out.

Leontyev turned to the nearest soldier, demanding his automatic weapon. He hesitated but gave it to her when Siyankovsky gestured agreement. Holding the weapon in firing position, she strode to-ward the nearest corpse, stopping just out of its reach, and then edged backwards slowly to maintain that relative distance. "You have to be thorough," she remarked for the soldiers to hear.

She fired point-blank at the corpse's head, as had Khrushchev back at the facility—the trigger clenched on repeat until the thing's skull broke open and disappeared in a cloud of bloody debris. It continued a few steps; she shot at one of its legs, tearing the knee to shreds. It fell then, twitching awkwardly, and went still. She felt satisfied.

"Like that," she said, tossing the automatic weapon to the soldier she'd taken it from.

The air filled with noise, smoke and blood as the soldiers riddled the corpses with round after round of bullets. The remaining two monsters staggered under the assault, the impact momentarily forcing them backward. But even with skin and flesh ripped from their bones, the corpses didn't stop.

"Their heads!" Leontyev shouted. "Shoot them in the head, for God's sake."

The soldiers adjusted their aim but without much accuracy, and as they were unwilling to get too close to the corpses, they kept missing their targets. But the final result was inevitable, despite cowardice and incompetence. After a few minutes of chaotic overkill, the slow-moving corpses had become so torn and shattered that further movement was impossible. They fell.

Leontyev watched the twitching scraps of flesh and bone as movement dwindled slowly in them. The ground was littered with blood and gore.

"What now?" asked Siyankovsky.

She looked at him, her beautiful features expressionless.

"Comrade?" he pressed.

She glanced aside then gestured toward the farmer. "Bring him to me."

Having believed himself safe in the protection of these defenders of the State, the man had relaxed somewhat and was slow to react. Two of the soldiers grabbed him; he struggled and moaned protests then. But he'd been made clumsy by sudden terror and they thrust him forward easily. Leontyev smiled.

"Relax," she purred, leaning toward him. "You want to serve the Motherland, don't you?"

He nodded.

"Good," she said. She turned to the soldiers. "Restrain him. Tie his arms and legs."

The man struggled, but it was half-hearted and despairing. He begged her for mercy. She smiled, leaning over him and stroking his forehead. "I'm not going to hurt you. This is your chance to be a hero of the state." His hands and feet were soon bound with rope. Fear choked the protests rising from deep in his chest.

Leontyev pulled a knife from within her coat. "You!" She pointed at a soldier. "Stab this blade into one of those corpses you just turned into wolf bait."

He did so, carefully carrying the bloody blade back to her. She took it, making sure none of the blood dripped onto her own flesh. Then she cut the blade across the farmer's cheek. The zombie blood mingled with his. He gaped in shock, wide eyes staring at her. He might have fallen if the men hadn't held him.

Suddenly he began to cough and splutter, as though his throat was being squeezed from within. Breath became a rasping wheeze.

"Lay him on the ground," she said. "Step back, but be ready."

The soldiers did so. Fear and uncertainty visible on their faces, they watched as the farmer died. When Siyankovsky began to question her, Leontyev gestured for him to stop.

Seconds passed in an uneasy silence. Leontyev's lips formed a smirking superiority.

"He's looks dead," said Siyankovsky. "Shall we check—?"

"Wait!" she cautioned.

A few more moments passed before the farmer's bound corpse twitched. A low grumble began deep in his chest. "The blood acts quickly," Leontyev remarked, as the farmer squirmed and struggled against his bonds, teeth gnashing and grinding. His eyes were cold and empty.

Leontyev looked toward Siyankovsky. "It's as I suspected. Have your men tie him to the back of the truck. Just make sure no one gets bitten. Then burn the rest of the bodies. All of them. The un-death is in the blood. None of it must remain in this place."

Reluctantly the soldiers obeyed.

"What was that all about, ma'am?" asked Siyankovsky as he and Leontyev climbed into their vehicle, the sound of the creature's snarls drifting around them and the flickering light of the burning mound of corpses giving the scene an eerie ambiance.

She scowled thoughtfully. "An experiment. We need to understand what we're up against." She gestured back toward the wriggling corpse. "This one might come in handy. Khrushchev is efficient at his job. Who knows how many will be left back at the facility? I need at least one to study."

She stared out through the windscreen, as though seeing a dark future somewhere down the road ahead.

IF HE'D EXPECTED his wife to fall into his metal arms in response to the revelation of his identity, Andrei was to be sadly disappointed. Instead she continued screaming at him, throwing anything that came to hand against his chassis. Even metal objects bounced off him without effect. He watched impassively until she weakened and the room went quiet. She held her son close, sobbing into his hair.

<It's me, Anouska,> Andrei said.

Tears filled her despairing eyes. "Why are you doing this? What are you?"

<Your husband.>

"My husband wasn't a...a monster—"

<I'm not a monster,> he said. <I'm trapped in this machine.>

The absurdity was clearly too much for her to accept, despite years of living with his prescient visions. She screamed a denial at him.

<Anouska?> The word rattled from the metal that encased him. His arm reached toward her.

"Leave her alone!" the boy yelled, wanting to be brave, to be a hero, but afraid to come closer. "You're not my papa!"

<I am—I'm Andrei Bryukhanov...>

Andrei felt something spark within him, like a contained burst of flame that swept from his chest to his head. Something had re-activated.

<Re-initialization underway. Warbot AI coming online in six minutes.>

<No!> he roared.

The jolt that spasmed through Andrei sent him staggering backward against a cabinet. The cabinet disintegrated with the impact. The woman and the boy shrieked. They desperately wanted to escape, but the only exit from the room was too close to him and fear made them hesitate. Just as well. Andrei wasn't at all sure what his robot host would do if they'd tried to flee past him into the village. In that moment he hadn't been in control—and not for the first time. He'd felt as though his mind was being pushed out of the circuitry.

<Five minutes to full re-boot.>

Re-boot? He didn't know what the word meant but he feared what would follow. He couldn't keep his thoughts straight. Glancing at the woman and the boy, he found he didn't recognize them any more, couldn't remember who they were, even though he was convinced he should. Where was he? Images flashed across his field of vision, morphing from a small cottage into a huge round gateway, beyond which vast powers boiled and churned.

<Enter the temporal vortex on my mark...>

Metallic joints grind into motion.

He detects new data. Electrical current jolts in his diodes, making him turn.

<Zombies detected. Command protocol OS 42.40 engaged. Override current parameters.>

He glances across the cluttered laboratory.

Snarling, bloody faces seethe around him.

In response the weapon on his right arm primes itself, its components grinding into action.

<No!> The warbot heard the cry of a different mind, one almost alien to it, yet familiar. It was warm, glowing, surging up from dark places in its cognitive matrix, pushing its mind away.

Andrei's consciousness bubbled into clarity once more.

<I...I'm sorry,> he groaned, his body weakening. He gestured toward his cringing wife and son. <Run! Get out of here while you can!>

The woman and the boy skirted around him, terror driving them on. As best he could, Andrei forced the other intelligence—the cold inhuman one—into a dormant state while he watched the only people he cared about escape from him. His control was tenuous and even as they disappeared he felt the robot's consciousness returning.

But they were out the door.

They were safe.

After a moment or two the warbot AI surged back.

<Full weapon activation. Zombie blood detected.>

Confused, Andrei tried to de-activate the machine-gun on his arm, to retract its cartridge. The drive mechanism rotated with a hollow growl.

For a moment, Andrei blacked out. In the darkness that swept over him, there was movement. He felt the presence of living humans. It was—No, not her! Not Anouska! Not the boy! He'd seen those two escape. Yet now they'd returned, forced back into the cottage by others. The woman, the boy—and the one who made him what he was.

The weapon that was his arm roared out of control and several rounds spat into the ceiling.

Anouska screamed.

"Bryukhanov! *Domovoi!*"

Something about the new voice stopped him. It was familiar and the words it spoke, naming the truth of him, gave him momentary strength to overcome the AI's growing presence.

"Bryukhanov, that *is* you, isn't it?"

The woman standing in the doorway with Anouska and Pavel was tall and dominating, dressed in a long leather coat, with dark hair drawn back under a black *ushanka*. She seemed familiar. He knew her—

"*You have been condemned for treason, Andrei* Bryukhanov," she whispers. A conspirator. "But I can help you."

"You can help?"

"I have need of men with your talents. Come work for me and neither you nor you family need suffer for your mistakes."

"I did nothing against Mother Russia."

She smiles. "All the more reason why I should help you escape your...misfortune."

<Doctor Leontyev?>

"Yes. You know me?"

<Doctor...> the robot rumbled.

She glanced at the military man behind her. "See, Siyankovsky. It's as I thought! I succeeded in transposing Bryukhanov's consciousness into another after all, even if it's not the intended target. He's alive in this machine." Her eyes narrowed. "Do you understand what I'm talking about?"

"Your research…"

"Indeed."

"Can you still control him?"

She smiled then. Andrei's head felt so fuzzy he was having trouble keeping awareness of his wife and child intact, while listening to Dr. Leontyev and watching the sensuous movements of her lips as she turned to face him.

—Soul Killer—

Leontyev suddenly adopted a flat tone: "Do you hear me, Andrei Bryukhanov? Do you remember the briefings we had together? When we discussed the heroic role you were to play in Soviet ascendency? Do you remember?"

<I…I don't know.>

"We spoke of the evil capitalist empire and how easily its foundation of hero-worship could be undermined, through one selfless act by a brave man. That man was you, Bryukhanov. Do you remember?"

<Yes, yes, I think I…>

"Do you remember the code word, the key that would signal you to obey?"

<I'm confused, Doctor. There was…is another voice, another whisperer in my head…>

"You hear no voice except mine, Andrei. Listen now. The code word is *domovoi*."

<Domovoi.>

AI reconstruction 90% complete.

<No, no, I can't…>

"You will do as I say, *domovoi* Bryukhanov. Lower your weapon!"

Slathering jaws, dead eyes, stench of living death. Overwhelmed, he falls backwards into the portal—

And the Soul Killer points the gun at him. A bullet spins out from the barrel. Bursts through his sternum. Spits out a spray of blood and fractured bone.

"Bryukhanov," Leontyev stepped closer. Siyankovsky clutched at her shoulder, a warning, but she shook him off. Why did they all these *men* think they could take such liberties with her? "Andrei, the Motherland is in great peril. The metal assassin you inhabit was sent by our enemies to destroy us."

<Assassin?>

"It brought death with it, and blood that raises the dead—not as living men, but as ravenous monsters, slavering beasts that feast upon the living. The zombie blood you have shed helps them create more. At the lab. On the road. In this village. If you don't come with me, you will damn us all."

<It's impossible,> moaned Andrei, <I don't believe you.>

Leontyev breathed out heavily. "I have no time for this, Andrei. I thought I might have to persuade you, so I have prepared a… demonstration." She reached out and shoved the boy, Pavel—Bryukhanov's son?—so that he stumbled a few paces into an open space. Suddenly the Soul Killer had a gun in her hand—*a bullet spins toward him bursts into his chest spits out blood and fractured bone*—and with it she shot the boy in his right leg. He screeched and dropped to the floor. His mother shrieked and moved toward him. One of Leontyev's men pulled her back.

Sick hatred burst in Andrei, a human desire for revenge that burned inroads into the robot's nonhuman circuits. The weapon on his right arm activated, its ammunition chamber cycling into a loaded position.

"Don't move, *domovoi!*" cried Leontyev. "Or my men will shoot him dead."

As she spoke the code word again, Andrei felt anger, the will to act, tighten around his limbs. He became motionless once more, paralyzed by the deeply embedded imperative.

<I—will—kill—you,> he moaned, fighting it.

"You won't. Just watch."

She took a vial from her pocket, opened the lid carefully and let a drop of its viscous contents fall into the wound.

"He will die, but this dead-man's blood will resurrect him."

The boy gasped. He clawed at his own chest and fell back, writhing.

"No!" growled Bryukhanov.

The boy groaned loudly and all movement stopped.

"Wait, *domovoi!*" demanded Leontyev, "or the woman dies as well."

Even as she spoke the boy was twitching back into life, a low growl vibrating from his deflated lungs. He slowly stood, awkward and unbalanced. Should Andrei have felt joy? Relief? Gratitude? The boy turned to him. Growled. Suddenly Pavel screamed in unearthly rage and staggered toward his mother, who had been weeping and cursing his murderer. Andrei saw into his son's eyes. They were cold and empty.

<Probability of zombie infection, 100%. Extermination protocols activated.>

The warbot's weapons jerked out of Andrei's control as his consciousness fell toward darkness. Before he lost sight of the room, the warbot's bullets tore Pavel's body into a fog of blood and flesh, spraying the walls crimson. Anouska screamed in white-hot hysteria and Andrei joined her, though his voice echoed only within the bounds of the virtual space to which he was confined. Surrounding circuitry flared and burned and faded—and he was lost in the lightless nothingness that replaced it.

COMING BACK TO the world seemed to take forever—a long, stressful journey that challenged his willpower over and over, and drained him of passion. Yet only moments had passed. As once more the warbot's AI—still not fully functional—slipped into whatever darkness had been reserved for it, and the outside world re-formed in the robot's absence, Andrei saw the torn remains of his boy, Anouska weeping—and Leontyev, gun pressed against his wife's head.

"Control it, *domovoi,*" the Soul Killer yelled at him. "Do as I tell you, or I kill her, too."

AI reconstruction 98% complete.

The world glitched. Andrei felt the robot's mind rising to prominence once again. He was strong, but it was stronger. Fully operational, it could expel him from its body with ease. Where would he go then? Certainly he couldn't control the mechanism any longer.

<I can't keep it down,> he rumbled. <It's…taking over. The other…>

"I swear I'll kill them—"

AI reconstruction 100% complete. Re-boot engaged.

Andrei felt himself wrenched away from the machine, rising up and out, hovering without orientation, not knowing where he was. His thoughts scattered around him like snow blown from a rooftop and melted into the shifting currents of air—

THE ROBOT-ASSASSIN shuddered, its limbs grinding to a halt. Leontyev swore at it, pressing her gun hard against the woman's temple. "Obey me, Bryukhanov!" she snarled. "Or she dies. I won't be thwarted—"

The robot's arm rose, mechanism whirring into place. <He is gone.> The machine's emotionless voice echoed around the room.

"What?"

<You cannot control me with these meaningless threats.>

"Bryukhanov—?"

<I am no longer Bryukhanov and no longer care about the woman. Warbot Model 3.2's memory structure has been re-built.>

Leontyev pushed the sobbing woman away and aimed her gun at the warbot instead, as pointless as that action seemed. She gestured for Siyankovsky and the others to do likewise. "Keep it covered," she ordered. The robot watched them impassively as they moved into place, weapons trained on it.

<Where am I?> it demanded.

"The village of Ustruya in the Soviet Union."

<What year?>

"Year?"

<What year is this?>

"It's 1963. You must know that—"

The warbot made a low rumbling sound that in a human might have been an impatient grunt.

<[crack, hiss] You speak a form of Russian common in [crackle] period.>

"And so do you, it seems."

<Yet the dead are here? They should not be. It did not happen. The plague began much later than this.>

"You brought the dead with you. I should warn you, assassin, this capitalist plot will not succeed. You took us by surprise, but now we are prepared. Give us the antidote—or tell me how to make it—and I promise we will not destroy you."

<*I* am the antidote.>

"You?"

<I was built to kill the dead. That is my purpose.> The tonal qualities of the robot's voice, which had been deep and harsh, rose several octaves and crackled into a whisper. Then it began to oscillate between the extremes, sometimes cutting out all together, sometimes echoing around the room. <*By accident I* travelled back...*I...Yes, can detect radiation*...emanating *from a portal... detect...[crack, hiss]...still open, but* dwindling. *Must kill the dead.* Stop the *plague*...kill the dead that are here. *Follow* the dead *into temporal stream* and hunt them...[crackle]>

To Leontyev, it was clear that the robot was malfunctioning. What it said made little sense. Words came from it like the grinding of unoiled machinery, punctuated by strange buzzes and clicks, like a radio that was losing reception. Perhaps Bryukhanov's presence had destabilized it. She needed to draw him back into prominence. Perhaps the code word...

"Enough, *domovoi!*" she demanded. "You will come with me now."

The two camera lenses recessed into the robot's metal surface swiveled toward her.

< [click]...interference *in the pursuit of command completion...* > A high-pitched hiss erupted from the machine. <...*will not be* tolerated [buzz]> Its gun-arm rose. <Threat *to human* safety detected. *You will*—[click] eliminated.>

Leontyev threw herself to the side. "Siyankovsky! Destroy it!"

Siyankovsky and his remaining men—one of them the rookie soldier Brodsky—opened fire on the bulky machine. Their bullets pounded against its metal surface, ricocheting in all directions, like physical manifestations of the sounds echoing from the walls around them. One of the soldiers fell, struck by his comrades' bullets. Leontyev grabbed the almost comatose woman whose house they were demolishing and pulled her to the floor.

"Domovoi!" she yelled. "Domovoi! Obey me!"

Half a minute passed before the death machine returned their fire. During the hiatus, she ran.

IN THE BLACKNESS to which he'd been exiled, Andrei heard voices. At first they were so distant he couldn't distinguish them from background noise. Then they were little more than a whisper—breath carrying only a hiss of sound. He began to see flashes of the outside world, so fractured and distant he could make no sense of them.

There was a sensation of vertigo, of fast descent, and then he heard Leontyev say: "Enough, *domovoi*! You will come with me now." Light sparked and through the eyes of the robot he saw the Soul Killer. The whispering sounds formed themselves into words.

<A threat to human safety has been detected. It must be eliminated.>

"Siyankovsky! Destroy it!"

Mist cleared as Leontyev's men turned their weapons on the robot. Andrei heard the clattering guns, saw the constant muzzle flashes, felt the machine's center-of-gravity shifting to compensate for the sustained impact of round after round. It wanted to engage its own weapons but Andrei fought it. For a moment his will managed to override the crippled machine's commands. Then he felt it pushing him aside. Andrei saw Leontyev grab his beloved Anouska, dragging her to the floor as a shield against the robot's attack. Fear for the woman who was his only link to the world cut through whatever influence he'd had. Activation began. He had to do something, to regain control of the robot and will it to stop. He reached out to it. During those moments when Andrei's will fought the warbot's AI for dominance, the warbot's arms-activation protocols paused. But Andrei was too weak. The most he could do was distract it, and that about as effectively as a mosquito buzzing around a horse.

Then Andrei saw Leontyev scramble back, pushing Anouska forward. She leapt up and ran out the door. The possibility of her escape filled him with anger, distracting him. His will released its grip.

The warbot's arm erupted in a blaze of firepower, bullets spraying across the room, cutting the soldiers to shreds.

Just as suddenly the gunfire ceased. The room filled with a smoky haze that turned the abundance of red blood that splattered the walls a pinkish blue. Nothing moved.

Anouska? Was she still alive?

He couldn't tell as the robot was looking elsewhere, but there were no signs of life between the death machine and the door. The attack had been so fierce, how could anything have survived?

<You cannot remain here,> the warbot said, words like scratchings on the inside of the skull he no longer had. <I have command protocols to follow and you hinder this unit's efficiency.>

<You killed them.>

<The dead proliferate throughout this time and place. It cannot be allowed.>

<You killed my wife!>

<My operational parameters cannot permit the plague to spread further. If the trend continues, the dead will consume all of human history.>

<You killed people, not zombies! You're the monster here!>

<Leave me now!>

Andrei felt the pressure exerted by the machine's AI matrix ripping at him, determined to eject him from its metal carcass. But he was equally determined not to leave so easily. Before he did, he would have his revenge—revenge against this killing machine, against Dr. Vasilisa Leontyev, against God, the country that had betrayed him and the world that had taken away everything he'd ever cared about.

And he knew how his vengeance would begin.

DURING THE HOURS he had spent confined inside the warbot Andrei had, without being totally conscious of the fact, seen into spaces within its neural networks that even the AI that ran the machine barely knew existed. Awareness of them clarified now. One of these spaces was a black hole completely invisible to the machine. Whoever he was, the warbot's creator had not entirely trusted the robot to do what it was intended to do. At first Andrei thought he had installed a negative contingency command sequence designed to "kill" the robot in the event that it went rogue. Perhaps the temporal transfer that brought it to Russia in the 1960s, and the trauma that event had inflicted on the robot's systems, had broken the logic chain governing the destruct mechanism. Otherwise it surely would have engaged by now.

But then he realized that it was more than this. The warbot's creator had wanted the robot to kill someone and had fitted it with a bomb. A small secondary brain hidden in a blind space within the robot's AI matrix would know when the warbot located its target— a scientist named Winterbottom—and would detonate the bomb in response. An image of the target appeared in Andrei's mind.

He could use this.

Being an intruder in the robot, a ghost in the machine, and hence not susceptible to its programmed blind-spots, Andrei could transfer an awareness of this Winterbottom—a bogus confirmation— into the machine's secondary brain, even as he felt himself being thrust from the robot's consciousness. He was determined not to go peacefully. <*You killed her!*> he screamed at the warbot, tossing his hatred like a grenade into the space that was its artificial consciousness—and letting that hatred carry the image of Winterbottom with it. Hopefully it would reach the secondary brain. It was all he could do. Then he was disembodied again, his consciousness tumbling away from the cold metal body. <*Die!*> he screamed, though even the robot could not have heard him.

Fading, he glanced toward Anouska, hoping to catch a final glimpse of her, praying that the robot would explode and the explosion would prevent his dead wife from returning as an undead monster. Yes, she was there all right, splattered with blood—her own, her son's or another's, he couldn't tell—unmoving amidst the debris. But suddenly her eyes opened—and he saw they were not empty, not cold. She was alive!

Elation turned to horror as a hot light flared from the warbot, bursting through joints in its carapace and tearing a hole in its chest. Its gun-arm flailed wildly, spitting bullets, and then the entire structure erupted into fire. A hot, violent wind smashed the walls of the cottage into kindle and swept through the village. Andrei's cry of despair was consumed in the blast.

COLD, ALL AROUND him, so cold it burnt. He felt it as pain, a deep bone-cracking pain, and knew despair had taken its final form. Not the chill of snow, or the lifelessness of metal. This was Death itself.

Yet he lived. He was in a body—a dead body. Whose, he wondered? Its muscles and sinews felt rigid and incapable of movement when he tried to flex them. An eternity passed as he stared from dead eyes across ground covered in red-hot mud, ash and debris, here and there bulging with blackened human shapes. All dead. Everywhere buildings were flattened, the rubble burning and the air thick with smoke and ash.

He levered himself up and stared down at his new body. It was a woman's and he recognized its clothing, despite burn marks and other signs of the violence that had engulfed it. Leontyev had run from the cottage before he caused the warbot's internal bomb to detonate. Apparently she'd made it far enough way to escape incineration, but like the rest she hadn't escaped death. Andrei's spirit had found refuge in the Soul Killer herself.

Yet he could feel the sickness in her flesh. She had been battered to death by the blast, irradiated, flesh poisoned. He would not be able to live in her long.

It was almost too much for him to take in. Not only had everything been taken from him, not only had he been tortured and those he loved killed, but now he was forced to live in the disintegrating carcass of his chief tormentor. The Soul Killer was dead, but it wasn't enough for him. He knew who was to blame, for everything. It was humanity that had created the plague—he had seen that in the warbot's fractured memories. It was humanity that had helped the plague to spread in the first place and had built violent warbots in a futile attempt to stem the tide of the infection. It was humanity that had pursued war throughout its history—had tortured the innocent, exploited each other and the world, seeded the future with evil intentions in the name of greed and cruelty. Humanity had taken life and dragged it to the brink of destruction, time and time again.

It could not continue.

ANDREI FORCED LEONTYEV'S cold, stiff body to stand and began the long trek back to the Centre for Non-Traditional Technologies Research, Installation 04.1. He had no idea how he would get into the building. His new body was slow-moving and awkward and Leontyev would have left guards to stop both exits from the facility and entry to the labs. Yet he went. This was his destiny and the way would open for him.

As he travelled and the going got more and more difficult, his resolve hardened. Snow drifted around him like fall-out from the explosion he'd just survived, blanched to match the coldness that had overtaken his soul. An arctic wind scoured his back. The external sensations seemed nothing to the cold within, and he simply kept moving, mind churning with visions of utter bleakness.

He'd found, clutched in Leontyev's hand, the container of zombie blood she'd used to murder his son. He had no idea if the radiation from the warbot's destruction or the cold or simply time would destroy the efficacy of the blood's transforming power—its uncanny ability to turn life into a cannibalistic parody of death. But it would be a backup for him. He had gained a new faith—a belief in the world's desire to rid itself of humanity—and he knew how it would happen. The warbot's last moments had revealed that the temporal anomaly through which it had arrived in their midst was still open, and around that absurdity Andrei had built a plan to rid the planet once and for all of the plague that was mankind. He would return to Installation 04.1. He would release the zombies confined there into this Cold War world. Let them hunt. Let them proliferate. If they brought death to this world, fine. If they were stopped, he would already have initiated a better, more thorough plan. Before the Soul Killer's body died for good, killing him in the process, he would let one of the monsters infect him—or failing that, use the blood Leontyev had collected to give himself a way into Death. Having become the cold, unforgiving monster he so wanted to be, he would throw himself into the currents of time. Go back—somewhere, anywhere—and take the zombie plague with him.

He imagined standing beneath a cross on a hill of execution outside first-century Jerusalem, staring up at the god-man whose resurrection was meant to save men's souls. He imagined biting the bloody foot nailed there and giving the messiah a new resurrection—a colder, darker rebirth. His legacy would not be divine forgiveness or the proliferation of violence and betrayal that Andrei had known, but instead the end of Man on Earth, an apocalyptic era cleansed of humanity's evil. *Humanity deserves death*, Andrei would cry, as he slouched toward Golgotha. *Death and a monstrous resurrection should be its fate. Where better to start an apocalypse than with the Messiah Himself?*

Or perhaps the time-streams would take him back further, to the prehistory of Man—and undeath could stop the evil before it had a chance to grow. Mankind had destroyed the future. Andrei would destroy the past. All that suffering would never have been. *His* suffering would never have been.

When he finally arrived at the Installation, not tired, for he could feel nothing but the chill of his inglorious vision now, he found the gates unlocked and everything quiet and still. No sign of zombies remained. There were no guards either. What had happened here? Had the zombies already escaped their confinement and wandered off to propagate their disease throughout Russia? That was fine with him, though as revenge it was half-hearted. Andrei's vision was more thorough.

Inside the building, there was evidence of the battles that had been fought, though no actual bodies—trails of blood, bullet holes and random burn marks stained the floors and walls. But no corpses, moving or otherwise. Neither the living nor the dead were anywhere to be seen. Surely not all of Khrushchev's men had been bitten and reborn as monsters? An eerie silence filled the corridors and disheveled rooms he passed, an emptiness that echoed with unheard cries. Andrei felt Leontyev's body deteriorating around him and so pushed himself to hurry toward the lab where this horror had begun.

Two guards appeared from around a corner. Andrei staggered away from them, but they merely saluted and continued on their way. Of course, they did. They looked at him and saw Leontyev.

No real attempt to reconstitute the laboratory had been made. It was a junk-heap of smashed equipment and scorched benches. What was missing was the bodies. Last time he'd seen it—how long ago was that? He couldn't remember—the place had been a slaughterhouse of torn limbs, blood and gore. Now the human remains had been removed (or had walked away) and where there had been gore, ashen smears formed indecipherable glyphs over the floor. The transdimensional portal remained though. He could see its glowing presence through the debris, staining the otherwise shadowy atmosphere—smaller and fainter, but still there. His plan could be set in motion, even if he had to chance Leontyev's flask of zombie blood, rather than something fresher, in order to become the Angel of Death that he knew he was destined to be. He hoped the insulated bottle had been enough to preserve the necrotic qualities of its contents.

"Well," said a familiar voice. "Look who's made it back home."

Andrei squinted into the shadows at a tall, solidly built figure about a dozen paces from him. The man was carrying some sort of weapon and appeared to be wearing a military uniform. It was torn and blood-splattered. The flickering light of the partially obscured portal highlighted one side of his face—enough to allow Andrei to recognize him.

"Comrade Khrushchev," he managed, though his throat had tightened to such an extent that the sounds coming from Leontyev's mouth were far from clear even to himself.

"Good to see you, Dr. Leontyev." Khrushchev stepped forward so that more light spread across his battered features. "Though you don't look too well right now."

Andrei didn't reply, hesitant about explaining just whom Khrushchev was really talking to. How would the man react? He'd had a strange affection for the Soul Killer, according to both guards and lab staff, with rumors suggesting that they'd been more than colleagues.

Andrei stumbled, making an effort to steady himself. The stiffening of Leontyev's limbs was getting worse. Andrei knew he had to hurry.

"What's happened?" he asked. "Where are the bodies? The dead men?"

"Khrushchev was good at his job, Vasilisa. I have to give him that." Andrei felt a tremor of disorientation wash over him at Khrushchev's strange third-person phrasing. "He worked out what was needed and made sure it got done. His men have been busy cleaning up and burning the bodies. Most of them are out looking for stragglers right now." The man held up the weapon he was holding. A flame-thrower. A small, blue flame wavered from its nozzle, flaring yellow then subsiding. "Fire, you see. The danger is in the blood. It must be burnt away. Even dying, Khrushchev destroyed them all."

"Dying?"

"It will come as a great disappointment to you, Vasilisa, to learn that Khrushchev didn't make it."

"But you—?"

"I am *not* Khrushchev. This is Khrushchev's body, as you can plainly see, but it's been re-inhabited by…myself. We were caught together in the blast that accompanied the arrival of the robot—I suspect the destruction of your ill-conceived psychic transmigration apparatus caused a wave pulse that tore me from my own body and deposited me in Khrushchev's." He shrugged carelessly, as though this miracle he was describing was the most ordinary thing in the world. "Whatever the cause, he'd been weakened and eventually my will proved the stronger."

"Who are you?"

"Marovic. Your dear whipping boy. The one you have depreciated for so long it's become a habit." His free hand extended to indicate not only the destruction here, but beyond the room and facility. "All this is your fault, Leontyev. You are a monster—cruel, sociopathic and treacherous. I've been wondering if you'd come back to continue your work. And here you are—ready to inflict more suffering and humiliation on those who find themselves in your clutches." He shook his head in mock despair. "So close, yet I see you've been infected. A pity."

"What?"

"I must follow correct protocols." He raised the flamethrower. The translucent flame dancing at the tip of it flared brighter.

"No, I'm—" moaned Andrei, "I'm not Leontyev."

"Sadly, that's true. Leontyev is dead. Now she is one of the monsters. And Khrushchev must do his duty."

"Wait! I'm—"

A wave of hell-red flame swept toward Andrei, consuming his words, burning the skin from his face and hands.

In that one endless moment the cold in him turned to unbearable heat.

THE HARROWING

Gary McMahon

Historical Note:
During the winter of 1069-70, William the Conqueror waged a series of brutal campaigns upon the north of England to subjugate the region. There was a scorched earth policy: the death toll is believed to be over 100,000.

FATHER NIGEL SIMMONS walked slowly to the front of the church. His footsteps were soft and measured on the stone floor; he carried his small frame almost somberly in the rarefied atmosphere of the old building. He approached the candle-lit altar and paused for a while, genuflecting slowly and closing his eyes to express a brief silent prayer. He wasn't quite sure what he prayed for, but whatever it was he hoped that it came quickly, before it was too late.

After a few moments he turned to face the interior of the church, and the silent woman who stood in the open doorway, waiting to be summoned inside.

"Please," he said, keeping his voice low. "Don't be afraid. Come inside and show me what you've brought."

The woman moved quickly, with small, eager steps. Her pale eyes darted left to right, examining the shadowy walls, the empty pews, the massive stained glass windows with their wire-mesh coverings.

"Father...I've found this out beyond the town gates. I know we aren't meant to go outside, but I been told you pay good money for this kind of stuff."

Nigel smiled. The woman's grubby face appeared to flicker in the lambent candlelight. "It's okay. This will be our little secret."

She nodded her head. She looked like she was about to cry.

Nigel reached out and took the package from her arms. It was heavy, and wrapped up in dirty rags. He used his fingers to trace the outline of the thing, looking for telltale signs as to the nature of what it was she'd brought him, but couldn't be sure what it was.

"It's in good shape," said the woman, taking a step backwards, away from him. Her face was dark and untrusting. Her shabby clothing made her look like a vagabond seeking sanctuary within these blessed walls.

Nigel turned around and laid down the package on the altar. He pushed away several candles and made some room. "Let's just have a wee look, shall we?" He unfolded the rags delicately, as if he were afraid to damage whatever was inside the wrappings. Once he'd uncovered the item, he allowed himself to breathe.

It was perfect.

"It's from a warbot." He stared at the limb, wondering if it would be possible to test fire the weapon before it was fitted. The arm looked to be in good shape; there was a mess of circuitry at the end where it had been severed from the robot, but the limb looked to be in working order. The brownish metalwork veneer was scratched and dented, but the core mechanism was undamaged. The joints moved freely when he picked it up to manipulate the elbow and wrist, and the oversized gun barrel which formed the hand was clean and free of detritus.

"Is it any good?" The woman's voice shook.

"It's marvelous. Thank you. Here—let me pay you." He reached over and picked up the charity box, using his penknife to jink off the lid. He took out a handful of notes and counted them, and then turned around and pushed them into the woman's waiting hands.

"From the poor box?" Her cheeks were bloodless beneath the thin layer of dirt; she was horrified.

"We're all paupers these days, my child. The meek that were meant to inherit the earth." He smiled, and he knew it was a creepy smile. He wanted to scare this woman, to ensure that she never spoke to anyone of the clandestine transaction that had occurred here.

Once the woman had left, Nigel closed his eyes and wished her well. God would look after her—at least some kind of God, if not the one he still tried to believe in. Didn't God always watch over the fallen? It was those who were yet to fall from grace that had to fend for themselves.

There was a sound behind him: a scraping noise, like metal on stone. He turned around and the robotic arm was moving. Somehow it had harnessed a residual power source and managed to perch up on its elbow. The wide-barreled gun was pointing right at him. Nigel took a step to the left; the gun followed him, smooth and steady. He took a step to the right; the gun tracked him again, not missing a beat.

He stepped forward, towards the altar, and the gun went off with a loud, empty click. It was either unloaded or decommissioned— he'd already inspected the mechanism when he handled the thing— but still his heart clenched and his steps faltered. Being shot at by even a damaged weapon was something he didn't like. The motion sensor in the limb was clearly still operational. They could make use of that, at least; even if the weapon itself proved ultimately useless.

He picked up the limb, wrapped it up in the rags in which it had been delivered, and walked to the vault door. He unlocked the heavy iron door, pulled it open, and then began to descend into the darkness of the church vaults.

Sergeant Zackary Rowlands was the last human being left alive in the battalion. He wasn't sure why he'd been allowed to live, but he knew that his situation was now untenable. The robots had turned on every living thing—they killed not just zombies now, but innocent people, the northerners they'd been sent to liberate. Something had gone wrong in the programming, and Bossbot—the leader—had turned rogue.

"This way." The rusty little battlebot waited until Rowlands was on his feet before sticking him with the knife. It was a warning; not meant to kill or even maim. Just a little nudge in the meat of the belly. It hurt, but Rowlands kept his cool. He refused to let them see his pain.

"I'm coming, you tin-pot shithead. Give me a chance."

The robot moved jerkily to the side, watching through its red cyclopean eye as he limped through the tent opening and into the darkening air. It kept pace with him on its caterpillar treads, crushing branches and small bushes in its refusal to deviate from a straight line.

They were all like that, these robots. They refused to deviate from the set route. And now, for whatever reason, the set route was to kill everything and lay waste to the very earth beneath his feet.

He was delivered to Bossbot's tent, pushed inside, and then the rusty little robot trundled off to somewhere else—probably a command post at the perimeter of the camp. Rowlands moved slowly into the tent. It was gloomy in there, with only a single battery-powered lamp providing illumination.

Bossbot stood behind a low folding desk, unmoving in the thick shadows. His silent metal bulk made him look like a statue, and he was certainly tall enough to be mistaken for one. He was as broad as the front end of a jeep, and stood at the tent's apex—yet the dome of his cylindrical head still brushed the canvas. Something bubbled inside that tube-like skull; Rowlands could see it through the strengthened glass panels. It was like boiling blood, but with machine parts visible in the oxygenated fluid. The small panel on the right hand side was cracked but not broken: nothing leaked out, not yet.

Rowlands made a mental note of the potential weak point, hoping that he might have time to put it to use.

"What do you want?" Rowlands was terrified, yet he maintained the illusion of command. He refused to accept that this machine was in charge, even if that attitude led to his death. "Why have you not killed me?"

Machinery clicked and whirred, and then Bossbot moved sideways, coming out from behind the desk that looked so much like a child's toy. His Kevlar-coated tracks moved silently, but the mechanics at his heart made a terrible din—some called it his battle cry, because when he was in full-on killing mode the sound was like thunder.

"Because I needed a witness." His tinny voice, devoid of tonal quality, was like the sound of nightmare. Behind his bullet-proof visor, the smooth-sculpted, unliving robotic features moved not an inch, but to Rowlands they seemed to be grinning. "But now I do not."

Rowlands felt his gut tighten. His hands began to shake. "So it's my time? My turn to be executed."

"Yes."

"You rogue bastard. They'll get you and they'll stop you, and they'll use your parts to repair toasters." Rowlands wished that he could believe the show of resistance he was acting out.

"I am not a rogue. This is my central program. My core directive. The Harrowing. Leave nothing standing. Leave nobody living. Eradicate all zombies and humans alike. The Harrowing."

Rowlands barely had time to question the robot's words in his mind, or recall the damaged visor, before his brains were blown out of the back of his head. All he could think of was the darkness that was billowing from Bossbot's multiple gun barrels...and then nothing. Nothing at all.

"The Harrowing."

NIGEL WATCHED WITH fascination as the white-coated men worked on the subject. They looked like doctors as they moved in choreographed patterns beneath the stark ceiling lights, but they were more like pioneers. To his knowledge, nobody had done this before. They were the first. When he had suggested his plan to the council of the Angels of the North, he had expected some kind of mockery, perhaps even outright derision. What he had not been expecting was congratulations and a free hand to oversee the project from the warren of church vaults beneath Oldegate.

This much power could go to a man's head. If that man were not a man of God, a man who answered to a higher power. Nigel had once been that man, but now the only power he answered to was that of the council. The Angels of the North had become his family and his church—the old ways were gone now; this was the new religion. Nigel had a new god. Force had taken over from love; violence had usurped the idea of compassion in Nigel's mind. No longer a teacher or a spiritual guide, he was now a warrior.

A boiler-suited orderly approached him but did not speak; he hung around in silence, as if waiting for permission to speak.

Nigel glanced at the man, realizing that he was afraid. When exactly had he started to inspire fear in people? How did that happen? "Yes?" The strength he heard in his own voice was terrifying. Even that one word had been enough to suggest what kind of man he had become—a man of certainty.

"I'm sorry, sir, but we've had word from a scout. He estimates that the rogue battalion is less than twelve hours away. Our scout witnessed a small advance party, and returned here as quickly as he could to give us an update." He grinned nervously; his mouth did not seem to know what to do.

"Thank you. We need to implement our plan tomorrow morning, then. Just ahead of schedule." Nigel was talking to himself; he'd forgotten that the other man was there.

The orderly nodded, waited, and then nodded again. Then, when it was clear that his presence was no longer required, he shuffled out of the room and along the corridor.

"How are we doing here, doctor?" Nigel approached the operating table. He looked down at the corpse. He knew that face—it belonged to one of his congregation. But the body beneath, clumsy and haphazard, a brutish amalgamation of flesh and machine, was almost unrecognizable as something that had once been human.

"The graft seems to have been a success." The doctor walked around the table and lifted the gun arm the woman had brought earlier that evening. "Once the aesthetic has worn off, we can run a few tests, but in my opinion it's safe to assume that this is another one we can tick off the list."

Tick off the list. He was so cold, dispassionate. As if he were working on animals instead of people. Or things that had once been people. But in a way, thought Nigel, he was. They all were. These subjects had ceased to be human once they'd been slaughtered by the undead. By using them in this way, and stopping them from becoming mindless eating machines, the Angels of the North were doing them a mercy. At least now they served a purpose; their deaths meant something.

That was how Nigel justified to himself what they were doing.

He left the operating room and walked along the corridor. There were bare patches on the walls where religious icons and portraits had been removed. Some trace of guilt had made him take them down. He did not want the Lord—even one he had almost stopped believing in—to witness what they were doing to His children.

The cages were up ahead. Nigel always felt uneasy around them, no matter how often he inspected them. He approached with caution, holding back. Then, unable to deliberate much longer without looking like a fool, he increased his pace and drew level with the iron bars.

These compartments had once been used to store the remains of the holy dead, old priests, men of belief. At one time, many decades ago, the relics of a now forgotten saint had been encased in a glass case behind these bars.

Now they were the home of bastardized creations: shambling, ungainly things that he and the Angels of the North had brought from the charnel house to dwell here. They were still vaguely human, at least in appearance, but robot parts had been expertly grafted onto the cold cadavers. This was a private army; a mindless legion of man-made demons. Part zombie, part robot, they were the only thing that stood between the rogue army of robots and the safekeeping of the town, and the riches stored here.

Rather than burn their dead, as the government regulations dictated, they had brought them here, and committed acts of scientific butchery upon the flesh…Nigel thought about what he knew of the process now, as he always did in the presence of these things.

It was incredible and blasphemous: men playing at being God.

The victims of a zombie attack had been subdued and tied down before they had a chance to reanimate. Then they were worked on by expert hands, and changed into something else, something new. They'd been installed with a brand of artificial intelligence which altered their basic instincts and turned them into soldiers. The morphic field that linked the zombies together, making them form packs to hunt down fresh human brains, had been interrupted and altered sufficiently to disconnect these specimens from their kind and make them behave in a different way. Nigel was not a man of science, but he understood that somehow the technicians had found a way to make these misbegotten creatures suggestible to commands transmitted via a central computer hub, which were then fed through circuits stored inside the skulls of two main dead-bots. This, Nigel often felt, was a modern-day Frankenstein story, but instead of one creature there were many, and they were under the control of dour men in white lab coats. ...

"Feeding time," said a voice from behind him. "Let's get them good and full and docile."

The slipshod figures behind the bars became agitated. Their rewired and rebooted brains recognized the voice, if not the words, prompting a Pavlovian response in the reanimated meat. They moved closer to the front of the cages, dragging their mechanized implants like mutations. He glimpsed a metal-cased arm, leg, skull plate; the glint of a gun barrel; a bank of flickering lights in a dead man's chest. No amount of circuitry or AI could ever negate their hunger. The need for fresh brains remained.

Nigel closed his eyes. He could not watch this. Not this. He could not stand to see them eat.

He walked quickly away as the red-dripping buckets were brought in.

ROWLANDS OPENED HIS eyes. It was a staggering feat of human endeavor just to do so, and he felt proud. Surely no man in the history of humanity had done so with half his head missing.

He was lying face down, with his half-head head pressed into the dirt. Around him were bodies. He knew this even before he remembered his own name. He was in a pit. With the dead. A dead pit.

He raised a hand, moving slowly, and cautiously touched the damage. It was not quite as bad as he'd thought. Not half a head exactly, but there was simply a large hole where a portion of it had once been. The right cheek was gone. He could feel his teeth with his fingers. The wound was moist. Meaty. But no pain; he was numb. There was nothing there.

He pushed himself up with his arms, as if he were commencing an exercise program. There was pain then, but just a little. Nowhere near as much as he expected.

He was alive, and that was all that mattered.

Feeling like the hero of his own story, Rowlands struggled, tipped to the side, and eventually coerced his body into a kneeling position. His paused there, proud of his accomplishment, and took a breath. Several breaths. He waited for his eyesight to focus, to establish some form of normality, and then, feeling odd and apart from himself, he stood. The sky was black as pitch. The moon was a silver sickle, and the stars looked as distant as dreams—or memories.

Rowlands pulled himself out of that pit, grabbing soft handfuls of soil and attempting to haul himself up, over the lip, and onto the flat ground. He wasn't sure how long it took; time had lost all meaning. He just kept on trying, falling back into the nest of corpses, and trying again. But some day soon, he knew, he would be out of the body pit.

Then, without even registering his success, he was lying flat on his back at the edge of the pit, white plumes of breath streaming from between his chapped lips, and staring at those memories of starlight. He blinked. His face was still numb. He hoped it would stay that way—prayed that he could stave off the pain until he was ready to die. He could not die yet, there was too much to accomplish. He needed to warn someone, anyone, about Bossbot and his plans to harrow the earth.

Standing, he felt giddy, light-headed. His vision swam. He set his feet on the earth, gripping the insides of his boots with his toes and pretending that it made a difference. The air was cold. He could feel it on the skin of his neck, but not on his face. His hands were clenched into fists, in which he was still holding handfuls of mud.

There was a small walled town not too far from here, a small place called Oldegate. It was located six or seven miles to the north; a forti-fied encampment of something like a thousand people. If he could get there, he could warn them. Maybe he could even raise a makeshift army to stop the rogues and halt them in their advancement north.

It was a vague hope—not much to cling to—but it was keeping him alive. If he gave up, he was dead. It was that simple. Rowlands had always been a man who knew his own limits, and this was the final limit, the single boundary he was yet to cross. He could see it up ahead, hazy in the distance: a line that he would be forced to walk or crawl or stumble over, but not now, not yet.

He started to move: one foot in front of the other. Push through the exhaustion; ignore even the hint of potential pain. He was a sol-dier, a warrior, and ahead of him stretched an invisible line of his fellows. Ghost soldiers, millions upon millions of the battling dead who had fallen in combat, during countless wars across the world and throughout the hellish halls of history....They were there for him now, urging him on. They were his brothers and sisters; they were his ghost legion.

"One foot," he said, through gritted teeth. His voice sounded strange, as if it belonged to someone else. "One foot. In front. Of. The. Other." He pushed on, walking, and then running somehow, into the night and the wide open spaces, looking for another war to save him.

THEY CAME TO an abandoned village—just two rows of houses and a post office with its windows smashed in; a few cars parked hap-hazardly in the street, a guttering fire up against a wall, old blood-stains on the pavements.

A light mist crawled across the ground like swarming ghosts, sifting between the buildings and the bases of the trees at the side of the road. The robots moved behind these small drifts of white, motoring slowly, scanning the area for movement. The massive frame of Bossbot was in the front rank, taking up his rightful position. His guns were primed; his pre-programmed mind buzzed and flickered with energy.

"Dead ones up ahead," said a small battlebot, tooling along the uneven ground at his side.

"Destroy them all. Fire at will." Bossbot would have smiled, if he possessed a mouth. Humor was not part of his programming, but someone, a bored technician perhaps, had customized one of his chips to appreciate the irony of killing those who were already dead.

They saw the first one a moment later, shambling slowly from between two semi derelict buildings. Its body was long and thin, the flesh sliding like fish scales from the bones as it made its way out into the open. The zombie stopped, raised its head, as if it were sniffing the air, and then turned to face the advancing robots.

The robots opened fire and the hailstorm of artillery took the walking dead man apart. First one of his arms vaporized, and then, as the rotting head tilted to examine the damage, both its legs went out from under it. The torso dropped, hitting the ground, and the rest of the cadaver was torn to shreds. Seconds later, all that remained was a scattering of meat and bones.

The sound must have triggered the others into action. They emerged from the abandoned houses, staggering through empty doorframes, and climbed from inside the rusting hulks of cars. Like a band of itinerant hobos, they began to crowd the desolate street in search of scraps.

The robots simply opened up their weapons, tearing the zombies apart. Chunks of dead flesh flew through the air like mutated birds; bits of bone and gristle splattered against the walls of the empty cottages. They didn't stand a chance; none of them stood anything like a chance. Not with Bossbot in charge. He was only disappointed that there were no living humans to kill. That would have made the skirmish more exciting. If a robot was capable of feeling such a thing as excitement—and Bossbot believed that he, above all others, could do that.

Then, as if by some greater power of will, Bossbot's wish was granted.

A small group of bedraggled people emerged from their hiding place within the ruined post office building. They climbed through the empty windows, helping and embracing each other, brimming with gratitude. They were smiling. Their hands were held out in supplication, ready to thank their saviors.

"Thank you…oh, thank you! You saved us."

Bossbot swiveled on his tracks, maneuvering himself into a better position. "Cease fire!" He screamed the words, wanting to enjoy this on his own.

The people—six of them: two men and four women—began to run towards him, realizing who was in command of the situation.

"Thank God," said one of the women. There was blood on the side of her face. Her hair was dirty. "I thought we were doomed."

"You are," said Bossbot, and then he trained his guns on the advancing survivors and made them dance for his entertainment.

NIGEL STOOD ON the wall looking out over his beloved Northumbrian countryside. Even in the past, before the world had truly gone to hell, this landscape was thought by many to be bleak and desolate. But Nigel had always found evidence of God in such desolation—there was a spiritual tranquility that he had experienced nowhere else. These days the spiritual side had faded, but still he saw beauty in the barren terrain, the rocks and crags, the gorse-swathed fields. And if that were not the face of God, then what was, especially in these days where He had abandoned His flock to their follies?

The sun had not yet risen to show its face, but a soft golden light limned the horizon. It would not be long now until morning, and everything had to be put into action before the people of Oldegate began to wake.

He turned and walked away, climbing down the wooden ladder from the lookout point.

He walked across the empty courtyard, glancing back at the

lookouts along the wall. There were not many of them left. Many of the town's small populace had already fled, heading south towards the promise of sanctuary in the nation's capital. Those who remained were weak and almost defeated by the situation they found themselves in. Food was scarce; morale was low. All that mattered now was protecting the church and what it symbolized: keeping the traitors from the gate.

He entered the meeting room to a wall of silence. His fellow representatives, five members of the Angels of the North, sat around a small oval table staring at their hands. Nobody looked up to greet him. This work was shameful, and none of them was brave or audacious enough to make eye contact until he spoke and broke the silence.

"Thank you for coming," he said, sitting down in the only empty chair. "We all know why we're here, so let's not get sentimental or dance around the issue. The plan has to go operational now, before sunrise."

The men—no women; just men—around the table nodded. One by one, they glanced up, and then around at eachother's tired faces.

"Do we vote Aye?" The question hung in the air for a moment, and then, finally, the vote was submitted.

"Aye."

"Aye."

Three more ayes, until the last man had added his voice to the chorus of approval.

Nigel stood without further comment, walked across the room, and went through the door, closing it softly behind him. There were tears in his eyes, but he could not allow the others to see him weep. That was for later, and to be done in private, after the horror had been unleashed.

Down in the vaults, everything was prepared. His people had worked through the night to get things ready, and patiently awaited his command.

"We're ready," he said. "Let's get this started."

Surgeons and technicians and untrained fighting men began to move in a pre-planned routine. They had rehearsed this many times, and it had become so much a habit that they were able to divorce themselves from their feelings of compassion and pity. It was a job, one that needed to be done, and as such there was no room for any kind of emotional attachment to the subjects.

Nigel walked the length of the main underground passage, past the cells containing the deadbots. These bastardized creatures, part dead flesh and part robotic scrap metal, were primed and ready for action. Their directives had been programmed by the technicians, their body parts represented the best that the doctors could do with such limited time and equipment. They looked rough, shoddy, jerry-built…but they were more than enough for the task they'd been built for.

"Let them loose." He reached the end of the row and looked through the bars. His wife's reconstructed form stood against the wall, and his daughter sat on the floor at her feet. Their faces were the same, but little else had been salvageable after the zombie attack that had left them ravaged. The doctors had grafted on a variety of parts, both human and robot, and when they'd replaced their brains with circuitry, they'd done their best to repair the skulls and leave no trace of interference. Their hair had been shorn, of course, and because they were dead it had not grown back. A year had passed since their deaths, but because they were still here, and he saw their faces every day, he had not been able to grieve.

"Release them," he said to the nearest man.

He kept staring at his family as the gate at the rear of the cell was opened. Drawn to the noise of levers groaning and the metal bars retracting, they turned and began to move towards the exit.

"May God go with you," said Nigel through gritted teeth. He watched until they'd gone through the doorway in the rock and entered the tunnel that would lead them up into the heart of Old-egate, where their programming would kick in and guide them to infect the entire remaining population and turn them into an army of the undead.

ROWLANDS WAS STILL running. He wasn't sure how he'd managed to keep going through the night, but somehow his body had gathered the strength to continue. He stumbled over tree roots, tripped on large stones and small boulders, but somehow he remained on his feet. If he went down, it was over. If he stopped for a rest, he would never start again; he'd just lie down and die on the hard, unforgiving northern earth.

The air was cold but he could barely feel it. His blood ran hot and free, the hunger for glory fueling him as he ran. Rowlands had always wanted to be a hero. Strip away all the psychological framework, the reasons why he did what he did, and at the very bottom, under the rocks of his psyche, was the basic urge to be like the (mostly fictional) men he had admired when he was a small boy. The soldiers he'd read about in magazines, the super-powered saviors from the comics of his youth.

He wanted to be one of them: a hero. And this was his chance to answer that deep calling, to grab it by the throat and become the dream.

Earlier he had heard gunshots behind him, and he knew that Bossbot and his renegade army were close behind, chasing his heels. If he kept up the current pace, he'd reach the walls of Oldegate first, and once there he could summon up some kind of battalion from the civilians he found there. He would lead them to a hard-won victory; the survivors would raise a statue in his honor.

Rowlands smiled, despite having few teeth left in his mouth. His mind was slipping, sliding away to reveal nothing but a comic book image of honor and glory. It was all he had left now, and he clung to it with a tired desperation.

His feet skimming across the short, dead grass, he approached a small stand of trees. The ground was rising, forming the base of a hill. Above him, at the top of the rise, he hoped to see the walls and gates of Oldegate.

Just as he drew level with the trees, and was preparing to cut around them, something lurched out of a thicket. It was a woman, and she was dressed in rags. Her face was a hole that was also a huge, gaping mouth: in his shocked state, he thought it resembled the maw of a monstrous lamprey eel.

"No!" he swerved, still unwilling to stop mid-flight. The woman grabbed his arm, her fingers sinking into the muscle, and he tried to bat her away with his right hand. She tottered after him, with him, her feet going out from under her as he dragged up from somewhere a burst of pace. Her other arm reached out, the fingers like claws, and she was able to sink her long, filthy nails into the flesh of his neck, and then follow up with a snapping bite that caused her teeth to scrape across the already broken skin....

Shrugging the dead woman off, Rowlands clamped a hand to the wound. It was bad, spurting: her fingernails had gone deep and that bite had been enough to infect the area. It was just another part of the greater damage of his head and face, but this time he knew that the infection was within him, even now working its way towards his heart. Before long, he would die, and then he would return as one of them—the things he had spent his adult life trying to destroy. The hungry monsters that had killed his mother and father, and then, years later, taken his young wife when she was three months pregnant.

He tried to cry out but he had no voice. The exertion had taken his words. He breathed heavily, pressing his hand against the side of his throat to stem the blood flow, and focused on his legs, his feet, the grim yards of ground passing beneath them as he continued to run. He was locked into this now, like a machine. Like one of those damned robots. There was no escape.

But if he hurried, Rowlands just might get to be a hero before he died.

IT TOOK EVEN less time than they'd allowed for when they'd drawn up the battle plans. Nigel stood on the wall and watched the carnage, feeling hollow and empty and dead inside. The hot-wired and chipped deadbots, under the command of the main transmitters stored within the skulls of his dead wife and child, stumbled from house to house, shack to shack, room to room, biting and killing and turning the populace.

Some of them came back within minutes, and joined the savagery. Others took a little while to revive, but once they had returned they caught on fast. Within forty minutes, and just as the sun began to slide above the rim of the world, there were only a handful of people left alive.

"Nearly there," said someone to his left.

Nigel closed his eyes. How had it come to this? What madness had possessed them in their last-ditch attempt to protect the town's treasures? Weren't these in fact the treasures they should be trying to save: the people, the home dwellers, the human lives who had come here in search of sanctuary? So many questions now plagued his mind....

Nigel knew that something inside him had broken on the day a small group of zombies had managed to break through the perimeter and enter within the walls of the town. His wife and child had been standing near the gate, talking with friends, and had been among the first to go. A mad woman who lived in a wooden hut on the far side of the square, an old hag everyone called a witch, had gone crazy and let them in...she said that her son was one of them, come back home to see her, to be near her.

Five people had been killed. Five loved ones, five souls that would never go to Paradise, if indeed that place even existed. The witch had been executed for her crimes.

Rather than burn the corpses, in the method the government guidelines had so clearly and carefully set out, the beginnings of a plan had taken root. Now, twelve months later, with people starving inside the gates because the food supplies had almost run out, desperation had aided the plan to fruition.

Rather than starve to death, the Angels of the North had decided that these people should be made into a rag-tag army, an undead troop under the command of machines and specially adapted chips and circuit boards, to protect the church and its historical treasures from the rogue battalion of robots headed their way....

It was insane. Yet he had been instrumental in making it happen.

"Forgive me, oh Lord," he whispered, and in that moment he realized that he still believed, that he had always believed and never stopped believing. He simply thought he had. "I'm sorry, Father." He clenched his fists. It was too late now to do anything but allow events to unfold, and when the time came he would attempt some kind of redemption, if only to ensure his place at God's side, where he could be reminded of his shortcomings for eternity.

Nigel so desperately wanted to close his eyes, to shut out the horror below, but he forced himself to watch the hell on earth that he had helped create.

A small group of zombies, headed by his daughter's tiny form, herded a screaming man and a woman into a corner formed by large pile of timber and a fallen down shack. They were trapped; their faces were pale blobs as they called out the name of God. The man looked up, at the wall, and his mournful eyes made contact with those of Nigel. He held the man's gaze; a punishment, an act of penance. The man's features screwed up into a snarl and he ran at the zombies, lashing out with his fists.

They tore him apart. Bony hands ripped into his soft, flat stomach, pulling out clumps of red. One of them tugged off his right arm, and he went down wailing. The others descended and began to feed. Nigel's daughter gnawed on the severed arm, her chin basted in crimson.

The woman was down on her knees. She could have tried to flee, dodging the feasting dead, but she chose to remain there and clasp her hands together in prayer. Her lips moved as she prayed quietly for salvation. Nigel mirrored her movements, his own hands coming together in front of his chest, and he mumbled the Lord's Prayer.

The woman closed her eyes and waited for death.

Oddly, the zombies moved away, in pursuit of other game.

The man rose, moving slowly and awkwardly with his ravaged body. He walked up to the praying woman, watched her for seconds that felt to Nigel like hours, and then knelt down in front of her, as if joining her in prayer.

Nigel finally turned away when he heard the woman screaming her husband's name.

AT LAST HE was almost there. Rowlands was flagging now, his feet were dragging in the dirt and his limbs felt heavy as metal rods attached to his torso. He pushed on, pushed hard, and aimed his dead-weight body in the direction of the walls surrounding Oldegate.

He could see figures along the top of the walls as he approached, lookouts keeping watch in case of danger. That was good; it meant that they had some kind of idea regarding battle and defending the high ground. He hoped that they were brave men and women, and they were not too frail from the rigors of this unforgiving land. He prayed that they were ready to fight.

He stumbled up the hill, still clasping one hand against the ragged wound in his throat. The flow of blood had abated, but the area was still damp and sticky. There was a strange buzzing sound in his ears, inside his head, but he tried to ignore it. Was it the sound of the infection, the song of the disease?

The sky was greyer than before, but perhaps that was the result of his eyes failing. He'd come a long way, travelled so far, to be a savior.

More figures had gathered above him, looking down from the battlements. They had spotted him. They pointed and called to him—he thought they might be welcoming him inside. One of the men—a young soldier by the look of him—raised something into the air, like a stick....

"SHALL WE SHOOT it, sir?"

The young man trained his rifle sight on the approaching figure. The zombie was in bad shape, perhaps a freshly reanimated corpse from the last couple of days. Its presence here meant that not only was the rogue battalion of robots nearby, but there were probably dead people walking around like lost children on the open ground between Oldegate and its attackers.

"Yes," said Nigel, staring down at the shambling thing. "Stop it dead." He felt nothing for this pathetic creature, not even hatred. Not even pity. "The only corpses I want to see moving are those *inside* the walls."

The young man squeezed the trigger. The sound of the gunshot was small, and there was a delay of a couple of seconds before the zombie fell to the ground, twitching, with the top of its head taken clean off by the shot.

"Good shot, son," said somebody behind him. He did not recognize the voice.

HE COULD HAVE been a hero.

He had no idea why he was down on the ground, his vision dimming and his legs making spastic movements in the dirt. But he could have...

...he could have...

...*should* have...

...been a hero...

THE FIRST LOOKOUT saw them advancing up the hill with the sun at their backs, casting their long mechanical shadows before them. They moved in a broad surge, with what looked like some kind of demonic juggernaut leading them. Caterpillar tracks and steel-studded wheels flattened the flora, mechanical limbs reached up, down and out to tear apart the earth and the nearby trees. They were a wave of destruction, a tsunami of chaos. It was obvious from just looking at the assembled robots that nothing which stood in their way would survive the relentless onslaught of their advance. Small, broad-backed ammobots moved alongside sleek warbots and amped-up combatbots, dragging their wagons filled with brass death behind them. The dome-headed juggernaut at the head of the group looked like some mythical monster glittering in the sunlight as it led the way forward.

The undead townsfolk roamed around the town square, walking up and down in search of more food, wailing and moaning in a manner that seemed like a strange combination of whale song and choral lament. They were gathering from habit, and, of course, because of the transmissions the deadbots were sending out. They were shells, husks devoid of anything but primal instinct, and somehow the technicians had found a way to harness that instinct and bend it to their will.

"Open the gates," said Nigel. Open the gates and let them in."

He moved quickly, running along the fortified battlements and down a ladder at the opposite end of the walled enclosure from where the zombies were massing. He hurried towards the church, followed by the five representatives of the Angels of the North, and entered by the main doors. They locked the doors behind them and headed down the stairs to the vaults, where they had prepared the secret cells that would hide them from the carnage taking place above ground.

Once the robots had moved on and the area was clear, they would emerge. It might take hours; it might take days. They had just enough food and water—supplies they had kept hidden from the rest of the hungry people of Oldegate—to last a week. But if they were forced to stay down there much longer than that they too would be starving by the time they climbed up out of the dark vaults into the blood-smelling air of the town square.

Just as they were about to close the doors and seal themselves up in that holy place, something happened that Nigel had thought he would never again experience. As the door was pulled shut, and the light from a votive candle flickered in the gap, he felt a sudden burst of faith. The light…it took on a shape, became the shuddering outline of a figure. He knew it was just light seen from an odd angle, but for the briefest of moments it looked like a kneeling man with his arms held out in the shape of the cross, and Nigel felt like he'd been given a glimpse of something pure and untouchable.

Was it Christ, or a reflection of His image, or was it merely wishful thinking?

Nigel did not have the time to consider this theological argument, so he acted decisively. "Let me out." He grabbed the edge of the door, mounted the stairs, and went back up into the church. The light still flickered, but it was just a candle flame. There was nothing ethereal here, only his will to gain redemption.

The door slammed shut behind him. "Good luck, Angels of the

North," he whispered, and then he ran out of the church and into the fray.

RIBBONS OF BLOOD seemed to hang in the air like vaporous sheets. Disassembled bodies lay scattered across the ground, zombie and robot indivisible unless you got close enough to see through the layers of gore. Smoke moved lazily across the stained ground, generated from the fires with the torsos of fallen robots.

Nigel ran across the courtyard, not even aware of what it was he needed to do. Was he trying to escape, or simply running deeper into the action? He did not know; he would never know…because he ran straight into scene from a nightmare, or a biblical painting of damnation.

And Bossbot was waiting.

"Ah, a holy man." The robot's voice was like the voice of a demon…it thrummed in the air like a swarm of giant bees. "Did you really think that this plan would prevent me from carrying out my directive?" The loud, frantic motion of machine parts sounded like contained thunder as the robot stood before the priest like a vision of Satan himself.

"Get back, devil."

"I am not a devil," said the robot. "I am Bossbot, and this is my command."

"All we wanted was to be left alone. These are our riches, and we are defending them." Nigel clutched the crucifix he wore around his throat and wished that he could do something positive. But he was just meat, and no match for the iron and steel of this mechanized monster. "Just leave us alone." He was crying. He saw robots mincing the cadavers of the undead army, and knew that somewhere in that mess were the brutalized remains of his wife and daughter. How could he have been so stupid, why had he thought this plan would ever work? Grief had clouded his resolve, turning him into a robot himself, a mechanical puppet of others.

"Riches?" The robot's voice grew louder. "I have no use for your holy riches. My mission here is to destroy and eradicate…everything. This, holy man, is the Harrowing, and when we leave nothing shall remain."

Nigel spotted a figure behind the massive robot, rising from its knees amid a pile of desecrated bodies. Like the figure of light he'd been given a glimpse of inside the church, the slowly standing man adopted a Christ like pose, with his arms held out away from his sides and his ruined head drooping down towards his chest. Smoke billowed behind him. His eyes were closed.

"Our Father…" Nigel fell to his knees, still clutching the small crucifix in his hands. This was it: he had rediscovered that which he had lost. He believed all over again, he had seen evidence of the Lord and his Mercy. "Our Father who art in Heaven…"

Bossbot stood there, his receptors firing out light, his internal mechanisms going crazy. "What is this? Why are you not afraid?"

"This," said Nigel, "is where it all ends."

The man with the torn apart face and ragged hole in the side of his throat had approached the massive robot from behind, staggering like one of those reanimated corpses—but he was not a zombie, he was a living man, a potential savior. The other robots were distracted, busying themselves with the clear-up process, so he managed to move up right behind their commanding officer. In his hand was a long metal pole, a section of the flagpole which had been broken off from the main gates. A tattered Union Jack flag still clung stubbornly to the shaft.

"I…" His voice was a wasted thing, pulled from his shattered jaws. The man's head was held together by gristle and willpower. Little else of it remained. "I…am…hero…" He raised the pole and brought it down at an angle, smashing into a damaged part of Bossbot's visor, right where the glass panel met his ironclad shoulder. It took two hits, but the glass panel came loose, cracked, shattered, and the pressurized fluid contained within immediately began to bubble from the gap. Then the pinkish fluid spurted, an elegant geyser, and the robot started to spin slowly and uncontrollably on his tracks.

The man Nigel had ordered shot as a zombie—he recognized him now—pulled back his arm and then thrust his hand into the shattered visor, where he tore up the wires and tubes inside the thing's conical skull. When he pulled his hand back out again, he was clutching something square and black—Bossbot's central hard drive, the place where all his data, his core programming, was stored.

The man—this glorious neo martyr—walked towards Nigel and then fell to his knees, the hard drive rolling from his open, bloodied hands.

Bossbot kept spinning, watched by his surviving troops. Their own systems began to fail, disconnected from the central hub, and they began to shut down like a series of lights going out. It happened quickly, as if without their commanding robot these others had no imperative of their own, and the entire impetus behind their mission had been housed within Bossbot's hulking shell.

Nigel bent down and took the black box from where it lay beside the dead man's hands. "Thank you, son," he said, closing the man's unseeing eyes with his fingertips. Etched upon the box was a familiar emblem: the Royal Coat of Arms.

This was an official mission. The Harrowing—or so the still-spinning robot had called it—was state-approved.

When he looked up, towards the heavens that he once again believed in, Nigel saw a fighter jet banking in the sky. He stared at the jet, and tried to make out some kind of reason in the puzzle of its contrail, but by the time he realized what the thin vapor trail meant, it was much too late to matter.

The mission was over; the real Harrowing had begun.

The bombs began to fall.

PRIME MINISTER MEREDITH Thatchell sat in the bombproof meeting room beneath Number 10 Downing Street in the fortified city of London. She watched the screen in silence. Her ministers and the head of National Security sat by her side, awaiting her reaction to the live footage taken by a camera in a small flybot spotter plane that flew alongside the fighters.

The northern outpost of Oldegate went up in flames. The missiles successfully found their targets, and human and robot alike were decimated by the thermal charges.

Reflected flames lit up the PM's narrow features, and illuminated her cold, cold smile.

"The loss of Bossbot is, of course, regrettable," she said. "But no one could ever be allowed to get their hands on that black box. I know this initial part of the campaign has lasted only a week or so, but the next one will be longer, and much more effective." Her smile was stiff, as if she didn't understand the rules of facial expressions. "Collateral damage aside, I think it's prudent to call this little test mission of ours a success." She turned to her colleagues, making an expansive gesture with her arms which included—and implicated—them in everything that had happened here today.

"The riches the priest spoke of, which are no doubt stashed away in the church vaults, will prove a nice little bonus when it comes to approaching the board for the funding of Phase Two of the Harrowing. Bossbot 1.1 will need to be more robust, I think." She laughed, but nobody joined her. They all looked uncomfortable, as if they were afraid of the sound of her insanity.

The PM spun back around in her leather chair, glaring at the flickering screen. The unseen concrete canyon walls of London hemmed her in, containing her madness. She, more than any other person alive, felt that she represented the capital, the glory of London—the city she saw in her fiery dreams as a citadel, and the chosen site of mankind's last stand against the plague of walking dead.

Everything else was to be sacrificed in order to achieve this goal.

"And then, fellow ministers," she said, baring her teeth in something that did not even resemble a smile. "Then, the really hard work can begin...."

TIMKA

Ekaterina Sedia

VALENTIN KORZHIK FELT a familiar lump in his throat as he watched the black government Mercedes, tinted windows and all, pull up to the front of the Moscow State University's Virology Institute. *Those days are over,* he whispered, not quite believing it. They were never over as long as the KGB or the FSB or whatever they called it these days drove around in cars with tinted windows and could show up out of the blue, at Valentin's place of work, and spook him so much—as if he was guilty of anything.

The man with the stripe of a general on his trousers came out of the back seat, tugged down his uniform jacket, and looked up at the windows with his also tinted glasses, directly at where Valentin stood. Valentin ducked away and felt foolish—it wasn't like the FSB general could see him through the glare, five stories up.

Maksim Vronsky gave Valentin a long, pointed look. "Seen a ghost?"

"Just about. FSB."

Maksim made a face, but remained standing by his bench, watching the thermocycler with his usual quiet intensity, willing it to work well, without failure. A finicky machine, that, and they all had little rituals to coax it into working. Valentin said little silent prayers to imaginary and funny gods, Lida Belaya sang to her samples—beautifully, Valentin thought. He always looked forward to Belaya's experiments, and today he was sad that she wasn't here to soothe him and yet happy that she wasn't, and wouldn't have to face the FSB general.

It was a large building, and objectively Valentin had no reason to think that FSB was here to see him. The secret yet universal belief in his exceptional status was verified when the frosted glass lab door swung open.

"Lieutenant general Dobrenko," the general said, and moved for Maksim. "Dr. Vronsky?"

"Yes," Maksim said.

"Dr. Korzhik," the general said to Valentin. "I'm here on business."

Maksim shifted on his feet, leaning uncharacteristically away from the thermocycler. "For me or for him?" His fingers were white around the stirring glass rod he had no reason to be holding.

"Both." The word plopped out of Dobrenko's mouth, lumpy and dull like a toad. "You both are virologists with a military past and bio weapons experience. You both served in Afghanistan."

Valentin did not know that about Maksim, and judging by Maksim's quick look, the ignorance was mutual.

The general sighed. "Another life, yeah? Back then, who would've thought that the Americans will be bombing the Afghans instead of helping them? Anyway, I'm here to request your expertise."

"What are you weaponizing now?" Valentin said. "Measles? Common cold? Herpes?"

"Nothing. In fact, we're attenuating." Oh damn it all to hell. Valentin managed not to say it out loud. Why can't you just leave shit alone? The less you stir it, the less it stinks.

"Let me fill you in." Dobrenko leaned against Maksim's lab bench, kicking out one long leg, his narrow behind resting against the black composite edge. Yet it was clear to them that listening was not optional. "You of course heard about the quarantine."

"I knew it!" Maksim whacked the glass rod against the palm of his other hand. "I knew it was a disease, not a food safety issue! Since when do they care about pesticide contamination, huh?"

Valentin nodded. Nothing ever changed—the newspapers lied just like they did in the eighties, and of course everyone guessed that the sudden stop of trade with the west was due to more than violations of environmental pesticide guidelines. Valentin groused that it was great Russia was not a WTO member, because if it was, who would let it boycott products like that? He realized that he was leaning forward, just like Maksim, eager to learn a secret, no matter how bad or distasteful, no matter how beholden it would leave him. Not like he had a choice anyway.

"There's a disease." Dobrenko's words slipped out measured, safe. "We believe it started in the US, and of course took little time to spread elsewhere. Of course, it'll take a while to burn through Western Europe—now that everyone is quarantining. Poland, the Czech Republic—they closed their borders too."

"How dangerous is it?" Maksim said. "What's the mortality rate? How does it spread?"

"Hundred percent," Dobrenko said. "Airborne, or at least we think so." Voice flat, face flat. "Of course, you can also say that the mortality rate is zero percent—it's all in how you look at it. According to our data, people who die from it don't stay dead too long."

"What, zombies?" Valentin grew irritable again, and heard his voice rising. "Next you'll be asking us to make you a vaccine for lycanthropy? Antibodies for vampirism?"

"This is serious," Dobrenko said. "Look."

He pulled out an envelope from his pocket. The pictures inside were of good quality: and depicted some unknown town, likely European judging by how clean the streets were—if one ignored the dead on the sidewalks, in the roadways. More disconcerting were several people standing—they all had an unusually slouching posture; some had missing limbs, others—ruined faces, bruises, long streaks of gore smeared on their clothes. And yet they stood.

"What do you want, a vaccine?" Maksim said.

"Sure, a vaccine would be nice. What we do want, however, is an attenuated virus—to grant immunity, and maybe produce…a milder illness, I suppose."

Maksim and Valentin traded a disbelieving look.

"Even if we could do that—and I doubt we can since viruses are tricky, and how many viral vaccines do you know anyway?" Maksim sucked in his breath. "Even if we could, what makes you think it's a good idea?"

"The election is coming. The virus seems to make people… brainless is not what we're after, of course, but more docile, easier to speak to. Easier to convince. Suggestible, I guess is what we're after. And if it's not airborne, it probably should be."

"This is United Russia's idea," Valentin said. "No way they're taking the majority of the Duma seats this time around."

"There is a way," Dobrenko said softly. "This is what I'm trying to explain to you—with your cooperation we might yet save the motherland."

Maksim shook his head and Valentin marveled—at Maksim's stubbornness, at his own impotent hate, at the ability to refuse to collaborate while simultaneously accepting the inevitability of doing so.

"Think about it." Dobrenko unfolded from his slouch by the bench and left. And why wouldn't he? Not like they had anywhere to run with the borders closed.

"Well?" Maksim was on him before the door closed behind the general all the way. "What's with you? You stand there and don't argue, and you were doing bio weapons before and never told me?"

"You didn't tell me either." Valentin sighed. "And arguing…you can't argue with the FSB. Not if you want to live or have any relatives."

"So we just let them infect people? This is just…I knew they were evil, but this is just ridiculous! Even they have to realize how bad this is, and we…"

"I didn't say we do it," Valentin said. "I said you can't argue. You have Lida's home number? Better call her, warn that poor soul."

As little as Valentin enjoyed reminiscing about his military service, there were parts of him shaped by it—as much as he managed to forget them at times, at others they manifested, almost violently, against his will, like claws and fur and teeth sprouting out of a werewolf. Valentin thought that maybe he was a were-soldier, like one of those shell-shocked vets that flipped out at loud noises and flashes of light. Only his flipping out was quiet, more orderly.

"So you served in Afghanistan," he said to Maksim. "Still remember any of it?"

"Every night." Maksim breathed through his mouth, suddenly slow and cautious. "I don't understand how they could do this to us—you can't just draft kids—eighteen-year-olds!—and toss them into hell. I don't care what Dobrenko said about the Americans—at least those are trained soldiers who volunteered to join the military. We…how could they?"

"They could and they did." Valentin stared out of the window overlooking the apple orchard planted by Michurin himself—or so the rumor had it. "And they'll do it again too. That virus…if they're talking to us about it, it means they brought samples for us, from god knows where. How long will those remain contained? How long until someone sneaks across the border? How many were incubating before the quarantine started?"

"You sure Dobrenko's right that it's airborne?"

"No idea."

"So what is it that you want to do? If you can't say no to the FSB and we're all gonna die anyway?"

"It's going to get bad. Can you imagine what it would be like, with millions of people turned into…"

"Zombies? You believe that?"

"I always believe FSB." Valentin managed a smile with one side of his mouth. "Even if they succeed and attenuate the virus, and release it…."

"We'll still be overrun with a horde of zombies." Maksim smiled too. "I'm starting to see your point. What do you suggest then?"

"We have to go into hiding. We can't run, and we cannot work for them, and I'm scared of what's going to happen. What we can do is to get armed and hide."

"Where?"

"Underground. Vorobyovy Gory subway station is closed now, it's under renovations. I know there's a side tunnel—a friend of mine works on the construction."

Maksim must've been taking Dobrenko seriously too, because he neither argued with Valentin nor called him insane. "Weapons," he said eventually. "We will need something...."

"The Biology Department used to have the ROTC program. There were Kalashnikovs, ammo, medical kits—the whole deal."

"And we'll get it how? Oh, don't tell me—you know a guy."

Valentin nodded. "I do. He used to run the program, Major Sechenov. He's old now, retired. But he has the keys—when he retired, he took them with him. The question now is, what are you bringing to the table? Do you still remember how to handle a Kalashnikov?"

"I can pull it apart in under eight seconds. And yes, I still remember what to do with it. And..." Maksim paused—as if a new life was being born in him right that minute, out of their fear and disgust, the bleakness that never seemed to lift away in this cursed place. "I think I can get us some heavy artillery."

"How?"

"I know a guy too."

IN THE FOLLOWING days, Valentin came to appreciate what his classicist ex-wife Lyudmila referred to as "Cassandra syndrome". He struggled. On one hand, one had to be careful while spilling classified info and yet trying to maintain the facade of collaboration with the government; on the other, as remote and cold as Valentin tended to be, there were people he cared about. He assumed the same was true of Maksim, but he never asked, allowing his colleague to negotiate the difficulty as he saw fit. The world was about to die, and Valentin hoped to hang on for a while. There was no news from Europe on TV, and he took it seriously. It would be good to have company, but ultimately it wouldn't matter: he never believed in a happy ending of the post-apocalyptic stories. If he did, he would've tried harder.

As it was, Maksim and he sequenced the viral genome to waste time during the day, and at night they sneaked into the old storage room of the Biology Department's ROTC. These back rooms, walls of gray cinder block and long shelves along the walls, housed so many relics of another time that Valentin wanted to linger, to look at the student-made posters satirizing Yeltsin's ascent, and to pet bald heads of the Lenin busts. Instead, they sorted through the boxes with Kalashnikov's parts, ammunition, handfuls of tracer cartridges. They also grabbed medical supplies and rubber gas masks, their trunks nestled embryonically in dark-green canvas bags. Detachable bayonets, poncho-tents, miners' helmets with mounted flashlight, cans of pre-Perestroika pork and condensed milk—countless forgotten treasures.

They made one trip per night, and took only what they could carry comfortably, using wooden crates they collected near supermarkets. Valentin hugged his crate to his chest and felt like crying over every item familiar on such an intimate level, like a shape of a lover's hand, carved into his heart by nostalgia for that lost time. He assumed Maksim felt the same. They walked then to the closed metro station, where Valentin's friend, Dmitry, left unlocked the side door leading to a set of service stairs and then a short side tunnel, with an abundance of warning signs and an empty electric shed. On their first night, Valentin took off the shed's padlock with the bolt cutters, and hung instead the one he bought. So far, no one seemed to have bothered to discover that the lock had been changed.

Thursday night was likely to be the last. They were almost done gutting the cinder block rooms, and Valentin looked forward to maybe spending the next night in his bed instead of skulking in the shadows and walking with a heavy crate for a good three kilometers. He breathed a sigh of relief when they reached the shed, and then almost jumped out of his skin when a shadow stepped from behind the shed.

It was a blessing that his hands were occupied—otherwise, he would've struck out blindly, before the figure said in an uncertain voice, "Dad?"

"Yes honey," Maksim answered.

Valentin's crate clanged to the ground. "You could've warned me."

"I'm early," the shadow figure said. "I was supposed to be here tomorrow, but I finished classes early, so I caught an early train."

In the dim light, Valentin was barely able to make out a face—a sharp chin, jutting bangs, a curve of a young cheek. "Your daughter?"

"Estranged daughter," she said with some emotion. "From St. Petersburg."

"Alisa," Maksim added.

Valentin didn't pry; other people's affairs interested him little, and he considered questions impolite, especially if they touched on such intimate topics as family and children. So instead he just nodded to Alisa and assumed that she would join them in their bunker. "Hope you like condensed milk," he said after they settled the crates inside the shed, and Alisa had a chance to appreciate the abundance.

"Now what?" she said.

"Now, home," Maksim said. "Tomorrow night, we're getting the heavy artillery."

Alisa nodded—apparently, her father already had told her about the museum. "I'll come with you," she said.

"All right." Maksim extended his hand, shook Valentin's. "See you tomorrow." He and his sudden daughter walked to the bus stop, while Valentin sighed and hoofed it back to the University metro station.

VALENTIN HAD ALWAYS had an ambivalent relationship with viruses: they were the worst of those pseudo-Zen koans, not really alive and not really dead. Finding a virus that could turn people into something like itself was both terrifying and a little thrilling, and Valentin couldn't help but get occasionally carried away, as the new bits of code came off the sequencer, and Maksim searched the databases for closest matches.

The samples Dobrenko gave them were all heat-killed, harmless, but still they worked with every Level 2 precaution. He couldn't help but wonder where the live specimens were kept, and how long it would take before they escaped. If there was one thing Valentin learned in his scientific career, it was that pathogens can never be contained. No matter how cunning the facilities and the locks, no matter what precautions, every microscopic life form would eventually break out of its confinement and run through the streets, chasing the shrieking throngs. He guessed that that moment wasn't too far off: newspapers wrote about contamination of produce with E. coli, necessitating the cordons all around Moscow. No one but the military had left or entered the city in the past week or so. Everyone complained about lack of eggplants in the market.

Maksim wandered over to Valentin's bench, to peek at the long strip of paper coming off the sequencer like a seismogram, with four colored lines, flailing up and down into peaks and valleys. "Pretty A-T heavy, huh."

"Yeah. What artillery did you have in mind?"

"I told you, a friend of mine is a museum guard. About to retire, so he doesn't give a shit. And they have a nice collection of old military technology. We can find what we need and walk away with it."

"So nothing too heavy."

"Or at least nothing without wheels."

"Your daughter...she can handle all this?"

Maksim nodded. "Yep. Bright kid, studies engineering in St Petersburg's University. Computer networks and all this jazz. She's certainly better at new technology than we are."

"We don't have new technology. Don't need it—what are we going to do, launch rockets from your laptop?"

"Do you mind?"

Valentin shook his head, then laughed. "Sorry. I just argue sometimes."

That night after work, they went to scope out the museum Maksim had been talking about. This time, they didn't have to walk too far. The museum was located near the metro station, a small building that looked like it was meant to be the part of the university but fell by the wayside somehow, and became one of those small, dinky museums that served as depositories of random specimens and donated junk no one had the heart to throw out. This one seemed to have received its fair share of WW2 relics, uniforms and helmets and rusted Katyusha shells sleeping under the glass. Most people clustered in the wing that had exhibited some porcelain dolls—Valentin thought with dismay that unless the exhibit closed soon, obtaining artillery would be difficult. He really was hoping for a sleepy, empty museum.

Alisa, who they had picked up by the metro, didn't seem impressed. Valentin studied her out of the corner of his eye, and she did the same. An alien, a small sharp-elbowed alien with a sagging backpack on her shoulder, barely covered by a shredded shirt. She seemed a bird with her ruthless bright eyes. "I want to see the dolls," she told her father.

"Go for it." He slipped a folded hundred into her hand and she sauntered off, in the direction of human voices and soft music, and flashing of theoretically prohibited cameras.

They wandered away, into the cavernous halls with the dangerously apathetic military technology. "Whoa," Maksim said, and pointed.

It was an entire T34, sitting, uncovered by glass or any other impediments, in a shallow niche. Far as tanks went, this was a lightweight, but maneuverable. "How are we supposed to get it out?" Valentin said.

"I used to drive one," Maksim said. "I think I probably still can."

"It's a tank," Valentin said.

"Precisely." The tone of his voice was not unusual, but the subtle setting of the jaw told Valentin that Maksim would accept nothing less.

"You have your heart set on it?"

Maxim nodded. "I doubt there will be anything better."

"Or more conspicuous."

When they left the museum, Maksim whispered into Alisa's ear, urgent. In response, Alisa only jerked her shoulder, not bothering to hide her distaste for the proceedings. Contemptuous, like her entire generation. Kids were such shit these days.

A sudden sound interrupted Valentin's fuming. A low, throbbing cry came from somewhere up ahead, at the entrance to the metro station. A small knot of people snagged at something, thickening and wrapping, and growing around the invisible epicenter from which the cry came. A drunk or an epileptic, Valentin thought.

"A woman's not feeling well." Some busybody whispered to Valentin, and went back to rising on tiptoes and craning his neck.

"No reason to hold everything up," Valentin said, and pushed ahead, his shoulder habitually plowing through the crowd.

He didn't have to push too hard: to his surprise, the crowd opened up around the alleged sick woman, as people stepped back. The woman in question, still thin and young-looking despite graying curls, wailed, but without much volume or enthusiasm, her cries interrupted by sobs like hiccups. She bent over, her arms raised behind her back, as if in some bizarre game of the airplane. She tottered a little, as if one of her heels had come detached, and then clutched a bloodied hand to her chest. Only then did Valentin notice that her temple was bleeding too—heavy black drops oozed from two semicircles imprinted just above her ear.

The onlookers hushed, a thing unusual in itself, as the woman continued to sob and grunt, and each sound grew more inhumane as she went. The sounds stopped eventually, the silence as alien to the usual thrum of the crowd as the stillness. *It would make more sense if it was snowing.* Valentin shook his head to chase away an unbidden thought. *Someone ought to do something.*

One of the onlookers who watched the woman with the same blank intensity as the rest of them, took a step toward her, reaching out with his knobby, sinewy hands—Valentin noticed these hands before everything else, the concave face and too-short jacket

sleeves, peeling threads on the checkered cuffs of the shirt. One of
the knuckles bore a bright crescent mark, slowly seeping blood. For
a moment, Valentin was relieved that someone had stepped up so
he wouldn't have to, but the man in the checkered shirt and old
jacket growled and grabbed at the woman, his jaws opening wide.
Before a few men in the crowd had a chance to step up, he bit the
woman in the face, his face blank all the while.

A few people gasped, a few backed away.

"What is it?" Alisa hissed into his ear.

"I...I don't know." Valentin looked over his shoulder, seeking
Maksim's input.

He wasn't far behind. "Shit. This doesn't look like anything..."

"I know," Valentin said. "Do you think...?"

Maksim took a step back, tugging Alisa's sleeve. She followed
him, too scared to get an attitude. "I think," Maksim said, "that the
farther we get away from this, the better."

EPIDEMICS WERE A bit of Valentin's hobbyhorse. The one that unfolded—no, unfurled violently, like a ribbon in a hurricane—was
perhaps the quickest. From the speed and the intensity of it,
Valentin guessed that Dobrenko either lied or didn't really know
that the virus has crossed the border some time ago: the cordons
around Moscow must've held back the tide for quite a while. It was
like a dam: once breached, the accumulated weight behind it bar-
reled down, and everyone wondered where it came from. They
barely had time to return to the museum, and already the streets
thronged with the confused and the overcome. The infected attacked the living, violently, savagely, and Valentin had to look away
more than once from a person screaming, clutching a bloodied ap-
pendage. He kept his gaze firmly up, never daring to look down on
the pavement where bones crunched and unspeakable things happened.

If Valentin was inclined to see the positives at the moment, he
would've been pleased with how easy it was to start a tank and drive
it out of the museum, wrecking the stairs and slightly widening the

side entrance in the process. Really, the tank was the least problematic thing in these streets, and his mind went to the late summer of
1990, where tanks in the streets were shocking and threatening. It
felt strange to crouch inside of one, seeing just narrow snatches of
the unpleasantness through the viewfinder.

Once they reached the bunker (T34 was surprisingly nimble on
the service stairs), Valentin surveyed their stockpile. He was glad
that they'd invested in less esoteric cans than thirty-year-old pork,
and drinking water wouldn't be a problem. The shed itself was
small, but the adjacent service tunnel was dark and cozy, and even
the light of their industrial flashlights did little to chase away the
velvety darkness. It did, however, snatch the outline of the railroad
ties, piled high and ready to be deployed to whatever track construction needed them, covered in yards of canvas.

"We could build a nice tent with this," Valentin said.

"Housing is the least of my worries," Alisa said. "In case you
didn't notice, there are hordes of zombies in the streets. Violent
ones. Did you see them maul that woman?"

Belatedly, Valentin felt bad for the girl. "How're you holding up?"

She barked a short, hysterical laugh. "Great. Fantastic. Probably
not as badly as I would be if my whole life didn't teach me to expect
a zombie apocalypse—thank you, Hollywood. But my point is, it
also taught me that zombies always show up, and you always run
out of ammunition or have to sleep, or have a weak point in your
defenses."

"So what are you suggesting?"

She crouched on the floor of the tunnel, her oversized backpack
pooled at her feet. From it, she started pulling dull pieces of metal,
and flat aluminum circuit boards with wires soldered on. "Believe
it or not, I specialize in AI. This is my thesis project—a simple command relay, but it'll do. You can put it on the tank, and it will per-
form a routine by itself."

"Like a remote controlled car," Maksim said.

Alisa rolled her eyes. "No, Dad. There is no remote control. More
like a Roomba. A Roomba with a big cannon. It'll eventually learn

where it needs to spend more time, to protect the perimeter. You know, like a real Roomba with cat hair."

Valentin nodded. "If you can do that...that would be helpful. There's an electric outlet in the shed if you need it. We stockpiled some diesel, but will probably need to get more after a week or so. Meanwhile, however, I guess keeping watch is up to us."

They left the girl to dig around in T34's metal innards, and turned their attention to the tunnel. The service tunnel ended in a dead end just half a kilometer past the shed, but the gaping mouth of it presented a problem: it led to the main tunnel and to the service stairs. The main tunnel was closed to the train traffic for the construction (it was eerily silent now, without the sound of the trains rambling past in parallel tunnels), but it was densely populated by construction equipment and, Valentin assumed, construction workers. Who may or may not still be there, and who may be affected by the plague taking place above. Valentin didn't want to think about the possibility of either himself or Maksim having been exposed—they took the subway every day, just like everyone else. Who knew when and how this outbreak had started? He wondered if Dobrenko was able to find more cooperative virologists; he even remembered a weird piece of scientific lore—the one that told of some institute in Chukotka, which was subsequently bombed to contain some horrifying outbreak. That was a while ago though; unlikely that a pathogen would survive for that long.

"We should probably build a barricade," Maksim said, "while Alisa's working on the tank."

They spent the rest of the day heaving the railroad ties and segments of old tracks into piles blocking the main tunnel, and a smaller one by the service stairs. The light of the miners' helmets lights was pale and uneven, and the shadows stretched long and menacing, snaked down the tunnel and disappeared into the silence, too dead to acknowledge. They spoke in hushed whispers, not so much out of fear of attracting attention but out of childhood superstition before the darkness. They positioned the metal tracks so that they protruded outward, to discourage any assault by the machinery. They only left a passage wide enough for the T34, and blocked it with a loose but formidable looking heap of ties and broken stone. They made sure that merely yanking the main weight-bearing tie would bring the whole section down, to a pile of rubble caterpillar tracks would have no trouble going over.

Valentin wasn't sure what time it was when the barricade was finished—wobbly and unwieldy, and hastily constructed, but solid enough to take cover behind. There were a few openings in between the railroad ties, big enough to take aim.

"I guess this is where we'll be sleeping tonight," Maksim said.

Alisa fell asleep on the pile of tents, wrapped in a ratty camelhair blanket. Maksim and Valentin picked out a couple of tent ponchos that smelled reassuringly of canvas and mildew. Both were too tired to use the hotplate, and instead they punctured cans of condensed milk with bayonet knives, and drank the sickeningly sweet mass through the triangular holes. If it wasn't for the starless sky and the smells of creosote, Valentin could've believed that he was still in the army. Although he didn't feel eighteen, and the twinges in his back told him that he would pay dearly tomorrow.

"It's amazing how some things never go away." Maksim was done with his condensed milk, and busied himself with disassembling of his Kalashnikov. He laid out all the parts in the narrow beam of his miner's light, textbook and meticulous. "I haven't touched one of these since 1986, and yet I recognize the pin and the magazine, and I know where everything goes. I couldn't tell you—my brain couldn't—but my hands just know."

Valentin nodded, and laid his Kalashnikov next to him, within an easy reach. "I remember those drills. We had to do it over and over until we fell asleep from the exhaustion and then we did it in our sleep."

"Yeah."

He wanted to sleep desperately, but even as his eyelids grew heavy, he reached over for the Kalashnikov, and made sure that the firing mechanism moved smoothly, and that the magazine was attached straight. "Nothing worse than a jammed magazine," he mumbled, and was asleep before he heard Maksim's answer.

A NOISE WOKE him: it took him a second to remember where he was, and the absurdity of the situation startled him like a glass of cold water in the face. Maksim shifted in the darkness—a distinct scrape of metal against wood and cinder block, but the sound that woke Valentin continued from the other side of the barricade, a quiet but persistent scratching and shuffling.

"Who's there?" Valentin called, barely raising his voice above the whisper.

The noise continued.

He flipped on his miner's light, half hoping to see a rat or a stray dog, which were not unknown in the bowels of the metro. The sharp beam snatched the railroad ties close to his face, and the opening into the profound darkness of the tunnel beyond—and an outline of a human head, just beyond the embrasure.

He took aim. "Who's there?" Louder, now.

Maksim's light flicked on, and the two crossing beams snatched out enough detail of the stranger. It seemed to be one of the railroad workers, the blue serge of his work shirt torn and splattered with mud, his face blue and swollen and decidedly not alive. The eyes shone dully in the light, without a glimmer of intelligence—or discomfort at the sudden stimulation.

"Hello," Maksim called softly. The man behind the barricade swiveled his head as if looking for the source of the sound, and continued his uncertain scraping at the barricade.

"It's not alive," Valentin reminded softly.

Maksim responded with a single shot from his Kalashnikov. The figure on the other side stumbled and staggered back into the tunnel, its face obscured by the slow dripping black liquid. They could no longer see it, but a soft thump reassured them soon enough.

"You think it's dead? I mean, really?" Valentin asked.

Maksim shrugged. "If a shot to a head doesn't kill it, I don't know what does."

"What if nothing does?"

Maksim flicked off his light. "Go to sleep. I'll watch for a while. I'll wake you when I'm tired."

Valentin closed his eyes. They could stay like this forever, he thought, waking each other up and going to sleep when tired, a constant unbroken circle of "Good morning" and "Good night," in the perpetual darkness of the underground. This life of conditional waking and sleeping cycles, predicated on living out of phase with his co-worker and, Valentin suspected, friend, held a degree of appeal. He smiled in the darkness then, and slept until a sharp jab in the ribs woke him.

"There're more of them," Maksim hissed.

Valentin bolted awake, flipped on his light. "More" was an understatement: the tunnel was alive with heaving flesh, the smell of unclean wounds and rotting teeth stronger than creosote. He flipped Kalashnikov to automatic fire, and took aim.

Maksim did the same, and for a while Valentin went deaf and blind from the gunfire, as it resonated off the roof of the tunnel.

A few of the attackers fell—all railroad workers, as far as Valentin could see—but more kept pressing from behind them.

"Get out of the way!" Alisa's voice cut through the moment the fire stopped.

Valentin looked back and saw the girl running toward them, next to the tank that was rolling slowly under its own power.

"Get the tie," Maksim yelled.

The two of them managed to wrench the weight-bearing tie free, and rolled out of the way as the tank hobbled over the rubble, leisurely, lopsidedly, and met the approaching wall of shambling apparitions. It was like watching an invisible child play with a toy tank—*vroom vroom*, back and forth, as it rolled over the workers, crushing, until there was nothing left to crash.

"Nice job," Maksim shouted to Alisa.

She smiled just as the tank turned and headed back over the barricade. Valentin moved away to give it berth but the tank went after him.

"Climb!" he yelled, before climbing higher over the beams.

The tank attempted to follow, then turned its attention to Alisa and Maksim.

Maksim turned to Alisa. "Can you disable it?"

"Yes! Just let it chase you!"

Maksim took off running down the service tunnel, and the tank followed. Alisa trotted behind, until she was able to grab onto the protruding part of the armor. Valentin followed, not too close but close enough to see. She climbed atop it, and then into the turret.

Valentin realized that Maksim was running into the dead end, and would reach it soon. There wasn't much space there for him to avoid the lumbering thing, and he prepared to distract the tank's attention if necessary. "Hey, tank," he called out as a test.

The tank stopped just as Maksim reached the wall of the tunnel.

"What was that?" He yelled at Alisa as soon as she emerged from the turret, red and panting.

"It's still learning." She sat on the caterpillar track, sullen, feet in black sneakers dangling. "I guess I could tweak it some more."

Valentin and Maksim returned to the barricade. Both were too tired to fix the collapsed section.

"You go to sleep," Valentin said. "I'll keep watch for a while."

After a few hours, the darkness grew irritating: whether he closed or opened his eyes, the view was the same, and every little sound, every whispering of the breeze, every echo of an echo, grew magnified and startled him. He wondered if Alisa had gotten any sleep, back there, in the safety of the blunt side tunnel. He decided to check on her.

She was not asleep—in fact, she looked as if she barely slept at all. Her miner's light snatched bits of metal lying on the ground, and her massive backpack lay open, spilling out the soldering irons and other implements of technology Valentin had no interest in.

He waited for her light to arc through the air in his direction, not to startle her with a sudden sound of his voice. "How's it going?" he said.

"Okay," she answered. The fatigue seemed to have drained most of her attitude, and her voice was small and hollow. "Almost done. Are there any more of those things?"

"Don't worry," Valentin said, mustering up what he hoped was a paternal tone of voice. "If there are more, we'll deal with them."

Alisa glowered at him. "I'm not afraid. I just need one of them, alive, for the T34 to learn to recognize them. You know, differentiation between a person and a zombie."

"That would be useful. How would it do that?"

"Temperature sensors," she answered. "I just installed them. But I also want it to recognize the moving patterns. If you see one, don't kill it yet; just wait until I'm finished here. Also, I named it Timka— T34 is too generic."

"All right then. I should probably go keep an eye on your dad," Valentin said. "When he wakes up, I'll go get you a zombie."

He shuffled back to the barricade, the taste of his words in his mouth. If it wasn't for the ridiculousness of the last word, it would've sounded so paternal, so domestic. Don't worry, little one, dad will go out and get you a toy. Not something he ever thought he would say, but the words felt right, appropriate even.

Maksim waited for him, awake.

"Alisa's fine," Valentin said. "You better tell her to eat or sleep or rest. She looks like a stray cat."

Maksim nodded. "She's a smart kid, but doesn't know when to stop. In high school, we had to turn off the lights and confiscate her flashlights to get her to stop studying. Imagine that? A seventeen-year-old kid wanting nothing more than to study engineering and to solder integrated circuits?"

"Better than the alternative," Valentin said. "Listen, take care of your kid, okay? I'll go to the surface. She said she needed a zombie to train the tank on, and I think it'll be easy enough to grab one."

"Be careful," Maksim said. "Do we think there's a chance it's airborne?"

Valentin shrugged. "It spreads fast, but with all the biting…and since none of us got it, I think it's likely fluids. But who knows, Dobrenko could've mucked it up some."

"Should I come along?"

Valentin shook his head. "And leave Alisa here? No, you stay."

"Be safe," Maksim said. "Don't let anything bite you." He didn't need to be persuaded, and Valentin appreciated that. There was nothing more tedious than pretend politeness, and back and forth and no, you take the last piece, I am fine. It was obvious who should stay behind, and Maksim had the good grace to not argue.

Valentin gathered his Kalashnikov and ammunition, ropes, metal clamps, thick gloves. He packed it all into the green gas mask bag. He had forgotten to wind his watch (the one that said "Commander's Watch," and was waterproof and weighed at least a quarter kilo), so he had no sense of what time it was. He wished they figured that part better. He crept toward the service stairs, to a small mound of shattered cinder block and half bricks Maksim and he had hastily piled up to create an illusion of blockage, meant to dissuade rather than prevent entry. He climbed over the pile, loose debris shifting under his feet. As he reached the bottom of the stairs, he turned off the light as a precaution, and pushed the door open, just a crack.

It was twilight outside, with pale scattering of stars just starting to manifest above the stairwell. The moon was still hidden, and long gray wisps of clouds stretched across the sky. The breeze rose and fell, like a sigh, and Valentin breathed in, closing his eyes without meaning to. Then he wished he'd brought a gas mask.

He shook his head and climbed the stairs, the Kalashnikov's muzzle resting on his shoulder, its butt snuggled into his cupped hand. He peered cautiously over the top of the stairwell, to see only the closed up building of the metro station nearby, and a dark outline of trees lining Lomonosov Prospect against the sky.

There were no cars in the streets, except for a few abandoned ones, and no people. He licked his suddenly dry lips.

What did zombie hunting have in common with science? It seemed very clear and reasonable before you started it, but once you did you realized that you had no idea of how to frame the question, what would be the best design, what sort of problems would likely arise, and so you blundered through halfheartedly until you made your first mistake and changed tack, circling around your definitions and gradually figuring it out.

He walked down Lomonosov Prospect, toward the University. He was reluctant to venture too far, and felt for the securely-looped rope in the bag on his shoulder, realizing that perhaps capturing a zombie would not be as easy as he thought. You couldn't knock them out. Just hope to tie them up and drag them along, staying clear of their bites. A gag would be nice. He hated himself for hoping to find a child.

There was a slow, gurgling growl to his left and he spun, Kalashnikov aimed before he had a chance to consider using it. Two women clung to each other as they moved toward him.

"Ma'am?" he said. "Are you all right?"

A stupid question. One of the women seemed intact, save for her broken heels and matted hair, but the other one had a ruined face, part of her nose and cheek missing, the hinge of her jaws moving visibly under the thin veneer of crusted tissue as she made the same growling sound.

He stepped back, taking aim at the growling woman's head. One would do, he thought, two would not be manageable.

She turned then, showing the undamaged half of her face. Lida Belaya, the one who sang to her thermocycler.

He shouldn't have been surprised: what were the chances that she would survive? Where else would she die but at work, in the lab, probably still singing?

"Poor songbird," he whispered and squeezed the trigger. There was no point in pity; it was only a matter of time.

As Lida fell, he swung the butt of his Kalashnikov's at the other woman's head. She spun and fell, and he was on her, his knee planted in the small of her back, twisting her hands behind her. The rope came out, miraculously untangled, and he looped it around the dead woman's wrists and arms, as she hissed and kicked and tried to scratch.

Her arms tied up behind her securely, she stopped struggling and lay still. Valentin jerked her to her feet, holding her elbow, pushing her in front of him. The Kalashnikov was jammed awkwardly under his arm, and he hoped that his trek back to the station would be brief enough to not require additional shooting.

The station was in sight, and he hastened his step, pushing the woman in front of him faster. She stumbled and fell forward; he grabbed her elbows, trying to keep her upright, but she jerked, pulled forward, and her left arm came undone—popped out of the socket and the bones tore through her flesh, the white of her blouse filling instantly with black blood. With only one arm holding her, she turned around, blundered into Valentin, and he felt her teeth closing just above his elbow.

He hit her with the butt of his Kalashnikov, sending her sprawling to the ground. Before she could get up, he shot her in the head. Really, there was no need for more than one zombie; he only needed enough time to explain. He tied a rope above the bite, pulled it tight with his teeth. This should buy him a few minutes— he hoped.

VALENTIN HOBBLED THROUGH the dark tunnel, checking his thoughts every few seconds. As long as he thought and remembered his thoughts, he was alive, and as soon as he couldn't remember, it would stop mattering. He thought about what was happening in other countries—if people there waited for their government to save them, if they were delusional enough to think that governments had their back. He had an advantage, he thought, of learning when he was eighteen that the government would not save him, but do just the opposite. He hoped that Maksim remembered it too— remembered where he was sent when he was younger than his daughter was now.

He listened to the metallic grinding behind his back—Timka, a tank, was learning now, like a kitten stalking a mouse hobbled by its loving mother. Valentin picked up his step. If Maksim learned the same lessons as Valentin, he knew of course that it was just a matter of time and there would be no salvation. He and his daughter could hope to live just a little bit longer. To maybe say things they had to say. Maybe he would explain to Alisa then—who really was of the wrong generation to actually understand these things—that Valentin didn't sacrifice anything. In fact, he was given a rare luxury—to choose his fate, something none of them had been able to do until now.

Valentin picked up his pace, even as his legs grew cold and leaden, and his thoughts dimmed and scattered. Behind him, the tank rumbled, and before he crumpled to the ground, he felt a brief wave of gratitude at the sense of relief that washed over him, and at the soft whispering of caterpillar tracks, fading into an indistinct lull.

BEHEADED BY WHIP-WIELDING NUN

Simon Clark

She's been fighting Viking warriors for years. She'll fight zombies for the rest of her life.

RUSWARP ABBEY, ENGLAND 938 AD.

THE VIKING INVADER had won the battle. The English army lay dead. King Towulph's viscera decorated the yew tree in the graveyard. Pink ribbons. Dripping pink ribbons.

The Englander stood guard in the doorway of Ruswarp Abbey. She was a young nun. Her clothes were torn. Blood ran freely from scalp wounds to glisten in her long, blonde hair. Her beautiful face was bruised, yet her bold defiance made her radiant. Little did she know what horror would soon unfold. Little did she know of the suffering to come....

The Viking chieftain strode through the graveyard toward her. A necklace made from the penises of the men he'd slain in battle today adorned his neck. From this string, bearing those crimson nuggets, blood dripped down his bare chest. Meanwhile, his warriors gathered behind him. They would enjoy watching their leader's encounter with this beautiful young woman.

The warrior thundered, "Stand aside!"

"Never," whispered the nun. "You will never enter this place alive."

"Oh?" The Viking raised his spear. "Who will take my life?"

"I will."

He laughed. "You, timid mouse? Little elf? Fragile virgin?"

Despite the pain of her wounds she stood upright. "I am twenty-six years old. My name is Sister Storm. Ten years ago I made a sacred vow to protect the relic of Saint Viatrix. I will do so until the day I die."

"Saint Viatrix? Is that your god?" The pagan warrior took a step forward. "Does he reside within this temple?"

Sister Storm held out her arms so they spanned the doorway. "I will not permit you to enter the chapel."

"I will enter whatever I want, whenever I want." The warrior swung the spear downward. The tip sliced down the long, black skirt of the nun's habit, revealing the woman's naked leg from hip to ankle. "Stand aside. I will gobble you up later."

The Viking warlord gestured for her to move from the doorway. He was keen to discover the treasure within. Sister Storm shook her head. She would not budge.

"You are brave," he told her. "And beautiful. But you'll be dead by sunset."

He used the glistening spear tip to cut the black fabric above her breast. Pale skin lay exposed. The man stared at the bare flesh with lust burning in his eye. That was the moment that Sister Storm raised her arm. She gripped the black handle of a whip. Its long, flexible tail trailed down her back. A glossy black strand of woven leather.

"A whip?" The Viking found this funny. "You threaten me with a whip!"

Those were his last words.

Sister Storm's arm snapped forward. The whip cracked. Its tip sliced through the man's muscular neck, severing bone, vein, and trachea. The head rolled toward her feet, the eyes staring upward in surprise. The headless body slumped.

Immediately, the Viking warriors that had gathered in the graveyard rushed forward.

Sister Storm readied her whip. "Almighty God, grant me the strength to protect this hallowed ground. Forever and ever, amen."

The warriors howled for revenge. Swords flashed. Faces filled with rage. Hearts surged with bloodlust.

Sister Storm swung the whip. She knew she'd die today.

RUSWARP ABBEY, ENGLAND. OUR TIME. THE TIME OF THE ZOMBIE. THE TIME OF DESTRUCTION.

THE ZOMBIE INVADER had won the battle. The English robot army lay destroyed. Prime Minister Walton's guts decorated the yew tree in the graveyard. Red ribbons. Bloody red ribbons.

Sister Storm gazed at the battlefield. She saw fields, trees, ruined houses, and empty roadways. Scattered across the landscape were smashed iron statues. Or, rather, she identified those metal figures as iron statues.

A mile away stood Ruswarp Abbey. Its sacred walls were broken. Only one stone tower remained.

"The Viking." She gripped the whip's black handle. "The bastard Viking."

But where were the Vikings? Why did she stand on this hillside? Just a moment ago, she had been in the abbey's graveyard. She had killed the Viking chief then confronted his army; she'd been determined to protect the shrine of Saint Viatrix. All of that had occurred just seconds ago. *So, where have the invaders gone?* Sister Storm wondered. *Why has the landscape changed?*

The beautiful nun gathered the torn flaps of the habit around her. Cold air played across the parts of her body made naked by the warlord's spear. A violent terror blasted the woman's senses. What cruel acts had been performed on her? What evil magic had transformed the landscape? What were these foul, fallen statues? There were hundreds…thousands….

A scream rose through her throat. She opened her pink lips to shriek panic at the world.

Then it came.

A great spirit passed over her heaving breast. She became serene.

The panic had gone. Her earlier prayer had been answered. God had delivered her to this place in order to safeguard the Holy Bones of Saint Viatrix. That was her mission here on Earth.

With a calm sense of purpose, Sister Storm walked through the battlefield. Amid those broken statues there were shreds of human flesh. Everywhere, there were the heads of men and women—skulls ripped open; brains gouged out.

Then came the sound of scuttling, clunking, a whispered sigh. The nun turned to see that one of the statues trundled through the meadow. This statue resembled an obelisk found in a pagan cemetery; the human form more a suggestion than a depiction. Attached to it was a long, narrow cart. When the statue paused, it used an iron claw to pluck a smeary, crimson human arm from the ground, or retrieve a hollowed-out skull from the long grass. The statue would deposit the sad fragment of flesh into the cart. That done, the statue moved forward again to collect more mortal remains.

Sister Storm wasn't frightened of the trundling obelisk. The spirit of the Almighty blazed within her veins. Sister Storm feared nothing.

"Wait." She pointed the whip's handle at the figure. "Tell me what happened here."

The obelisk plucked a skull from the dirt before inching forward again.

"Stay where you are!" Sister Storm pressed her hand against the statue's chest. "I asked you what happened here."

The statue spoke in a deeply melancholy voice, "Madam, I am Funeralbot. Purpose of self is not conversation. Purpose of self: to gather the dead."

"But you do speak. Tell me what happened."

"Purpose of self, madam: gather deceased. Purpose of self: bury the fallen."

"Who invaded our land?"

The statue moved away. "I am Funeralbot. Dissemination of information not my purpose."

"Tell me who killed these people."

"I collect the dead."

"Did Vikings slaughter these warriors?"

"I must fulfill my purpose."

"Tell me!" She slammed the whip's handle against the statue. The blow rang like a bell. "Who destroyed this army?"

"Zombies." The voice didn't come from the creature known as Funeralbot. This voice had a scratchy, thin quality. There was a note of cunning. She instinctively knew that this individual possessed a cleverness with words. She allowed Funeralbot to resume its solemn harvest.

"A funeralbot will tell you sod all. They're miserable little bleeders."

"Who's there?" She raised her whip. The black flex glinted in the sunlight. "Who speaks?"

"I do."

"Come forward, or I will find you." She cracked the whip in the air to discourage anyone from playing games.

"I have come forward. Truth is, I'm a minimalist design. In other words: titchy."

The nun looked down into the long grass. A metal vessel sat there. This could not even be described as a statue. The object was rounded like an inflated pig's bladder, and no larger than a basket that could accommodate five loaves of bread. What appeared to be a bronze trumpet was fixed to the top of the vessel. A corroded trumpet at that. Studded all over the curving body were clear glass beads of different sizes. Some were missing from the sockets. A few were cracked. The vessel had been roughly patched with oblongs of copper.

She examined the vessel more closely. Black letters were painted on its gray, metal shell.

"What do you have inscribed there?" she demanded.

"My name and purpose," the vessel replied in its thin, scratchy voice. "It says: I AM TRUTHBOT. MY PURPOSE: TO SEE EVERYTHING, HEAR EVERYTHING, TELL EVERYTHING."

"The language is not familiar."

"The words are in English."

"I am English."

"Not modern English, you're not. You were brought here through a trans-dimensional gateway. I only understand you because I'm fitted with a translator program."

"Explain using plain terms."

"The humans are becoming extinct. They're desperate for more human beings to repopulate the planet, so they use a machine to reach into the past and nab any poor sucker they can."

"You claim that I have been brought from my time to this world of the future?"

"Yes."

"Are you lying to me?"

"I am Truthbot. I cannot lie."

"Bastards."

"You look like a nun," said the vessel, "but you cuss like a grunt."

"My name is Sister Storm. My purpose is to protect the shrine that contains the sacred bones of Saint Viatrix. Now a little tin pot tells me that I have been stolen from my God-given days in order to be fucked by strangers? To be like a sow destined to push piglets from its body!"

With fierce determination she strode toward the abbey ruin. The long black skirts of her habit swished, her blonde hair shone in the sunlight.

Truthbot followed. "Just hang on there, Sister. You can't simply amble up to that stone heap."

"I will do as I have vowed."

"It's not safe for humans."

"That is holy ground. Of course it is safe."

"Not any more, it ain't. The place is jammed to the rafters with zombies."

"Zombies? Are they invaders?"

"In a manner of speaking."

"Like Vikings?"

"No. Much worse than Vikings."

"I will drive them out with my whip."

"Please, wait. I need to tell you the truth."

"What truth?"

"All of it." The iron vessel sighed. "I am a robot. Specifically a truthbot. Humans manufactured me in order to gather information, then impart it to other humans."

"I have no need of your information. God manufactured me in order to protect Saint Viatrix. His shrine is in that building." Sister Storm could plainly see the abbey. What she could not see were the invaders…these zombies.

Truthbot scurried after her. "Please wait. I must tell you what I know."

"Then talk."

"You're heading into danger. Those zombies will go crazy for your brains."

"They want my brain?"

"Oh, yes."

"Why?"

"They eat brains."

"These zombies are demons?"

"They were human beings once. They have been infected by plague—this turns them into animated corpses that relentlessly hunt your kind. They can smell a human brain from miles away. Yesterday, the zombies came into the valley. They killed all the people and destroyed the robot army. You see, robots were built by humans to protect humans. Please slow down, Sister. There's so much truth inside my memory depository it hurts. I am constipated with fact."

The nun climbed onto the carcass of a huge robot and walked along its torso. "If all the humans here are dead, why do the zombies continue to occupy the abbey?"

"Their behavior is a mystery."

"Some purpose holds them here," she said. "This place must be important to them."

"They are fascinated by the abbey ruin. Obsessed."

"It's as if they have undertaken a pilgrimage to the shrine of my saint." She stood on the head of the smashed robot. Shreds of her habit fluttered in the breeze as she considered the facts. "Zombies were human beings that have been transfigured?"

"Yes. Now they are disgusting lumps of meat that can walk and fight. They talk a little. But their minds are just crud."

"No more facts, Truthbot. Let me think." She continued to stand on the giant robot's head. One of her sandaled feet rested on the curving dome of its eye. The head gave her an elevated platform to view the abbey ruin…the seemingly deserted abbey ruin. She nodded as she began to understand. "I have information for you, Truthbot."

"Tell me, tell me!"

"The mortal remains of Saint Viatrix lie beneath a stone slab of the chapel floor."

"Ah…" He sighed with pleasure as the information gently penetrated his brain. "Nice."

"Saint Viatrix is the patron saint of the rampant dead."

"Hmmm…"

"Can you understand what I am saying?"

"I record without understanding."

"The sacred bones of Saint Viatrix radiate a holy power. The zombies can feel it, just as I feel the Spirit of God. The zombies know that my saint is special to them. They want to exploit its power."

"Zombies are stupid. They won't understand that."

"But they instinctively sense it! They want his bones. They intend to violate his tomb."

"There is nothing you can do to stop them, Sister. I've got telephoto visual receptors. I've seen the filthy little bleeders in the ruin. There are hundreds."

"Nothing will stop me."

But something did stop her. A hand reached up from the brambles that grew beside the robot's gargantuan head. Fingers closed around her ankle. She saw ripped fingernails, peeling skin, exposed bone. And she felt the power of the hand. A face peered from the brambles. Mad hatred. Mad hunger.

"Feed…gukk…feed…narr."

"This is one fact that you need to know, Sister!" squealed Truthbot. "THAT IS A ZOMBIE!"

The zombie had been shorn of its legs. All that remained was a torso, a head, one arm, and one powerful hand that gripped her ankle. Sister Storm's sharp eyes absorbed what threatened her.

So, this is a zombie? The beast had been mutilated in battle. The sweet smell of decay reached her nostrils. Yet a life-force still blazed in that rotten apple of manhood.

Sister Storm was smart. She understood that the demon wanted to drag her into its nest of brambles. Once there, the creature could rip open her skull, then tongue out her brains.

"Truthbot, stand back." She uncoiled the whip.

"No!" cried the bot. "If one drop of blood from the zombie touches your skin you could be infected, too."

"Kkurk…" The zombie tugged her ankle. "Feed me…kill the hunger."

"Let go!"

"I smell brain," oozed the monster. "S' good. S' nice…."

She cried out to Truthbot: "Help me!"

"I spoon facts; I can douche you with information. But I can't physically help."

She yelled in frustration. Then she lashed downward with the whip, aiming at the grotesque face. The whip shredded plants; gobs of green leaf flew everywhere. Yet those spiky vines were so thick and so tangled that she couldn't strike at the creature.

"Please remember!" squeaked Truthbot. "Don't get its blood on you. Not one drop!"

"Tin pot! You've already told me!"

"You will become a zombie."

"One of the rampant dead, I know!"

Instead of using the whip's lash to attack the zombie's head, Sister Storm turned the handle of the whip round. She then used the large, bulbous handle-butt to pound the fingers that encircled her ankle. Sister Storm gambled on breaking bones—not the skin. With God's help no blood would be spilt.

"In the name of the Father!" Crunch! A zombie finger snapped. "The Son!" Crack! Its thumb shattered. "And the Holy Ghost!" Scrick! Her next blow dislocated the middle finger.

Sister Storm pried the remaining fingers away. There was no

blood, thank Heaven. The instant she was free she leapt clear of the flailing hand. Quickly, she jumped down from the robot's giant head and marched across the meadow.

"Where are you going, Sister?" cried Truthbot. "I need to record your intentions."

"I'm going to the abbey. I will protect the holy shrine of St. Saint Viatrix. Mark my words, Truthbot: Blood will flow. There will be war. So help me, God!"

RUSWARP GLADE. NOON. BRITBOTS: DREADNOUGHT CLASS.

SISTER STORM, THE whip-wielding nun, took a path through Ruswarp Glade. The abbey was no more than five minutes away. The single, burning thought in her head was to protect the shrine of Saint Viatrix, patron saint of the rampant dead. As a sixteen-year-old novice nun, she had sworn an oath to defend his grave to her last breath, to the last drop of blood.

Truthbot scuttled along the woodland path. She figured out that those glass beads set in that little robot were its eyes, while the dented trumpet bolted to the top was its ear.

Truthbot, meanwhile, had pertinent truths to share: "Sister Storm. The zombies have nested in the abbey. There are hundreds of the scuzzy little fuckers."

"So you've already told me, Truthbot."

"They will kill you, Sister. Or they'll turn you zombie. You'll roam across England, hunting down humans."

"I have my whip."

The tin pot surged on, eager to douche her with fact. "You'll spend the rest of your existence obsessed with human brains. Eat human brain. Gobble human—"

She pointed with the whip. "What are those?"

The little creature skedaddled forward to peer at what stood beneath the trees. "Those are British warbots. Dreadnought Class. Big fuckers, aren't they?"

"Why do they have such big noses?"

"That isn't a nose, that's the barrel of a howitzer."

"Howitzer? For me, the word has no meaning."

"Artillery? Big guns? Shooters? Weapons of war?"

"Ah, weapons. These iron men are warriors?"

"You've got it, Sister. Warbots! Built for battle!"

She approached the pair of warbots. Standing over twenty feet tall, the massive bodies were a dull gray. Rust stains ran down their torsos. Steam hissed from the ball-joints of their limbs.

"These warbots are still alive?"

"Yeah, Sister, but their ammo silos are empty."

"Does that mean they cannot fight?"

"It means they're junk."

"No, Truthbot." Her intelligent eyes examined the iron giants. "If they do my bidding, they are still useful."

"Oh...kay." Truthbot sounded doubtful. "They're pretty stupid, too."

"How so?"

"Look at 'em. Because the commandbot's kaput they just stand here, waiting for orders from someone."

"Then I shall be that someone." Sister Storm tapped the whip handle against a massive iron leg. "Warbot! I am a human being. You will obey me!"

Steam gushed from vents in the warbots' flanks. Both robots slowly turned toward her. And both roared: "WE OBEY."

"Warbots. The time has come to fight."

"We have already fought," rumbled one of the machines. "The human and robot army battled the zombie here. We have lost."

"You will fight again. This time we will win."

"We have no shells for our howitzers. We cannot wage war without shells."

"You have me," Sister Storm told them. "And me is all you need."

RUSWARP ABBEY. ONE NUN, THREE ROBOTS VERSUS
FIVE HUNDRED ZOMBIES. THE HOUR OF BATTLE.

"WHEN I WIELD the whip, some other hand than mine guides the lash." This is what Sister Storm told the three robots as they moved across the meadow.

One of the twenty-foot-high robots wheezed, "We are warbots, Dreadnought Class, Mark I. We do not understand."

"Sister, I told you the big iron blockheads were stupid," shrilled Truthbot. "You'll be stupid, too, to fight zombies with just a whip and these two junkyard refugees."

Sister Storm stoked the whip's black handle. "When I fight the Lord breathes strength into my arm."

"We have no shells for our howitzers." The warbots released forlorn gusts of steam. "We are empty. Our guns, silent."

"The Lord also breathes wisdom into my mind." She strode forward with determination. "I will find this shell weapon you speak of."

"Where?" sighed a warbot. "All ammo trucks have gone away"

Sister Storm regarded the lumbering warbots. There was something elephantine about them—the way the large metal tube jutted from their faces.

"Warbots, stop." They obeyed her command. "You! Pick me up. Lift me as high as you can." One of the machines did as it was told. The giant scooped her up in its iron claw and extended its arm above its head.

Sister Storm was now thirty feet above the meadow. She could see the abandoned houses, the empty roads, and the scenes of devastation where the battle had been fought. She also saw dozens of broken robots lying on the battlefield. Then she noticed one robot in particular. This was the important one.

"Take me to the river. There by the bridge."

The huge warbot obliged.

Truthbot scuttled through the grass, looking pretty much like an iron crab, his little legs scrabbling like crazy to keep up. "Tell me your plan, Sister. I need to record for posterity what you intend."

Sister Storm rode astride the warbot's thick wrist as if she rode a metal serpent. "I am intending to do something terrible." The breeze blew her long blonde hair. "I intend to violate that which I treasure most in the world."

"And that is?"

"You must have guessed what it is?"

"I'm not built for guesswork; you must state clear fact."

"I know what my beloved saint really is."

"Then tell me, Sister. What is he?"

"You will see for yourself, Truthbot."

The robots halted by the bridge. Sister Storm ordered the one that carried her to set her down. As soon as she'd alighted on the riverbank, she pointed at a warbot that lay face down in the water.

"When you lifted me high above the ground I could see your comrade lying here. There…in the container on its back? Are those the shell weapons you need?"

The two warbots vented steam. The sight of the shells filled them with what must have been the robotic equivalent of pleasure. "Yes," roared one of the giants. "Those are what we need."

Truthbot gave a dismissive grunt. "There are only two shells. You won't win a war with just two howitzer shells."

"They shall have one apiece." Then she frowned. "Tell me, Truthbot, what is the effect of these shells?"

As the warbots helped one another slot these yellow cylinders into the pipe that extended from their faces, Truthbot quickly explained what a shell was capable of. The sound they made. The devastation. The explosive destruction.

"Ah," breathed Sister Storm. "Golden arrows with lightning bolts in their bellies. Yes, I have a use for those."

The warbots marched proudly now. Each metal giant had one shell apiece. That was enough to restore their combative spirit.

One of the warbots declared proudly, "England expects…"

"…every robot to do his duty," added the second.

Then both released a roar of steam: "LET SLIP THE BOTS OF WAR!" Their combined shout echoed along the valley.

"Sister, I hope you weren't planning a surprise attack," Truthbot commented drily. "Every zombie in a hundred miles will have heard that." The robot gestured with a delicately articulated limb, which might have been his attempt to shake a fist. "Idiot block-heads! Stop making so much noise!"

To Truthbot's surprise they stopped their hollering. He took the opportunity to ask a question that troubled his synthetic mind. "So…Sister Storm…this treasure you are so intent on violating? What is it?"

"You must have guessed?"

"As I've already told you, Sister, I'm a truthbot. I'm not made for the guessing game."

She paused as she gazed at the ancient ruin. "In the year 633 AD, the nuns of my order entombed a man by the name of Viatrix inside Ruswarp Abbey. He was venerated as a holy man. A man who could never die."

"I see…"

"So, Truthbot, I am finally beginning to understand the nature of Saint Viatrix, the patron saint of the rampant dead."

"Tell me—I will record your words for history."

"The truth is, the saint I have sworn to protect is, in fact, a zombie."

"My memory cache contains no record of a zombie found in Britain fourteen hundred years ago. How can you accurately verify Saint Viatrix was a zombie?"

"Not was a zombie. Is a zombie."

"Zombies did not exist in antiquity."

"Wasn't I brought from my time to the future, little tin pot? Might not the same process have catapulted a zombie from this present-day world into the past?"

"You have evidence?"

"In the Year of our Lord, 928, I became a nun. Every night I held a vigil at the saint's tomb in the chapel. When silence fell I would hear the same sound beneath the slab." Her face became grim. "*I heard him moving.*"

A warbot released a whoosh of steam. "Target within range." Its howitzer pointed in the direction of the abbey. "Request permission to fire."

"No, not yet," she said, "we must be much closer. There is something I have to see with my own eyes."

As they continued through the meadow the truthbot scuttled closer to Sister Storm. "Why would a holy order of nuns claim that a zombie is a saint?"

"They knew that zombie Viatrix was dangerous. So where better to imprison it? If you can, picture those brave nuns. Somehow they captured Viatrix and then sealed the monster into a tomb. Once there, beneath the stone floor of the abbey chapel, it could not escape. If those in holy orders were told the tenant of the grave was a saint, then the nuns of later years would protect the building. They, like myself, would dedicate their lives to stopping trespassers from breaking into the tomb."

"Couldn't those women who captured the zombie have destroyed it?"

"Fourteen hundred years ago, would they know how?"

"Maybe not."

"And the abbess of Ruswarp Abbey might have decided that the Almighty Father tested her faith. Perhaps the abbess believed it her sacred destiny to keep the zombie confined beneath the chapel."

"What do you plan to do now?"

"To find out the truth," she said. "Saint Viatrix is important to the zombie invader. We should find out why." Her fist tightened on the whip's handle. "If we don't, the people of this world will be in even greater danger."

She urged the warbots forward. Their movements weren't silent in the least. The machines clanked. Steam escaped from rusty vents and ball-joints with a loud hissing.

"Lumpheads," scolded Truthbot. "Can't you make less noise?"

The warbots grunted, "This is war...no time for stealth, no requirement for caution...attack...attack." They lumbered onward.

Truthbot scuttled after them, complaining bitterly about their rumbustious approach to battle.

Sister Storm's long legs kicked out through the skirts of the habit. She murmured prayers for strength, courage, and wisdom. *This is it. The hour of battle has come. Heavenly Father, guide my whip. Charge my heart with courage.*

As she approached the abbey she could see more detail of the ruin. Though many of the walls were in a state of great decay, the chapel that housed the shrine of Saint Viatrix was almost intact. The roof had no holes. The walls were sound. Just one small door at the side had been forced open. Not that she was interested in the door. She had other ideas about gaining entry to the building.

Sister Storm raised her whip hand. "Stop!"

The two warbots immediately froze on her command. Although they weren't silent, they were breathtakingly obedient.

Truthbot managed to catch up. "Sister. The warbots have only one miserable shell each for their guns. You won't be able to defeat the zombies with two shells."

"I do not intend to defeat the zombies. I have only one target in mind." She turned to the second warbot. "I shall ride you into battle. Lift me onto your shoulders."

The twenty-foot machine quickly hoisted the nun aloft and sat her on its broad, iron shoulders.

"Truthbot," she called, "bear witness to what happens here today. Then go forth and tell the world what I have discovered."

"And what have you discovered, Sister?"

"Soon you shall see for yourself."

"This is too dangerous!" cried Truthbot. "You will be killed."

"If my death saves human lives, then that death shall be glorious."

"What if those rotters turn you zombie?"

"Don't worry, little tin pot, I have a remedy for that." She sat with her legs tightly clasped against the warbot's neck, as if she rode a mighty stallion bareback. "Warbots! Advance! Take me to yon building!"

Her iron steed snorted. Jets of steam blasted from this engine of war. The two giant robots thundered forward. Truthbot scuttled behind.

"You," she shouted at the other warbot. "Use your weapon to break down that wall!"

She pointed at the chapel. Obediently, the warbot aimed its howitzer.

Then the giant robot stopped moving.

Has something gone wrong? she asked herself. *Why doesn't the warrior attack?*

Truthbot sang out, "Stupid blockhead needs the order to fire."

Sister Storm yelled, "FIRE!"

The warbot complied. With a colossal bang the howitzer discharged its shell. A split-second later flame burst from the wall. Sister Storm had never heard a sound so loud. Chunks of masonry were hurled across the graveyard by the explosion. The stone head of an angel bounced down into the grass in front of her.

The smoke cleared, revealing a huge hole in the structure. Sister Storm was familiar with the chapel. She recalled the austere interior, the bare stone walls, the slab floors. A simple wooden shrine to the Saint stood against one wall. There, candles would burn.

When the wall collapsed it revealed that the chapel was no longer the barren-looking chamber. Instead, the House of God was crammed with bodies.

"Zombie combatants sighted," hissed first warbot. "Ammunition spent. Request further orders."

"Ye Gods," squawked the truthbot as he scanned the chapel full of zombies, "there's hundreds of the fuckers."

The robot that Sister Storm rode grunted, "Do you grant me permission to fire?"

"Not yet." She unfurled the whip, so its glossy, black tail hung down the robot's chest. She called to the first warbot. "Enter the building. Fight the zombies anyway you can."

"Order understood."

The elephantine machine lumbered through the collapsed wall of the chapel. Immediately the zombies attacked. They clawed at its iron body.

Then something strange happened. Something strange enough for Truthbot to cry out in surprise.

Several zombies began tearing open their stomachs in order to rip out their own entrails. They used the snake-like gut as tripwires. Soon they managed to make the first robot fall. Dozens of zombies had armed themselves with chunks of masonry that the high-explosive shell had blasted from the wall. They used these improvised hammers to beat the first warbot into scrap metal.

Truthbot screeched in panic. "This shouldn't be happening! Zombies don't use tripwires; not even their own bloody guts. And they never use weapons. Something weird's going down. It's as if the zombies are under remote control!"

"Take me inside!" Sister Storm pointed at the chapel. "I must see what's in there!"

"Please, Sister!" shrieked Truthbot, "Don't go in there! They'll tear you apart!"

"Permission to fire," grunted the warbot.

"Not yet," she said. "Not until I know the truth."

She urged the warbot forward. As she rode on its shoulders, she began to swing the whip. The zombies that used their guts as trip-wires moved toward her steed. The creatures' piss-yellow eyes locked onto their target. They intended to use their bloody intestines again to upend the warbot.

Sister Storm would not allow them so easy a victory. She had a surprise for these brain-hungry demons.

"March forward," she urged the warbot. "Strike them with your claw."

The warbot slammed its metal claw down on the zombies. Skulls burst like eggs. Foul-smelling zombie head-shit sprayed across the chapel floor.

Zombies with loops of intestine clutched in their grotesque hands shuffled forward. Before they could deploy their tripwires Sister Storm deployed the whip. And with devastating accuracy.

Crack! The whip sliced away the top of a zombie's head.

"Gnurrr..." The zombie slammed onto the floor.

Snap! The lash exploded a zombie face.

"Keep moving!" she yelled at the robot.

The Dreadnought-class warbot steamed forward. White vapor blasted from its vents. The heat caused the faces of the nearest zombies to bubble. Zombie eyes popped right out of their sockets.

The huge iron claw continued to pound zombie meat.

Sister Storm, riding high on the behemoth's shoulders, wielded the whip with power and precision. The lightning-fast tip lashed away heads by the dozen. Soon zombie bodies squelched under the massive feet of the robot. Meanwhile, Truthbot zigzagged behind, recording what he saw.

The other zombies that carried their hunks of rock lurched from the shadows. Snap-burrrr-crack! The whip struck again and again. Sister Storm did not miss. Skulls ruptured. Bodies tumbled. Blood flowed. The groans of dying zombies filled the air.

"Move forward," she urged the warbot. "I must see the tomb of Saint Viatrix."

The huge robot slithered over oozing gore. The chapel was so slippery underfoot that the machine almost lost its balance.

And if it should lose its balance now? That would spell disaster for the nun's plan. She willed the robot onward. Her metal warrior was so tall that she had to duck to avoid being hit by the timber roof beams. Even so, she still wielded the vengeful whip.

Yet her weapon couldn't defeat all the zombies. They began to climb up the flanks of the warbot.

She couldn't allow the demons to reach her until she'd fulfilled her quest. The warbot must carry her into the heart of the chapel. She had to see Saint Viatrix's grave for herself.

"Move!" She kicked her heels into the robot's chest. "Just another ten feet, then I shall see."

A hand grabbed her foot. Crack! The whip parted hand from wrist. The severed hand still clung to her foot with a crushing power.

Pain wouldn't distract her from her quest. God willing, even death would not stop her now.

She prayed over and over in soft tones: "Not yet, Father—please not yet. Grant me but a few more moments of life in this world." Then in a loud voice she cried, "Warbot, take me three steps forward!"

The machine took a single step. Steam whistled only thinly from its vents now. Its strength had almost gone. The warbot weakened. This noble giant sagged beneath the weight of zombies climbing up its body.

The robot labored to take another step, then abruptly stopped. This engine of war could no longer move.

Zombies clambered up over the iron hulk toward Sister Storm. More zombies lurched forward. They began to push at the warbot in the hope of toppling the iron beast.

Sister Storm deployed the whip again. This time she aimed at a timber roof beam. The moment the lash curled around the balk of timber she swung away from the robot, using the whip as a lifeline. Quickly she hauled herself upward onto the roof timber.

Now she could see the shocking truth. Sister Storm inhaled deeply as she made sense of what lay below.

The sacred tomb had been engulfed—she couldn't phrase the description in any other way to convey the sheer number of bodies. Zombies had clustered tightly around the slab that covered Saint Viatrix's grave. More zombies had clambered on top of their own hell-breed, so that she looked down on what seemed to be a donut constructed of stinking death-flesh. And yet these creatures were alive—at least they were alive in their own demonic fashion. Some compulsion had drawn them here. They'd sought out what Sister Storm had once believed was a depository of sacred bones.

The circular wall of rotting flesh pulsated. The zombies had become a matted ring standing ten feet high. They craved to be close to Saint Viatrix, King Zombie of the rampant dead. Somehow they were irresistibly attracted to this place. So what happens next?

Would Saint Viatrix rise from the grave in all his blasphemous glory? Perhaps to become their master? The malignant head of this foul swarm? If the zombie army acquired a leader that could intelligently plan wars against the human race, then that would make them infinitely more dangerous. Humanity would be even more hard-pressed to survive. The zombies would be close to ultimate victory.

In truth, she decided, what these foul creatures require in order to become the lords of this earthly realm is a calculating mind to control their actions. Then the kingdom of Man would fall beneath their putrescent heel. The Zombie would reign forever and ever.

Was it possible that meager thought did trickle from their minds, like pus from a sore? Or had these creatures fallen under a spell that directed them to slavishly turn the chapel into a fortress? Either way, this inner ring of defenses built from the monsters' own bodies was clearly intended to protect the saint's tomb. Were they now biding their time until Viatrix's resurrection?

From this height she could look down into the center of that protective ring. She glimpsed the stone slab that covered the grave. The zombies appeared to revere the tomb so much that although they clustered around it tightly, and a dozen deep, they refrained from physical contact with the slab—their holy of holies.

Sister Storm called down from where she perched herself on the roof beam. "Truthbot! I have vital information for you. The zombies are protecting Saint Viatrix. I believe he possesses not only intelligence but the ability to draw them here. Saint Viatrix moves these demons as a man can move pieces on a chessboard. He controls them. That is why they do not act in what you say is the usual zombie manner. My greatest fear is that Viatrix will rise from the tomb to lead them."

Truthbot zipped to and fro to avoid being caught. The tin pot might be small, but it was nimble. "Scientists believe that the zombies are connected; linked by a morphic field generated by the residual brain activity that animates them. Truthbots aren't built for speculation, although I can tell you this: the clues are stacking up that you're absolutely right about your damn saint being the puppet master. Somehow he's hacked into the morphic field. He's sucking these shit-heads into the chapel, because he realizes he can control them. Who knows? This Viatrix guy, if he is a zombie, might have spent the last sixteen hundred years working on the telepathy thing as he lay in that stinking pit. Now he's going to use his zombie bitches to break him out of jail. Whoa!" He darted away to avoid being clubbed by a large wooden cross that a zombie had ripped from the altar.

Sister Storm cried out, "Flee now, Truthbot. Go into the world. Tell people what we have discovered here. Warn them that there could be more ancient zombies waiting to escape their tombs, and that they may have the power to exercise their will over the morphic field. If these creatures from older times are able to marshal the zombies into organized armies, then the human race will be in even greater danger."

"You better do some fleeing of your own, Sister. Those creeps are a-creeping up on you!"

Sister Storm glanced at the creatures that had begun to scale the chapel's stone pillars. Soon they'd reach the timber roof beam. Then they'd reach her.

She gazed down at the ring of zombie bodies—they pulsated and squirmed. They were excited at being so close to the tomb that had drawn them here. The heap of rotting yet living meat convulsed. Did they sense that something wonderful—to them—stirred in the cavity beneath the grave slab?

It was starting. A sense of anticipation crackled on the air. The moment was electric. He was coming. The patron saint of the rampant dead.

The whip-wielding nun cried out, "Flee, Truthbot! It's time for you to leave!"

"Sister, you come, too."

"No, I must give one last order. Just be sure that you tell everyone about what we have found here today." She used the whip to behead a zombie that shuffled along the roof beam.

For a moment, she became lost in memory. How many times had she fought the Viking invader to prevent those savage pagans from desecrating the abbey? Did Zombie Viatrix lie there in his grave, laughing at her misguided devotion? The foolish nun who mistook the profane for the sacred?

Sister Storm felt she was drowning. The dense cluster of zombies surrounding the tomb grew blurred. She tried to inhale. Her heart pounded. She couldn't draw that vital lungful of air so she could shout the final order. If she couldn't do that, her plan would fail. All would be lost.

The timber she stood upon over twenty feet above the chapel floor trembled. The zombies approached from both ends; they would catch her in the middle.

The dying rays of the sun shone through the chapel window. That glorious light touched her. And it seemed as if a voice passed over the world to enter her heart.

The mental confusion vanished. Sister Storm became focused. Sister Storm took charge. And Sister Storm took that crucial breath.

Her eyes locked onto the tomb of Viatrix. Then her voice rang out with that all-important order.

"Warbot. Aim at the floor in front of you!"

The tube that jutted from the front of the giant robot's face clanked downward. The machine used its final life-breath of steam.

"FIRE!"

The explosion was enormous. The ball of fire outshone the sun. The last warbot had fired its last shell.

Sister Storm was blessed with a moment of grace. To her eternal satisfaction, she witnessed the blast that destroyed Viatrix's tomb— and its evil tenant.

ENGLAND. SEVERAL MONTHS LATER.

"AND, TRUTHFULLY, THAT is what happened." Truthbot had told the story of Sister Storm many times before. He had just told it again to the men, women, and children who huddled around the forest campfire. This little group of survivors clung to life out here in the wilderness, desperately evading the zombie hoard. Truthbot continued: "I witnessed the destruction of St. Viatrix's tomb. The explosion smashed his body to pieces. However, there could be others like him out there that have the power to draw the zombies to them. One day there might be zombie generals who can organize those creatures into armies. If that happens, the zombie will be even more of a threat to your survival. Remember what I've told you tonight. Be vigilant. Always be on your guard."

The time had come to leave. Truthbot lifted himself up onto his stumpy legs as his audience nodded their thanks.

"Sister Storm was an extraordinary human being," he declared. "A legend. She gave me a new purpose: to find people who survived the zombie invasion. My mission is to share the story of Sister Storm with you all. Because there are occasions in this life when hope is hard to find. But hope can always be found in a story. And there are times when hope is the only weapon we have to fight Evil in this world."

EXCLUSION ZONE

Dale Bailey

THEY FLED IN a stolen flatbed with three tarp-swathed warbots strapped across the back. Four of them: Dr. Rasikov, his wife Darya, his daughter Larisa, plus Dmitri, the harelip. The harelip followed close behind them in a tractor trailer, also stolen, and packed with canned goods, powdered milk, and as much of Rasikov's lab equipment as they could wedge in: a portable generator, three laptops, an assortment of alembics and circuit boards, and six severed human heads in cryogenically-enabled bell jars.

Also the dog, Bolick.

Rasikov could have done without the dog; a big German shepherd that always reeked of the oily fish-flavored offal Larisa fed it, no matter how often he implored her to bathe it. But he also could have done without the harelip, had a lab assistant of some sort not been critical to his work. And given the nature of his work—not to mention the zombie hordes that every day multiplied exponentially around them—lab assistants were hard to come by. The two things he could not do without were the two women squeezed, with Bolick, in the cab beside him.

Stealing the flatbed had been less difficult than Rasikov had feared. It was mostly a matter of gathering the courage to face streets teeming with looters, zombies, and the freshly imported warbots that stumped among them. The bots were lethal, but not particularly choosy. They mowed down looters and zombies alike, and Rasikov and Dmitri did their best to avoid all three as they stole through night-plunged streets to the warehouse district, where it was the work of a quarter hour to appropriate a flatbed with keys still in the ignition. Nobody had been especially careful about locking up as the chaos escalated.

They had a single close call, he and the harelip, when a lone straggler from the horde surprised them, lurching out of an alley as they slipped by. The thing was a slavering monstrosity, its hair greasy and lank, its face gaunt, ravaged by the virus. When it saw them, it cast aside the ulna it had been sucking the marrow from. It staggered toward them, groaning, ravenous. Dmitri felled it with a single shot to the forehead, and together they watched it shudder, gnashing its bloodstained lips, and die.

Then they were in the truck. On the way back to the flat, Rasikov dropped three warbots with an ingenious device of his own design. A simple flip of a switch generated a magnetic field that interrupted their connection to the master server. Rendered essentially brainless—and considerably less indiscriminate in laying down fire—the robots staggered around like drunks, and then clattered to the weed-grown pavement, the yellow light in their eyes dimming, dimming, dark. From there it was a matter of wrestling them up, strapping them down on the flatbed, and gunning the truck back to pick up Rasikov's family.

They had stolen the tractor trailer and loaded it up during the first chaotic days of the plague—before the power had gone down and people had abandoned the city in droves. Russian officials had pled for patience. Conventional wisdom held that the zombie plague would run its course—that the brains of new victims would be devoured before they could revive, that the crisis would soon draw to an end. Rasikov had feared otherwise: hands and teeth were poor tools to penetrate skulls. Most victims would revive long before brain-injury rendered them inert. So the size of the gathering horde that staggered down the street toward Rasikov's flat did not surprise him. Rasikov gunned the flatbed. One zombie lunged onto the hood of the cab and slid away; it burst like a ripe pomegranate as it hit the pavement, spraying blood, curdled brain, and bone fragments across the windshield. The truck crunched others like insects or hurled them aside, partially dismembered. They waved the stumps of their arms, tottered like wind-up toys. Darya shrieked beside him. Bolick barked.

Rasikov laughed grimly.

He'd put himself through medical school suturing up the festering gunshot wounds of Russian mobsters in the meanest streets of Moscow. After that he'd done a stint with the Russian army in Chechnya, stuffing the entrails of the wounded back into their abdominal cavities and hacking off the jetting limbs of young men too grievously wounded to risk anesthesia. He had been tested in blood and seasoned with screams. The death of a virus-plagued cannibal on the hood of his truck moved him to bleak hilarity, nothing more.

Then they were free, nosing their way through streets littered with abandoned vehicles as dawn broke over the ruined city. A car alarm blared in the stillness. A warbot wheeled around to watch them creep by. Now and then another horde of zombies would stumble toward them from the depths of some sordid den where they feasted on human flesh and brains. But they shambled too slowly to catch up to the speeding vehicles, and soon enough—after ramming aside half a dozen wrecked Zaporozhets, and maneuvering their way around an overturned tanker on an entrance ramp—they reached the motorway.

They fled west, and the roads were clear, because west was death.

Chernigov fell away behind them.

A hundred kilometers ahead of them lay the Exclusion Zone.

A hundred kilometers ahead of them lay Chernobyl.

THE TRAINS HAD stopped running. The checkpoints were unmanned. Chernobyl was a dead, doomed place, but—despite the hastily deployed robot warriors in the streets—the world was more doomed still. Rasikov had seen the truth of the matter while other men were still glued to the reassuring statements issuing out of Washington, Beijing, Moscow. The robots—the last spasm of a military-industrial complex that would rather profit from the epidemic than destroy it—were inefficient and primitive, as dangerous to their human makers as to the zombie hordes they were intended to contain.

And so, in the first weeks of the catastrophe, while the world still slept, Rasikov laid his plans. Hoarded supplies. Downloaded specs of the warbots. Studied the rank of severed heads in his university laboratory and pondered the future.

"They are too primitive to save us, these American machines," he told Darya one night in bed. "Without true artificial intelligence they will never be able to make the fine distinctions the battlefield requires."

"Let the experts handle this," she said, punching him in the dark. "You go to sleep, you silly man."

But the silly man did not sleep. He lay awake, staring at the bloodless moon that peered through the blinds. True AI was too far away. Something more was needed. Something only he—Mad Rasikov, his colleagues had branded him, banishing him to the dank, windowless university basement he called a lab—something only he could provide. Rasikov swelled with pride in the dark. He had never backed down. He had drawn no quarter with his enemies. He had continued his research despite all obstacles, despite even the business with Lubricov. And now he, Sergei Rasikov—Mad Rasikov, he thought with bitter amusement—would save them all. He just needed time. He just needed a place to work—a place empty of humanity, where the walking dead would not pursue him.

He needed Chernobyl.

Now, as they cruised the decaying streets of Pripyat, Darya said, "What a terrible place you have brought us to, this city of the dead."

Rasikov demurred. He saw beauty in this irradiated and decaying city, in the shadow of the vast cooling towers of the abandoned nuclear plant. The sarcophagus that had been built to enclose the melted-down reactor loomed high in an unwashed blue sky. Nor was it a dead city, not to the observant eye. Tangles of radiation-poisoned vegetation towered everywhere around them, engulfing the houses, heaving up the asphalt of the street in slabs, and turning blight-reddened leaves to the lemon-yellow sun. Birds called, and something slid through the undergrowth. As for the absence of humans, well what of it? Humans had irradiated the land for thirty square kilometers around the nuclear plant. Humans had unleashed the zombie plague upon the earth. And where humans fled in any number, the zombies would follow.

"We'll be safe here," he said.

Darya just gazed out the window. "But safe from what?"

Rasikov didn't answer, not directly anyway. He merely pointed at a dilapidated house down the street, one relatively clear of the jungle that was slowly enveloping the abandoned city.

"There," he said, "that one will do."

THEY SIGHTED THE first of the spiders the following Tuesday.

They'd spent the previous three days unloading the trailer and getting the house in order, stacking the canned goods in the kitchen and storing away the distilled water in the basement. "Yes, and what shall we do when the fuel for the generator runs out?" Darya had inquired at one point, lugging a canister of gasoline into the adjoining garage. "What then?"

"We scavenge the abandoned reservoirs of Pripyat," Rasikov said. "That should sustain us for some time. Failing that, Dmitri and I will retrieve more from Chernigov."

"Chernigov belongs to the dead."

"Soon enough the entire world will belong to the dead, Darya."

"And the radiation. Have you thought of that?"

"I'd rather risk radiation than being eaten alive. Besides," he said, "the ambient radiation in the Exclusion Zone is fairly low. We can endure it without fatal damage for some time. Other things, small things with many generations—" He shrugged.

"What?"

"They may not be so lucky."

"I should have stayed behind. Larisa and I both."

He dropped a container of gasoline clattering to the floor. "I've made it perfectly clear that you're free to go. I can do without you, especially after—" The name lodged in his throat like a stone. "After Lubricov," he spat. Lubricov, his greatest rival at the university, and she had—she had—

His mind treated him to an imaginary little movie of them writhing together.

He had spoken a lie. He could not do without her—nor she him.

And then she was beside him. "No, you are right. What I did was unforgivable. I have no words to describe it."

She touched his clenched arm. After a moment he relented.

After Lubricov, she had said in the days following the anonymous note that had betrayed her, after Lubricov, anything. Anything to preserve the marriage—for Larisa, for them all, for the true love she bore for him.

Now she inclined her head. "You are right," she said. "I am sorry."

Anything. Anything.

And so he took the living room and dining room for himself. He set the harelip to knocking out the wall between them. When that was done, they lugged in the lab equipment. Three behemoth steel slabs, hinged at the base for vertical adjustment, commanded the center of the room. They hoisted the bots—stinking of burnt oil and spent ammunition—clanking atop the slabs. The rest of the equipment they squeezed in as best they could: the surgical table near the windows, the storage cabinets along the extended wall Dmitri had opened with his sledgehammer. And the heads, the precious heads, immersed in their green preservative fluid: the idiot gaze of their bleached faces, the seaweed coils of their hair. Dead but not dead, Rasikov sometimes raved. They merely awaited sufficient advances in technology to wake them to life afresh. The heads went in a mesh-caged, bracket-mounted storage shelf on the wall, as safe as they ever were on their erstwhile shoulders. Rasikov carried the key everywhere he went, though he seldom used it, for as long as the cryogenic coils didn't leak the heads required little maintenance. It was the theory, the possibility, of immortality, not the design or refinement of the preservative coils themselves, that engaged Rasikov's scientific curiosity—that consumed it still.

But the heads held Dmitri in fearful thrall.

How many times had Rasikov returned to the lab after some errand, to discover the harelip gazing rapt at the heads swimming in their green amniotic solution? Two dozen? Three? Four? And that just in the last few months. Calculating the hours lost on his work transcended even Rasikov's considerable mathematical skills. Loud deliberate throat clearing didn't solve the problem; nor did a quiet talk over the bone saw; finally a cuff was in order.

Rasikov still remembered the day he had first struck the harelip—the way the cur had spun around, rage flashing in his narrow yellow eyes, his hands half lifted in self-defense.

"How dare you raise your hand to me," Rasikov had snapped, and cuffed him again, a hard blow to the temple. That had dulled the fury in the dog's eyes. Thereafter, Dmitri developed a fawning, anxious manner in his presence. Rasikov's work gathered momentum. Yet still he occasionally caught Dmitri gazing with bewitched horror at the heads on their locked shelf—and occasionally a cuff— or two—was necessary to get Dmitri moving once again.

Twice already today, Rasikov had been forced to lift his hand to the harelip, first when Dmitri dropped his end of one of the precious tables, and again when he'd shattered a box of test tubes. He'd been on the verge of cuffing him yet again—this time the harelip had let slip his end of a tool case, sending a drawer of sterile instruments skating across the floor—when Darya and Larisa began to scream in the kitchen. Dropping his own end of the case, Rasikov seized the nearest weapon that came to hand, a six-inch surgical lancet, and dashed into the kitchen.

He found his wife and daughter cowering from a black and golden spider that rested pulsing on a wooden cutting board. The body of the thing alone must have been the size of a dinner plate.

High splayed legs, thick as a man's finger, or thicker, supported a great domed back bristling with dark quills. Its pulsating fangs— its *chelicerae*, Rasikov automatically corrected himself, a man of science to the last—glistened with greenish venom.

His wife screamed again.

Larisa shrieked.

Bolick leapt barking around the room.

"Everyone be still," Rasikov said.

"Sergei—"

The spider flinched at the sound of each voice, adjusting its stance with swift incremental movements. Atop its head eight soulless red eyes glared at Rasikov with murderous intent.

"Be still, I said," Rasikov repeated.

This time it took. Even Bolick fell silent. Darya's breathing labored in the silence. With each lightning shift, the spider's talons clicked on the wooden cutting board. Rasikov inched closer. He lifted the lancet, his heart hammering. In the same instant, the spider leapt at him, its legs outspread. With a grunt, Rasikov lunged at the thing. Using the lancet, he speared it through the abdomen with a chitinous crunch. The arc of the blow carried the spider backward, skewering it to the cutting board. Pinned there on its back, the thing thrashed, its legs clawing the air. Thick yellowish puss oozed from the wound to pool on the cutting board.

Darya breathed a heavy sigh.

"My God," she said. "My God, such a place this is."

Tentatively, Rasikov reached out and touched the quivering lancet. The spider's legs closed about it reflexively, and then relaxed into death.

"Get it out!" Darya said. "Get it out of my kitchen!"

"Dmitri," snapped Rasikov.

The harelip pushed forward. He stood at the counter and swallowed audibly. Then, with trembling fingers he lifted the cutting board. The lancet shuddered, and for a moment Rasikov thought the spider was going to drop and burst on the kitchen floor. He actually saw it happen: saw the thing tumble to the worn linoleum, exploding in a geyser of jaundiced slime. He had actually lifted a hand to strike the harelip for his stupidity, when the little orc of a man righted the cutting board. Shuddering, he lurched toward the back door.

"Dmitri!"

The harelip looked over his shoulder, wincing.

"Take it to the lab. We'll need to dissect it."

Grimacing, Dmitri swung toward the laboratory. His precipitous change of direction swung the spider like a wheel around the axel of the lancet, and for a moment Rasikov thought once again that the loathsome creature was going to splatter to the floor. He had an image of Dmitri's boot plunging down upon it, with a moist squelch that left bristled legs and shattered fragments of the thing's *cephalothorax* jutting from its jellied innards. He closed his eyes, swallowing. The door swung closed behind Dmitri.

"Daddy," Larisa said. "Why was it so big?"

"It was a mutant, dear. The radiation from the meltdown caused it."

"Will we see more of them?" Darya asked.

"I suspect we will. Them and more, I should imagine. Anything small and short-lived, with many generations a year, may have mutated significantly. The background radiation from the meltdown is sufficient to exact a significant toll on something so tiny."

Darya picked at her blouse with nervous fingers. "Why did you bring us to such a place, Sergei?"

This again, he thought.

"What would you have had me do? The cities are falling. Wherever survivors settle in numbers, the dead soon will follow. We have choices to make, Darya. We are safer here."

"Safe enough to do your research, right, Sergei?"

Did he detect a hint of bitterness in her tone?

"Would you have us cower in our flat, Darya?" How quickly Lubricov's name came to his lips, unspoken—not in front of Larisa. But Darya sensed it there anyway and bowed her head in submission. Gentler now, Rasikov touched her shoulder. "It was only a matter of time before the dead devoured us. My research alone offers us a chance—the whole human race a chance." And while this was true, it was also profoundly disingenuous. For Rasikov science had always been about the search for knowledge. Practical applicability was a secondary concern—*could* a thing be done, was the central question, not *should* it.

"What is it you are planning?"

"I am going to give my clients immortality," he said— "and the warbots the true intelligence they need to defeat the dead."

AFTER THAT, RASIKOV decreed that no one—not even Larisa—go unarmed.

"But she is so young," Darya protested one night in their bedroom.

Though no others had invaded the house, the spiders had proved not uncommon in the days since that first incident in the kitchen. Once Rasikov had looked up from his work with one of the warbots—he had cracked the cranium to examine the primitive wiring inside—to find one clinging to the outside of his lab window. And at least twice more he had been summoned by screams to dispatch other denizens of Pripyat: ants the length of a man's finger, beetles the size of his palm. Each he dutifully dissected; each had unfolded the same story. Internal organs twisted by generations of mutation. The self-evident tendency toward gigantism. Yet in no case did the creatures pose any serious threat. The ants were merely oversized ants, the beetles merely beetles; the spider's venom would sicken, but was unlikely to kill.

None of these findings did anything to allay the irrational terrors of his wife and daughter. And while Rasikov's work was too pressing to bother stringing lights in the basement or searching out heavy-gauge mesh to reinforce the windows, he did sacrifice an hour every day to train Darya and Larisa in the use of firearms.

As to his wife's fear that Larisa was too young: "The world makes no allowances for youth now, love," he said.

"But she *is* so young."

"She must grow up, then. We must all grow up, Darya," he added, hoping that she would understand the implication: that she must adjust to this new life's unpleasant realities, oversized insects among them.

"But is there not some other place where we could seek refuge?"

"Within our reach, there is not. Humans have colonized every corner of the planet. Where humans survive, the horde will follow."

"How can you be sure, Sergei? You are always so sure of everything." A hint of reproach had crept into her voice.

By force of will, Rasikov ignored it. He did not mention Lubricov—dead now, no doubt, devoured by the horde and risen up to join them. The world was not entirely without justice.

"My reason tells me so," he replied. "The evidence informs me."

Darya was silent for a long time. While he waited for her to respond, Rasikov studied the shadows, thinking of their wedding day, the bright beginning to what was to be a new life—the brilliant young scientist and his lovely bride, herself a rising executive in a new Russia, more free and fair. Instead he had wound up relegated to his basement lab by colleagues disdainful of his work ("immortality, indeed," one of them had sneered); she had seen a promising career cut short by an untimely pregnancy. Desperate for funding, Rasikov had come to rely on the generosity of a wealthy clientele that lived in terror of death. And Darya? She had surrendered her career to care for Larisa. Perhaps that had been the beginning of the thing with Lubricov, her bitterness and sense of betrayal.

Yet even in his fury, the guilt of her sacrifice every day weighed upon him, and so he had forgiven her as best he could. So he tolerated, indulged some might say, the unreasonable, even the hysterical, when it cropped up in her: her terror of insects, for instance, and not merely overgrown ones. And he did his best to lighten her load in a thousand tiny ways: or he had, anyway, before this present crisis. Now his research pressed upon him: the problem of robot intelligence, its bearing on his prior work, its potential for human salvation, and the rehabilitation of his reputation.

Darya shuddered. "How horrible," she said. "How terrifying.

Better that I should die—that we should all die—than suffer such a fate. The world is a terrible place to demand of us such a choice."

"But a brighter hell to have you in it," he said, smoothing her hair from her brow. He kissed her gently.

"I love you, Sergei," she said. Nestling her head into his shoulder, she slept. Rasikov was sleepless though, his mind dizzy with warbot circuitry and the more complex biological circuitry of the heads encased in their cryogenic jars on the floor below. And if he heard the surreptitious sound of something moving in the basement far below him, he dismissed it as his wife's hysteria infecting his far more rational thoughts.

Tomorrow the true work began.

MESSY WORK IT was, too.

Picture it: Rasikov and Dmitri in their makeshift lab, while elsewhere in the house, Bolick frolics, distracting Darya and Larisa from Larisa's lessons in English, the passport language to a better world, as if there is any longer a better world to hope for, or the need of passports to traverse it.

Picture the lab. Picture the harelip in a dingy white coat, swinging back the hinged braincase of a disabled warbot, tilted up on one of the enormous steel slabs. Picture Rasikov himself, gloved, masked, in a butcher's apron smeared with gore. The bone saw whirs as he prepares to decant a brain of his own—the second of the day. The first—the gray matter of a wealthy mob kingpin, and Rasikov's first essay in immortality—had curdled into the consistency of headcheese due to an imperfectly sealed bell jar. With this, the second of the day—the brain of a female telecom executive dying of cancer—Rasikov has more luck. The bone saw silenced, Rasikov lifts off the top of the woman's skull as effortlessly as another man might lift the lid from a can of mandarin oranges. The brain inside is a healthy pinkish gray and, when Rasikov gives it a tentative poke, firm to the touch.

Working against time now, Rasikov expertly snips away the network of nerves and blood vessels that bind the brain like a net, and lifts it out of its host skull. A few short steps carry him across the room to the slab. Dmitri recoils, transfixed, his eyes ashine with horror and fascination, one hand lifted as if in supplication. Ignoring him, Rasikov, his arms bloody to the elbows, lowers the brain into the bot's open skull. After that it is but the work of moments—and he has but moments to complete it before the freshly thawed brain dies in his hands. His mind reeling with schemata of warbot circuitry, Rasikov wires it into its new home. Electrical leads from the robot's optics he sinks deep into the brain's visual centers. Other leads he runs into auditory, olfactory, and tactile hubs.

Then the tricky work, the really experimental stuff: wiring the brain's spinal terminus into the bot's primitive nervous system, a process more art than science and one—Rasikov admits to himself—unlikely to be successful, at least on first attempt. Yet as he swings closed the bot's braincase, optimism fills him.

Rasikov switches the warbot on.

A moment passes. Then another.

The bot's yellowish eyes flicker, flicker, and alight.

"It's alive," Rasikov whispers.

But the next breath brings a blinding electrical flash and the sizzling stench of roasting brain. Turning in rage and frustration, Rasikov strikes Dmitri again and again, until a thin rivulet of crimson snakes out of the harelip's twisted nostril.

Alive? Alive?

But no.

Decidedly, irrevocably, undeniably dead.

EVENING THEN.

As he did most nights, Rasikov sought refuge in the company of his daughter. At twelve, Larisa had begun to take on some of the dark beauty that had transfixed him in her mother thirteen years ago. Yet she was still a child and he sensed how the day wore upon her—the long hours studying English and algebra under her mother's supervision when even she must have known it was a

doomed enterprise; the dearth of friends. That most of all, he supposed. He had himself been a lonely child, virtually friendless, and
the absence had weighed upon him like a stone. To have had
friends—and Larisa *had* had them—and lost them, how much
worse that must be.

And to see, as a mere child, the things she had seen. Vessa, her
classmate, torn apart in the schoolyard as the rest of the class fled
screaming. Elena, her closest friend, gore dripping from her sunken
face as she feasted upon a hapless pedestrian in the street below
their flat. And Inna. Gone. Just gone.

It was Inna she turned to now as they walked the broken street
outside the house. The westering sun drew down beyond the plant's
great cooling towers. Bolick gamboled through streaks of light and
shadow. He paused now and then to bark, rear raised and tail wag-
ging, luring them on. It was of Inna that she spoke, reaching up to
put her small hand in his as she had not since she was a true child,
two or three years gone now.

"Is she alive, do you think?"

The father's dilemma: to be honest or to lie? He chose the third
path, honest enough in its way, he supposed, but disingenuous at
the core. "I don't know."

Larisa pondered this for a moment.

Then, matter of factly, "I think she's dead."

"And how does that make you feel?"

"Sad, I guess. But there is so much sadness in the world now. We
have been lucky, that's all."

Rasikov shook his head.

"You must never attribute our survival to luck, Larisa. We are
here, safe, because we acted with intelligence. We formulated a plan
and executed it."

"And the bots?"

"When my research pays off—and it will pay off"—said to reas-
sure himself as much as his daughter, Rasikov supposed—"when it
does pay off, then we will reclaim the world for humankind. We
shall be famous, eh?" he added, nudging his daughter and smiling.

She smiled back, a weak and starveling thing, but a smile nonetheless. "How?" she said. "How shall we become famous?"

"The robots are very stupid now, yes? I make them smart. And then they will protect us as they were intended to do—and maybe all humankind."

"What is left of it," his daughter said.

"Yes. What is left of it."

Bolick dashed back from the end of the street, his tongue lolling. He danced about them. Larisa knelt to wrap her arms around the dog's neck, snugging her face into the animal's ruff, and Rasikov, mindful of the dog's omnipresent fishy stench—he could smell it now—laid a hand across her shoulder. He spared an uneasy glance at the radiation-poisoned jungle, higher and more tangled here, swallowing the houses whole. The sun hung low in the sky, a swollen red disk, half hidden behind one of the plant's looming cooling towers.

"We should go back," he said.

"Just a little farther, Dad. Please. It seems like we've been cooped up in that awful house forever."

Against his better judgment, Rasikov assented. "Five minutes, no more, yes?"

They ambled on hand-in-hand. Bolick, dismissed, ran ahead once again.

"And until your research pays off?" Larisa asked.

"We take care of ourselves. Remember your lessons?"

"Mutant, aim for the center of the mass," she said, rolling her eyes. "If you run into an infected, do your best to put a bullet in the center of its—"

She never finished the sentence. In the shadows, something dark and swift—Rasikov took it for a rabbit the size of a beagle—darted across the pavement. Barking, Bolick jetted off in pursuit, disappearing into the mutant jungle.

"He'll be back," Rasikov was saying when the stillness broke.

From somewhere deep in the thicket, the dog let out a strangled yelp of dismay. A heartbeat later, it was silent. The brush thrashed for perhaps a minute—certainly no longer—then all was still.

"Daddy—"

"He will return," Rasikov whispered. "Just wait."

"But—"

"Wait, I said."

In the silence, Rasikov counted slowly to sixty, then to a hundred and twenty. The dog squealed again. The undergrowth shook violently. A horrible sound rose in the stillness—the worst sound Rasikov had ever heard in his life, worse even than the screams of a man being torn asunder and devoured alive by monsters that only days and hours before had been as human as himself. It was a gnashing chittering sound that went on and on and on. Rasikov thought it would never end.

Larisa's voice brought him back to himself.

"You have to save him, Daddy."

"Dmitri—" he said weakly.

"Daddy."

Dmitri, he started to gasp. But there was no time to fetch the harelip. It was already too late. An image seized him. Not his daughter's best friend gorging herself on a neighbor in the street below their flat, but his daughter's face as she watched from the window. Horror and inconsolable loss, an expression such as no man should ever have to see on his child's face. *She is so young,* Darya said inside his head. And how much horror—how much loss and sadness—could a child endure?

And so Rasikov found himself wading into the thicket, gun drawn, to save a fishy-breathed mutt he despised in his heart—a mutt that he knew in the same heart was beyond saving—and not for the mutt's sake either, but for his daughter's. For whatever shred of innocence she retained in this ruined world.

He went in.

Gnarled, mutated branches lashed at his face in the darkness—in here the bloated red sun might as well have been warming the planets of Betelgeuse. His feet tangled in bracken. He held the gun out before him like a talisman, his heart hammering—

—and found the dog in a shaft of crimson sunlight lancing through a gap in the canopy overhead. He had a confused impression of something shiny and lean, impossibly fast, skittering away into the shadows. And then—he had never been this terrified, some still functioning portion of his mind observed—he shoved the pistol back into his belt, leaned over, seized the dog by the ruff of its neck, and pulled. It wouldn't budge at first, stuck fast, and then, suddenly, it gave with a sticky squelching sound that set his guts churning.

Unharmed, Rasikov stumbled into the street, dragging the dog behind him.

"Daddy!" Larisa screamed. "Daddy!"

Rasikov looked back to see what manner of horror he had dragged out of the brush. Not a dog, oh no, but the merest shell of a dog, a dog torn asunder, its fur tacky and matted with blood, its entrails strung out like spaghetti and half-devoured.

"Bolick!" Larisa cried.

She lunged toward the dog, but Rasikov was quicker. He snatched her away—who could say what kind of venom the beast had been pumped full of?—and then, glancing about the quickly darkening street, he pulled her into an embrace, running the fingers of one hand through her silky dark hair as he whispered soothing nonsense into her ear and carried her back to the house.

LARISA COULD FIND no sleep until after two the next morning, and even then she seemed to have reverted to a stage of development deeper than mere childhood. She curled fetal underneath her sheets, her skin pale and splotchy from tears, her thumb corked in her mouth.

Downstairs, Rasikov poured himself a stiff scotch. When he opened the refrigerator for water—he could hear the generator burbling away outside; at least one thing had not gone to hell—he found it empty.

"There is none up here," Darya said. "I couldn't bring myself to go into the basement and fetch any."

If Larisa had retreated into childhood, Darya had aged a decade or more in the last eight hours. Her dark hair hung in ragged snarls around her shoulders and her eyes gazed up at him from wells of shadow. Deep lines bracketed her lips. Nor had Rasikov survived the experience unscathed. He'd caught a glimpse of himself in the rust-stained mirror of the downstairs bathroom. His graying hair hung over his eyes in greasy strands; his eyes themselves glittered through this veil like diamonds in fathomless, black pits. They are right, my colleagues, he thought, I am really and truly mad, a mad man trapped in a world gone crazy.

Sipping his drink, he ruminated on the events in the street. His daughter's grief. His own horror. Could he have saved the dog if he'd only acted sooner, if he could have broken free of his own paralyzing terror? And what kind of man hated his daughter's dog in the first place?

What kind of man was he?

Rasikov took another sip, holding the whisky in his mouth until it released its soothing bouquet of flavors, oak and cherry, peat. It wasn't so bad neat, he thought. And: would this night never end?

Darya had said something.

"What?" Rasikov said.

"We'll need some in the morning."

"Need what?"

"Water. For breakfast."

He leaned against the counter, thinking this through. "Do you think I could have saved him?"

"Bolick?"

He nodded.

"I don't know, Sergei. I wasn't there."

Rasikov sipped scotch.

"Probably not," Darya said.

"I saw the thing. Just a glimpse. But it was big. And fast."

"Why did you bring us here, Sergei?"

"What would you have had me do? Did you want to see Larisa eaten alive? Or worse yet, one of them?"

No response. But something in Rasikov made him press the issue.

"Did you?" The words came out harsher than he intended.

"No, Sergei. I wouldn't want to see those things. But surely there was somewhere else—"

"Where? Tell me. Where? Human beings are everywhere. Meat, that's all we are anymore, Darya. Just meat, everywhere. Our only chance is isolation. Only if I finish my work can we survive." He turned away, flapping his hand, thinking of Lubricov. "Go, if you want to go," he said. "Do you think there are not days when I wish you would? Days I can think of nothing but what you have done to me?" He turned to face her, fists clenched. Then, by sheer force of will, he relaxed his hands. Whatever his inclinations with the harelip, Sergei Rasikov had never raised a hand to his wife or daughter. There had been a time when he hardly ever raised his voice. He crossed the room, placed his hand over hers where it rested, trembling, on the scarred deal table. "I'm sorry," he said. "I'm doing the best I can."

Darya pulled away. She cradled her face in cupped palms. "I'm sorry, too, Sergei. You cannot know how sorry I am."

He sighed. "I will fetch the water," he said.

RASIKOV SWUNG BACK the basement door.

A breath of chill air breathed out of the darkness, the smell of must and damp earth. They should have left the supplies in the trailer. Locked away. Safe from the denizens of this terrible place.

Too late.

Rasikov flipped on the overhead light. A flashbulb glimpse of the basement—the shaky staircase, the dirt floor—dazzled him. Then the light blew out in a shower of brilliant sparks. He had never bothered to repair the wiring. The pressure of his research, the dearth of time. They had used the space only during daylight hours, in the dim gray radiance of the open doorway. Another mistake. So many mistakes.

He fetched a flashlight and shone it down the backless wooden risers, soft with rot. The darkness deepened around the roving beam. The basement was little more than an earthen pit. He shuddered to think of the things that lived in such dark, damp places. Things with many legs. And mandibles. Things ravenous with hungers he did not care to think about.

An image of the spider leaping at him came to Rasikov's mind, its legs extended liked a great eight-fingered hand. How lucky he had been with the lancet. He thought of the thing pinned on its back to the cutting board, its legs clenching, the expanding pool of thick yellow guts.

Rasikov swallowed. He swept the beam around the room once more. Gnarled wooden support posts sprang into momentary relief. The low ceiling unveiled itself, a tangle of floor joists, age-yellowed pipes, and moldering wire. The water was stored in interlocking stacks of cardboard boxes against the far wall, soggy from the damp.

Why hadn't he woken the harelip on his upstairs cot? he asked himself.

Because someone needed to guard Larisa's door (or so he had told himself)? Or because he hadn't wanted to appear cowardly in front of the woman he loved? Wasn't that what had kept him from racing after Bolick into the undergrowth, when there might have still been time? Cowardice?

Shamed, Rasikov put a foot on the first riser. It creaked beneath his weight. Slowly, he descended, first one step and then another, his heart pounding. Halfway to the bottom, he thought he heard something rustle in a distant corner. He stabbed at it with the light—was that a swift scuttling he heard in the dark?—but there was nothing there, just cobwebs and crumbling earth.

Just imagination, nothing more.

Rasikov took the remaining steps two a time. He strode across the basement with a confidence he didn't feel, wedged the flashlight into a half-open box, and seized it in both hands. The light leapt erratically with each step—for a heart-stopping moment Rasikov thought it was going to crash to the floor—now illuminating the scorch-stained water heater, then the rusting furnace in quick strobic flashes.

And now he did hear something: a stuttering chitter, high pitched. Something black and iridescent, something large, flashed through the light. And suddenly the basement was alive with sound and movement—that awful chittering keen, the damp-muffled scuttle of swift taloned feet across the earthen floor. Dozens of them—whatever they were—by the sound of it. Surrounding him.

An image of Bolick—torn apart, his fur tacky with blood—possessed him.

Sergei Rasikov, still clutching the box against his chest, ran. The flashlight jarred loose, its beam wheeling. It hit the floor, flickered, and went out, plunging him into darkness. He skidded to a halt. In the same moment, the box burst, spilling its freight of gallon jugs. They fell like bombs, exploding in whooshing geysers. In the darkness, Rasikov wheeled around, his hands outstretched. His breath seared his lungs. Around him, the chittering picked up in intensity. He could sense the things—whatever they were—closing in. He'd lost his bearings in the darkness. It pressed upon him, oily and thick. He spun wildly, searching for the doorway.

Then, high up in the darkness, he spotted it, a faint gray rectangle of light.

Rasikov lunged toward it, trying to gauge the distance, but he slowed down too late. His foot caught the first of the risers, sending him sprawling. Breath burst from his lungs. His knee punched through a rotten riser, unleashing an inferno of agony.

The chittering drew closer, louder, the circle tightening.

Something heavy scurried across his calf. And fast. So fast that Rasikov barely had time to register anything but its weight, the chitinous scrape of its underbelly across his leg, and then it was gone. Panting, Rasikov scrabbled up the steps on hands and knees, the risers creaking ominously beneath him.

He hurled himself into the hallway, kicked the door closed

behind him, and scrambled to his feet. In the next breath something hurled itself against the other side of the door. The wood shuddered in its frame.

Rasikov stiffened, panting, waiting for the next shuddering blow. But it did not come.

THE PACE OF Rasikov's research quickened. Setbacks followed success.

The next morning—after forcing the reluctant harelip to lug two boxes of water from the empty basement (had he imagined it all? Rasikov wondered)—Rasikov managed to elicit a moment or two of stuttering, incomprehensible speech from one of the brain-implanted warbots. The brain died soon after—he'd still not managed to wire the spinal terminus correctly, a matter of trial and error—but Rasikov pressed on, encouraged. The brain that followed the next morning, that of a wealthy industrialist who had died of a massive heart attack at age forty, proved more successful still. This time the brain survived for nearly five minutes. Confused—some brain damage from an imperfect preservation process, Rasikov presumed—the thing did not speak. But then its yellow eyes dimmed and the bot's head clattered to the table.

Rasikov resisted the impulse to cuff the harelip for this failure. It wasn't his fault, after all, and Rasikov did not think of himself as a cruel man. But his frustration built. The next brain—the penultimate brain, he saw with dismay—had been damaged by an imperfect seal as well. And the sixth—on the day that followed—proved disastrous.

It began, ironically, with a breakthrough—Dmitri's breakthrough. The harelip had been studying the nervous column of the nearest bot when he abruptly straightened.

"Dr. Rasikov," he said, grinning.

The sight—ugliness compounded with joy—inspired a wave of disgust in Rasikov. Yet he managed to stifle the reaction.

"Yes, Dmitri."

"The wires. If you reversed red and green—"

"No—" Rasikov said, but he strode across the room and peered into the spinal cavity for himself. He thought he had mastered the spinal column, a thick column of wires encased in a flexible rubber sleeve. Yet...

Swiftly, he decanted the last of the brains—that of an octogenarian who had died of old age—and hurried back across the room, bobbling the slippery oblong of flesh. For a moment he feared that he would drop it. It was all too easy to imagine it splattering against the floor of the lab, gone soft with dry rot. Then he lowered it into the bot's metal cranium.

Deftly, Rasikov ran the wires. Yellow to the visual center, orange to the auditory hub, brown to the tactile. He plunged the speech ribbon into the whorled pinkish-gray flesh. Then he turned to the tangled column of wires that extruded from the bot's spinal column. First the thick mobility strip, then the snarl of ancillary wires—white, blue, black, on and on. Finally, the red and the green, reversed as the harelip had suggested. Then, with trembling hands, he latched the bot's cranium. He triggered the start-up sequence.

Its yellow eyes lit up immediately. Its fingers flexed. Still strapped to its table, it turned its head to stare at him.

"Alyona?" it said.

Rasikov smiled. "Sergei Rasikov," he said slowly and loudly. "Remember me, Mr. Sidirov?" Of course, the moment of awakening would be confusing. Explanation would be required. "We had an arrangement to preserve you through cryogenic sleep. Do you recall that?" And pushing on cheerily: "Welcome back."

The bot did not respond to cheer. In fact, it ignored him.

It rotated its head—a full 360 degrees, Rasikov noted with delight; the bot-brain interface was perfect—to take in the lab. Then it said, "Alyona, the dog has gotten in the flowers again."

"Mr. Sidirov," Rasikov said with a sinking feeling.

The harelip had crept up to Rasikov's shoulder, anxious for praise.

"Mr. Sidirov, you're okay. Everything is okay."

And then—could a bot's speech box express panic? If so, then Mr. Sidirov's did—then the bot said, "Alyona? Alyona? The dog is in the garden again—"

"My name is Sergei Rasikov," Rasikov said.

"Mr. Rasikov," the bot replied, and Rasikov almost relaxed. All it took was a brief period of adjustment, he should have anticipated—

"Rasikov, you fool. You're late again, Rasikov. This is your final warning—"

"Mr. Sidirov—"

"Is this the eighty-year-old?" Darya said from the doorway.

"Yes. Now if you'll just—"

"It's useless, dear. He's suffering from senile dementia."

No, it could not be true, Rasikov thought. But some deeper voice—the scientist's voice—told him that it was so. The eighty-year-old brain had been compromised from the start. A red fog enveloped him. Rasikov turned and struck the harelip, struck him and struck him again, he couldn't say how many times. When he came to himself, Darya was clutching his shoulder, dragging him back.

"Enough!" she was screaming. "Do you wish to kill him?"

Rasikov stepped away and saw what he had done. He had driven the harelip into a corner of the lab. Dmitri hunched there, his hands raised to ward off further blows, his face a mask of blood, snot, and tears. The harelip had pissed himself. Rasikov could smell the stench of it, acrid and sharp. The deformed lip curled in helpless fury. His yellow eyes burned with hatred. Rasikov had half a mind to beat the expression off the cur's face, but then, turning, he saw Larisa standing in the doorway to the kitchen. She had seen his display of strength then. Good. Cruelty was another matter.

"Get to your feet," he snapped to the harelip. "What kind of man are you?"

And then, to Darya, "Tomorrow at dawn we will take the tractor trailer into Chernigov, Dmitri and I."

Darya held him by the arm. In the doorway, Larisa's eyes filled with tears.

"But why?" Darya asked.

"We need more brains."

THE CITY OF Chernigov had fallen to the dead.

To Rasikov, high up at the wheel of the truck with the harelip beside him, it seemed like the whole world had fallen.

He drove recklessly, a drumbeat of doom starting up inside his heart.

The trip had been doom-haunted from the start.

Darya had wept before they left. "Must you go?" she cried.

"What would you have me do?" Rasikov responded. "The bots are our only chance."

They were in the kitchen, at the deal table, Rasikov and Darya and Larisa, her eyes downcast. Never before had she seen her parents at such odds. Rasikov had been the unquestioned head of the family until now. Darya had ceded authority to him as naturally as she had ceded her career twelve years ago. Especially after Lubricov. To see her protest like this—it was a measure of her terror.

"And if the horde comes while you are away? If the things that took Bolick come? If the things you heard in the basement—?" She turned away, her face as pale as the cold gray light of dawn outside the windows.

"Daddy, please—" Larisa said.

And this was the hardest thing of all, this paradox: to deny his daughter his protection that he might better protect her still. He laid his large hand across her small one and squeezed gently.

"You have your weapons."

"And scarcely know how to use them," Darya said.

"We shall be back within the day."

"If you come back at all."

"Yes," he said, quietly angry at Darya's weakness for the first time in—how many years? "Yes, if we come back at all."

The harelip had come in then: the truck was loaded with the

tools they would need to defend themselves from the horde. Rasikov ran through his mental checklist—the weapons, the ammunition, the machetes, honed to such sharpness that a single touch of their edges would draw a crimson bead down a man's finger.

"We must go now."

Larisa withdrew her hand in silent protest. Darya waved her hand in disgust.

"Go, then."

Rasikov stood.

At the doorway, she called him back.

"Is this what you have become then, a murderer for your research?"

"No," he said, "a murderer for your salvation." And when she did not speak: "I love you."

For a long time, she did not respond, and Rasikov felt a dike collapse inside him, spilling heartbreak through his veins, sweeping all away in the deluge. The old business with Lubricov reasserted itself, the shock on her face when he discovered the truth and her pledges to do whatever it took—*whatever it took*—to make up for her betrayal. And so at last, again, she relented, and when she did he felt flood through him not triumph, but a vast gray ocean of guilt and disgust. For he had betrayed her too in his way, demanding of her servile obedience to his wishes, and she had betrayed herself in surrendering it.

"I love you, too," she said, turning away, tears in her eyes, before accompanying them outside. As he climbed into the truck she kissed him, saying, "I really do love you, Sergei." Yet even as the warmth of forgiveness spread through him—for everything, even Lubricov—Darya screamed. Rasikov bounded from the running board, spinning, uncertain what new nightmare to expect. Three zombies staggered up the street toward them, their eyes burning with hunger. He brought his rifle to his shoulder, and dropped them one by one.

He took her in his arms, kissed the top of her head. "They're dead now," he said. "There's nothing to fear." And then: "Use your weapons. Be safe. I will return soon."

To the truck then.

Pripyat soon gave way to the radiation-blasted waste of the Exclusion Zone: sprawling thickets of iridescent trees, black and twisted, interspersed with barren stretches of swampy scrub. The sun hung low in the sky, a gray cinder. Yet still a seed of anxiety germinated within Rasikov. When he saw another walker—a crawler, actually, leg-shattered and wasted with starvation, dragging itself along the highway toward Pripyat—that seed bloomed into full-blown dread.

Rasikov ran the thing down like a dog, but already he sensed it was too late, already a horrific suspicion was dawning in his mind. For there were more of the monsters. Two or three lurching through a grove of trees to the west. A cluster of seven—or was it eight?—staggering through a fen to the east. A score or more, not a dozen yards from the motorway, stumbling toward Pripyat.

Toward Pripyat.

"They communicate," he whispered.

Even as Rasikov said it, his mind sketched the scenarios. Some primitive morphic field, perhaps. Or worse, and more likely: perhaps the things had been engineered by some clandestine military researcher, weaponized to seek new brains when local stores were exhausted. In a flash he understood. Migrant as birds, they roved the devastated countryside in great packs, throwing off lone walkers as scouts. And when one of those walkers spotted prey, the nearby horde converged, summoned by some crude telepathic mechanism encoded into the viral genome itself.

He swallowed and turned to look at the harelip.

"They've discovered Pripyat," he said, pushing the accelerator to the floor. "We need brains. And we don't have much time."

NOW, AS THEY came into Chernigov, that drumbeat of doom intensified in Rasikov's heart. Everywhere around them loomed the wreckage of a dead civilization: shattered glass and the abandoned booty of looters, an overturned shopping cart in the middle of the street, the burned-out husks of cars, and, most tragic of all, the Savior Cathedral, more than a thousand years old, a blackened ruin. Not to mention the contending forces that battled sporadically for the streets: the occasional warbots, halfway functional, laying down streams of ineffective ground fire, or, more often still—despair seized Rasikov just seeing it—banging senselessly in corners they could not navigate their way out of. And then there were the dead themselves, limbless and whole alike, dragging themselves after the truck, their faces smeared with gore, their starveling eyes ablaze with unholy appetites, their hands outstretched like curved and grasping talons. They shambled out of alleys and stumbled down stairs as the truck lumbered down debris-clogged streets, finally grinding to a near halt as Rasikov navigated a snarl of burnt-out Volgas, Moskvichs, and troop carriers.

As the zombies drew closer, Dmitri threw himself in terror away from the van's window, smashing Rasikov against the door.

"Off, dog," Rasikov cried, thrusting him back, uncertain what repulsed him more, the craven harelip or the converging horde.

"How are we to find survivors in this?" the harelip cried.

Rasikov wrestled the wheel. "They'll find us. They'll hear the sound of the truck and come running."

And then the damned were upon them. Bodies slammed the sides of the cab. Window glass spiderwebbed and shattered. The dead clambered upon the running boards to thrust grasping hands through the broken glass. A single zombie, its virus-wasted cheeks green with rot, black teeth loose in its gums, shoved its face through the medusa coils of clutching hands arms. Rasikov smashed it away, feeling its nose crunch beneath his elbow.

Another of the dead had clawed its way, head and shoulders, through the passenger window.

"Do something," Rasikov shouted. Out of desperation, the harelip seized his machete. A single blow left the zombie's head rolling on the floorboard, its teeth gnashing like those of a rabid dog. Another sweep of the blade severed arms, hands, fingers. The passenger side of the cab was suddenly an abattoir, the window empty.

Still the zombies grappled at Rasikov on the driver's side, tearing at his clothing, his arms, his hair. He reached for his own machete, then wedged it halfway under the seat. A better idea had seized him. He flung the wheel hard left, shaking loose some of the dead clinging to the side of the truck, crushing others under the wheels. Another yank of the wheel brought the driver's side tires shuddering onto the sidewalk. The cab smashed into the neighboring building with a screech of distressed metal, leaving behind a long streak of jellied blood and bone. A single eyeball, embedded in the gore, gazed blindly after them. Rasikov swung the truck back onto the street. It smashed aside an overturned limo, spinning it like a top, plowed through another wave of the dead, and then—for a moment, anyway—the road cleared and the horde fell behind them.

Rasikov whipped the truck into a residential neighborhood, taking the corner too fast and feeling the tug of the trailer wanting to overturn. Here the streets were less clogged with debris and he could pick up speed. The horde fell farther behind. Yet still the gore-smeared head in the floorboard rolled around, snapping its yellow bloodstained teeth.

"Get rid of it!" Rasikov shouted.

But the harelip merely cringed, hugging his knees on the seat, and what came back to Rasikov was the dense creature standing in horrified awe before the cryogenically preserved heads in their racks on the laboratory walls—and what it had taken to get him moving. He struck the harelip with an open hand across the face.

"Now!" he hissed.

The blow jarred the harelip into motion. He leaned gingerly over the edge of the seat—nearly losing his fingers for his trouble—dug his hand into the head's greasy hair, and lifted it high. For a moment the thing held Rasikov's gaze with mad appetite, its eyes rolling. Then Dmitri flung it out the window. Rasikov glimpsed it bouncing on the pavement through the passenger side mirror; then it was gone.

After that, they caught glimpses of the occasional rover, but saw nothing more of a congregating horde. They cruised for hours, block after empty residential block, scaring up packs of feral dogs; once, as the afternoon sun sank toward twilight, they saw an emaciated cat curled atop a set of porch stairs, as if its owner had only just stepped out and would any minute return.

But they saw no survivors.

Rasikov wrenched the wheel away in despair.

The dead city of Chernigov fell behind them and the Exclusion Zone hurtled closer.

ZOMBIES.

Squinting through the shattered windshield of the sorely abused tractor-trailer, Rasikov saw not the familiar house he had come to expect over the last couple of weeks, but a scene out of a Bosch painting sprung hideously to life. Zombies fought like animals over scraps of flesh. Zombies sucked the marrow out of shattered bones. Most of all—and most terrifying, he thought, his heart lurching in his breast—zombies converged from all sides on the vulnerable windows and doors of the house.

But the girls had not been idle in his absence.

Windows had been boarded over, doors jammed.

Rasikov processed the scene in the space of a breath. In the next he knew what he had to do. He had to wreak destruction on the horde, and he had to get himself inside the house. Better yet, he knew how to do it.

"Hold on," he snapped at the harelip.

Rasikov punched the gas, running down zombies as the truck gathered speed. The harelip reached out to stop him, but Rasikov knocked the hand away, and hammered the accelerator. The street outside rocketed by, foliage to either side blurring into a black screen, spliced through with flashes of dilapidated houses. Wind tore through the shattered windshield. The house hurtled toward him. At what seemed to him the very last moment—he could only hope he didn't misjudge and crack the house open like an egg—

Rasikov wrenched the wheel hard left and gave the gas one more adrenalized punch, trying to drive it straight through the floorboard. The truck's left wheels came up, and for a moment it hovered in perfect equipoise. Gravity swung through him like a pendulum. Then the scene before him rotated a perfect twenty-five degrees. The truck slammed down, snapping his head against the dashboard.

Rasikov had hoped to clear out an arc of zombies with the skidding trailer—he had felt it slam over the sidewalk and into the yard—and use the opening to dash inside the house. It was just a matter of scrambling vertically up the seat and out of the cab. Instead, suspended in his seatbelt, he groped awake to find the harelip hurtling toward the driver's side door. Fingers gouged Rasikov's arms. He caught a boot to the chin. Then the door screeched open, revealing a dark square of twilit sky. The harelip was gone.

A distant chorus of moans arose in the still air.

A moment later, Rasikov fumbled loose of his own harness. As he plummeted toward the passenger side door, he snatched at the wheel. One floundering boot landed on the gearshift, giving him leverage. With the other hand he groped around on top of the upended seat for the machete he'd wedged there. Then, using the wheel, he launched himself toward the gray square of sky. A breath later, Rasikov, leveraged himself out of the cab. He stood atop it—

—and saw a massing horde of the dead.

Perhaps a hundred had already gathered around the house. And more were coming: thrashing their way through the thick mutant foliage, lurching across neighboring yards like loathsome insects, stumbling down the street from both directions, as far as the eye could see.

For a moment, Rasikov marveled at the complexity of their biology—the sheer power and swiftness of the morphic field that the zombie virus generated in what remained of their brain. Then any time for thought was gone. The living dead were upon him. They yanked him away from the truck. He saw the door recede above him, like salvation lost—and then he was going down, dragged to the ground by dozens of cold dead hands. The terrible stench of decay—of disease and rotting flesh—filled his nostrils. He swung the machete in a great circle. Zombies collapsed around him like felled trees, their legs severed at the ankles. Even as they dragged themselves toward him on their elbows, Rasikov scrambled to his feet. He kicked them away with a booted foot, and brought the blade around in another whistling arc. A rotting head—its jaws clacking—bounced to the earth at his feet, and a path opened through the melee. Rasikov sprinted for the house. By then, full dark was closing down upon the Exclusion Zone, and as he slammed onto the porch, he sensed the mutant denizens of the night stirring to life. The enveloping thickets churned with swift, chittering movement, and the night terror of the basement, those circling dark-plunged monsters, momentarily engulfed him—then Darya flung open the door. He lunged through the bright yellow rectangle. He kicked the door closed behind him, let the machete fall clattering to the rot-softened floor, and swept Darya into an embrace.

Larisa hovered at her mother's side, weeping with terror.

Rasikov knelt to take her face between his hands. "No tears," he said, kissing her forehead. "Now is the time for courage."

"Your face," Darya said, and standing on tiptoe she kissed away the blood on his forehead.

Then, snatching up the blade, Rasikov dashed to the lab.

The harelip cowered in the far corner. Rasikov lashed at him with fists and boots. "For your cowardice I might have died!"

He turned away then, snatching the last semi-automatic out of a drawer and shoving it into the harelip's trembling hands with the few remaining magazines. "This is the last of them. Make good use of them," he said.

By then the air rang with commotion—the zombies as they shambled moaning toward the house and that awful chittering noise, as though the engine roar of the truck's arrival had stirred the terrible creatures of the Exclusion Zone to greater than usual activity. His experience in the basement flitted through Rasikov's mind—the horrific encircling strategy of the mysterious predators, the chitinous scrape of an armored belly across his calf—and then it was too late for thought.

The horde was upon them.

DOORS BUCKLED UNDER the mass of bodies. The nails holding the wooden slats over the windows groaned. Other planks shattered altogether, and grasping hands shot through newly opened crevices.

In a hurried conference they worked out a plan: the harelip would defend the lab, Darya and Larisa would take the kitchen, falling back as necessary. As for Rasikov? His job was to restore the warbots to functionality.

With fumbling hands he slammed open a storage cabinet and retrieved one of the positronic brains. Across the room, he unhinged a warbot's skull. Now he saw how premature his conclusions had been, how limited his investigations, by time, by resources—by forces he could not have anticipated, such as the mutated monsters that inhabited this hellish place. Should they repulse the zombie attack, how long could they hold at bay the assault of the creatures in the basement? Or the thing that had torn Bolick apart? And should they beat back that storm, what then? Where could they go in a world where even the Exclusion Zone had fallen? Always their enemies would seek them out, always a time would come—and soon—when they would wake to find themselves besieged once again by the dead.

A reinforced window gave utterly way—Rasikov saw Dmitri move to defend it, machete in one hand, pistol in the other, his craven face twisted with terror and desperation. A door screeched and trembled on its hinges. Cursing, Rasikov turned shaking fingers back to their task. How simple defense against an enemy so stupid and so slow should have been! Yet the headshot was so uncertain, and they assailed you in such numbers that even well-armed and well-trained men fell before them. As for Rasikov and his family—what hope did they have?

Every moment the horde swelled. Every moment that insectile

cacophony grew louder. Dark shapes, armor glinting in the rising yellow radiance of the moon, wove sinuously through the teeming zombies.

And from the basement, the same chittering clamor grew ever bolder.

Rasikov flipped on the first warbot. It ran through its start-up sequence. The eyes lit up—Rasikov's heart surged within him. Then they flickered, and went dark. Hurried, riven by terror, he'd miswired the thing. Screaming in frustration, he flung open the hinged cranium and seized the brain. He gasped as it slipped away, watching in dumb horror as the delicate circuitry shattered, sending shards of metal skating across the laboratory floor.

At the rear of the house, the generator clunked ominously.

The next moment it died altogether.

The lights dimmed and dimmed further still, then went out.

The stench of cordite stung Rasikov's nostrils as he wheeled back toward the cabinet for the second brain.

Guns roared, spitting fire, but in the swirling darkness, headshots were hard to come by.

Now, in shadows he turned again to his work—

The snap and pop of semi-automatic fire broke out in the kitchen.

Darya and Larisa retreated into the lab, guns blazing at the oncoming horde. A terrible gnawing sound reverberated from the rot-soft floorboards beneath Rasikov's feet. The armored monsters too were coming.

He worked on, wires slipping through his nerveless fingers, knowing that the warbots were their only chance. But already he felt the despair of the condemned man sweeping over him like a shroud— the despair that had driven him to this fresh avenue of research in the first place, the despair that had seized him again that afternoon in Chernigov when he had seen the robots slamming themselves into corners, unable even to maneuver themselves to freedom.

Then the sheer pressure of massed bodies on the porch began to break through.

Assailed now on three sides, Rasikov's defenders steadily retreated.

He slammed shut the warbot's skull, activated the start-up sequence, and armed it. The thing's eyes illuminated, bright yellow squares in the darkness. Then it heaved itself erect, its barrel-shaped torso snapping the straps that bound it to the table. The gimbals in its rubberized knees wheezed as it clanked to the floor, leaving its mates strapped to the tables on either side. It opened fire, guns blazing in the darkness.

Chaos—even greater chaos, Rasikov thought, if such a thing could be imagined—erupted in the cramped lab.

Bullets whined in the flashing dark, plaster and woodchips flying as they *whumped* into walls and cabinets. Glass shattered. Metal shrieked amid the hot sizzle of burning oil. Rasikov caught strobic glimpses of zombies falling back before the initial ferocity of the assault, and then surging forward again, damaged, delimbed, but still actively undead, their brains uninjured.

Then Darya was screaming.

For a single panicky moment, Rasikov thought one of the zombies had taken her—

—but no—

Words came screaming out of the darkness, *"Turn it off, turn it off—"*

And in the next blinding flash, he saw that one of the behemoth automaton's bullets had creased a line of blood under her high Slavic cheekbone. The afterimage of the blood dripping black down her face burned itself into his retinas. In that moment, all was forgotten, all forgiven. Lubricov was but a distant nightmare. They'd had so much time and he'd thrown so much of it away in fury. No more. With a cry, Rasikov flung himself at the warbot's broad metallic back—it made a hollow boom—hit the deactivation switch and rode the thing clattering to the floor. He rose to a crouch and stood astride it, his hands raised, like a man who has just wrestled a lion to bloody death.

Seizing his machete, he leapt into the fray.

He drove them back, severing limbs, but he rarely had a good angle for decapitation, so still the dead came, staggering armless, unbalanced, or dragging themselves forward with blackened nails in the sponge-like wood.

Now the lone bursts of the harelip's pistol filled the air. Darya had run dry, then Larisa. Rasikov heard their screams as the living dead overwhelmed them. He turned, abandoning his post, and drove the zombies back from them with his frenzied blade.

But it was too late.

Already they had succumbed to bites. Darya's was a bloody hole in her thigh, Larisa's a ragged tear in her upper arm. Their screams mingled in the smoky air. In mere moments the virus would infect their brains, taking them both. And in that same instant, a terrible idea was born in the mind of Sergei Rasikov:

He could save his wife and child—how could he live without them?—and they could save him—

"Dmitri—" he cried. "Cover me!"

The harelip backed slowly toward the center of the room, spinning to lay down fire in three directions, holding the zombies at bay.

Two quick strokes of the blade was all it would take, yet Rasikov hesitated. "No, Sergei—" his wife whispered, her eyes shining up at him.

"Would you become one of them?" he responded, and then, with horror at what he had become, he brought the machete down in a terrific blow. Her body shuddered, jetting blood, as her head rolled away. Rasikov spun then, without thinking—he could not bear to think about this thing he must do—and brought down the machete upon Larisa's thin, white neck.

"Daddy!" she cried, and then she was gone, her lips still moving with the half-unspoken word.

Weeping, Rasikov drove his fingers into the hair of the severed heads. He lifted them high and pressed their already cooling lips each to his own for an agonizing heartbeat, and then a heartbeat more. And then—the detonation of the harelip's pistol shots still ringing in his ears—he dashed across the room to the surgical table. By now experience had made him proficient with the bone saw. Through a blur of tears, he unzipped his wife's skull and removed her sacred brain. A moment later, he lowered it into one of the war-bot's metal craniums. Experience made wiring it but the work of moments—yellow, orange, and brown to the sensory centers, then the speech ribbon and the more complex work at the spinal node, his fingers slippery with perspiration. Twice— three times— four— he had to turn and use the gore-streaked machete to fend off a zombie that had slipped through the harelip's perimeter. Then he latched closed the cranium, activated the bot's start-up sequence, armed it—armed *her*—and hurried back across the room to repeat the process with Larisa. Even as the Darya bot's eyes flickered to awareness, her daughter stirred on the table. For a moment, a terrible fear seized Rasikov—that they would turn upon him their righteous fury.

Instead they rose up, their weapons spitting flame. Zombies fell back before the onslaught, and Sergei Rasikov felt a surge of triumph. At last his research had born fruit! With the superior firepower of the bots, the dead, not to mention the terrible things under the floor—he could see boards bulging as the monsters began to break through—could be driven back and defeated. And most of all, Darya and Larisa—his wife and daughter—could be with him forever, their brains, their essential selves, transferred into ever more sophisticated bots as humanity reclaimed the planet for themselves—

With renewed fury, confident of victory, Rasikov lunged into the fray.

The machete slashed silver arcs in the air as he drove the dead back, hacking away hands and arms and legs. Heads rolled away, snapping in ravening madness. Sweat broke out on his brow and ran in rivulets down the channel of his spine, and he reveled in this evidence of his humanity.

And then—dear God—the floorboards began to give way at his feet.

That awful chittering rang in the air, loud, loud, then louder still, a high stuttering whine that first competed with and then drowned out the moaning of the hungry dead. Floorboards cracked, then gave away. Still his wife and daughter stood by the slabs where he had given them life, firing into the throng of viral-ridden zombies.

And then the first of the monsters thrust its way through the floor, visible in flashes of gunfire: a sleek bullet-shaped head, armored like some dreadnought of old, furred antennae waving in the smoke from the firearms. Huge mandibles—*maxillipeds,* Rasikov's mind screamed, *maxillipeds* hungry for living flesh— champed ravenously, slinging viscid yellow venom that would paralyze their victims even as they tore them apart with those slavering jaws. Screaming, Rasikov fell still farther back, the machete hanging useless from his nerveless fingers. So big, the thing was so big—the size of a man or larger. Its taloned legs scrabbled for purchase as the chitinous, iridescent body drove its way through the floor, segment after armored segment after armored segment. Dear God how long was the thing, and in that screaming moment, Rasikov knew, he knew—

Radiation-mutated centipedes, monster centipedes—

Monster centipedes crowding down in the darkness under the house, starving and stupidly malign, dormant by daylight but roused to action by the cacophony of the battle upstairs, seeking the prey that had so long eluded them. Another burst through the floor and then another, splinters flying. Then they were everywhere, half a dozen of them, a dozen skittering up the walls, across the ceilings, and over one another's writhing bodies. They plunged blindly into the ranks of zombies, tearing them limb from moaning limb—

"Darya!" he screamed. "Larisa!"

But even then, despairing, he knew. His family's bodies—magnificent testaments to the genius of humanity—had changed, but their brains—their brains had not. And above all his wife and daughter feared insects. Mouth grills emitting metallic bleats of terror, the two bots stumped past him and into the voracious horde beyond, their cylindrical metal bodies impervious to zombies and centipedes alike. With their massive strength, they plunged through the walls of the house—

"Darya," he cried. "Larisa—"

But they were already gone, the destruction they had left in their wake admitting still more of the horde.

By now the harelip's pistol had gone dry as well.

The two men stood, back to back, machetes at the ready, by the great slabs where Rasikov had given his family life, and in that moment, Rasikov knew what he must do. Gritting his teeth, he turned his back to the horde of zombies and giant arthropods, lifting the machete.

In the same instant, the harelip, turning, must have reached the same conclusion.

"No, Doctor—" he cried, his hands uplifted.

Too late.

With a single sweep of the razor-sharp blade, Rasikov sent the harelip's body tumbling to the floor. Grimacing at the shock of greasy hair, he snatched up the head. At the surgical table, he buzzed open the skull. It was a bloodbath by now, the zombies staggering back before the onslaught of the enormous centipedes that slipped among them, bearing them to the floor and sucking huge gobbets of bloody flesh into their clattering maws. Rasikov stumbled across the room, mad with terror. Shouldering over the fallen bot, he tore open its cranial cavity and ripped free the positronic brain. He lowered the harelip's slippery brain into the metallic skull. Standing, he drove back a handful of encroaching zombies—one, two, three—with his blade. He fell to his knees and wired in Dmitri's brain with trembling hands. He armed the warbot, and flicked it on.

The harelip's eyes lit up, yellow beacons in the gloom.

He heaved his massive frame up, his cylindrical head rotating to take in the chaos, and then he brought his arms to bear. Bullets tore through the zombies, blowing them back. Centipedes exploded in fountains of ichor.

"Yes, Dmitri!" Rasikov cried in triumph, swinging his machete. His experiment had succeeded at last!

Dmitri fought with a vicious intelligence Rasikov had never seen, squeezing off single rounds with inhuman accuracy. The backs of zombie heads blew out in gouts of blood and brains, their bodies convulsing on the floor. Others staggered into the holes in the floor and fell silently into the basement, their arms grasping. Centipedes exploded in spectacular fountains of yellow pulp.

Back to back, they fought, the doctor and his assistant. Heads rolled. Venomous maws fell snapping to the floor. How long the battle lasted, Rasikov could not guess. His arms grew heavy. The smoke from Dmitri's guns stung his eyes. Yet a time came when the battle shifted. The horde dwindled. The black armored monstrosities drew back into the darkness of the porch, then the street beyond. He advanced across a floor slick with viscid ichor, with blood and brains, driving back the last of the dead.

The roar of Dmitri's weaponry died away.

At last only snapping heads remained to pose any danger. Rasikov made the rounds of the room, kicking them into the centipede holes. For the moment his victory held at bay his grief for his wife and daughter. Dimly, far down in his brain he nursed the hope that they would someday be reunited. Respect and gratitude for his deformed assistant ran through his conscious thoughts.

He heard the clump of metal feet at his back.

He turned to congratulate the behemoth machine. "Dmitri—"

"Dog," the thing said, the voice in its speaking grill inhuman, and abrupt understanding seized Rasikov: the machine had helped him destroy the invaders only so it could have him for itself. He darted across the room and flung back a supply cabinet door. Inside, nestled in a foam-lined box, lay the clever device he had used to bring down the three warbots back in Chernigov, when this had all begun. He snatched it up even as the Dmitri-bot seized him in its metal pincers, lifted him high in the air—Rasikov's feet dangled kicking a full meter off the floor—and slammed him down atop the nearest table.

Breath exploded from Rasikov's lungs.

A single word issued from the thing's speaker grille. "Dog," it said.

Rasikov punched the button on the device, punched it and punched it in desperation, but nothing happened. The bot was its own creature now, severed from the master server by virtue of its human brain. *Too late*, Rasikov thought. *Too late*.

"No, please—" he gasped, tears welling up in his eyes. To come so close to achieving everything he had hoped for, and have it all turn to ashes in his mouth. "I'm sorry—"

The bot did not respond.

Or perhaps it did: actions speak louder than words.

With one massive claw the robot pinned Rasikov to the table. With the other it strapped him tightly to its surface. Then, with surprising delicacy for such a massive machine, it tore off Rasikov's pinky. The pain was screaming agony—and Rasikov *did* scream. He screamed and screamed as the robot worked its way slowly around the fingers of both hands, taking its time, savoring the moment as it plucked each one and dropped them to the floor by the table.

"Dog," the Dmitri-bot said.

Sergei Rasikov screamed for a long time.

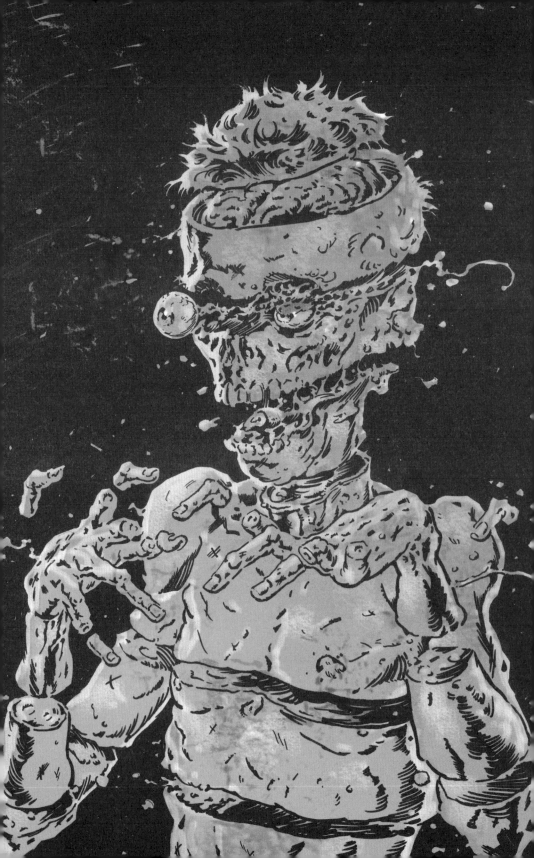

SPINBOT

Simon Kurt Unsworth

ONE

THE PIT WAS huge. Thornhill stood as close to its edge as he could get, looking in, watching as the flames leapt around the bodies and the smoke rose in greasy, black twists that fragmented in the rain. Water dripped from him and spattered onto the muddy ground, fell hard from the grey sky and hissed, sibilant, as it hit the flames. It smelled; no, it *stank*, of roasting meat and burning hair, and rottenness and baking excrement. Occasionally, there was a dull pop as something expanded and ruptured. *Bowels*, he thought, *or maybe bellies*.

The road to the pit was busy, the sanibots queuing in neat lines to drop in their loads. They were simple robots, wheelbases mounted by tilting platforms and a single movable armature topped by a mechanical claw. *Typical*, he thought sourly, *they can't build their own warbots, but they can manage garbage disposal*. Even that, though, they'd made inefficient; back in Philadelphia, he'd heard that they'd converted iron-smelting plants, using workbots to scoop out the slurry at the end of the day and keep the furnaces burning, incinerating thousands upon thousands of corpses every day with a minimum of fuss or mess. Here, they'd dug this vast pit and were simply dropping the zombies into it.

Other sanibots ringed the pit, occasionally squirting plumes of flammable liquid into it to keep the fires burning, their trays loaded with barrels and hosepipes. *Barbarism*, Thornhill thought, *with neat queues.*

Devon, the *left-tenant* they'd sent to meet him, was still arguing with the cleribot when Thornhill got back to the jeep. One of the papers was stamped wrong, or in the wrong place, and the bot was refusing to let Thornhill leave the compound. "He is not cleared," the bot insisted, its voice toneless. "Without clearance, he cannot pass."

"He has government clearance," said Devon, waving another piece of paper in front of the bot. "Look, special clearance. Captain Thornhill is here on official business, at the invitation of her Majesty's government."

"He is not cleared," the bot said again.

"Christ," said Devon, turning to Thornhill. "I'm sorry, sir, but do you have your US army identification with you?" Wordlessly, Thornhill handed it over and then went back to watching the thick coils of smoke rising, the rain falling, while Devon carried on arguing with the bot. Gunfire sounded, sporadic and distant.

"We can go," said Devon from behind him after another couple of minutes.

"The bot cleared me?" asked Thornhill.

"No," said Devon. "I bypassed him." Behind him, the cleribot was motionless, the red glare of its LED eye dulled and empty, a small brass plate in the side of its head open, wires dangling. Devon picked up Thornhill's kitbag and carried it to a distant jeep. As they pulled away from the compound, Thornhill's last view was of another sanibot tipping its load of twisted flesh and tangling limbs into the pit and the flames jittering hungrily up to accept the offering.

They drove for hours; well, *left-tenant* Devon drove and Thornhill rested, his head leaning against the window and jolting whenever the jeep bounced. The landscape changed as they went, from the grey urban sprawl of a town whose name Thornhill didn't know to drab hills covered in stunted trees, gorse and grass. He saw no zombies, although they did see a squad of warbots at one point, tramping down the road back towards the town they had just left. They slowed as they passed the bots and the lead, spotting Thornhill's uniform, snapped off a salute and said, "Hiya, Buddy!" Thornhill did not reply.

For the last part of the journey, Thornhill dozed and dreamed of home; in his dreams, it was quiet and calm. The last time he had seen it, it had been on fire, its streets thronged with the dead, the air full of bullets and screams and mechanized voices, its streets running with oily water from the hoses playing water across the fires. Ash and cinders from the burning buildings danced in the noise above his head, falling in lazy, plunging spirals like dirty snow, covering the world in a skin of shadow and grime.

"WELCOME TO MINISTRY POINT," said Devon.

Thornhill had slept longer than he realized and the landscape had changed yet again. The road was now in a valley, louring hills with grey stone scree slopes at either side, a huge metal fence ahead. They had come to a halt in front of a gate in the fence, which was shut. There was no sign of movement, except for the swiveling of the remote guns on the top of the gateposts; both were pointing towards their vehicle. The fence was a recent construction, hastily done, and already the atmosphere was working on it so that streaks of rust were appearing around the welded sections, stretching down towards the ground. Thornhill climbed out of the jeep, looking around warily, stretching and making his back creak. The guns moved again, tracking him.

"There aren't many here," said Devon from the other side of the jeep. "It's one of the reasons Ministry Point was chosen. There are no habitations nearby, just abandoned fishing villages, so there's no reason for them to come, not really, and their numbers are low. It's not so bad now, but in winter the weather's fucking horrible. That helps, though; the cold keeps them away and makes them slow."

"Yes," said Thornhill. It made sense, when he thought about it, somewhere quiet and with space to work.

"We fenced all around the Point, so that the only way in is through this gate or by the sea. We kept the harbor operational because we use a couple of the smaller islands for field work, and sometimes we get deliveries that way."

"Field work?"

"Testing the bots. The islands are uninhabited, so they're ideal testing grounds."

Thornhill waited as Devon went to the gate and held their IDs up, wondering if the same issue that had so bothered the cleribot would delay them here, but it did not. The gate swung open, revealing a further stretch of road and a guard's hut, padlocked shut. One of its windows was broken, the glass held in place by strips of silvery duct tape.

"It's another half mile," said Devon. "Come on." The two men climbed back into the jeep and drove on.

TWO

"WE'RE A SMALL Team," said the woman, Victoria James, who had introduced herself as the Civilian Liaison Officer. They were standing in front of a set of low prefab buildings, painted in dull greens and greys. She was tall and slim, tired-looking, but pretty. When she turned and led them through the main doors, Thornhill found himself watching the sway of her buttocks appreciatively. Looking up, he caught Devon doing the same thing. The man smiled at him, sheepish, and said quietly, "She's not a senior officer, I'm allowed to look." Thornhill grinned, the first smile he had formed in how long? Days? Weeks? It made his cheeks ache and he dropped it.

"We're isolated here," continued James as she walked, swaying nicely ahead of Thornhill, "so we run on a skeleton staff, with support from the bots. We have war- and troopbots protecting the fence, although not as many as we've asked for, and a couple of aquabots covering the dock and making sure nothing comes in from seawards. We have workbots and a docbot, but we still have to do things mostly the old-fashioned way, by hand." She glanced back over her shoulder as she said this, flashing Thornhill a tired, low wattage smile. He didn't smile back.

"I don't mean to sound ungrateful," James said, "but we're at a loss. We don't have enough staff, or time, or stores, and on paper everything's perfect, it should work."

"But it doesn't." It was a statement, not a question.

"No."

"You better show me, then," said Thornhill. "And I'll need to meet the rest of the team."

Wargle was perhaps the tiredest looking man Thornhill had ever seen. The flesh under his eyes was black, sagging like loose sailcloth, and his hair was greasy. Unlike James, who looked clean despite her tiredness, Wargle looked like he hadn't showered in days, and smelled like it. When they shook, his grip was clammy and it was all Thornhill could do not to wipe his palm on his jacket after releasing the man's hand. The roll of plans he passed to Thornhill was battered and creased, held together with a tangle of elastic bands. Unrolled, they looked like a mechanical palimpsest, the original drawings lost under notations and overdrawing and doodles.

There were seven of them in the refectory. As well as Thornhill, Devon, James and Wargle, there were Bolton and Patel, Wargle's assistants, and Jackson, who described himself as the "general dogs-body and zombie farmer." All of them looked exhausted to varying degrees, and when they spoke, their voices carried the despondent notes of failure. They had spread the plans for the spinbot out on the refectory tables, weighting the corners with salt and pepper pots and tubs of ketchup that had scabs of old sauce crusted around their rims. Despite the complexity of the plans and the confusion of additional marks and notes, what Thornhill was seeing made sense; it should work.

"And you say it's never worked?" he asked eventually.

"No, that's not true," said Wargle. "It works very well, *perfectly* well, until we try to give it self-direction."

"Self direction?"

"When we turn on the AI," said Patel. "There's something about

the algorithms that doesn't fit with mechanics, and it goes batshit."
Patel's accent was lilting, gentle, and Thornhill liked it. Recently, he
seemed to have only listened to American voices, human and bot,
and being here in England (*Scotland,* he reminded himself, *we've
come over the border into Scotland*) was pleasant if only for hearing
these new tones. Wargle's was gruff, cockney, James' the clipped
tones of someone who had tried hard to lose an accent and Devon's
something that Thornhill didn't recognize, all glottal stops and ab-
breviated vowels. He wondered how he sounded to them.

"What happens?"

"It goes batshit," repeated Patel. "Loss of motor control, erratic
and disjointed movement, and a final collapse. Two earlier models
burnt out their engines, trying to carry out opposing actions at once
we think. We're trying to fit US AI technology into British engineering, and it's just not working."

"Whether it's actually intelligence or not is a matter of discussion," said Bolton, speaking for the first time. "The way the warbots
act, you have to doubt it. It's more like artificial stupidity than artificial intelligence."

"Indeed?" asked Thornhill.

"The Spinbot is designed to take account of what we see as fun-
damental flaws with the warbots," cut in James smoothly. "Perhaps
it's easier if we show you a practical demonstration?"

"Yes," said Thornhill. "I think perhaps you'd better."

"Agreed. Jackson, could you organize it?"

"Yes, ma'am." Jackson's accent was soft, a hint rather than a
bludgeon, and it made Thornhill think of peasants and farmwork-
ers for some reason. "It'll be ready in the morning."

THERE HAD BEEN a line of bullet holes stitched across the harbor
wall, and there were more across the mooring dock at the island.
As they disembarked, Thornhill following James down the unsteady ramp, followed by Bolton and Patel wheeling something
under tarpaulin, the periscope eyes of the aquabots tracked them
from further out in the bay.

"Have they helped?" Thornhill asked, intrigued. He had only ever heard about aquabots, never seen them in action. They didn't have a great reputation.

"It's hard to tell," said James. "We have no idea what they do under the water, because they don't report in to us, so they might be stopping all sorts, but my guess is no. A couple of times we've had dead whales wash up on the beach covered in bullet holes, and we're fairly sure they shot at the transport boat once, although they didn't do any damage." Thornhill looked back at the stemmed eye, glinting in the early sunlight. Its red pupil contracted as he watched, tracking them as they moved up the beach, bobbing in the swell.

"Did they shoot the harbor? The dock?" asked Thornhill.

"That was the warbots," said Bolton. "Both times, firing at things that they thought they'd seen but hadn't, damaging things when they didn't need to. We've managed to wash the blood away, but it took a while."

"Blood?"

"They killed a technician called Talbot," said Bolton. "Accidentally. When we complained, we were told that it was a regrettable death, unfortunate but to be expected, collateral damage, and that it was to be ignored. The warbots trundle about the place, all shiny and bright and gleaming and massive and wisecracking, but you know what? They're fucking useless things. At least the troopbots will take orders sometimes."

"And your bot will be better?"

"It'll be less destructive," said James, "to the environment at least. Warbots aren't exactly discriminating when they start firing."

"No," replied Thornhill. "I don't suppose they are."

The island was small; viewed on the map it looked little more than a dot of grey against the blue background. In reality, it was a an outthrust of dark, scabrous rock covered in gorse and sparse sea grass, the beach a shingle strip leading up to the open land. There was a long fence encircling the beach and a portion of scrubland beyond with observation towers on its seaward side. At the fence's center was a large gate, and at the gate was Jackson. He was dressed in an outfit that looked like fisherman's waders, rubber legs and belly cinched tight around his midriff. He waved at Thornhill; Thornhill, almost despite himself, waved back.

James climbed up the ladder to the top of one of the towers and Thornhill followed, glad that James was wearing trousers as he went up behind her. He was attracted to her despite the fact that she was nothing like Mary; perhaps that was the point. It had been thirteen months since he had seen her last, thirteen months since the falling ash and the screams and the bullets.

Thirteen months since Mary died and since the child at her side, Thornhill's and Mary's child, died with her.

As Thornhill and James settled themselves against the railing of the observation platform, Wargle appeared on the next tower along. Patel and Bolton pulled the tarpaulin off the thing they had man-handled down to the beach, revealing a tall metallic cylinder mounted on a wide caterpillar tracks. Sensor arrays were mounted around the top of the cylinder, and below this a series of grooves like a screw thread were cut into the metal frame. As they busied themselves with it, Wargle called over, "It'll be under my control initially." James raised a hand in silent reply.

"Ready," called Patel, and both he and Bolton ran to Wargle's tower and climbed up to join him. Jackson waited until they were safely on the platform alongside the older man and then turned and opened the gates.

"Hey!" he shouted, his voice loud in the island's peace. "Hey! Food, you dumb bastards!" Thornhill watched, intrigued. Jackson had walked through the open gateway and was still shouting, danc-ing and jigging, waving his arms about. Making a target of himself. "Hey!" he called again. "Hey, fuckwits! Hey morons! Lunchtime!"

It's breakfast time, thought Thornhill abstractly, and then stopped thinking as the first of them appeared. It was always like this, no matter how many times he came close to them; a moment where the sheer impossibility of it took his breath away, where the sheer *absurdity* of them was numbing.

He heard them before seeing them, a low moaning that rose on the wind, and then they came out from the gullies and shambled out from behind the rocks, staggering and lurching, heading for Jackson. In only a few minutes there were dozens, converging on the dancing man in a shuffling frenzy. Most were long-dead, Thornhill saw; their skin grey and ruptured, but one or two were newer, fresher, their skin the color of curdled milk. A gull swooped in, snatching at the torn flesh of one of the shambling things and then falling upwards into the sky, a greying string dangling from its beak; the dead man ignored it.

"Come on!" shouted Jackson. The nearest of the things reached him, holding out clutching hands, fingers curled like old twigs and keening furiously, and then Jackson stopped dancing and ran. He dashed back in through the gates and to the tower inhabited by Thornhill and James, climbing the ladder rapidly, leaving the gates open behind him. The zombies followed, clustering in the gateway, pushing and flailing as they poured through and chased the man.

"Watch, please," called Wargle. There was a loud whirring, and the machine on the beach jerked to life.

As the bot rolled up the shingle, the air around its cylindrical body seemed to blur, a silvery sheen appearing to encase it. The zombies ignored it, as they always did the bots, concentrating on Jackson. The first of them had reached the bottom of the tower now and were shaking at the ladder and the thick metal legs. Their attentions reached Thornhill as tremors, shivers that he felt through the soles of his feet, and a scent of corruption and spoil. There were loud, wordless groans and shrieks surrounding them. He reached for his gun but James placed a restraining hand on his arm and shook her head. "Watch," she said.

The spinbot came closer, was perhaps twenty feet away, when the closest zombie's head exploded. No, thought Thornhill, not exploded, *disintegrated*, pieces of desiccated flesh stuttering into the air as a noise like the whine of flies sounded. The noise deepened and the next zombie's head collapsed, spliced and torn, flesh and bone spraying to its side. Just beyond it a female zombie's hair fluttered briefly and then her head, too, came apart. For a moment her brain was revealed, a decayed white mass inside the flailing hair, and then it, too, was gone. The noise of flesh and brains falling to the ground was like rainfall, a dull pattering, and the bot came on, reaching into the mass of zombies at the foot of the tower. Clouds of fragmenting flesh rose, the stink worsening as their rot was fully released, before falling back into that silver blur and spinning off sideways. *Wires*, Thornhill realized, *wires like a giant weed-wacker, a monster strimmer. Oh, that's good; no, that's* brilliant.

There was a clang as the wire hit the leg of the tower. A spark the size and color of a flaming egg leapt from the tower, and immediately the bot turned. The whirr of the spinning wire dropped, its pitch lowering as it retracted slightly, the halo reducing, and the zombies continued to jitter and burst, stripped to nothing in seconds; it took less than a minute before the cluster of zombies around the tower was reduced to a pile of torn flesh. The bot turned, its caterpillar tracks grinding over the fallen bodies, and moved towards the gate.

"I'll switch to AI," called Wargle. He held up a control that looked oddly like the kind of thing Pete's remote-controlled toys had used, and pressed a button on it.

Immediately, the bot faltered. It jerked forwards and stopped, jerked again as the arrays around its top flared to life, and then it carried on rolling towards the gates. There were five zombies near the entrance, spread out in a thin line; more were approaching from beyond the gate. The bot began to spin again, the whine picking up, and the first zombie was felled as the wires tore into it. The bot altered direction, cutting across the ground towards the next zombie, a child. The blur around the bot lowered, dropping down the groves in its body until it was the same level as the dead child's head, which splintered into chunks and a shower of maggots and dusty skin. Its legs cracked as the bot rolled over them, turning on its base. The next zombie came apart from the shoulders up as the wire raised itself along the bot's frame, but the fourth managed to stagger past it and towards the first tower.

More of the dead poured in through the gates, the bot spinning and flailing, some of the zombies falling to it but others getting past. The body spun on the tracks, the mosquito burn of the wires growing louder and more frantic. Thornhill could smell it even over the stink of dead flesh, the smell of burning oil and metal, of things overheating. The bot's eyes glared and the antennae on its head twitched as it tried to track the zombies. Something groaned inside it as it tried to turn itself, the wire blurring faster as it cut into a woman's arm, severing it in a puff of dried blood and shredded material. She fell sideways, crawling and pitching like a drunk on the deck of a ship.

As the first of the zombies reached the tower's foot, black smoke started to pour from the bot's insides, coming out in thin, capering streams from the slots. There was another loud groan, a clunk, and then the bot ground to a halt. The wires spun for a moment longer and then, with a wheezing sound, they slowed but did not retract, falling lower and lower until they dragged across the ground, pulling furrows through it before stopping completely. More smoke poured form the bot's body, the thick clouds reminding Thornhill of the smoke rising from the charnel pits he had seen the day before.

"Fuckery!" shouted Bolton, his voice echoing in the morning air. Jackson leaned over the railing, aiming his rifle at the zombies below. Quickly, and without fuss, he shot each of them in the head and then climbed down the ladder. Thornhill realized why he was wearing the rubber waders; the mound of torn and dead flesh at the bottom of the ladder was deep, and by the time he had made his way over it to open ground, Jackson was smeared up to his belly with black slime and clinging lumps of skin and muscle and fat. He quickly picked off the rest of the zombies, using a single shot on each one as he walked to the gate. As he closed them, pushing back the ones still outside, Bolton and Patel were already climbing down the ladder of their tower and going to the spinbot. Wargle remained on the platform, his shoulders slumped and his head down.

"What's wrong with you, girl?" Thornhill heard Patel say as he climbed up onto the bot's caterpillar tread and peered into its body, still spewing smoke slowly from the slots in its side. Bolton went to the machine's rear and peered under it, lifting a hood in the cowling and starting to poke at whatever was inside.

"It's burned out," he said, "although not completely. We can salvage some of the components, I think."

Thornhill holstered his gun, which he'd not realized he'd drawn. James offered another tired smile, saying, "Again. This is what happens every time, this or something like it. The AI doesn't take, the machinery fights itself, and then it goes offline, breaks down."

"It's not off," said Thornhill, looking at one of the camera sockets on the bot's head, where a pale glow was visible. The socket jerked, dropped, jerked up further, flared and focused on Patel. "Move!" shouted Thornhill. "Patel, move! *Move!*"

The man looked up, his expression confused, and then the bot's engines coughed once, the wire leaping from the ground as it span violently around. Patel's expression disintegrated into a red misted thing, the mist flowering out as the wires span rapidly through it again and again, wet flesh spraying across the front of the bot. Patel's body remained standing for a second and then collapsed, slumping across the bot's tracks and rolling to the ground where it lay a patch of grass growing rapidly darker as his corpse bled out.

Wargle was shouting something, holding the remote aloft again and pointing it towards the Spinbot as Bolton staggered back from its rear, twisting and stumbling as he went. The bot jerked again, the ground-glass noise of its gears agonizing, and Bolton screamed. The wire dropped, flaying the top of the man's skull off, hair and bone and skin and brain rising above him in a wet cloud, his scream lurching upwards and then crashing down. He managed to crawl several feet before he collapsed onto what remained of his face. Brains slathered across the ground around him, tangling into his sodden hair.

James screamed, the sound jolting Thornhill. The bot made another lurch forward, towards Jackson, who loosed off a round at it. The shot glanced off with a metallic crack, burying itself into the earth to the machine's left; Thornhill saw a clod of grass leap as though stung. Wargle shouted again, still waving the remote, jabbing at it. Jackson ran, the bot making a uneven movement to cut him off, more smoke spurting from it, one set of wheels coming loose from its track, the top tilting, the wire slashing diagonally now, churning the earth as though searching for the buried bullet. Jackson darted back towards the gate and the zombies beyond sent up another low groan, fingers wrapping around the thick metal posts and rattling it as Jackson came close. One managed to slip a hand through, a woman, wrists slimmer than the others, and grasped at Jackson, the fingers slipping from the rubber back of his suit. He shrieked, jumping forwards to escape the grip, and the wire hummed above his head, a silvery arc in the morning light.

Jackson dropped and the bot tried to follow, its tubular body leaning. More earth leapt in chewed pieces as Jackson tried to roll away, and then the bot leaned too far and collapsed completely; the body tore away from the tracks with a sound of bolts and metal fracturing, the wire clanging around the treads and tangling as it fell from the base. More smoke poured from it, thick plumes alive with the firefly dart of sparks and electrical lightning, and then, finally, it was still.

THEY HAD THE robot opened out on a table in the lab, several floors under the refectory. On three tables, actually, one for the base, one for its body and one for the wire. The latter was covered in lumps of flesh both fresh and old, and Jackson had handled it wearing thick rubber gloves. Clumps of mud had fallen out of the treads as they had wheeled the base in, leaving an imprint of itself across the floor. The room smelled of blood and torn earth and oil.

"There's nothing," said Wargle, dispiritedly. He was peering into the body's innards like a pathologist at an autopsy. *I suppose it is an autopsy, of a sort,* Thornhill thought, and said, "Let me look."

The AI unit, connected down and up via a series of wires and tubes to the base and the sensors, was set in an armored box in the center of the bot's body. Opening the box revealed circuits and processors that Thornhill didn't recognize. "I thought you were using US technology?" he asked.

"We are," said Wargle. "But what you sent us didn't fit with the new operating system that the government purchased for use in our bots, so we've had to rework it."

"What new operating system?"

"The one we use," said Wargle, as though speaking to a child. "The government tendered out for companies to provide the operating system when the need for one became apparent, and we use the one that won the bidding process."

Tendering? Bidding? What was this? As far as Thornhill and his colleagues knew, the Brits were using the system they had provided them with; this was the first he'd heard otherwise, and he said so. "Well, why would we tell you?" said Wargle. "We don't belong to you, you aren't our lords and masters. We made a choice based on cost and efficiency, and it wasn't the system you provided us with."

"Cost and efficiency?" repeated Thornhill. "It was cheap? And so efficient that it couldn't run the AI software we sent? Christ, what a mess. No wonder the fucking thing doesn't work."

"The diagnostics told us that there's no real compatibility problem between the programming and the system we use," said James quietly. "That was Patel's main area of expertise, the interface between the two. Bolton was his assistant, and the expert in the mechanics of the spinbot, linking the processors and the physical machinery so that one did what the other said."

"Oh, so you do use computers?" he asked, thinking of the rolled and tattered plans they had shown him.

"Of course," said Wargle, his voice rising. "We're not completely uncivilized, you know, we do have some technical know-how. However, when it became clear that we had an on-going problem with the bot, I required the team to return to paper calculations rather than rely on computer thinking, as we couldn't be sure where the error was."

"Fair point," said Thornhill, peering again into the machine's guts. "What's this?" he asked, pointing to a small black chip that was nestled like a spider on one of the circuit boards.

"I don't know," said Wargle, "I'd need to check Patel's plans. He and Bolton made lots of changes as they went along. As Victoria says, it was Patel's area of expertise rather than mine."

"Check," said Thornhill, poking at the chip with a screwdriver. It had no maker's mark, its black skin a dull plastic. He began to pry the chip away from the board. "I don't recognize it, and I need to. If Patel's done this, I need to understand the What and Why of it."

"Patel," said James quietly, and began to cry. Thornhill looked at her; everyone looked at her, Wargle and Jackson and Devon, and none of them moved. Eventually, Thornhill went to her and put his arm around her, and she fell against his shirt and wept.

By nightfall, Thornhill was exhausted. After James had stopped crying, they had regrouped in the refectory over coffee; none of them had felt like eating. The rest of the day had been spent going over each plan, comparing it to the dissected bot on the tables, picking through the tangles of wire and burned out servomotors, tracking filaments down from the sensor arrays in and out of the various junctions of cabling and wire. Much as he hated to admit it, Thornhill could find nothing that would explain the bot's behavior. It simply didn't work.

Thornhill was on his bed, was almost asleep, when there was a knock on his door. Opening it, he found James standing in the corridor.

"Can I come in?" she asked. After a moment, Thornhill stood back and let her pass. She entered the room, looking around it but finding nowhere to sit. Finally, she sat on the edge of the bed and said, "They're not welcoming, these rooms, are they?"

"They're rooms," said Thornhill. He had stayed in worse, and better, over the past year. It was under cover, there was a bed, and it was safe; there wasn't much else he could hope for, not really.

"I suppose," said James. "I came to say thank you for today. For taking care of me, I mean."

"I didn't take care of you," said Thornhill. He hadn't; James had only cried for a few minutes before she had pulled the tears back into herself, her breathing hitching back to normality.

"You did," she said. "We've been here for months now, and it's like we've been forgotten except for the shittier and shittier messages asking when we're going to produce something that works. You're the first new person any of us has seen in months, only Devon gets off the base."

"You're safer here," he said, thinking of columns of smoke, of the warbots heading back towards the city, of dancing flames and the marching, shuffling, inexorable dead. "It's getting worse out there."

"I know," she said. "We get the news, the official stuff and the unofficial, truthful stuff. We have the internet still, and can talk to people out there if they're around."

"Who do you talk to?" he asked. Because there was nowhere else, he sat next to her on the bed.

"No one," she replied. "I haven't had a conversation that isn't about bots or the dead in months. There isn't anyone, not any more. I was married, but he—" She broke off, struggling. Thornhill placed a hand on hers and said, "I know. I know."

"I thought being here would help," she said. "Away from it all, safe, no memories. It doesn't make any difference, though."

"No," he said, thinking of Mary, of Pete, of the way their ghosts chased him wherever he went. He didn't let go of James' hand. She turned towards him, leaning in so he could smell her scent, clean and fresh.

"Can I stay here tonight?" she asked.

"Yes," he said, and they spent the night curled into each other in the narrow bed, touching but doing nothing more, and they were not disturbed until morning.

THREE

THORNHILL HAD ONE of the dreams he had come to regard as nightmares. In it, Mary and Pete were in their kitchen, the sun coming in through the windows and warming them so that they glowed and smiled and smelled good. Although he couldn't see himself, Thornhill could feel that he was dressed in shorts and a loose shirt, that he was relaxed. They had a day ahead of them to spend together, and although no one in the dream spoke, they nodded and smiled at each other and he somehow knew that the sun would shine all day and where they went would be peaceful and that it would create memories for them that would last a life. In the dream, Pete was unmarked, Mary was unmarked; both were alive. Life was normal, boring, simple, and when he woke the memories of the dream clung to him and for a moment he didn't remember about death and fires and bots, there was just Mary and Pete and the life they had made before everything fell apart, and then it fell apart and he was crashing back into the world.

Victoria was warm in Thornhill's arms. They were spooning, he curled against her back, his left arm over her and his right under her neck. Neither was naked; she had kept her panties on and borrowed one of his T-shirts, he was still in his underwear. His vision filled with her hair, cut short so that the curve of her skull was visible through it. Mary's hair had been long, auburn, thick. It wasn't fair, he told himself, to compare Victoria to Mary, it did them both a disservice. They were different in looks, in shape and smell.

In life, and in death.

Victoria moved, rolling slightly and pressing herself back against him. Her legs were long, smooth, and her buttocks firm. He shifted slightly, moving away, creating a gap between them, only inches but enough. She twisted and as she did, he closed his eyes and breathed slow, sleepy. He felt her look at him for a long time before she carefully disentangled herself from his arms and rose from the bed. Thornhill risked opening an eye and watched her, long and lithe, dress quickly. He closed his eye again as she pulled the T-shirt over her head, listening to the sound of material rustling and papers turning as she went around the room. After another minute, she brushed his cheek gently.

Thornhill did his best impression of a waking man, mumbling as he rose from slumber.

"Thank you," said Victoria quietly. She leaned down and kissed him on the cheek. "Thank you for last night. For yesterday."

"My pleasure," Thornhill said, but wasn't sure whether it had actually been a pleasure or not. It was a betrayal, wasn't it?

"I have to go," said Victoria. "Work work work."

"Yes," he said, sitting. "I suppose there is."

"I'll see you later," she said and with that, she was gone.

HE FOUND THEM in the workshop.

"We need more help," Devon was saying to Victoria as Thornhill opened the door. "We need replacements for Patel and Bolton, and we need them urgently."

"I know," Victoria said. "I've tried talking to them this morning, but they say there's no one."

"They sent the American," said Wargle.

"They did," said Thornhill from the doorway. Wargle didn't look bothered that Thornhill had overheard him; Devon looked embarrassed and Victoria smiled at him. Jackson was at the rear of the room tinkering inside an open bot, and saluted. Thornhill didn't salute back.

"Why you?" asked Wargle. "Why not more manpower, scientists or engineers?"

"Because there's only me," said Thornhill. "You're up here, away from everything and it's quiet, but out there? It's gone to shit."

"We know," said Wargle.

"No," said Thornhill, "you don't. The bots help, but it's a losing battle and the US can't keep providing hardware to the UK. In the US, entire cities are overrun, no-go areas, and the UK is going the same way. High density population areas are the worst hit; London, Manchester, Liverpool, Birmingham, all gone, all dead."

There was silence in the room. "Gone?" said Devon eventually.

"Gone," said Thornhill. "We don't have the ammunition or the bots to hold the lines of the dead back in our cities, let alone yours, so your project is critically important. This country needs to develop its own defenses, and urgently. That's why I'm here."

"Why weren't we told?" said Jackson.

"Told what? That your country's on its knees? That our country's on its knees? That the whole fucking world's on its knees? I don't know. Ask your government, they make those decisions. Me, I've come to find out what's happening here, and nothing else. So, how's the spinbot?"

"Fixed," said Jackson. "Well, I've put it back together and replaced the damaged parts. Whether it'll work or not is another matter." He looked at Wargle; Wargle didn't reply.

"If the spinbot's fixed, what are you working on?" said Thornhill, looking past the man at the splayed bot on the far table.

"A troopbot," said Jackson.

"Why?" The bot was lying on its back on the table, its arms draped wide and its chest cavity open. Its legs dangled off the end of the table.

"Servicing it," said Jackson. "The coastal air plays havoc with their guts, so we open them up and make sure nothing's corroding. We do it for all the bots assigned to us."

"The bots self-repair," said Thornhill, walking to the crippled machine. "We don't provide spare parts."

"Don't we fucking know it!" said Jackson. "You also didn't give the buggers the ability to cope with damp sea air. It's British air, see? Tough stuff, eats through anything, high in salt. I have to make all the parts myself. Well, me and Bolton did, but he tended to concentrate on the spinny and left me to the repair work."

Jackson gestured to a workbench at the far end of the room. On it were strings of metal coil, circuits, pieces of servomotor and assorted pins and screws and bolts. Computer monitors showed revolving 3D pictures of the bot's insides, the traceries of connective wiring and mechanical muscle picked out in different colors. Thornhill took it all in, sighed, and said, "Is the spinbot ready to go?"

"Yes," said Wargle. "We've made some amendments to the design, and I'm hopeful it will work this time."

"Then let's run the test," said Thornhill.

"No can do," said Jackson. "The island's running low on zombies. We need to go fishing."

THEY WERE IN the cab of an old troop transporter, its canvas sides removed and replaced with chicken wire wrapped tight to the rusting metal frames. The wooden benches had also been removed, and the tailboard had been replaced by a larger ramp that reached to the top of the frame when it was up, and which was attached to a winch that was bolted to the cab's roof. The engine was noisy and old, and its breath came in rank gasps through the air vents. Jackson's cigarettes smelled worse.

"There's a story about these," Jackson said, looking at the burning tube clenched between his fingers. The paper was grey rather than white and it burned unevenly, occasionally spitting tiny embers out from itself.

"Yes?"

"We can't get proper cigarettes any more, because you Yanks stopped exporting them to us, and our cigarette factories haven't got enough tobacco to feed everyone's needs. Story is, the government rang the factory owners in a panic and said, 'You've got to make us some more cigarettes, the addicts are getting restless, and most of our soldiers smoke!' 'What can we do?' say the factory owners, 'we've got fucking nothing to make the cigarettes with.'

"'Nothing?' asks the government. 'Nothing,' says the owners, 'except the sweepings from the factory floor.'

"'Well, use that, then,' says the government. 'We can't, it won't stick together,' say the owners. 'Don't worry,' says the government, 'we have just the stuff', and sent the owners tons and tons of cowshit.

"'We can't use cowshit,' say the owners, 'people will notice.'

"'Just do it,' says the government, so the factories start to make cigarettes out of sweepings and cowshit, and eventually they ring the government and say, 'Well, they look like cigarettes, and they smell like cigarettes, but there's a problem.'

"'What?' asked the government.

"'They still taste like shit,' and there's a moment's silence from the government, and then they say, 'Never mind that, we'll call them Victory V's, there was a wartime brand called that. It'll generate some of the old blitz spirit! Besides, addicts will smoke shit if it feeds their addiction.' So that's what they did, rolled up factory sweepings and cowshit and called them Victory V's, and you know what? We do, we smoke them, all us stupid bastards, because we're British and we put up with things."

They were driving slowly on the roads around abandoned villages, passing three since leaving the base, and fields in which no laborers worked.

"There's no one left around here, just us," said Jackson. "The government moved them out, because we couldn't protect them. Some stayed, silly bastards determined not to leave the houses they were born in or something, and we did what we could, but most got eaten fairly early on. Now, there are just us and the sheep and the cows and the grass and the zombies. And there aren't many sheep or cows left."

It was true; Thornhill had only seen a few cattle, scrawny beasts standing dejectedly in the fields around them. Without humans to care for them, they were struggling. Everything was struggling. Even the dead in the fields seemed lackluster, watching the truck as it rumbled past but not following. Most of them were rotted close to immobility, he saw, their flesh liquefying as they stumbled around. Here and there, dark shapes were crumbled to the ground, but whether they were animal of human it was impossible to tell.

"There used to be enough in the fields around here to keep us stocked," said Jackson, "but now there aren't. We've used them up, so we have to get them another way." They were approaching a large field surrounded by the sort of fence Thornhill was beginning to recognize, a hastily constructed metal barrier of unevenly spaced poles about six feet high. It leaned drunkenly out at some points, held together by additional twists of baling wire and, at one point, a thick blue wrap of nylon cord. Rust wept down the metal from the bolts holding it together.

Where it ran along the road, the dead were pressed up against the inside of the fence, watching. Another truck was parked at the far end of the field and Jackson pulled up next to it. As they climbed down, he said, "This is how we get our zombies now."

A man climbed down from the second truck, another canvas-sided troop carrier without canvas. Its rear was half-full of zombies. Jackson walked along the side of it, looking in at the dead, and then said, "Christ, MacAllister, is this all?"

"It's getting harder to get them," said the man, presumably Mac-Allister.

"Harder? Is it fuck! He," said Jackson, jerking his thumb at Thornhill, "tells us that it's gone to shit out there and the dead are a bumper crop!"

"True," said MacAllister, looking warily at Thornhill, "but that means it's harder. There are more of them, they're in mobs, it's fucking dangerous because I can't get them all in the truck and the ones that don't fit tend to want to fucking eat me. You think you can do better, you go and get them yourself."

"Where do you get them?" asked Thornhill, going to stand by Jackson at the truck. The dead inside moaned, pressing out the wire stretched between the metal struts, their fingers tearing, their lips ripping where they pressed against the thin cabling. Some were new, some older, their eyes rheumy and raw.

"The suburbs," said McAllister. "The towns are too fucking hot these days. Most of them are no-go areas. You're a Yank? Fuck, your warbots are as bad as the fucking zombies! You get in the middle of a street with the dead on it and you've got more chance of being shot than the zombies have!"

"So I'm told," Thornhill said.

MacAllister turned back to Jackson, dismissing Thornhill. "Come on," he said, "cough up and let's get this done." Jackson passed him a thick roll of crumpled notes, which the man spirited away into a pocket. It was oddly shocking; commerce, even now. *We don't change,* thought Thornhill, and felt a black urge to grin.

"Get in the truck and get ready," Jackson said to Thornhill. "When Mac pulls his truck away, back into the gap and drop the tailgate fast, understand?"

"Yes," said Thornhill.

Jackson went around the field, banging on the metal fence as he went, and most of the zombies inside followed him in a loose stagger around the perimeter. At the same time, MacAllister went to a section of the fence and removed two bolts; Thornhill realized it was a crude gate, hinged not at the side but across the bottom. MacAllister got back into his truck and reversed up to the fence, using the truck to push the hinged section flat. The tailboard of the truck, released from within the cab, fell down but the zombies didn't move, still attracted by MacAllister and Thornhill, grasping at them in a vain attempt to latch on to them.

At the far end of the field, Jackson opened a smaller gate in the fence and slipped though, closing it behind him. He began to shout and jump, much like he had on the island. "Hey, fuckfaces!" he yelled. "Hey, you! I'm right here! Come and get me!"

Immediately, the zombies in MacAllister's truck turned, stumbling to the rear. "Get ready, Yankee!" shouted MacAllister and revved his engine as Jackson carried on shouting and jumping. The dead already in the field followed him as he moved. Thornhill climbed into the cab of his truck and started the engine, feeling its ragged motion through the pedals under his feet.

The dead came down MacAllister's tailgate, some falling in their eagerness to get to Jackson, the ones behind trampling them and falling themselves until most were lying in an ungainly, struggling mound on the ground. Slowly, they pulled themselves forward, wriggling free of the heap like maggots, clambering to their feet, lurching forwards. They were focused on Jackson, who was close to the center of the field now, Thornhill and MacAllister forgotten. As the last of the dead fell from MacAllister's truck, he gunned his engine and jerked the vehicle forwards. Amidst the oily exhaust smoke and clattering, he raised a hand to Thornhill and he drove away. Thornhill raised his hand in return, and jammed his own truck into gear.

It was heavy, the shift resisting for a moment before crunching into place. Thornhill drove the truck forwards, lining it up with the gateway, and then reversed into place. There was a winch handle attached to the dashboard, the cable wrapped around its drum and stretching out through a hole cut in the cab's ceiling, and Thornhill released it. Behind him, the truck's long tailgate fell open, the impact shuddering through the vehicle with a crash.

Thornhill twisted in his seat, watching through the window as Jackson ran across the field, still shouting. The dead followed; a phalanx of rottenness and decay that moaned as it went, zombies falling and rising, clutching and grasping. Jackson stayed ahead of them, darting this way and that, before moving back towards the rear of the truck. He carried on calling insults and enticements, random words, human sounds, and the zombies came on.

When they were close, Jackson retreated up the tailgate, entering the body of the truck, becoming a blur moving behind the mesh, the zombies following. They crowded against the entrance, falling and reaching out, Jackson dancing ahead of them. The smell was overpowering, of meat left in the sun and of dirt and flies and shit. Some of the dead missed the entrance, clawed at the outer edge of the truck and slipped between a gap Thornhill had left between it and the fence, staggering along the side of the vehicle and banging on the cab doors. More of them pressed themselves against the cab below Thornhill's window, the faces twisting and mouths opening, teeth blackened, skin shredded and peeling, eyes dry and pale. He knocked the lock down, just in case one of them managed to open the door by accidentally pulling the outside handle.

"Come on, you dead bastards," Jackson called, finally reaching the back of the cab. "Start the winch," he shouted through and then jumped, catching the top of the frame and lifting himself so that he was on top of wire mesh. Thornhill hit the winch control, which slowly lifted the tailgate. Zombies tumbled from it, some falling into the truck and others to its exterior.

"Drive us out," called Jackson from the top of the truck. Thornhill didn't move. The zombies inside the truck were looking up, seeing Jackson through the wire, reaching for him, their fingers mere inches below him. The mesh buckled a little and he shifted, moving to another place. "Drive," he called again, but Thornhill still did not move.

It always came to this point, he thought, the point of decision.

How to act? How to behave? The zombies by his door banged on the glass, leaving smeared prints, the mesh under Jackson buckled more, dropping to scant fractions of an inch above the grip of the tallest of the undead, and Thornhill trying to decide, *Which way now?* The mesh bowed further, dead fingers beginning to brush against the metal, snag at it.

There was only one way, really, he knew that. Thornhill slipped the truck into gear and moved it forwards. For a few feet it bumped, knocking the dead down and rolling on top of them, jolting over the mortified flesh, and the jolts sent Jackson lower, the frame itself beginning to bend, the zombies starting to tear at the mesh, wrapping their fingers through it and pulling it down. The truck picked up speed, escaping the clump of the remaining dead, leaving them behind. The noise of the engine made the things in the rear moan louder.

He drove for several minutes, finally reaching a point where he could see none of the dead around them and stopping the truck. Jackson clambered across the top of the cab and dropped to the ground in front of it. "Why the fuck didn't you drive?" he said, climbing back into the cab as Thornhill vacated the driver's seat. Thornhill didn't reply.

Jackson lit a cigarette and then accelerated the truck, heading further out into the countryside. "We can't go back yet," he said. "I'll have to go back and try and herd the loose ones back into the compound."

"Fine," said Thornhill. "I wanted a chance to talk to you anyway."

"What, to explain why you didn't fucking drive us away?"

"No, to ask: how long have you been sabotaging the project?"

It was a mistake, Thornhill realized. Not his suspicions, they were confirmed instantly, but in asking in such an offhand way, in underestimating the situation and the individual. Jackson lashed out and jabbed his cigarette at Thornhill's eye. Thornhill didn't so much see as sense it coming and jerked his head back, cracking it against the window as the lit tip of the cigarette scoured across his cheek. Sparks leapt in front and behind his eyes as Jackson punched again, shreds of tobacco fluttering into the air. The truck swerved, throwing Thornhill back against the window for a second time, the crack and slice of it loud in the cab, and then they swerved back. The momentum drove Jackson against his door and Thornhill against him, and he punched at the man, his fist connecting against the soft meat of his belly and then again against his temple.

The truck swung again, jolting off the road and onto the field, banging hard against a stone wall and then coming away in a swarm of sparks bigger and brighter than the ones from the cigarette. Jackson lashed out, hitting Thornhill in the throat and then the truck was back on the road and over to the other side where the ground sloped away, and it was tilting, the balance shifting, dropping Thornhill on top of Jackson. He used his weight to pin the man, grunting as he was struck again, and then butted him, his forehead setting Jackson's nose to a new angle, spraying blood in a silken runnel across the two of them. There was a groan from the engine, a violent lurch as Jackson's foot stabbed at the accelerator, and then the vehicle was over and rolling and the cab roof was jumping to meet Thornhill.

FOUR

MARY CAME IN from the kitchen, carrying a beer. It was sunny and warm, and the beer looked cold; condensation dripped down the side of the bottle and trickled over her fingers. She held it out to him and he took it, and it *was* cold, gloriously so, the glass biting at his skin, slippery and brittle. He took a mouthful, malt and rich on his tongue. Mary held out her hand and he took it in his own, but her skin was cold and hard, and when he looked down, he was holding a bot's hand, the metallic fingers twisting around his own. "Mary?" he asked, but received no reply. "Pete?"

Silence. The beer turned foul in Thornhill's mouth, drying and thickening, clinging to his teeth and gums. He coughed and Mary juddered, her hand harsh and metallic and tightening around his. He coughed again, the liquid in his mouth congealing, Mary juddering more and then she was gone and he was in the cab and his mouth was full of cigarette ash.

The cab was over on its side. Thornhill was lying against the passenger-side door, which was now the floor, with the contents of the ashtray on his face, up his nose, in his mouth. He spat, retching, and tried to remember the last time he had drunk a cold beer. A year ago, certainly; probably more. How long since he had held Mary's hand? Pete's hand? Easier: thirteen months and four days, and he missed her and missed Pete and wanted to hold both their hands again.

His face throbbed. Raising his hand to his cheek, Thornhill found a crusted wound that opened at his touch, his fingers coming away from it slick and wet. Twisting around hurt his ribs but he could breathe, which meant that they probably weren't broken, and he managed to get his feet under him and stand. The driver's door was missing.

Jackson was missing.

Thornhill poked his head cautiously out of what was now the top of the cab, angling his shoulders past the steering column. The truck had come to rest at the bottom of a slope, lying on its side. Darts of pain jumped through his body; he would ache tomorrow, and just for a moment wished he was a bot, that he couldn't be hurt, that he couldn't miss people. He still had ash in his mouth and he spat again, and then someone shrieked.

He was halfway out of the cab, knees precariously on the edge of the doorframe, when the remembered the zombies. Turning, he saw that the frame and mesh over the rear of the truck had bent as it rolled but hadn't completely torn loose. The dead writhed behind it like maggots, questing at the tears and holes in the metal, pulling, groaning. A trail of the moving dead was scattered up the slope behind them, torn and battered but still wriggling, trying to stand, stumbling forward. A pall of smoke rose from the engine, a thick column of darkness that reached into the sky like an accusatory finger.

There was another shriek.

Another.

It was Jackson; he was twenty feet from the truck, crawling. His legs were turned half back on themselves and were smeared with blood. Thornhill dropped out of the truck and went to him, un-holstering his gun as he went *I should've done this before,* he thought, his fingers rising to the weeping injury on his face and then dropping away again.

Jackson was on his front but his feet were pointing back; he'd soiled himself and the smell of blood and shit was rich and clinging even in the open. Taking hold of his shoulder, Thornhill rolled him over, Jackson shrieking as he did so. The man's face was a caul of blood, a flap of skin torn loose from his forehead hanging down over one eye. When he opened his mouth to shriek again, his teeth were slick with blood and his breath was red.

"Why?" asked Thornhill.

"Fuck you."

Thornhill reached out and took hold of the flap of skin dangling from the man's head and pulled at it, tearing it further away from the man's skull. As he did so, he pushed the barrel of his gun into Jackson's mouth to stop him shrieking. He glanced back over his shoulder. A couple of the dead had tumbled from the truck and were thrashing weakly on the ground. Further up the slope, one of the zombies fell, rolled and stood, ungainly yet inexorable. He didn't have long. "Why?" he asked again.

"You fucking Americans," said Jackson, blood slathering across his chin and bubbling from his nose. "You send us your bots and your money, and they're no fucking good, and they're not for our benefit, no. This is an island, and you're colonizing us."

Thornhill didn't reply, didn't deny it; he couldn't.

"It doesn't matter now," said Jackson. "This is my country, ours, and I won't have it invaded by you, so I've stopped it."

"How?"

Jackson laughed, an unhealthy slurry of noise that sounded like it was coming from deep inside a tin of mud and glass. The zombies were closer.

"How?" Still no reply, still that wrenching, gurgling laugh, and more blood was spilling from the man now, his eyes were weeping red tears, one pupil huge the other a tiny pinprick.

"How?" and pulling on the skin again and this time Jackson didn't shriek. "Fuck you," he said, breathing out a surf of warm loosed blood. His left hand fell away from his body and opened and a small remote control fell out, a black plastic casing with a single button set into it. The button was depressed.

The nearest of the dead was only feet away and more were behind it, the mesh around the truck's frame ripping away completely and more collapsing to the stony ground. One of the jutting rocks was covered in blood, which Thornhill supposed was Jackson's. Taking a last look at the broken thing at his feet and thinking about Mary and Pete and trying not to feel the blood on his fingers, he rose from his crouch. Jackson might delay the dead for a while; the nearest of them was only a few feet away and more followed, hungry. Always hungry.

As Thornhill started back towards the base, the sound of things eating was behind him. Jackson screamed again. Thornhill walked, not quite knowing the man he had become.

IT TOOK HIM three hours, walking at the fastest pace he could manage, before Thornhill reached the base. The journey was made slower because, although he followed the roads, he had periodically to slip into the fields either side to avoid the dead, scurrying past them hidden below walls and hedges, or waiting for them to amble past him. Once, on a road further down the slope, he saw a warbot, motionless, but he didn't approach it, wary of how it might react to him. There would be no irony in being shot by his own side's machinery, only death.

As he approached Ministry Point, Thornhill heard sirens, atonal and bleak, and they carried with them the scent of burning. A hank of smoke rose from somewhere on the other side of the metal fence, from near the buildings and the gate was open. Zombies shuffled along the road and banged into the fence, bouncing along it like fretting bees until they found the entrance and lurched inside. He watched for several minutes, crouched behind the nearest wall, as more and more zombies appeared, called by the noise and the smoke and…what? Their unerring sense for disaster, for where there was weakness to exploit.

For where there was food.

Where were the bots? They had warbots patrolling, he remembered, and troopbots, and even the guns on the gateposts were primitive bots, designed to shoot anything without a heat signature or that they didn't recognize. The base should have been protected, *was* protected. The guns were motionless, though, their barrels tilted down to the ground, silent.

The fence was unclimbable, so Thornhill had to either go through the gate or travel all the way around to the coast and try and get in via the sea. He had his handgun and spare ammunition for it, and was tired with the walking he'd done. His face ached, his head ached, his whole memory ached, and he wanted to know what was going on. *Fuck this,* he thought, and rose.

The first shot lifted the top of a dead man's skull, ropes of hair and brain jumping from it like an octopus's legs, and his second tore through something's cheek and ripped the jaw loose as it exited; male or female he could not tell under its cover of dirt and decay. His third knocked a child back and then he was moving, threading his way through them, twisting his shoulders and hips, dancing, dodging their outstretched hands and gnashing teeth, using his arm to push them aside, kicking at their knees to shift them aside, and then he was through the gate and onto the road beyond. Another two shots took care of the walking flesh nearest him, clearing a path that he moved through. Move fast but not recklessly, sure but not panicking; simple rules to survive. Don't think, don't remember, don't wonder, just *do.*

There was a jeep crashed further down the road, its driver's seat awash with blood. Devon? Wargle?

Victoria?

There was a stutter of gunfire ahead of him. Thornhill jogged, continually glancing over his shoulder and around him. The dead, where were they all coming from? There seemed hundreds, knots of them, a wave of them behind him, more ahead and to each side.

They turned to look at him, started for him, attracted by his smell, by the blood on his clothes and the pus weeping from his cheek.

By his life.

He passed a utility building, a storage shed of some kind, with the dead pressing against it, dragging hands that left black streaks down its walls. More of the creatures saw him, left their places and joined the crowd following him. He fired at one coming in from the side, the shot tearing a path from its eyeball to the back of its head, spinning it, dropping it, the echoes of the shot cavorting around him, and still no one came.

Where were the fucking bots?

They were around the next curve; well, two of them were. The warbot was standing at attention in the middle of the road with zombies drifting around it. Behind it was a workbot. Both were motionless, ignoring the dead. For the workbot, that was normal, it would carry out whatever task it had been assigned without other concerns, but the warbot should have been shooting, following the primary instruction written deep into its metal and electronic soul: kill the dead.

Only a few zombies had reached the main buildings, and most of them were clustered around the large roller doors through which the vehicles and bots moved, and which were down. Thornhill went to one of the smaller doors, pushing aside the dead to get to it. It was unlocked, opened easily, thank God, and he slipped in and shut it behind him. The dead started to hammer on the outside of the door, an irregular tattoo, their groaning a dreadful descant to the rhythms of their assault. There was nothing to block the door with; it opened into a featureless corridor lined with neon strip-lights in yellow and red and blue. Under the sound of the banging from behind him, Thornhill heard voices from somewhere ahead. Ignoring the swift alarms of pain sounding in his body, he began to run.

He found them two levels down, in the workshop.

They were all there; Devon was on one of the table, sitting up and shirtless, bandages wrapped around his torso. Wargle was sitting at the far workbench, goggles around his head, and he barely looked around as Thornhill entered. Victoria was standing by Devon, but came to Thornhill and folded him into a hug. "We saw the smoke and thought you'd both been killed," she said. "Where's Jackson?"

"What happened?" asked Thornhill.

"Everything went to shit," said Devon. "I was outside near the gate, doing a check on things, when there was funny fucking noise."

"Noise?"

"Like a high-pitched whine, and then a series of pops and sizzles like things burning, circuits shorting out. All the bots stopped working, just stopped, every last one of them."

"And then?"

"The gates opened. They're electronic as well, and when they failed the locks disengaged. They aren't supposed to do that, in the event of power loss or anything like that the locks are supposed to stay sealed to protect us. Fuck."

"Where's Jackson?" asked James.

"Dead," said Thornhill, trying not to think of the flap of skin peeling back, tearing, slippery between his fingers. "He's been sabotaging the project. I thought he was just trying to prevent you developing your own bots, but it's worse than that. He's done something to every bot here."

"Why?" asked Wargle without looking around.

"It wasn't clear, but I think to stop you working with us. With America," said Thornhill. "He wasn't making much sense at the end."

"What do we do?" said Victoria. She was flushed, her cheeks reddened, her eyes wide and her pupils large and dark.

"What weapons do we have?"

"We have a whole armory," said Devon, easing himself off the table. "It's full. Rifles and grenades, ammunition."

"Were you bitten?" asked Thornhill, raising his gun and pointing at the man.

"Do you think I'd be alive if I had been?" said Devon. "I swerved the jeep and lost control after the gates opened and cracked my chest against the steering wheel. It was a shock, seeing the gates open and the bots stop. The warbots just sort of…went limp and the guns on the gates just dropped. I'm so used to seeing them moving, constantly turning and walking and looking."

"Yes," said Thornhill. "Take me to the armory."

ALL THE WEAPONS were damaged. Jackson had carefully plugged each barrel and removed the insides of the grenades; it must have taken him months. Whatever signal he had sent out via the central matrix to the bots in those last damaged moments had killed the communications networks as well, burned out the monitor screens of the security system, destroyed their defenses.

"Did no one suspect?" asked Thornhill. "You gave him full run of the place, he did all the repairs and maintenance, he was a there all the time, was involved at some level in everything that went wrong, and none of you thought it was funny? Odd? A bit damned suspicious?"

"We were all part of everything. There was only ever six or seven of us at any one time, everyone was into everything," said Victoria.

"Christ," said Thornhill, "what a mess. We need to arm ourselves somehow, and get out of here. What have we got?"

"The spinbot," said Wargle. "The AI doesn't work, Jackson's seen to that, but I've managed to repair the mechanics and I can control it using the remote."

"Good. We'll use it to clear us a path."

"There's a problem," said Wargle. *There always is,* thought Thornhill, *always. Problems after problems, coming like breath, like clouds. Like zombies.* "The spinny will only be able to go a short way, and probably not all the way to the gate. The repairs I've done are only temporary, spit and string jobs, and I can't guarantee how far or long they'll last."

"Then we go backwards," said Devon, "to the dock. The boat's ready to go, I prepared it this morning ready to take the crop to the island."

Crop? thought Thornhill, and then realized that he was talking about the zombies he and Jackson had been collecting. *Christ, these idiots have forgotten how things are,* he thought, *stuck up here in the middle of fucking nowhere playing with toys and talking about crops and fishing and the spinny and letting one man do all their practical work while they talked and doodled and he crept about and quietly fucked them all. Christ.*

"Then we go that way," said Wargle. Thornhill nodded; what choice did they have? None, as ever. This was life now, no choices, few chances and little hope. "When can we be ready to go?" he asked.

"Now," said Wargle, removing his goggles and picking up the clumsy remote control. "Spinny's as ready as she'll ever be, even if we're not."

THERE WAS A service lift at the rear of the base and they went to it, the spinbot trundling ahead of them down the wide corridors. The battered metal cowling caught the strip-lights in broken lines, and the smell of its engine was thick and made Thornhill's eyes water. The clank of its caterpillars was loud, echoing off the stone and metal walls in dull waves.

The lift opened out into a huge hangar, mostly empty, but with the base's vehicles in the far corner; two more trucks and a couple of jeeps. "Can we use a truck?" asked Wargle, but Thornhill knew the answer. Jackson had been busy last night, he thought; it didn't take long to confirm that the remaining vehicles had been immobilized, their engines damaged beyond repair.

"Did you know which jeep you were going to use today?" Thornhill asked Devon.

"Jackson told me," said Devon. "He said that the other needed tuning up."

"I'll bet he did," said Thornhill. "He's been planning this for a while, but I think my arrival brought things to a head."

"Can you hear them?" asked Victoria. "Outside?"

They could. In the time they had been inside, the dead had surrounded the base, homing in on the entrances like wasps attacking a creature's eyes. The hangar doors were shaking, rattling under their assault, their moans amplified by drumhead-taut metal, filling the space with noise.

"The dock's another quarter of a mile or so," said Devon. "How are we going to do it?"

"Spinny can clear the path," said Wargle confidently. "We'll follow in its wake."

"How fast can it go?" asked Thornhill.

"A fast walking pace," said Wargle, "but I'd be wary of pushing it too hard. We should make the dock in fifteen minutes."

"What weapons have we got?" They had side arms, nothing more. Jackson had done a genuine number on them, trapping them here, isolating them and removing their defenses extremely effectively, and for a moment Thornhill was glad the man was dead, and horrified at himself for his gladness.

"Open it," he said, gesturing to the enormous hangar door. "Let's get this done."

As the doors rose, the spinbot's wires coughed to life, the motors jerking grittily for a second before their rhythms smoothed out and the grey blur appeared around the machine. Wargle moved it forwards and they came together behind it, and then the dead were in and moving towards them.

The sound of the wire whipping through the air, a high-pitched whine, changed as it met the first zombie, deepening and slowing before speeding up again. Flesh, old and dry, leapt from the creature's head as its body pitched sideways. The flow of zombies widened around the spinbot as it went forwards, the wire chewing through them, sending skin and bone and hair and brains into the air. The caterpillars crawled over the fallen, pushing a gap through them and Thornhill and the others followed.

Thornhill fired at the dead that came close, spinning them away. Devon, hampered by his injuries, stayed close to Wargle, shooting at anything that came close and James stayed by Thornhill, using a wide sweeping broom to keep the dead away. They moved on, clambering over the finally dead, their feet slithering in entrails that had decayed to grey and black slime, the smell of rot and the spin-bot's exhaust writhing around each and into Thornhill's nostrils in thick, queasy strings.

How many of the dead were there? Hundreds? A thousand? There seemed to be a never-ending clot of them, the spinbot cutting through them only to have more appear, stumbling and weaving, sliced away into chunks by the wires, the sound like an axe chopping into dry wood, the air filling with dust and floating hair and fragments of skin, choking Thornhill, the sound of the engines and the shots huge, echoing from the distant room and the floor, catching them in the middle of waves of sound, and the dead moaned and came on and on and on.

It didn't last; as the spinbot emerged from the hangar, clouds of black smoke started pouring from the metal cowling of its body, weeping from around the bolts and from inside the slots and twisting around the wires in thick, fracturing strands. The wires, still rotating but slowing, started to tangle around the zombies they hit, tearing through them and dragging them around, their weight slowing the engines more. Wargle screamed something, hitting the controls and shaking them, but the engine in the bot gave a lurch, jolting it with a sound like gears crunching. More of the dead caught in the wires, no longer being destroyed but simply yanked off their feet and dragged so that Thornhill had to step further back to avoid the flailing limbs. Victoria screamed, and he fired over her shoulder at a dead soldier, opening his head like an old apple. Devon shouted and then Wargle was running, dropping the remote behind him, breaking to the side. The dead knotted around him, clutching and gripping and then the man was down, and his screams were louder than any other sound in the world. Devon went to him, firing, but the spinbot gave another lurch, turning so that the sweep of tangled dead bore down on Devon.

"Run," said Thornhill, pushing Victoria. "Run to the dock, I'm right behind you."

Devon managed one scream as the mass of the zombies and wire hit him, clung to him, and then was silent, submerged. The bot rolled on for several feet, pacing Thornhill and James and then slowed, the smoke pouring more thickly from its body and from under it, leaking oil and hydraulic fluid like blood. Then, with a last, agonized screech of metal it came to a halt.

They ran, dodging and weaving, the road opening up ahead of them, freer of the dead who were gathering around Devon and Wargle, tearing at their heads, fighting for a morsel of brain. Thornhill finished a clip as he ran, dropping it and loading another into his pistol, trying to clear their path, Victoria using the broom like a staff, knocking aside a shambling child's corpse and a female that might have once been its mother, thrusting it against outstretched arms and torn faces and open mouths, and they made their way to the dock.

The boat was already overrun; two zombies were on its deck, a third wandering along the gangplank. All three were dripping, and more shapes were pulling on the anchor chain and shifting in the murky water around it. The was a dull crunch as one of the shapes got caught between the boat and the dock, the swell lifting the boat into it and then pulling it away. Another shape took the place of the crushed one, which sank away, fragmenting. Beyond the boat, one of the aquabots floated, belly up, bobbing in the worsening surf, carried in towards the shore on the tide. Thornhill, seeing their escape was gone, turned back but the road was filled with zombies, a loose wall of them coming towards them.

"There," he said, pushing Victoria towards the steps at the side of the dock. They led down to a shingle beach, narrow and short. They descending, reaching the beach in seconds and crossed to its middle, where they stopped. Victoria fell to her knees, weeping. Thornhill sat next to her. The first of the zombies appeared at the top of the steps, wobbled, fell as Thornhill shot it.

"How could it have ever ended up anywhere but here?" he asked quietly. Victoria raised her head, looking at him but not replying, and he shot her in the belly. She screamed, was thrown back to landed spread-eagled on the beach. A vast bloom of red opened up across her front, its petals spreading quickly down to her waist and up towards her shoulders.

"Jackson couldn't be working alone," said Thornhill, "he needed help. You helped him. You're good, I'll give you that, distracting me when I was asking about his little additions to the AI systems, and then again in my room when I might have had chance to think things through more clearly. You were never married though; I had access to your files before I came, to all of your files."

"We were supposed to be away from here before he triggered it," gasped James. "Out to sea." She spat a piece of bloodied saliva at Thornhill but it fell short, dropping between the stones between his legs.

"Why?"

"Because this is our country, not yours," she said. She struggled into a sitting position, her breathing ragged, and then used the broom to crutch herself upright. He stood too.

"So you destroy the research rather than accept help from the US?"

Another zombie appeared at the top of the steps, tottered and lost its balance, collapsing down them in a series of drunken cracks. Thornhill didn't bother to shoot it; it couldn't stand when it reached the bottom and simply dragged itself forwards but made little progress across the stones.

"It's never help, there's always a price," said James. "And we decided we weren't going to pay it this time, so no, not just the research and not just the bots here, but everywhere in Britain. A single pulse, sent up from the matrix and out, to the satellites and out from them, and all your fucking bots die. We make this alone or not at all, we aren't a base for you to use as a commodity or a bolt-hole, we are not 'acceptable collateral damage.'"

Thornhill thought of satellites orbiting the earth, pointing themselves at London, at Manchester, at all those other towns and villages he had never heard of, would never hear of, sending out Jackson's signal, practiced and perfected over the past months. They had provided him the equipment to do it, unwittingly, given him and Victoria time and security. All over Britain, bots were freezing, the warbots' guns falling silent, the sanibots motionless on the road to the pits. Or would the sanibots and cleribots carry on, unaffected, run by a different system, waiting for instructions that would never come? All over Britain, were people realizing that the dead were no longer being stopped? That there were no defenses left?

It didn't matter.

Grey shapes were emerging from the sea, lank hair dripping with water and seaweed, clothes sodden, skin sagging and bloated and gnawed. More of the dead had appeared at the top of the steps, were scrambling down them. Thornhill had very few bullets left, not enough to escape.

Another thing that didn't matter.

There's nothing beautiful left in this world, he thought. The sun was washed out these days, never appearing with any brightness, never casting its light on anything but the dead and dying. The sea was a leaden sheet, broken by the emerging, staggering figures of the dead, the air itself was stale and used. James was ugly, anger and pain twisting her face, blood dripping from her mouth and down her chin in long, swinging trails. He shot her again, this time in the head, the spray soaring into the air bright and vibrant, glittering red and pink and white, so unlike the zombies' dank tones. Thornhill thought of Mary, of Pete, of a country he had only ever visited in wartime, of a woman he had known was a traitor but had held anyway because he wanted to feel warm, to feel loved.

More zombies came down the steps, more emerged from the sea, the first of them crunching across the stones towards him. He raised the gun to his head, knowing that God would understand, that Mary and Pete would understand, and wishing above all else that he could see something beautiful again.

"Diplomacy — The art of letting other people achieve your ends."

автор рассказов

EKATERINA SEDIA RESIDES in the Pinelands of New Jersey. Her critically acclaimed novels, *The Secret History of Moscow, The Alchemy of Stone, The House of Discarded Dreams* and *Heart of Iron* were published by Prime Books. Her short stories have sold to *Analog, Baen's Universe, Subterranean* and *Clarkesworld*, as well as numerous anthologies, including *Haunted Legends* and *Magic in the Mirrorstone*. She is also the editor of *Paper Cities* (World Fantasy Award winner), *Running with the Pack* and *Beware the Night*, as well as forthcoming *Bloody Fabulous*. Visit her at www.ekaterinasedia.com.

"I grew up in Moscow, so it's only logical for me to write a story set there. I remember the whispers surrounding the war in Afghanistan very clearly, the dread of my classmates before the draft—anything but Afghanistan. I remember how no official channel ever spoke about that war. So my mind went to the Afghan veterans and their chance to re-live the dread and paranoia of those times, and to realize that governments remain deceitful, and people get victimized no matter who's running the show. Pessimistic? Perhaps, but in the character of Dr. Valentin Korzhik I tried to embody the value of remaining honorable even if you don't believe in happy endings." — *Ekaterina Sedia.*

Simon Clark wrote *Blood Crazy.* This novel of mayhem and parents hunting their own children has been published in translation, optioned for filming, and still recruits legions of loyal fans. Simon's latest book is *Blood & Grit 21.* This is an expanded and enriched eBook of his first collection of bruising stories that are absolutely for readers with hearts of steel. His other novels include *King Blood, Nailed by the Heart* and *Death's Dominion.* Call in on Simon at www.nailedbytheheart.com.

"I grew up in the blood-soaked landscape of Yorkshire in the North of England. A place invaded and colonized by Vikings a thousand years ago. So when I set out to write a ZVR story full of zombies and robots I realized that brutal Viking warriors would be a powerful addition to the mix. My home county is rich in mythology. One particular legend that caught my eye involves a nun that lived in the ancient seaport of Whitby fourteen hundred years ago. Single-handedly she is supposed to have defeated an invasion of snakes by cutting off all their heads with a whip. So: a whip-wielding nun, Vikings, robots, zombies, and my abiding fascination with the weapons of war—all these elements ignited my imagination as I sat down and wrote 'Beheaded by Whip-Wielding Nun.' " — *Simon Clark*

Simon Kurt Unsworth lives on a hill in the north of England with his wife and child where he awaits the coming flood and writes essentially grumpy fiction, for which pursuit he was nominated for a 2008 World Fantasy Award for Best Short Story. His work has been published in a number of anthologies, including the critically acclaimed *At Ease with the Dead, Shades of Darkness, Exotic Gothic 3, Gaslight Grotesque* and *Lovecraft Unbound.* He has also appeared in three of Stephen Jones' *Mammoth Book of Best New Horror* anthologies (19, 21 and 22), and also *The Very Best of Best New Horror.* His first collection of short stories, *Lost Places,* was released by the Ash Tree Press in 2010, and his second, *Quiet Houses,* came out from Dark Continents in 2011. He has a further collection out from PS Publishing in 2012 (*Strange Gateways*) and his as-yet-unnamed collection will launch the Spectral Press *Spec-*

tral Signature Editions imprint in 2013, so at some point he needs to write those stories. You can follow him on Facebook or Twitter and he might eventually get his website up and running, but don't hold your breath.

"Writing a story for the *Zombies vs Robots* universe and setting it in the UK was great fun. It contains some of the grouchier feelings I have about how the country of my birth is run and about how nationalists and extremists think and act. Zombie mayhem, however, fits nicely anywhere and seemed a good way of taking out some of my frustrations without actually harming anyone. Spinbot seems like it'd be a great machine, and I'd love to see it in action, if they ever get it working properly." — *Simon Kurt Unsworth*

RIO YOUERS IS the British Fantasy Award–nominated author of *Dark Dreams, Pale Horses.* His short fiction has appeared in numerous anthologies, and his latest novel, *Westlake Soul,* will be released by ChiZine Publications in spring 2012.

"I was drawn, creatively, to the graphic novel's use of primary, task-specific robots—so unlike the hi-tech gadgetry and flamboyance of robots seen on the silver screen today. I immediately envisioned these basic machines in a World War II setting. Fortunately, the Trans-Dimensional Gateway introduced in *ZVR: Which Came First?* afforded me the opportunity to do just that. Thus, "For King and Country" came to light…and while existing in Chris and Ashley's fabulous ZVR universe, it owes much to any number of classic British war movies." — *Rio Youers*

ROBERT HOOD IS an Australian author whose stories have appeared in magazines and anthologies both downunder and overseas for several decades, most recently in *Exotic Gothic 2, 3* and *4, Zombie Apocalypse!, Scenes from the Second Storey* and *Anywhere But Earth.* He has been described as "Australia's master of dark fantasy" (Sean Williams) and "Aussie horror's wicked godfather" (Black Magazine)—epithets that reflect a long-term predilection for weirdness and dark monstrosity. This obsession is apparent in the collection *Creeping in Reptile Flesh*, which has just been re-edited and re-published by Morrigan Books, in his earlier collections *Day-dreaming on Company Time* and *Immaterial: Ghost Stories*, and in a dark fantasy novel contracted for publication sometime in 2012/2013 by Borgo Press, *Fragments of a Broken Land: Valarl Undead*. His website can be found at www.roberthood.net, where there is a link to his award-winning blog Undead Backbrain. Feel free to shamble by.

"Zombies and robots are thematic favorites of mine, so when asked if I'd like to contribute to a ZVR anthology the response was a no-brainer, especially given the retro, wonderfully pre-digital nature of the robots in the IDW franchise. At the same time, I had been contemplating the bizarre "psychic warfare" experiments undertaken by both US and USSR governments during the Cold War, and decided to take advantage of the trans-dimensional portal that was already a feature of the ZVR world to explore the sense of absurd nihilism that runs through most of human history. I had massive fun creating both the exploitation-flick ambiance of the Soul Killer and her hapless victim, and filling a pre-existing political landscape with undead monsters and a clunky robot." — Robert Hood

DALE BAILEY LIVES in North Carolina with has family, and has published three novels, *The Fallen, House of Bones,* and *Sleeping Policemen* (with Jack Slay, Jr.). His short fiction, collected in *The Resurrection Man's Legacy and Other Stories,* has won the International Horror Guild Award and has been twice nominated for the Nebula Award.

"What I love about the whole Zombies vs. Robots franchise is the sheer absurdity of the premise—the shambling zombies of the Romero era in combat with automatons from the age of Robbie the Robot. The challenge—or the challenge I took upon myself—was to embrace this absurdity, then to treat it with deadpan seriousness. I took a mad scientist with a bunch of heads in jars, gave him a hare-lipped assistant, and threw in a bunch of giant centipedes, sure, but I also tried to work out the logic of the plague and to inhabit the story with genuine characters. I set the piece in the early stages of the outbreak, when no one really understands what's going on—including the exponentially increasing numbers of zombies, who it turns out just can't get those pesky brain cases open with their rotting hands before their victims revive as zombies themselves. And I gave my mad scientist a genuine emotional core—or I hope I did—as he struggled to deal not only with his colleagues' utter disdain but with his wife's extramarital affair. The result, I hope, is pulp fiction with heart. I hope you had as much fun reading this one as I did writing it." — *Dale Bailey*

GARY MCMAHON IS the award-nominated author of the novels *Rain Dogs, Hungry Hearts, Pretty Little Dead Things, Dead Bad Things* and *The Concrete Grove*. Forthcoming are a short story collection from Dark Regions Press and the novel *Silent Voices*. His acclaimed short fiction has appeared in *The Mammoth Book of Best New Horror, The Year's Best Dark Fantasy & Horror,* and *The Year's Best Fantasy & Horror*. He lives with his wife and son in northern England, an area which inspires many of his tales. Follow him on Twitter or Facebook, or visit him at www.garymcmahon.com.

"I've always wanted to write a story that used William the Conqueror's 'Harrying (or Harrowing) of the North' in a modern setting, so when the invite for this project came along I saw it as the perfect opportunity. The history of England is long and bloody and brutal—a lot of that brutality is still here, but it's more subtle. With 'The Harrowing' I wanted to explore the fact that some things about my country's leaders never change; the ZvR world was, surprisingly, the perfect way to tackle these themes. Many readers might vaguely recognize the character of the woman Prime Minister. Believe me, the similarity is deliberate. As a sidenote, musical accompaniment to this story came from P.J. Harvey; her album *Let England Shake* is bold, beautiful and terrifying." — *Gary McMahon*

STEVE LOCKLEY IS a British Fantasy Award nominated author and editor whose novels include *The Ragchild* and *The Quarry*. With

Steve Savile, he is also responsible for the Sally Reardon Supernatural Mysteries series. Steve has served as a judge for the prestigious World Fantasy Awards.

"I'm a bit of a history buff and have always been fascinated in the way that battles can be won and lost due to the weather, and 'The Last Defense of Moscow' gave me a chance to fool around with a scenario that defeated both Napoleon and Hitler. I've written a few zombie stories in the past but this, without doubt, was the most fun." — *Steve Lockley*

M IKE DUBISCH IS a fantasy illustrator with his roots in golden age horror comics and pulp sci-fi. Mike began his illustration career contributing to *Science Fiction Age* and *Realms of Fantasy* magazines, as well as small press horror anthology comics *Gore-Shriek*, *Cry For Dawn*, and *Raw Media Mags*. His art has been used in toy design and illustration for Star Wars and Dungeons and Dragons, covers for *Aliens vs. Predator* comics, and graphic adaptations of *The Boxcar Children* and other children's literature. Mike also creates fine art, prints, and experimental films exploring H. P. Lovecraft's Cthulhu Mythos. Other projects include interior art for *Classics Mutilated* from IDW, cover and interior art for *All-Monster-Action* and *Blackhole Rainbows*. Mike lives in Phoenix, Arizona with his wife, Carolyn, and three daughters where he teaches online at the Academy of Art University. Mike is on Facebook and can be found at www.Dubisch.com.

"Zombies vs. Robots gave me a chance to explore a number of different influences from old black and white horror movies to the garish propaganda posters of WWII. Fifties science-fiction comics blended with my life-long obsession with the Living Dead. One of the great pleasures of this project was playing in Ash Wood's world. His zombies are, to a bone, a desiccated, hungry looking bunch. His robots have this great life to them. They somehow manage to be evocative of a child's rendering of a robot, yet reference classic science fiction; all while keeping a leg in gritty mechanical realism, but still sporting wonky giant screws and bolts holding them together." — *Mike Dubisch*

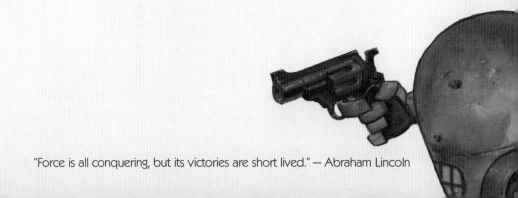

"Force is all conquering, but its victories are short lived." — Abraham Lincoln

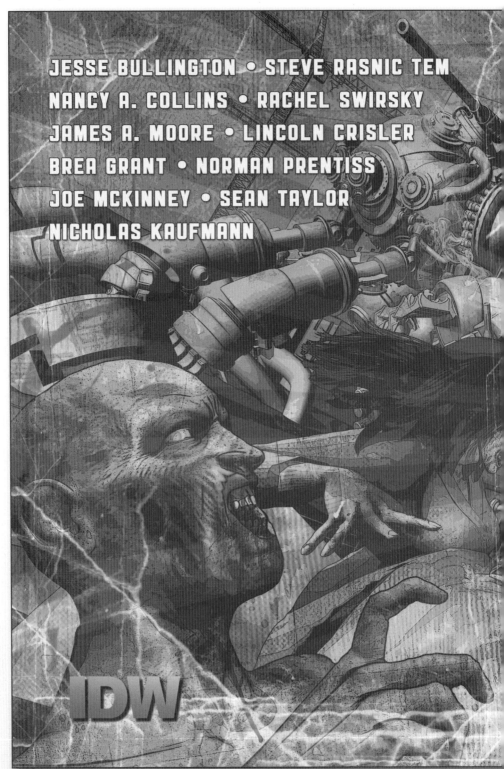

BOLTS • BULLETS • BRAINS
THIS MEANS WAR!
A ZOMBIES VS ROBOTS ANTHOLOGY
EDITED BY
JEFF CONNER
ILLUSTRATED BY
FABIO LISTRANI

ZOMBIE TERROR · ROBOT MENACE

ZOMBIES VS ROBOTS

WOMEN ON WAR

AMBER BENSON
BREA GRANT
RHODI HAWK
RAIN GRAVES
YVONNE NAVARRO
KAARON WARREN
EKATERINA SEDIA
NANCY A. COLLINS
RACHEL SWIRSKY
AMELIA BEAMER

Edited by Jeff Conner
Illustrated by Ericka Lugo
Introduction by Nancy Holder

IDW

Enjoy this and other unique *Zombies vs Robots* collections — available now.